The Shamrock Shore

HEROES OF THE MISTY ISLE

The Shamrock Shore

In the Footsteps of
Patrick Through the Hills of Erin

SANDY DENGLER

MOODY PRESS
CHICAGO

Contents

NOTE:

When Patrick stepped ashore sometime in the fifth century, Ireland had places and place names aplenty, but no towns. Places and physical features bore Gaelic names unfamiliar to most modern readers. For example, the Cill Dara (Cill is "church") of Saint Brigid is Kildare today. For simplicity, familiarity, and those readers who enjoy following along on a contemporary map of Ireland, I shall use the modern English place names. Do bear in mind that that's almost certainly not what the places were called back then, or even what they are called today in Gaelic.

1

Mussels

"Come away and drown in me," roared the sea below.

The land, mute before the pounding surf, offered no better suggestion.

"End your hopeless, senseless flight!" Violent white spray slammed against the rocks beyond the craggy head.

No response came from the battered land.

Gray haze blotted out the line between gray sea and gray sky. In the offshore mist, barely visible, a gray blob of island hung suspended, all alone, isolated.

Padraic of Lambay stood on the brow of the rocky headland gazing at the misty isle and listening to the wicked sea at his feet. He had traveled now as westwardly as he could go without getting wet. He had literally walked to the end of the world.

And yet he could hardly pause. So far, the silent land had offered him no cover. Fiendishly clever and resourceful as Padraic was, strong as he might be in his youth, he had not been able to escape his pursuing black nemesis. He had hidden in forests, among rocks, and out in the uninhabited peat bogs. He had crossed rivers and mountains. Still his hunter came.

He dare not steal a boat. Should the man on the black horse learn from the locals that a boat was missing, he would know instantly where Padraic had gone. That would end Padraic's life. For if he could not permanently elude his pursuer in all the wilds of Erin, on an island he would be as vulnerable as a pony in a farm pen.

In fact, if any locals spied Padraic, and that intelligence reached the man on the black horse, the fellow might guess Padraic's whereabouts. He must flee now, immediately, before he was seen.

Carefully, carefully, he worked his way down the broken rock of the headwall. The sea growled and hissed, promising doom even as it beckoned him. Slippery moss threatened every moment to yank the land out from under him. And now he had run out of stepping-stones. He glanced back and could not see the top of the cliff where he had stood moments ago. At least now he could not be seen except from seaward. No fishing smacks, no curraghs bobbed on the restless surf. Safe for the moment.

A fleeting moment. A very fleeting moment, in fact. Now what? He couldn't go up. He couldn't go down. The sea churned among the rocks below, waiting with a dastardly twinkle in its eye for him to make the slightest misstep. When he thought about it—and Padraic in all his seventeen years rarely thought about anything in advance—this wasn't such a good idea after all.

Perhaps his evil pursuer's luck had at last run out, and Padraic could hide in safety among the copses on this westernmost jut of land. Perhaps he could crawl back up these slick wet rocks to safety.

Perhaps cows fly.

With a practiced eye he watched the boiling swells slosh against the black rocks and fall away. He watched the way the loose ends of the blue-black mussels moved, tied to the rocks as they were. The directions they shifted revealed far more about swirls and currents than did the chaotic water itself.

From a lifetime of intimate proximity to the sea in her many moods, he knew the behavior of tide and surf. A few feet below the surface, invisible, lurked flat rocks that would break every bone in him if he jumped. But there, a few yards out—that was a deep hole, a dark, swirling hole. If he leaped out from here, and did not slip, and managed to plummet himself into that hole, he could begin his swim to the ultimate safety of the gray and distant island.

Of course, if he missed it he was pudding.

The wind was picking up. It lifted spray and rippled the water surface, making the rocks beneath much harder to read.

He watched the swells a few minutes longer, gauging the time between them. He must launch himself out from the rocks and drop into the hole at the very moment the swells filled it fullest. Not difficult for such a nimble fellow as himself. With fear clutching his throat so tightly he could not breathe, Padraic leaped.

* * *

A quarter mile away, where a sweet rill cut down through its rocky gully to the salt sea, Bridey dragged her curragh up into the grass above tideline. She really must caulk the little boat with tallow before she ventured out in it again. The seams in its leathern hull leaked horribly. She flipped it upside down and stared morosely at its moldy bottom. Whoever thought to make a curragh out of rawhide ought to ride in one awhile. They'd think better and stick to wood next time. The hem of her simple brown wool chemise was wet to above her knees from the bilge in the leaky vessel.

She hated wet clothes. They made a cold day so much colder. The rising wind chilled her legs so that her bare toes ached. Whenever she mentioned the cold she despised so—not complaining, just mentioning—her stepmother always retorted, "Nonsense, Bridey! A girl of eighteen is full of warmth and vigor. Your body doesn't know cold. Now when you're my age, you'll appreciate what cold is."

Appreciating quite well what cold is, she climbed down the rocks to the waterline to retrieve her basket of mussels. With the seaweed packed about them they would last till tomorrow. Chicken tonight. Steamed mussels tomorrow. Perhaps her stepfather would get around to butchering the lame calf in the next day or two, and they could have calf's liver.

Bridey paused to look out across the gray sea, her farewell to the day, as the breeze caught her wool shawl and whipped its edges about. Her brown hair—a rather mousey brown, she thought—tangled in her eyelashes as the air flicked her perpetually short wisps around her face. For a lingering moment she watched white water pound the headland to her left, and she marveled at its power.

Then she frowned. It couldn't be! And yet, no bird was that large. What looked like a man in a white shirt appeared to have just jumped out from the cliffside, arms flailing. A faulty appearance, surely. No one would be so foolish. Yet a strange sort of yelp floated in on the wind.

It could not be faerie folk. By reputation they were known for their grace and intelligence; this fellow displayed neither.

For a few moments more she watched the swells rise and shatter themselves against the black rocks of the headland. Then she ran back up the lea and dropped her basket of mussels. She flipped the curragh right side up and dragged it down into the mouth of the creek. Cold creek water wicked up her skirt and her linen shift to well above her knees. A curse on cold! She waited until the surf was about to crest. As the sea rose, she shoved out into it and hopped into the boat of holes. As it backed off, she sculled away from shore.

Bridey could scull a boat as well as anyone, but with the wind rising and the sea growing rougher by the minute, she decided to use both oars. She put her back to it smartly and drew the curragh out beyond the breakers before they broke her.

The boat lifted high on a swell, dropped precipitately into a trough. Up . . . and down. She kept the bulbous prow headed into the swell and craned her neck to watch the water beyond the headland.

Yes, there it was. Rather, there *he* was. The head of either a man or a seal bobbed in the cold water. She rowed out another hundred yards to where the swells rose more gently, and watched.

A long arm struck out, took a swimming stroke. Another. Another. The brainless donkey was trying to swim out to Skellig Michael! She wagged her head at the very thought. Obviously he was one of those inlanders from the mountains who knew nothing about winds or tides or the vagaries of changing weather.

Bridey knew a thing or two about the sea, and she knew the danger in which she was placing herself. The wind, bucking against the tide, was raising the swells higher and higher. Whitecaps were starting to break over much too frequently. The skies beyond the Skelligs had darkened ominously. She had best return to land before the storm line caught her. Already two inches of water sloshed in the bottom of her puny craft, and she had nothing to bail with. She shot one last glance toward the tiny swimmer in the tumultuous sea. She watched the water surface for the right moment. As a swell subsided she set one oar deep and stroked powerfully with the other. The curragh pivoted half a revolution. She headed back where she belonged, toward shore.

Well beyond the breakers now, Padraic struggled onward. Once in his childhood days, back when he was reckless and foolish, Padraic of Lambay had swum from his island home all the way to the mainland to its west. He did it on a dare from his best friend, who turned right around and betrayed his best-friendship by tattling to his father. It was the warmest time of year and a sunny day. Even so, Padraic almost did not make it. His father, storming with pride and rage, came over with a sailing smack to fetch him home.

Then the Behr appeared, a ruddy clan magnificent in their strength of arm, and with them came death and destruction. Col of the Behr ruled Lambay now, and that, ultimately, was the reason Padraic now struggled in icy water. It was Col's fault and Keiran's and . . .

Padraic rolled over to rest and swim backstroke awhile. Gray sky hung just out of reach above him. Gray water sloshed in his aching ears. He accidentally inhaled some and nearly went under in a coughing fit. Every muscle in his body hurt from the cold.

And it began to dawn on Padraic that quite possibly that misty gray isle was farther away than he could manage. This was not an altogether prudent plan. When his head sank so far that water broke across his face, he reversed himself to upright and began swimming more earnestly, coughing and choking.

The cold had slowed him to a crawl. He could not stroke strongly. He could not move fast. He could not kick hard. When he forced his head up high enough to see anything, the headland he had left looked as far away as the island he wanted to reach. A pox on such trickery of the eye! With landfall so far behind him, now he was surely close to his destination. He swam slower. And slower. He could not unclench his teeth enough to cough properly. Water rattled in his chest.

Suddenly some behemoth of the deep nudged him. A whale? Here? Did whales attack people? When he paused to look he went under again. Water filled his ears and face and rushed through his hair. He kicked frantically to the surface.

The whale took a huge mouthful of his tunic and tugged. He

fought back, struggling as much as his cold, cold arms would let him. The water in his eyes blinded him.

Then the whale barked in a soprano voice, "Hit me, and I leave ye to the fishes! Stop fighting me!"

He responded with a fit of violent coughing. He slammed against the whale's side, too spent to resist. Strong hands gripped his clothes. Strong arms hauled him upward.

A boat. This was a boat, not a whale. Now he was being dragged up over the curved stern gunwale into it, still coughing. The boat lurched wickedly and came to an even keel. Water sloshed over him.

She was small and slight as women go, much too frail looking to be out here alone in a curragh. Her thick brown braids reached her waist. Thicker yet were her long black eyelashes. And her freckles—between the freckles and her upturned nose, she looked like a child.

She was no child, obviously. With grim determination she set an oar and turned the boat around in a single stroke. She rowed for shore with long, powerful pulls, scowling at him all the while.

To Padraic's intense embarrassment, his coughing turned to nausea. Fortunately he had not eaten for nearly two days, so he had little to lose. What he had, though, he lost, and he hated himself for his weakness.

He felt a bit better then, though still quite as cold. He sloshed a hand in the bilge. "About as much water inside the boat as out."

"If ye don't like this boat ye may jump out and wait for another." Her voice snarled tightly, angrily, as if lunging through this rough sea were his fault.

"This one will do, lady, and nicely."

She watched the horizon behind him as she worked.

When he twisted to see what she was looking at, the curragh lurched dangerously. Its bilge water slewed from side to side, throwing the boat all the more dangerously off kilter. She was looking at an approaching wall of darkness and rain.

"Ye would do well to bail, I trow." She glanced behind.

Padraic noticed that with the wind behind them they were approaching the rocks with unnerving speed. He couldn't stop coughing. Still, he knelt low and began scooping water with his forearms, his elbows pressed together, splashing it up and over the side. The bailing seemed to do little good.

They appeared aimed not for the headland exactly but for a tumbling creek and steep hill hard beside. Not that it mattered. The rocks along that shore were just as lethal as the rocks at the base of the headwall.

She paused, resting no doubt, and studied the sea behind him. Casually, she dipped an oar. The curragh broached suddenly, wallowing sideways in a deep trough. Padraic's terrified yell dissolved into still another coughing fit. So near to shore . . .

She calmly, expertly, planted the other oar. The curragh rotated another quarter turn and caught a huge swell exactly right. It carried them up and over the worst of the rocks onto the stony strand. She stood swiftly and leaped out, grabbing the gunwale to keep the boat from riding back out on the next swell. With a few jerks and tugs she dragged it up nearly to grass.

She stood a few moments, arms akimbo, looking at Padraic. "Ye might consider getting out now. 'Tis drier outside the boat."

He tried to stand, but his cold legs would have none of it. She tipped the boat, and he leaned, and together they dumped rescuee and bilge out onto the stones.

She pulled the boat well above tideline and turned it bottomside-up.

He crawled up into the grass, flopped onto his belly, and closed his eyes. Lying face down, he didn't seem to cough as much. Or perhaps he was finally clearing the seawater from his tortured lungs.

He heard her wet skirts slap against her ankles as she left. He didn't want her to leave, but he was too spent to raise a protest. The swishing skirts returned and settled to silence beside him. He opened his eyes to a basket of mussels packed in seaweed. The basket nestled at an easy downhill tilt within the green of cropped grass, dainty weeds, and emergent shamrocks.

He rolled to his back. Every body part he owned ached.

She was watching him with huge, opalescent blue eyes beneath those magnificent lashes.

What should he say? How should he say it? He of the glib and ready tongue suddenly found his tongue stiffer than his weary

15

limbs. "How did you know I needed help? Were you coming in from that island?"

She shook her head. "I saw ye jump in."

He watched and waited. Sometimes silence loosened a person's tongue better than questions.

It loosened hers. "I almost didn't bother. I even started to return to shore. But I knew ye'd not make it half way, so I turned around again, and waited."

"Waited! Why?"

She shrugged. "Ye'd just proven what a silly goose ye are, to try to swim out there. I assumed ye were silly enough that y'd not take m' help the first time offered. So I waited till ye realized m' help was needed. Saves argument."

Padraic pondered all that awhile. He couldn't fault the logic. Still, her casual disregard for his comfort and safety angered him. Incredibly thoughtless girl, this.

The rain arrived then, with occasional drops and then a steady fall. He shoved himself clumsily to sitting. He was so cold now that he no longer felt cold.

She bounced to her feet and picked up her basket. "'Twill be dark before long. Ye best come along with me, for ours is the closest rath. Well, nearly the closest."

In a wild paroxysm of effort he flung himself to his knees. Gaining his feet took a bit longer. Stiffly, numbly, he followed her as she strode away up the hill. His toes hurt with every step. His fingers tingled painfully. His lungs ached.

They picked up a path through the grass. It wound over an oak copse and out across a grassy lea to the top of the headland. He stopped and turned to look behind.

Still suspended in the mist between sea and sky, the vague gray island called to him. *There is safety here. No matter how big and black, no horse can swim here. That is not the end of the world. This is. Come to me.*

He would love to come, but there was no longer any point in going. This strange girl with the long braids knew he was here. She knew he had attempted to swim to the island. An innocent word from her would send his nemesis out there straightway, and he would be trapped.

16

He felt incredibly alone. Abandoned. He could run no more. He didn't even care anymore. He would let fortune cradle him or cast him out as she chose.

Wearily, his feet dragging, he followed his rescuer through the gathering darkness.

2

Cattle

So you are Padraic of Lambay."

The farmer, Bridey's stepfather, looked for all the world like a badger. Beady eyes crackled in a thin, pinched face. Below his narrow shoulders, his body widened, broad and chubby. His long, pointed nose and clumsy waddle completed the effect. He was probably half a head shorter than Padraic, but he seemed bigger. He had backed his stool against the wall so that he could lean against the dried mud and stretch out his legs. "Where is Lambay?"

"'Tis an island just off the eastern coast, sir."

It was a good thing, probably, that Bridey shared no blood or heritage with these her stepparents, for who would want to bear a physical resemblance to a badger and a hedgehog? Her pudgy, stubby stepmother rocked back and forth on a tiny stool by the fire. Not only did she possess the long narrow nose of a hedgehog, her short, gray, backswept hair bristled in little peaks and spikes. She must have been dreadfully ill in the last year or so to have cut off all her hair. Now it was growing back in fits and starts. She perched as near as she could get to the fire in the center of the room. She drew her wool shawl close around and asked innocently, "Rocky?"

"In a few places. Mostly it's cobble shores and sand or mud beaches. Excellent clamming."

With a hazel broom, Bridey was sweeping out the little one-room farmhouse. She said nothing, and Padraic could see no indication that she was listening. Still, how could she help but listen in a room so small?

"So there's not many rocks to jump in amongst. Eh?" The stepfather's crackly little eyes skewered Padraic.

Padraic glanced away, suddenly embarrassed. It had been a silly thing to do. He had been desperate then. He still was.

The old man opened his mouth to speak, and from the look on his narrow face Padraic could see he was about to become the recipient of another barb.

But just then Bridey lurched into her stepfather. The broom struck against his knee.

Swift as a stoat, the stepfather swung his arm out. It hit her at about belt level and shoved her back. "Clumsy wench!"

Padraic wanted to leap up and knock the old badger off his stool. The fellow's legs lay sprawled out over the floor, he not so much as lifting his feet to aid her in her work, and he dared call her clumsy!

Peace settled again almost as abruptly as it had been shattered. Bridey went on with her sweeping, with no change of expression whatever on her face. The stepmother rocked gently back and forth, muttering to herself.

Whatever the old fellow had been going to say must have fled with the peace, for he began anew. "'Tis far from home you are. Why are you here, if your kith be on Lambay?"

"My kith be no longer on Lambay. We were driven off the island by interlopers."

"Do I know them?"

"The Behr, a warring clan from the north, around Louth. They hold that land still, as well as Lambay."

The man grunted. "Cu Chulainn country. A land of heroes."

"And ruddy proud the Behr are to be a part of it."

Bridey must have been listening, because she paused in her sweeping. "When did ye last see your home?"

"Seven summers ago."

"That's sad. And ye've been wandering ever since?"

Should he explain? The less these people knew, the safer he would be. And yet he wanted to tell. He yearned for someone to know, and he could not explain why he wanted that so intensely.

He kept his mouth closed for a moment only. Then it spilled out his story against his better judgment. "The Behr drove us into the sea. We journeyed in two curraghs to a landing near the Liffey. There, roving bandits murdered the adults among us and took us children captive. Sold us into slavery, of course."

Bridey was studying him intently. "Your parents? Were your parents among the dead?"

"Aye."

"Be ye certain they died?"

"My first task as a brand new slave was digging their graves."

She watched his face a moment longer and turned away to her sweeping. Her eyes caught the orange firelight; they were moist. Why would she weep for a stranger in a strange land? Padraic was none of her concern.

The old man harbored no such sentiments. Curtly he asked, "Sold, eh? So you be an escaped slave, aye?"

"I am a free man now."

"Hardly," the old man snapped.

Padraic was not about to let this sneaky fellow know he was right. Free? Escaped indeed, and free only in that he had run beyond his master's reach. A man? Some would say he was still untried and not yet fit therefore to be called a man. Yet Padraic had seen more, and done more, in his seventeen years than most men see and do in a lifetime.

"A free man, sir."

The badger grunted. He pondered the waning fire and the iron kettle nestled in its coals. "If you wish to eat with us, freeman, you might help Bridey bring the cattle in before dark. Soon's the milking's done we'll sup." He nodded toward Bridey as she put her broom aside.

"I'll do that, sir." Padraic leaped to his feet, glad that he no longer had to sit on that cold, hard floor of beaten earth and glad to be done with this conversation.

He followed the silent girl out the door into the clammy evening air. He could not see the sun for the thickness in the sky, but the west glowed a little brighter than did the east. His clothes had not quite dried yet, and the icy wind cut through them.

Damp cattle smells hung on the air, pungent, penetrating smells of fresh green grass and fresh green manure. From the sucking mud of the farmyard they walked out into stubby pasturage.

She wandered across an open lea, aimlessly it would seem, and not a cow in sight.

20

Padraic jogged a double-step and fell in beside her. "As I was traveling to westward, to this end of the earth, I crossed a severe mountain range. Snow on the peaks, high passes."

"The reeks, aye."

My nemesis on the black horse followed me across those tangled mountains, with never a hesitation. I am doomed. "Those mountains to the east, the sea to the west and south. What is north?"

"More sea, they say. I've not been there m'self."

So. This bit of land jutted out into the ocean, a peninsula with its throat plugged by mountains. With the black pursuer on this side of the reeks, Padraic was nearly as trapped as if he were on an island.

They topped out on the crest of a smoothly rounded hill. To the south, several miles beyond and below, the sea washed in a rippling white chalkmark against a ragged shore. Beyond the flat line of water, other distant, rounded hills rose dark against the horizon. Everywhere he looked from the windswept hill, Padraic saw barriers. The barriers stayed his progress; they didn't seem to slow down his nemesis at all.

He gazed across the water to islands in the southwest. They were fairly large and gentle islands. They appeared far too inviting to serve for escape.

Bridey was watching him watch the sea. She twisted to look at the islands in his line of sight. "If it be islands ye want, and ye are so determined to reach them, I'll be taking supplies out to Skellig Michael in a week or two. Ye may go along."

"Skellig Michael?"

"That pointy little chip of an island ye seemed so determined to swim to today."

"That would be wonderful!" He paused and licked his lips. "You hardly know me, and it's insane of me to ask a giant favor, but I will. When we go out, can you leave me there? More impor-tant, can you not tell your parents—your stepparents, I mean—that I've gone?"

She stared at him. "I would not've guessed ye're a Christian."

"A Christian?! Whatever put that bit of fluff in your head?"

"Skellig Michael is a monastery. A retreat for men of the

21

Christian faith. They've no land or soil on which to farm, so they depend upon the raths round about here for supplies."

"I had no idea . . ." A Christian monastery. What a splendid place to hide! Padraic's pursuer would never think to seek him there. That would be like seeking an eagle in a henhouse. "Yes! Yes, I want to go."

She bobbed her head, a terse little gesture that said quite plainly, "Very well. It's as good as done."

They continued down off the brow of the hill into dense woodland. Padraic saw cattle tracks all about now. The beasts' cloven hooves had cut deeply into the mud, punching black, wet holes in the woodland floor. Near the bottom of the wooded slope, cut stumps replaced trees, and the sky opened.

Placid cattle stood about all over the glade. Calves with round, curly faces watched Padraic curiously, their ears flung forward. With impatient nudges, their mothers shoved them into motion even before Bridey began to wave her arms at them.

Padraic jogged downslope, moving around behind the knot of cattle. Well uphill of him, the lead cow stuck her nose in the air and took off toward the trees at a trot. Her dewlap flung itself back and forth with every stride.

"I suppose," Bridey called, "the rest are down by the tarn. Follow these—they'll go home if you stay behind them—and I'll fetch the others."

Padraic called something cheery and affirmative and forced his tired body to a trot. He felt neither cheery nor affirmative. He did not want to follow ten cows across this hill, even if they slowed to a lethargic walk. He wanted to rest. He wanted to eat.

Eat. Yes. That he wanted most of all.

The lead cow slowed and ambled up the wet hill into the trees. A few cows off to the side stopped; for what, Padraic could not imagine. He jogged through the mud and yelled. They thought better of their idleness and fell in behind the leader.

The hill was much taller going up than coming down. Padraic noticed that almost right away, even if his weary thighs hadn't started to tell him so. He struggled up through the welter of trees and holly bushes and hazel and bristly raspberry tangling his ankles and thin little saplings and low-hanging branches. At one point he found himself surrounded on all sides by cattle. He was supposed to be staying in back of them, driving them ahead of him.

The lead cow topped out on the crest, leaving the forest behind. Another half dozen animals with their calves sauntered out into the open. Good! They would all be home soon, home to that cauldron on the fire and supper. In just a few strides, Padraic himself would clear this miserable woodland.

Suddenly the startled lead cattle ducked aside and bolted back toward him. Furious at the stupid beasts, he fought his way across the hillside to cut them off.

And then Padraic froze, terrified.

It was he.

From the northeast he came, on that horse. That black horse. That huge black horse with feet like anvils and nostrils big enough to inhale a pig. They came rising up out of the ground over the crest, the warrior and his horse, as one would imagine Lugh would emerge from his underground hill palace.

The rider wore his black tunic and vertically striped black-and-white leggings. His black cloak he had tossed carelessly over his shoulder. The silver inlaid work in that intricately wrought sword at his hip gleamed, even in the overcast. The silver trim on his bridle shone. The enamelwork glowed. Instead of the usual gold torque, he wore a thick silver necklace, bold and heavy.

Padraic melted silently earthward and bellied out where he had stopped. The warrior followed no trail—Padraic had no way of knowing where the fellow was going or whether he would pass close enough to see a terrified lad flattened down among the raspberry vines. Thank whatever gods that be that this warrior owned no dog.

Padraic pressed the left side of his head tightly into the mud. He held his breath as he listened with his right ear to the heavy, measured tread of the horse. What would he do if the cadence slowed? What if the ogre paused to investigate? Should he leap up and run? Stay hidden?

A cow loped past him not two feet away. He stayed frozen. The hoofbeats faded without slowing. Still he remained.

Silence, but for a couple of agitated cows with their irregular scurrying.

Cautiously he raised his head. The warrior had passed to the northeast, down over the side of the hill toward the unknown, away from the coast and those comfortable looking islands. If he stayed his present course, approximately, he would not pass anywhere near Bridey or the rath of her stepparents. Both now lay behind him.

Padraic leaped to his feet. He ran down into the covering mantle of the woodland, into the safety of closeness. He heard cows round about in all directions, but he did not care. He remained as desperately hungry as ever, but it no longer mattered.

He had just come within a whisker's width of being discovered by the man who had crossed the breadth of Erin to destroy him.

3

Mares

Gwynn gripped her ax two-handed. She felt very, very close to lopping heads, and her husband's would be the first to roll.

Next to go bouncing down the hall would be that hussy's!

Her husband was holding court in the banqueting hall today, and no wonder. Truth, and he was entertaining half of Connaught with this debacle. His friends and cohorts and partners in crime ringed the great and echoing room, seated in all their opulence and folly, with smug grins and an obvious tendency to dropsy. How she hated them all!

"And thereby," her husband droned, "I proclaim our severance."

His moustache was graying, but only in places. His beard and moustache had always been darker than they ought to be, and the silver hairs made the darkness all the more obvious. He was getting flabby too. He was shorter than most of his retainers. All in all, he was not a prize to start with. What the hussy saw in him, Gwynn could not guess.

Gwynn herself was larger than this snippet of a girl, width as well as height. None of her weight was fat, and her breasts did not yet sag. Her hair still shone golden despite her forty years. It dropped in a single bulky braid down her back nearly to her knees.

Gwynn addressed not her husband, or even the room in general, but the blonde wench already seated at his elbow. "Your face tells the world that you pride yourself in your good fortune. You have ensnared a king of kings—a ri ruirech. You have achieved great power by making yourself consort to a man of power. You poor little fool! He will pillage your wealth and then tire of you as he tired of me and two others before me."

"Thank you," her husband interrupted. "You are dismissed."

Gwynn raised her voice and put the edge of a sword on it. "I am a queen, and I am speaking." She glared at him sufficiently to cow him and continued. "Of the three husbands I have taken, he is by far the saddest of the lot. You will find that the marriage bed will quickly lose its appeal—in fact, about as soon as you marry. I entered our union with two hundred cattle, eight bulls, and five horses. He is generously allowing me to leave it with my two favorite mares. I am cast out, departing his house with no lover, no wealth, and no prospects. I no longer have him." She paused. "Which, my dear, makes me infinitely more fortunate than you."

Still gripping her ax, she turned with disdain and began the long, demeaning walk the length of the hall to the doors at the far end.

"Mums!"

She hesitated, then turned. Her husband's voice would not have stayed her, but this was his youngest, Aidan. Of her husband's three sons, she had always liked Aidan best.

From his father's side, Aidan left his chair and stepped forward. "Two mares and a son, if you will have me."

Her husband roared, "Aidan! She is not your mother."

Aidan wheeled on his father. "By blood, she is not. My blood mother you drove out. It is Gwynn's hand that fed me, her arm that taught me the use of ax and sword, her lap where I listened to the tales of our fathers. She is my mother."

"Leave with that conniving, wretched woman, and you're out of my house. Not one cow will you ever see of mine, nor will you ever sit in this chair."

At seventeen years, the lad still had not achieved his full growth. His white hair tumbled about his head, constantly unruly. With his thin neck and gangling legs, he looked more a child than a man. But as he turned away from his father, a smirk graced his lips. With a man's casual boldness, he sauntered down the hall to his mother's side.

They left the hall together, from smoky darkness into the cold, fresh air of spring, and Gwynn's breast swelled with pride. She was losing this power struggle, but she was winning too.

Her husband's retainers stood about, holding her mares for her. Obviously they were here to make certain she took with her nothing of her husband's. The gods forfend that she should be allowed a cow or two! Donkeys. They were all such donkeys.

She paused at her gray mare's shoulder. "Aidan. Are you sure about this? Much as I would love your company, I advise against your coming."

"I am sure." His voice sounded solid, not the least hesitant.

Gwynn bobbed her head. "Very well, my son. Off we go adventuring." She slid her ax into its loop on her saddle and swung aboard.

The lad possessed no cattle of his own. Until this hour he had spent his life in idle, happy pursuit not of wealth but of music. His skill with lyre and bagpipe surpassed that of the fili, the minstrels. A penchant for poesy would not improve their holdings or their status now. She wished he had shown more initiative in developing a good herd.

He crossed to the picket line and untied his little roan mare. He slung himself astride, leaned over, and untied the bay mare beside his. He brought it along on lead as he joined his mother.

The grizzly, pot-bellied old retainer named Ronan seized the bay horse's lead line. "This is your brother's mare, young prince."

"Nay, it's mine. He was borrowing it." Aidan spoke boldly but not too loudly. "Did you receive orders to refuse me my property?"

"I received no orders at all concerning you, prince. I did not know you would be coming, nor were you mentioned."

"Then, dear Ronan, follow orders."

Ronan loosed the horse and stepped back.

Aidan dug in his knees, instantly urging the roan to a jog. The bay trotted along behind, her ears flopping.

Gwynn extended her arm. The retainer beside her handed off the lead line of her other allowed horse, the black pony-mare with the roach mane. She drew the line in a bit, that it not tangle in her gray mare's tail, and rode beside her son, out across the muddy milking yard toward the track.

Gwynn waited until a league of open ground separated them from the ears of the retainers. "You're throwing away all—your bloodline, your inheritance. I hate to see you abandon your heritage on my account."

The lad grinned. "And what am I throwing away? My father's

27

firstborn has already sired two sons. Sooner or later, one of them will seize the headship. Papa thinks his secondborn is a wise husbandman, the man to manage his herds. I'm his baby, his jester, his burden. He's never treated me seriously. Eventually, he'll throw me out as he threw out my mother, and I'll have nothing."

"Perhaps, eventually. But you'll have nothing instantly if you follow me."

And the boy smirked again, his lips curling. "But I have prospects, dear Mums. My future prospects. Under your aegis, I'll get wealthier and more powerful much faster than I would under my father's wing."

"The aegis of a woman with two mares and a battle-ax to her name?"

He smiled and reached over to grip her arm. "You are the only person, man or woman either one, who has successfully stood up to my father. And you are a queen not only by marriage but in your own right. Father is not just trading you for that little vixen at his side. He's getting rid of a potential enemy before she can grow any stronger, and he knows it. I know it. You'll not stay destitute for long."

The lad's assessment of her abilities fairly matched her own. So did his assessment of her situation and the danger her ex-husband saw in her. Probably the man would not stop with driving her out. Probably robbers or assassins were waiting somewhere for her even now, under his direction. She could use the boy's strength, untried as it was, and his sword.

She nodded toward the horse he was leading behind them. "That bay mare isn't really yours, is it? It's your brother's."

Aidan grinned. "Not only that, this roan too is borrowed."

* * *

Two days and twenty-five miles away, Donn of the Thicket waited nervously. His son, Donn of the Moor, seemed even more nervous. And no wonder. This would be an unpleasant task by any measure.

She had to pass this way. Steep, cumbersome mountains, difficult to cross, channeled man and beast alike into the valleys between. All valleys an eastbound traveler would use save this one were either filled with lakes, or boulder-strewn to excess, or choked with peat bogs. The woman was a queen and accustomed to taking the easy way. Therefore, she would travel through here, for this was the easy way.

Donn of the Thicket did not particularly like this assignment, but he had his orders, and the ri had been specific. The queen was not to die within the territories of her husband, or anywhere near, lest suspicion fall upon him, the ri. But she was to die. When she left the doon at Connemara, said the ri, she would be allowed no retainers or cattle on her journey. She would be traveling unprotected. Her demise would not be difficult to achieve.

The ri had said nothing about ladies in waiting, and Donn had forgotten to ask about companions other than retainers. She might bring along some ladies in waiting. Donn made an independent decision: he and his men would sell any ladies in the company of the banished queen and keep the proceeds. They certainly were not being well rewarded otherwise for this bit of skulduggery.

"Father?" his son murmured low, despite that murmuring was unnecessary. "Two travelers just cleared the slieves, heading this way."

"Two?" Pity. Only one lady in waiting. On today's market, one slave was not much return for a murder, particularly the murder of a queen. With Donn's typically scant luck, the slave would be fat and ugly to boot.

Donn's four companions were able to conceal themselves behind trackside brush. Donn himself was not so fortunate. He was a huge man, burly and wide, with a shaggy red beard. He stood out of the surroundings, as it were, in nearly any landscape. The hazel scrub of this open limestone country did not easily hide him, so he slipped back behind the hillock to the south of the path.

"Donn!" a companion called back. "Seven colors on them both!"

"Seven!" Donn blurted out an unholy word. Royals, and royals only, wore seven colors. This ri had sired no princesses; therefore a prince attended the dethroned queen. Donn knew the ri's opinion of his three sons respectively, and he knew their relative prowess as warriors. Only if that prince were Aidan would Donn dare attack.

* * *

Less than one hundred fifty miles to the southeast, a great black stallion picked his way down through the rocks to a swirling, rushing stream. He thrust his mighty muzzle into a pool among the boulders and drank heavily, with much slurping, for he wore bit and bridle.

His owner, ever proud, perched on a moss-decked stump and watched his stud horse drink.

Two times now, Keiran of the Great Horse had traversed this peninsula, south to north to south to north. So far he had heard no murmurs about a stranger from the east. He knew the lad had crossed the reeks and was out here on this jag of land somewhere. He now was confident the boy had not doubled back and recrossed the reeks, escaping eastward. Padraic of Lambay was here. Somewhere.

It was curious how his quest had taken on a life of its own. When Keiran first undertook to capture the runaway and return him to his masters, the assignment sounded simple. How far can a sixteen-year-old lad get before a seasoned hunter catches up? The price on the lad's head—ten cows—was the original goad, of course. Why undertake so mundane a task for any less than ten cows? With ten cows and this stud horse, Keiran could build himself a fine life.

That had been a year ago, almost to the day. The date when the lad ran had been two weeks before Beltaine, and Beltaine was coming up again in about two weeks. A year. Who would think it? That slip of a lad had given Keiran the slip, so to speak, over and over. It was humiliating. And Keiran of the Great Horse was no more humble than was his stallion. Perhaps that was why the need to recapture the slave now burned so brightly. The stake had grown to more than ten cows. Infinitely more.

Stumbling, his horse rotated and clambered back up the gully. He stopped, dropped his head, and nipped the top off a small, pale shrub. Keiran stood and stretched. Let the horse browse awhile.

Somewhere up the rocky gorge, water rushed. Keiran went exploring, stretching to climb over boulders, striding up through

30

the tanglewood over thick, soft, forest duff. The water roared more loudly, directly ahead. A pink jay clamored in the juniper above him and flew away on a rush of wings. Great tits, little round chunks of blue and yellow amid the spring green, chirped and tipped their black caps toward him.

A good time of year, spring.

The mist in his face told him about the waterfall ahead before ever he reached there. He followed a faint game trail out across flat rock until he stood in a notch in the land at the brink of Earth's beginnings. With magnificent white power the stream cascaded, plunging, dashing, from a ledge into a churning pool. Its spray roiled high and drifted downstream on the waterfall's own breeze. Glistening in constant wet, ferns and moss covered the craggy walls of the gorge.

Keiran stood awhile in this mystic hollow, drinking in the dark, melancholy beauty of it, as the gray mist blew in his face. No doubt he was surrounded this very moment by elves and perhaps a leprechaun or two. The wee folk made him nervous. They held such power in their tiny hands and twisted little minds. One never quite knew how to stay on their good side.

He turned away, eventually, and started back downhill through the streamside forest toward his horse. He thought he heard wee footfalls in the duff beyond the rowan and hazel. He did not look in that direction.

His horse had wandered away. He picked up its tracks and followed without so much as slowing or bending over. Clipping leaves and tender shoots as it went, the stallion had angled down through the trees and out into a wooded vale.

The wildness of this country impressed Keiran. Often in his journeying he passed through land untouched by farmers with ax and fire and plow. Rarely did he feel this sense of brooding mystery. He quickened his step.

Keiran saw his black saddle seat loom above a spindly rowan up ahead. His stallion raised his head and thrust his nose high. His ears tilted not toward Keiran but behind him and then to the side—everywhere at once. The stud horse was nervous too. He started to move away, but his dragging reins caught in a bush. He stopped.

Keiran reached the great black hindquarters and ran his hand along the horse's rump to his neck. He scooped up his reins and flicked the loop over the stud's head. Keiran moved to the horse's near side to mount, lest his sword tangle and bend.

The horse started forward the moment Keiran's feet left the ground, nearly sweeping him off with a low-hanging oak limb. That was not at all like the stallion.

Keiran wrenched the horse's head around and dug in his heels, sending them forward through the trees to westward down the vale. He wanted to get out of this gloomy forest quickly, though he could not say why.

The last he heard of Padraic of Lambay, the lad was headed south and west, well this side of the reeks. Keiran would return to the south edge of the peninsula, where the land was brighter, more open, windswept. He was confident Padraic had not come up through here. He knew where the lad was not. Now he would discover where the lad was.

4

Stoat

Once upon a time, evil Fomorians ruled Erin. In an epic battle, the People of the Goddess Dana, the Tuatha da Danaan, once and forever defeated the Fomorians. Then came the Celts. The blond invaders and the Tuatha da Danaan found they could not coexist, so they struck a bargain stained in blood—the Tuatha da Danaan would live in the Erin belowground, and the Celts would claim the Erin aboveground.

Through the cold, gray pastures and forests of the surface, Celtic herdsmen drove their cattle and sheep. Silence surrounded them, silence and wind. Nights and sunlight came and went. They made love and war with equal ferocity.

Even as the affairs of men played out in damp forests and muddy leas, far beneath their feet the Tuatha da Danaan feasted. For his fellow gods, the hero-god Dagda built great, mounded hill palaces. The Celts knew them as barrows and tumuli—burial mounds. But down within them, beyond the sight and reach of mortals, heroes laughed and sang in perpetually bright banquet halls. They feasted without end, lifting horns of ale to toast their own passage from death to immortality. Upon those tumuli of the gods and demigods, Celtic kings built their great halls, that the wisdom of god and man might share common ground.

And the greatest of all was Tara.

"Good. We need all the wisdom we can get."

Morosely, Cuinn of Emhain Mhacha looked about the lesser hall at Tara. In the dark shadows lining the walls, the assistants and apprentices huddled. Denied the fire in the middle of the room, they hunched up inside fur robes and cloaks. No font of wisdom yet, today they served as aides to the brehons. Tomorrow they would become the law of the land.

Of the dozen brehons gathered here, Cuinn could probably

be called preeminent, despite that Emhain Mhacha was being eclipsed as a seat of power. He could certainly be called the oldest.

And brehons were not, by nature of their position, young to begin with. Many years' study of law and philosophy, every detail and every word committed infallibly to memory, was only the beginning of a brehon's life. Kings were merely warlords. They neither framed nor administered the law of their own lands. The brehons did. And the august body here tonight would prepare a list of prospects from which the council of nobles would choose a new high king. The ard ri. King of kings.

Cuinn's body had dried up years ago. His spidery legs and arms trembled constantly as long as he was awake. His lower lip tended to droop, and he was not always clear in his pronunciation. He was gray now and nearly bald, though his oldest friends remembered his long, blond hair. On occasion they still mentioned his legendary speed and agility and the way he could slip soundlessly through thick woodland. His nickname for many years, until age slowed him to a walk, had been Uasal—the Stoat.

He sat nearest the fire in the center of the lesser hall, his pillow and its wolfskin cover as close to the warm coals as he could manage. Despite that Beltaine would be upon them in a fortnight, the cold, raw wind and rain outside made the night feel like winter.

Indeed, all twelve clustered close around the fire.

Blaine of Clones added, "Wisdom and much luck. No matter whom we nominate, fighting is bound to break out somewhere."

"Doesn't it always, when there is a change of high kingship? Of any kingship, for that." Muirdoch of Ailech, representing the northern Ui Neill, was probably the youngest of the men assembled. Even so, rare wisdom rested in him.

Cuinn admired Muirdoch's quick mind and brusque manner of getting immediately to a point. Less so did he admire the man's impatience. To be fair, Muirdoch's impatience might stem from the fact that he was somehow different from others and no doubt grew up with no little teasing, as children are wont. Tall, lean Muirdoch possessed a face that tanned quickly in summer, and his hair, a strange dark brown, grew long and shaggy. His nose, an eagle's beak, dominated his face. In theory, he was a purebred cousin of a grandson of Niall of the Nine Hostages. In fact he was probably the product of a happy romance somewhere beyond the sea, perhaps Spain.

"I mean worse fighting than usual." Blaine drew his woolen cloak closer around. "Every candidate has his faction, and every faction is altogether too enthusiastic about its own man."

Muirdoch studied the coals in front of him, or perhaps he studied one of Dagda's great palaces deep below. How far did those crackling eyes see? "My cousin died at an untimely moment. He left too much undone. He should have been grooming a replacement. A tanaiste. The man he wanted to succeed him."

Blaine made a noise like a baby blowing bubbles. "That's no guarantee of an easy succession. Many's the time I've seen the council ignore a tanaiste and espouse some lesser choice. Or better choice, in some cases."

"How many candidates do we have to take over the high kingship, all told?" From behind Cuinn, the brehon from Laigin to the south spoke up. He attended tonight as a courtesy, since the Ui Neill and the ris of Laigin struggled at desperate odds with each other.

Politics. Cuinn despised politics.

"Six serious contenders." Cuinn responded without twisting to look at the man. His arthritis bothered him terribly in clammy weather.

"And all six have an armed unit ready to put them on the throne?"

"Eager to put them on the throne. Yes." For a few moments, Cuinn mulled a new possibility, an intriguing possibility. "So who is a seventh, a man without arms?"

Blaine brightened. "Of course! A compromise."

Cuinn nodded. "Muirdoch. Your fileh. He knows the bloodlines of all our chief candidates. Who shares the blood but not the hunger for power? Whom can we put forward as a compromise candidate?"

Muirdoch raised his eyes to Cuinn. "I disagree strongly. Adding a seventh cord complicates the six-cord braid unnecessarily. Let us deal with what we have, without adding the aspirations of still another man."

35

"I'm not putting it forward as a request yet. I'm exploring the prospect."

Muirdoch grunted noncommittally. "I'll fetch him." He raised his hand. He hardly moved, actually. In an instant, two of his attendants hovered at his side. He sent them off to seek his fileh.

"Comment?" Cuinn addressed the room in general.

"Yes." Muirdoch scowled. "The family of the Ui Neill have served capably. Why are you so eager to change dynasties?"

Blaine answered before Cuinn could get his faltering mouth to respond. "If your candidates rise above the crowd, all well and good. I will gladly put them forward. But Ui Neill or not, they must demonstrate a readiness to lead. We'll not hand anything to them."

Everyone else offered a comment or two, but no one added much. Cuinn didn't expect much yet, not until these men had let the idea incubate awhile. Tomorrow he would receive the good comments, the thoughts of depth and wisdom. By the time Muirdoch's fileh arrived, everyone was fairly well off the subject.

The poet seated himself at Muirdoch's right. He appeared a slight, singularly composed man, and young, considering that a fileh prepares for his vocation twelve years at least. And yet he knew not only the complete genealogy of his clan but those of most of the other ruling clans as well. Another twenty years or so, and he would be the wisdom of all Erin.

Muirdoch introduced him as Finbar. White Head. It fit his fair locks well.

Finbar looked placidly from face to face. "How can I serve you?"

"We need," Cuinn began, "a seventh candidate to present to the council. He should be related to a kingly line, preferably the son or grandson of a regional king, but have no aspirations to the high throne. He ought to lack a fighting force."

"I can give you genealogies. I cannot guess at aspirations."

"A point well made. You see, though, what we're seeking."

"I see." The fair-haired poet looked a bit confused. "Other than Ui Neill?"

"Not limited to Ui Neill."

"Mm." He studied the fire a few moments.

Cuinn possessed several useful mnemonic devices for committing unrelated information to memory, but this young man must know more than a few. What is more unrelated than strings of names?

"You have candidates from Airgialla and Ulaid. Laigin. One from the northern Ui Neill and two from the southern." He pressed his lips together. Thin lips they were, practically nonexistent. "There is a family in Cashel —"

"No." Muirdoch cut him off. "Too far. Unwise to invite them into our midst. We don't need to complicate matters."

"Mm. Could you accept another line from the southern Ui Neill?"

"Who?"

"There is a family of royal descent, the Slevin."

Muirdoch wrinkled his nose. "Mountain men?"

"Their name bespeaks their origins." Finbar paused again to stare at the fire. "For about five hundred years they ruled the vales and mountains south of the Liffey. The line split into three, and two sons emigrated. The Slevin who remained in the mountains merged with the Slaney, royals with royals."

"We dismissed the Slaney from consideration."

Finbar nodded. "One branch traveled south and now rules near Cashel. He is a ri ruirech in his own right and also by marriage into the Tiernach. The other branch settled north of the Liffey on the coast and on the island of Lambay. The Slevin of Lambay are the most direct line back to the original royal house."

Cuinn shook his head. "We also dismissed the Behr."

"The Behr of Louth are interlopers on Lambay within the last few years. Upstarts. The ancestral family there is the Slevin. They were the princes of eld."

"You speak truly. 'Were.' The Behr destroyed the prior inhabitants of Lambay."

"Drove them out. The line still exists, though I have not yet heard where."

Cuinn studied the towheaded poet a few moments. This could be the solution. "Gavan? That's your territory. Where did the Slevin go when they left Lambay?"

Behind him, Gavan's gravelly voice growled in the darkness.

"Cutthroats murdered the escaping adults and took the children into slavery. At least two of the children, very young ones, died. That was seven years ago, and we still haven't stamped out the brigands. Like water they are, flowing silently, disappearing into the earth, bubbling up somewhere else. There's some wild country there—they can lose themselves easily."

"Who purchased the surviving children?" Once upon a time, Cuinn flowed like water. Now the Stoat waddled clumsily, a badger at best.

Gavan called to his aides. In rumbling tones, he muttered with two of them. He raised his voice. "The uncle of my assistant Brian here purchased one of them. I'd say he's the one you want. Unfortunately, he escaped from the uncle last year. Ran away."

Muirdoch glowered. "Then he's at large, who knows where. Not worth considering. Too much trouble to find him, particularly since he won't wish to be found."

"Brian?" Cuinn called. "Come forward."

A remarkably sturdy looking young man slipped between Muirdoch and Cuinn by the fire. Cuinn had trouble for a moment identifying the rush of emotion he felt. Envy. Cuinn envied the lad's youth, his strength and energy. Cuinn would never himself see the likes again.

"Brian. Tell us what you know about the runaway slave."

"He's quick of mind, sire, and quick of body too. He and I played together when my uncle first obtained him, before he was old enough to carry a full work load. He was always able to run faster and jump higher than I. And yet he was very clever. We did some dastardly things, and his quick wit saved us many a caning."

"A good playmate." Cuinn considered this. A young man who could outdo this vibrant, virile fellow before him.

"A good friend, sire. Then I entered study to become a brehon, and he took over my uncle's stables."

"Managed them? At what age?"

"Fifteen, sire. Not quite that. As I say, he's quick."

Muirdoch wagged his head. "No. We have enough sneaks in high places. We don't need another. And he's too young. What is he now? Sixteen? Seventeen?"

"He's exactly what we want," Cuinn contradicted. "No aspirations to the high kingship, no partisan fighting force, no lands to protect at others' expense. Youth is an advantage. He'll have excellent advisers at his side to guide him. And if he's as quick as Brian suggests, he will be able to gauge between friend and foe, good advice and bad. And he'll grow with the crown. Think what we could do with a high king trained from the start as high king and giving the crown the full vigor of a long manhood. Tara is not yet recognized as a unified seat for all Erin. We need that kind of stability if we would permanently establish Tara as the seat of seats. The true ard ri. The king of kings."

Murmurs and muttering all around him told Cuinn that his opinion enjoyed at least partial approval from his fellow brehons.

Muirdoch grunted. "We need heroes, not political buffoons. Your politics is sound, but politics does not make high kings or any other kings for that matter. Ability does. A strong arm, swift feet, and a leader's skills outdo politics any day."

"If he's successfully evaded capture so far, 'tis an excellent indication of ability."

Muirdoch persisted. "Nor are bloodlines the key to making a king. They help, but they mean nothing in the end, where fighting skill determines the man. If he's a runaway, I'd not call him a leader."

"Neither would you call him a slave by nature." The more he defended his idle idea, the more Cuinn himself believed in it.

Blaine of Clones bobbed his head. "I think we should at least examine this young man and test his prowess—mental prowess as well as physical strength. If he has the makings of a hero, Cuinn's idea bears close scrutiny." He twisted around to face Muirdoch—Blaine still enjoyed the flexibility of middle age. "You are the man to convince. May I suggest you direct the search personally. You'll receive some immediate impression of his native talents. If he wins you over, splendid! If not, you can report to us concerning your misgivings, based on your firsthand impressions."

Muirdoch pursed his lips momentarily, then licked them. "Good point. Excellent point. Very well, Blaine, I shall. Brian, you will tell me all you know about this young man. Everything. From that I will know how his mind works and therefore where he may be found. Finbar, you will remain at court here. I'll take only three retainers with me. I want to travel fast and light."

Blaine beamed. "Good. Good. Brian, tell all of us, not just Muirdoch. We need all the information we can get concerning him."

Young Brian studied the fire. "Well—uh—to start with, his name. He doesn't use his family's name of Slevin but rather the Lambay designation. Padraic. Padraic of Lambay."

5

Fieldfares

Gwynn, once of Connemara and now of Nowhere at All, pondered the fragile uncertainty of trusting in the strength of man's arm—mostly to keep her mind off her saddle sores.

Gwynn and Aidan rode now between two great, rounded, glowering mountains, down a narrow valley defile. Though a few trees studded the open valley floor, the truly dark forests did not start until the mountains began their upward slope. The valley appeared fairly flat, but its stream, hardly more than a brook, danced so swiftly and merrily among its boulders and riffles that one knew it was descending rapidly.

Beside her, Aidan sprawled in his saddle. His mare's reins lay flaccid on her neck, for he needed both hands for his panpipes. He tooted idly, putting together some odd little tune. It was maddening.

Gwynn could not relax so thoroughly as did her son. She could not shake the feeling that sooner or later her ex-husband would try to send woe upon her. She certainly would have, were the situation reversed. As they rode down the valley, Gwynn made sure they remained in the open corridor. Here along the streambed, away from the trees, she could see trouble coming from quite some distance away. There was one disadvantage, of course; trouble could see her coming too.

A few hundred yards downstream, a loose flock of fieldfares and redwings lifted out of the streamside brush and flew across the creek into the forest. Moments later, with a sharp *chee!* a kingfisher shot itself straight from a downstream alder to a clump of alders hard beside the riders.

"Aidan! Act nonchalant, and put those stupid pipes away!"

"Huh?"

"Brigands! If they be but five or six, we've no problem. More than that and you've some fancy swordwork to do."

41

"Mm." The callow lad stuffed his pipes down into the linen bag on his saddle.

Gwynn fervently wished she'd been more diligent in enforcing Aidan's martial practice. Panpipes, for all that's sacred!

She drew in a couple feet of the black mare's lead line and tucked it firmly beneath her thigh—the leg without the rubbed sores—bringing the pony's head in closer. She dropped her looped reins. From now on she would direct her mare with knees, calves, and heels. She would need both hands free if the disturbance ahead was what she thought it to be.

Gauging from where she'd seen the fieldfares rise, she rode ten yards more, cued her mare to a halt, and yanked her broad-ax. She raised her voice enough to echo off the hills behind them, directed it downstream, put her most imperious edge to it. "You in the brush there. Present yourselves to the queen and declare your business."

Uphill of the track, a sapling yew rattled. Nothing else moved.

"Very well, rogues. I assume you are up to no good and intend to fall upon some hapless traveler. I really don't think that sort of thing should be allowed. My prince, to arms! We shall rid the land of this nuisance."

Aidan drew his sword so swiftly it whispered. He, too, had tucked his lead line beneath his thigh, but apparently the roan he rode required a hand upon the reins. That surprised Gwynn. If the roan really was borrowed from a brother, she would expect it to be better trained. Aidan's brothers loved working fine war horses into shape.

She balanced her ax beside her ear, gripping it with both hands so that she could swing it instantly to either side of her mare's neck. To improve her purchase, she drew both knees up tight under the saddle's bulging pommel. Henceforth she would direct her mount with her heels and body weight.

Her head high and her ears working, the gray mare moved forward on command. The black pony mare skittered nervously beside Gwynn's left knee.

Gwynn's ears were no longer as sharp as they once had been, and Aidan's were untrained and untested. She wished she could hear above the noise of the four horses now, the way she once could. Their hooves wiped out such subtle sounds as grass rustling, as a man drawing a deep breath just before his charge.

Gwynn, however, was not the only warrior hampered by an untried assistant. With a howl, a fair-haired young man leaped out prematurely from behind a dense green bush ahead. Moments later, beyond him, another came screaming out of the shrubbery. She heard cries across the track beyond Aidan, but she would deal with these two upstarts first.

Deftly she took out the first young man simply by rotating her mare instantly, very nearly in place. The broad gray rump swung around wide to the left, quite unexpectedly; it broke the lad's charge in midstride and knocked him off his feet. She knew that lad. Donn of the Moor. His whole family served as retainers to her ex-husband. And where Donn of the Moor was would his father be.

She roared at the scenery in general, "Donn of the Thicket, you attack me and you're a dead man!"

Even as she spoke, she swung her ax one-handed toward the second attacker, giving the haft a twist and a hook. She didn't have to watch where it was going. She was already turning her attention across the track to the other shouts, to pick her next target. The ax in her hand jarred to a heavy pause; the twists and hook she had made carried it on, then, in a wide arc up past her horse's neck.

She grabbed its haft with her right hand and sat poised to strike again, but no targets rushed toward her. Blood from the ax blade dripped onto her arm. She could smell it. She was ready! But the skirmish was stayed.

From partway around a small hill, Donn of the Thicket had already shouted to his men to hold. So it was Donn and five underlings, including his son. They all stood frozen, like a strategy diagram hastily drawn in battle dust.

"Your loyalties are sadly misplaced, Donn of the Thicket, if you would attack your queen, and she so far from the throne she once held. I'm sure you know I've been dismissed. The ri would have had to tell you his plans when he sent you ahead. 'Tis no longer your business nor my former lord's whether I live or die, for I've left his territory."

Aidan's sword too was bloodied. A rather pudgy, base-looking fellow sat in the wet grass beyond Aidan's roan mare, his head sagging, his right arm wrapped around his ribs. The front of the man's tunic dripped red. Aidan swung his roan around to watch behind them, becoming the eyes in the back of Gwynn's head.

She nodded toward the fair-haired lad struggling to his feet behind her. "I spared your son once, Donn, but I'll not bother to spare him again."

"I hear your meaning, lady. But if I let you live we dare never go home again."

"Then don't. You served me yesterday in Connemara. Serve me tomorrow where fate leads us."

"Our families . . ."

"Go and fetch your families and your cattle."

Donn opened his mouth to reply, but a raggedy old mountain man nearby crossed to him and muttered something. Donn frowned. He motioned "Come" to his son and the others. They gathered around Donn on the slope, an impromptu council of war—four men, where moments ago there had been six.

Gwynn sat comfortably, easily, on her nervous mare, ready in an instant to make that none where once there had been six. The very nerve of these brigands . . .

They turned as one to face Gwynn. Donn nodded. "You need retainers. We need a more certain source of necessaries. We're agreed. We will join you, to the betterment of our fortunes and our families.'"

Gwynn bobbed her head once. That was sufficient to indicate approval. "A fortnight hence, Aidan and I will be found where the salmon gather in the River Corrib."

"Too brief a time, I fear. We will be traveling with little ones. But we'll hasten."

Gwynn could wait. She had the time free. "Your fortunes will not suffer."

Donn bade good day, giving her the obeisance due a queen. From beyond the hill, a man brought down their mounts—three small ponies. The dead man and the injured fellow were placed aboard them. Great, burly Donn of the Thicket rode the third. It appeared he ought to be carrying the pony. The brigands, with no further comment and no looking back, started up the valley toward Connemara.

Aidan slid off his mare and wiped his sword in grass tufts before drying it on his shirt. "I fear you're very foolish, Mums, to tell him we'll travel to the Corrib. He'll run right home to Father with the news of where we are."

"Stop and think, my prince. Your father owns scores of fine war horses, most of them mine. What were these men using?"

"Cull ponies." A grin spread across Aidan's face. "You're saying my father is too miserly for Donn to confide in him?"

"Your father, my prince, is the cheapest of churls. I brought him wealth, and he claimed I squandered his property. He grasps. He never proffers. Donn knows that."

With a final glance up the valley, Gwynn felt content that Donn was not going to try to double back and catch her by surprise. She started her mare down the track again. "Besides, your father is vindictive. If Donn were to let slip that he had me in his grasp and let me go, your father would flay him. No. Your father won't know that Donn's party returned home until a week after they have gathered up their families and chattels and left again."

Half a dozen fieldfares rose out of the streamside brush ahead and flittered up into a silver birch by the water's edge. As Gwynn and Aidan approached, they burst out of the tree and continued downstream, exactly what fieldfares would be expected to do if no one lurked ahead.

The queen and her prince rode in silence for perhaps an hour. She kept a close eye and ear to the land. No danger threatened for the moment at least.

She glanced now and then at Aidan. The lad appeared lost in reverie. The discussion about his parsimonious father could not have been what set him dreaming this time.

"Your thoughts have drowned you, prince."

He grinned at her. "The skirmish back there. Six to two, the odds, and we won handily. Now I understand why poets would devote so much time to glorifying the feats of heroes. I've been in fights before, and drawn my share of blood, but—"

"Far less than your share, lad."

"Very well. I've drawn blood. But I never realized how exhilarating a clear victory like this is."

Gwynn smiled. Silent, without voice, her heart spoke. *I rejoice with you, lad, and I envy. Never ever let yourself lose that sense of exhilaration, as your stepmother has done.*

They would arrive at the Corrib long before Donn. They had plenty of time. Gwynn called a noonday halt. They munched dried crabapples with honey, finished the last of the barley loaves, and discussed that night's supper.

On the trail again, they left the vale and cut up over a dark and craggy slieve to the southeast. Gloomy forest engulfed them almost instantly. But the gloom kept the understory open and sparse. The horses climbed the rugged slope, following more a game trail than a proper track, without a lot of difficulty. They crested out on a treeless crag. They would follow the mountaintop ridge a couple hundred yards and begin their descent down the other side.

The forest was safe. Her ex-husband had sent Donn. He the cheap one would not send two bands.

Or would he? She and Aidan drew in their horses simultaneously. A company of nine men, all well armed and mounted on sturdy war-horses, came riding up the mountainside, probably a mile or less ahead. Gwynn would never have spied them had they not been crossing an exposed lea. They followed a faint track, no doubt this very trail. Another quarter hour and they would pass this point.

Aidan muttered, "Recognize them?"

The band disappeared into the forest on this side of the lea.

"No. I doubt they are of Connaught."

"Do you suppose, like Donn, they are seeking us?"

"Probably not." Gwynn pondered prospects a moment. "My eyes are not what they once were, but I think I perceive that the man behind the leader wears three colors. I would guess it is simply some chieftain returning home from raiding. Or planning to raid into Connaught."

"Why do we tarry? Six is one thing. Nine is another. They are too many to overcome."

"You will take my horses and conceal yourself up beyond

those rocks. I shall handle this." She left her ax on her saddle and slid to the ground.

"Nine to one? Mums. . . "

"You will learn, Aidan, there is more than one way to win a skirmish." She waved an arm off to the southwest. "Go, down over the side, before they draw near enough to hear the horses."

She listened to the mares lurch and stumble across the rocks. Then the forest muffled their hooves. Already she was unplaiting her long braids. She let her rippling hair fall loosely to her waist. She shed her shawl and unbuckled her broad leather belt. She could hear horses approaching through the forest downhill of her. She untied the thongs on her calves and tossed her sandals aside. The mountaintop breeze lifted and fluttered her loose tunic. Her fine linen shift, flowing from neck to knee, billowed in the light air. She loved the soft kiss of fine linen.

Transformed from the tightly bound and braced warrior queen into a soft and feminine Everywoman, she seated herself on the squared, mossy limestone crop beside the track. The startled war party rode out onto the open crest. She arranged a smile on her face with which to greet their leader.

6

Sow

I am a wind of the sea,
I am a wave of the sea,
I am the sound of the sea.

I am a stag of seven tines,
I am a hawk on the cliff.

I am a teardrop in the sun,
I am the fairest of fair flowers.

I am a raging boar,
I am a salmon in a pool.

I am a lake upon a fair plain,
I am the spear that roars for blood,
I am the god of inspiring fire.

I am . . .

Pure, cold darkness was fading into the first feeble light of early morning. This enchanted hour just before dawn seemed to give the chief druid's poem a special magic.

Padraic knew the incantation by heart. He'd heard it often enough, ever since infancy. It was the poem the first Irish Celt, Amergin, intoned as he set his right foot upon Erin to claim the land for humankind. Despite its familiarity, it never failed to move Padraic, to fill his heart and sometimes even to put tears in his eyes.

This broad, gentle hilltop had been denuded of trees quite some time ago, it would seem. The few stumps remaining were weathered and overgrown. Rich grass now covered the knob, for the cattle had not yet been brought here to graze it down. And between the meadow and its encircling forest, thickets of haw-thorn were springing up.

No wonder the druids and abbots of Currane chose this spot for Beltaine observance. Hawthorn was never more sacred than at this moment of the year, on this first day of May. Numerous strips of dyed linen festooned the thorny branches, tangible evidence of intangible invocations to the spirits of the land.

Every person in the tuath stood about on the hillcrest, the young and old, the rich and poor, the highborn and base. The abbot of the Currane monastery nearby invoked his God's blessing upon this first day of May and upon the people gathered here about. In the name of God he blessed all the beasts and children. It was quite beautiful.

The chief druid of Currane pointed dramatically toward a pile of tinder and sticks. With a muffled *fwoof!* the pile leaped spon-taneously into flame. Children oohed. He turned and ignited the second bonfire with a pointing finger. More oohs and aahs.

From downhill, cattle lowed. Padraic could smell them com-ing in the moist air of predawn. From now until noon, every ani-mal in the district would be driven between the two fires. That passage through the fire would protect them from disease during the year to come. Would that men could be so easily protected!

With further incantation the chief druid greeted the sun as it shot its first golden shafts of light out from beyond the northeast-ern hillcrest. Almost immediately, it slipped upward behind a thick overcast just above the horizon. No matter. The celebration of Beltaine was off to a good start.

Assuming that Padraic's black nemesis was still seeking him —a totally safe assumption—the man would sooner or later come here, where everyone else had come. He might be sniffing about at some other Beltaine observance at this moment, but he was near. Not finding Padraic there, he would come.

Padraic stayed back among the trees that crowned the hill on three sides.

Then a mighty yell snapped his head around. The son of the ri tuatha was executing a perfect salmon leap over the near bon-fire. Expertly he snapped his body just as he alighted, making no sound at all upon landing.

Padraic could do that. He could leap, in fact, every bit as high as did this young prince—and land quite as silently. Padraic carried the blood of kings, although one would never know it from the way he had to run and hide.

A girl who must be the prince's bride—she didn't look much more than fourteen—jumped over the fire behind him.

The leaps themselves ought to be sufficient to bestow fertility, their intended purpose. But the prince and his bride then knelt before the abbot. Muttering unintelligible Latin, he laid his hand first upon the man's head and then upon the girl's. The bride and her prince must really hunger for offspring, to seek blessing by every possible means!

The first boaire to drive his cattle between the fires, here came Bridey's stepfather. He carried his pig board on one arm and led his prize herd bull. The chief druid's assistants, white robes flapping, struggled mightily to keep the rest of the herd in a straight path. These were men who knew cattle too. Padraic could have told them about the recalcitrant beasts. He had been herding them for nearly two weeks. How Bridey put up with the moody milkers escaped him. Cows reflect their masters, it would seem, and these beasts were sullen and uncooperative.

Druidic assistants on the far side of the fire redirected the cattle, some of them with great difficulty. Padraic saw one assistant catch his companion's eye and wag his head disgustedly. Padraic would drink to that.

For some reason, Bridey's parents felt called to bless some of their hogs as well. It would seem their boar was on his own, for he was not in the herd. Just as well. The truculent beast would as quickly tear a man as look at him. They had brought the three sows and the shoat they planned to raise into another brood sow. The boaire was having a more terrible time with his four pigs than with all his kine, and the cattle were ills enough.

The man's wife followed behind. She carried her pig board too. Why did they not enlist Bridey in this? Bridey ended up with all the other work around the rath.

The stepfather managed to keep his side of the swine herd headed in the right direction, alternately poking with his prod and fending the animals aside with his broad pig board.

The stepmother did not fare so well. She lunged back and forth, sticking her board into the face of first this hog and then that one. She would no sooner turn one than another would dodge aside. She was always a few moments too late to really be effective. Apparently, in order to herd swine one must be smarter than the pigs.

Her most fecund brood sow stopped suddenly and changed directions. The sow was headed for Padraic. He need only leap out and flail his arms, probably, to turn it back toward the fires. He did not. He slipped behind an oak. The hog came crashing into the woods. He listened to its progress through the trees and brush as it left the frightening crowds behind.

But its flight had drawn attention this way, and attention was the last thing Padraic needed. He turned and followed the sow down the hillside through the crackling woodland. From the back, in the early morning half-light, he would appear to whomever bothered to notice him to be a simple peasant hurrying off to retrieve the wayward sow.

He kept going, all four miles back to Bridey's rath. The feast of Beltaine would have to continue without him.

As he passed beneath the wych elm near the gate, the errant brood sow came bucketing across the lea toward home. Padraic stopped and stood very still. He had no board with which to shield himself from her teeth, should she decide to attack. But she did not. She charged past him through the mud and ran inside.

The egg basket on her arm, Bridey paused by the gate as the sow galumphed by. "Home so soon?" With a bemused half smile, she turned and walked off toward the sty.

As Padraic entered the ring wall, Bridey was closing the sow's pen. "Careful of that pig," Padraic called. "She's not been through the fire."

Bridey turned to him and almost smiled. "She never has been. She always gets away and comes back home. Doesn't like crowds, I suppose."

"She has good taste, by and large. Neither do I." Padraic fell in beside Bridey as she walked off toward the gate. Half the chickens laid outside the earthen ring wall, try as Bridey might to train them differently.

Padraic knew where one of them laid—under the hazel bush by the wall. He parted the grass and retrieved an egg.

Bridey picked up the speckled hen's egg beneath the wych elm. "I'm surprised ye went. Ye seem afraid to be seen."

It would be prudent at this point to change the subject. Padraic asked, "Why didn't you go?"

"I mind the farm. Someone ought. I threw out the old fires and swept the hearths. They're prepared now for the fresh Beltaine fire the Papa will bring home. M'stepparents had not done that when they left this morning." She paused the barest moment. "Besides, if I go, I might find someone to marry, and I'd leave here. Then where would m'parents be?"

"You mean stepparents. Or is one of them a natural parent?"

"M'mother died, and m'father remarried. Then he was killed, and m'stepmother remarried."

Padraic felt he ought to say something. But his nimble tongue, which so frequently got him out of strange corners, decided to abandon him this time.

She turned and studied him. "Who are ye? I mean, who are ye really? Not just an escaped slave."

"Yes, just an escaped slave. But that was a long time ago. In theory I am free—or soon will be."

She studied him a moment longer, not the least convinced, and headed off toward the gorse thicket. "I overheard m'stepparents talking last night. The Papa has heard of a stranger in the area, Keiran of the Great Horse, who was enquiring about a newcomer with an eastern accent. Papa supposes that would be y'rself. He's going to try to find the fellow today and see if there's a reward."

"I'm sure there is." If Padraic's heart had ever lingered on some fond nubbin of hope, that nubbin was gone now. Why did he keep running? Why didn't he just turn himself over to the black hunter and be done with it? He was so weary of running.

Like a hog seeking acorns, Bridey knelt low and rooted about in the gorse. She didn't seem to notice that her hands and arms were getting scratched. She retrieved an egg and then, from the other side, another.

Padraic almost missed a creamy egg nestled in a bed of

shamrocks by the wall. He paused a moment before he picked it up and let his eye linger on the curious beauty of the smooth white egg against the brilliant green of those little round leaves.

Bridey ambled off toward the gate in that casual way of hers, as if she had nowhere to go in a hurry. And yet, she always arrived, wherever it was, quickly. "I was going to row out to Skellig tomorrow. The curragh is about loaded, save for the eggs and cheese." She looked at Padraic beside her. "The tide will be right for another hour. Shall we go today instead?"

He searched her face for any sign of what she might be thinking. Her blue eyes said nothing, and they said everything. She knew nothing about his situation, and she understood all.

He did not hesitate. "Yes. Let's."

* * *

They nestled the eggs in amid the barleymeal. The wheel of hard cheese they slipped under the center seat. The crock of salted soft cheese was wedged just so up into the bow.

Two pairs of oars lay under a bush by the boat. Padraic picked up the second pair reluctantly.

"No need," Bridey said. "If I take two sets of oars, it will tell anyone on shore here that I have a companion. Only one set gone suggests I went alone."

Padraic grinned. That had been his surmise as well, but he had been prepared to help with the rowing. Oarless, he gratefully clambered aboard as they shoved off.

"Tuck down," she suggested. She hauled backwards on her oars. The leaky curragh lunged forward against the swells. She had to be the most powerful rower Padraic knew.

There was no room in the overloaded boat for him to hunker down fully. But by tucking his head below his knees and lying well forward, he would look to the casual eye like just another bundle.

Bridey improved that appearance by throwing her cloak across his head and shoulders. Any fishing smacks that passed would see nothing more than Bridey and her load of supplies. A companion in the boat with the girl? Why, no. I don't think so.

He sighed. "I feel incredibly unheroic. Here I cower in the shadow of a girl. Hiding. It grates on my very soul."

"At least your soul is still connected to your body. Be ye certain this Keiran is trying to kill ye?"

"He tried to the last time he nearly caught up to me."

"And ye say he's been dogging ye for a year? The reward must be high indeed."

"My assessment as well, though I don't know how much he promises. Your stepfather strikes me as a man who will seize the slightest chance to profit from me."

"Rest assured."

Despite the overcast, the day had seemed calm. Scant breeze, quiet waters. In the tiny boat, the waters did not seem calm at all. The craft pitched and bucked with each stroke of the oars.

Padraic was not a seafarer. His stomach began a lengthy explanation of the folly of leaving solid ground.

He tried breathing deeply. "The waters are very rough. Storm coming in?"

"The waters around the Skelligs are always rough. The rocks set up countercurrents that shift with the tide. I've no notion at all how ye thought ye'd swim out here."

He would this very moment much rather be swimming. Deep breaths were not helping his distress in the least. "Are any boats about?"

"None."

He came up from under the cloak in a thrice and managed to lean over the side in time. If he felt unheroic before, he felt utterly foolish now. There she sat in quiet composure, rowing steadily. And here he sat in disgusting discomposure, sweaty, light-headed, his palms clammy, his stomach openly rebelling, his throat locked into a nearly permanent gag.

She smiled at him as a mother might smile down upon a feckless child. It was the first smile he had ever seen on her. "A sailor ye are not," she purred. "But that makes ye no less interesting."

Interesting! She called him interesting. Was that the best word she could come up with? He glanced out past her shoulder. They were still a long, long way from the craggy islets of the Skelligs.

The swells evened out into great rolling humps. Up and over and down with a *whoosh*. Up and over and down. Up and over and down. He lost his stomach twice more before they drew within hailing distance of the island.

He threw the cloak aside. "I'll go it alone from here."

"Be ye daft? The waves will smash ye into the rocks."

"I'll take my chances." He rolled out over the stern. The chill water pierced instantly to his skin. It filled his ears and eyes. He didn't care. It sloshed in his face as he struggled, swimming desperately. He arrived at a drywall stone dock five minutes after the boat did.

The tidal rip sucked him under twice and threw him against the rocks. It flung him wherever it pleased. As it hurled him toward the jetty, men in gray tunics reached down and pulled him out of the water.

His stomach felt no better, but neither did it feel any worse. He sat on the solid wall. He knew better, but his body kept insisting that he was still bobbing out there in that horrid sea. When he closed his eyes, he could feel the motion as vividly as he had in the boat. What evil tricksters were the gods of the sea!

A large fellow with a rumbly voice was saying something about how Bridey was a day early. And who was this stalwart chap who swam along behind, ha ha?

Padraic began to shiver. And he also began to notice that these jolly men were laughing at him. Not with him—he wasn't laughing. *At* him.

He didn't care.

Yes, he did.

He felt miserable, body and soul.

Far beyond the roiling sea—but not nearly far enough—the mainland they had left hung in the gray haze. On that jut of land, his black nemesis sought him. Probably the fiend and the stepfather had already found each other. Most probably, the fiend knew by now where Padraic hid.

And here he sat with no escape route, waiting for the ax to fall, a lonely cormorant perched on a much-too-tiny rock. And Bridey and her companions laughed at him.

Happy Beltaine, Padraic of Lambay!

He glanced back at them. No, bless her heart. Bridey was not laughing.

7

Cockerel

This was not real. This was one of those ridiculously impossible dreams that seem vivid and true for about fifteen minutes after one wakes up—and then you regain your senses. People didn't really do these things, or live in these places, or subject themselves to these austerities. Surely not.

Padraic picked at the tasteless stirabout in his bowl. He sat cross-legged on the damp cobble floor with a dozen men in a beehive-shaped hovel of dry-laid stones. No one had bothered to so much as fit large and small stones together. It was a heap. Why it did not come tumbling down around these monks' ears, Padraic had no idea.

He could see daylight between some of the stones near the top of the curved roof. It was raining now. Why did the water not drip down through those holes?

The monks dressed carelessly in the plainest of wool. Apparently they used whatever wool came off any sheep. Black, brown, white and yellow, coarse and fine, all were carded together without regard to color or texture. The resultant fabric, if it could be called that, must itch mightily. It was lumpy, and it pilled. Most of the men went barefoot despite the perpetual dampness. And although most and probably all were free men, possibly of rank, none wore a torque around his neck. None advertised his rank.

If trees had ever grown on this conical rock, they were gone now. What did these men burn for fuel and light? With what did they cook this tasteless gruel?

Ages ago this morning, when Padraic set off from the mainland, he thought eagerly of remaining here in hiding. The prospect grew less inviting with every mouthful of porridge. This was the company food, the good fare. What did they eat when no visitors were around to bring out the cook's best?

56

He must have been looking about the cramped room a bit too critically, for the monk beside him smiled apologetically. "It's temporary. We've only been here a short time. We're going to build with greater care higher up the slope."

"What, pray, is the advantage of clambering higher up this crag?"

"There are some very nice sites there, more level than this one. Not extremely so, but more so."

"Forgive me, sire, but a sheep's back is flatter than this floor."

The fellow grinned impishly. "A hurley ball is flatter than this floor."

What this man's Erse name was, Padraic didn't know. He called himself Gallus, a Latin designation. The man had mentioned that the Latin name meant "cockerel." Why would this fellow call himself after a chicken? As tough and strong as any trained warrior, he possessed a quick wit and open mind. Padraic could not shake the thought that this man, as well as the others here, was utterly wasting himself on this minuscule cone of rock. All the man and his companions had to do was ride into any tuath in Erin and take over as a stranger in sovereignty. And the tuath would be all the better for the change of kingship.

"Uh," he asked, "just what do you all do here every day?"

"Matins in the morning, then work at the building."

"Matins?"

"Morning worship."

"Ah. Then build things."

The fellow's head bobbed. "We plan a clochan for each monk, that he might spend time in contemplation alone. An oratory, of course. It will take some time."

"Where will you find the wood?"

"We'll build in stone, like this building, but with greater care and effort."

I should hope so. Padraic filled his mouth with more of the unpalatable gruel. Some things are best left unspoken.

Gallus continued, "Study in the afternoon. Vespers in the evening, and to bed. Four of us here read Greek and Latin well, and the rest are learning."

"Greek. For the prayers."

"We say our offices in Greek or Latin, either one. Depends on who is leading the service."

"There are no women here."

"None of us was married when he came."

Padraic finished his stirabout as his mind and body fought bitterly with each other.

This is a safe haven, among Christians, his mind insisted. *Whether you admire Christians or not, Keiran is not likely to seek you here.*

Subject me to the privation and terrible food in this benighted colony, his body fumed, and I'll never forgive you. I'll make your life a misery.

My life already is a misery, and has been for a year. I want respite. Padraic was somewhat surprised that his body objected to the situation here so strenuously. It was his body that had suffered most in this flight, paying endlessly in weariness and aches, in bad food and irregular meals, in that recent disastrous episode of seasickness. Indeed, to leave here would subject his delicate stomach to the rigors of another crossing. Too much! Too soon! The tasteless stirabout aside, didn't his body want the rest?

Not here! his body insisted.

He excused himself following the meal, such as it was, and wandered outside. The rain had eased off. A coarse, misting drizzle persisted, making the dark rocks glisten. He stood awhile on a small, jutting outcrop and studied the steep hillside. The island rose out of the sea and up into a single pinnacle. It appeared pointy and bare from shore. It appeared even more so here, although the more Padraic studied the craggy slopes, the more dwarfed trees and scrawny bushes and patches of grass he saw.

A tuft of shamrocks sprouted from among the boulders at Padraic's feet. Imagine that. In this barren scape! The vivid green softened the stark rocks and whispered "Hope."

He could see where some of the new buildings would go, high up there. Ridiculously aloft. The monastics were in the process of constructing a staircase to the sites, up through the tumbled rocks of the hillside. They were building dressed-stone steps here and cutting them out of the living rock there. Hundreds of steps. The fools!

He turned a half circle to survey the rocky shore below. The sea could not be called high or dangerous today, and yet it churned violently amid the rocks. Birds, it would seem, were just as foolish as monks. The place was alive with them. What did they find so attractive about this ugly rock pile? Gulls and an occasional kittiwake dipped and soared. He spied a pair of white gannets fishing offshore to the southeast. Glossy black crowlike birds with stunning red beaks hopped about in the boulders to the northward. Padraic could not recall having seen anything quite like them on Lambay.

Lambay. Mum with her broad smile and voluminous lap. His sisters and cousins. Soft, gentle shores, tasty clams, wind-riffled pastures. Lambay. A thousand miles away, a thousand years ago, a thousand ways different from this miserable cairn. Lambay.

A hundred feet below him, Bridey was readying her curragh at the crude little quay. She turned suddenly and called up to him. "Padraic? I must leave, to be home by full nightfall. Be ye coming or staying?" She had known he was there all the time.

Padraic picked his way through the boulders and occasional grassy patches to the path and down it to the quay. His body said, Not in a million years will you remain behind. But his mind seized his tongue before his body did and blurted, "I ought stay a while, don't you think?"

"I think 'tis not m'decision or yours, but theirs." She dipped her head and looked past Padraic's shoulder.

Powerful, square-built Gallus and a chubby companion were making their way down the path. The companion wore a curious small leathern cap painted with intricate, intertwined plaits. Each carried a sturdy pole on his shoulder. The fat monk walked barefoot. How the roly-poly fellow managed to do that in these sharp crags escaped Padraic, but it gave him one more reason to suspect the sanity of the whole colony.

Gallus the Cockerel smiled cheerfully. Cheer. In this corner of barren waste. "This is Pileatus. I don't believe you've met Pileatus yet. He's our cook."

In theory, stirabout was a porridge that one simply could not ruin. It virtually made itself. Were Padraic the cook, responsible for the stirabout he ate today, he would have hidden the fact as carefully as possible instead of crowing it to the world.

Pileatus chuckled, every bit as relentlessly cheerful as his companion. "They thought that since I am so broad, I love food. Therefore I'd make the most of our simple rations."

A scheme that failed, obviously.

Gallus stepped out onto the quay. "We'll see you safely off, Bridey." He tossed a leathern scoop into the boat. "A bailer."

"I thank ye."

Pileatus attempted to flatten out on his stomach on the quay with his head out over the water, but there was no such thing as lying flat on that paunch. He flexed his knees, dug his toes into the rock, and gripped the gunwale of Bridey's curragh with both hands. His leathern hat slipped slightly askew. Gingerly Bridey stepped down into the boat.

Padraic nodded toward the construction project. "How many steps, pray tell?"

Gallus mused, "We calculate there will be about six hundred by the time we're through."

"With that much work or less, could you not quarry out a comfortably level spot down here?"

"We could, but 'twould just not be the same." Gallus's smile spread out across his face again. He smiled amazingly often for one in so dismal a circumstance. "Ah, and you should see the sunrises from up there!"

Padraic grunted. Sunrises indeed. "Then you need every strong arm you can muster. That's a wondrous amount of toil, and precious few men to see it completed in a timely manner. Let me remain here a few weeks, and I'll help with the work."

Gallus's eyebrows rose. "We value and appreciate your most generous offer. We'd enjoy having you, and we certainly could use the help, but we purposely limit our number. Already we have as many mouths as we can feed, and others ashore waiting for an opening, so to speak. Besides—" he shrugged "—we've no need to hurry. If we don't complete it in our lifetimes, those who follow will."

Padraic caught himself staring, and he could not stop. "Others wait to come here?"

"Eagerly." Gallus nodded. "We had a death just last month. A sad case. He was a vibrant fellow, and constantly on the move. One morning he suffered severe headache and his left arm and leg ceased to function. He couldn't talk save to sing praises to God. He lingered two days and slipped away. A brother from up near Killorgin took his place within the week."

Padraic stared a moment at Bridey and her boat, unseeing. She snapped her head impatiently.

He lurched forward, still gripped by confusion.

Pileatus held the boat as Padraic climbed in. Gallus again thanked him for his generous offer and with the sign of the cross blessed Padraic, Bridey, and the boat.

Pileatus let go as Gallus stretched out his pole. Padraic seized it and used it to stabilize the boat as Bridey set her oars and turned them away from the rocks.

She twisted to watch the swells behind them. "Now!"

Padraic let go. The boat surged forward, away from that small chip of land in the oceanic expanse. Pileatus lurched to his feet, waving happily. Gallus raised his arm in a warm farewell gesture. They watched, obviously content, as the boat pulled away.

Perhaps if Padraic were active, as Bridey was, his stomach would fare better. "While we are so far from land that no one can see the number of heads in this boat, let me row awhile." He perched on the thwart ahead of her.

She hesitated a moment behind him, then said, "No. 'Tis too dangerous. We'd have no control as we were switching back and forth. The curragh would broach in the heavy swells and dump us out."

He mulled this a few moments. She was right. Still, he intensely dreaded this crossing. He was almost ready to risk capsizing if his stomach would purr more contentedly.

What was it about the island that bothered him? Something strange. Something at sixes and sevens. "I didn't see a boat there!" That was it! "They had no boat drawn up on shore anywhere on that island that I could see. How can they return to the mainland, should they choose?"

"Why would they do that? They're already where they want to be." She rowed with easy grace.

"But they're trapped! What if . . ."

"If the sea is too heavy for us to bring them supplies, it's too heavy for them to leave. And if the sea is mild, we carry to them what few things they need."

"Yes, but . . . "

But what? Here was a contented clan of men from diverse places and diverse circumstances, building for the future even as they carefully hid themselves from it. They cheerfully went about stacking stones, learning to read, and saying their mysterious words of Latin and Greek, as if that were all life need offer to make one happy.

And they didn't want him.

They didn't need another set of brawny arms. They didn't want another quick wit. Go home, Padraic.

He had no home.

They rode swells as high as the swells of morning. Sea . . . horizon . . . sky . . . horizon. Sea . . . horizon . . . sky . . . horizon. Sea . . . horizon . . . sky . . . horizon.

His stomach only briefly caviled over the faulty nature of the stirabout before off-loading it. Why, oh, why, could those monks not accept his presence at least long enough for his stomach to recover from the indignities heaped upon it this morning?

Bridey's opalescent blue eyes watched Padraic without really watching him. She watched beyond him, keeping Skellig Michael just beyond his left ear, navigating, at least for most of the time, by using the island as her point of reference. How did boats get out there when fog reduced visibility to two strides? Why did the mainlanders so eagerly suffer these wild seas to bring provisions to foolhardy men?

"What drives men and women so?" Padraic found himself voicing his questions aloud, and he hadn't meant to.

"What?" She had been buried in her own thoughts. She surfaced enough to look not past him but at him.

"What horrible forces are at work here? You risk your life to take a boatload of things out to men who throw their lives away on a remote rock. It's madness."

"Not at all. 'Tis the faith. As the apostle Paul said, the body of Christ is formed of many parts. Those men have given their lives to Christ in that particular way. A blessing they are, and a blessing they render to us all. I give m'life to Christ in this way."

"For what reason? What do you receive for all this?"

"We've already received, and bountifully. We're promised eternal life, and that's no small thing. We cannot repay that debt, but we can live in God's love."

"Madness."

"Have ye never heard the preaching of Patrick?"

"No."

"I knew so, for if ye did ye would understand."

Patrick. His whole life, Padraic had been hearing about Patrick. He was sick of hearing.

There were others abroad in the land who extolled the Christian faith, some of whom died before Padraic was even born. The ris and the druids preached roundly against those others. Interlopers from outside, they called them. Ah, the tales of bitterness and rancor Padraic heard about an arrogant churchman named Palladius, the poems of ridicule that the fili composed about him.

A few years ago during a visit to the rath where Padraic lived as a slave, the ri ruirech of Armagh had inveighed for two hours straight against a Briton, Secondinus. One would have thought the man was planning to plow all Ireland and plant weeds. All he did was plant a sort of colony at Armagh and then preach against the ri. From what Padraic had seen of the ri ruirech, Secondinus was probably not far wrong.

But Patrick. Few spoke against Patrick, and fewer still disputed him. The fili seemed strangely reticent about mocking him. Did Patrick wield some mystical power over the Aes Dana, the intellectual castes? If so, whence the source of that power? And above all, what power drove otherwise reasonable people such as Bridey and Gallus and his companions to these acts of insane sacrifice and effort?

And they did it all in the absence of Patrick. He was not there to oversee, or goad, or praise, or condemn. He had no idea what was happening here. Yet they labored on, cheerily, as if he stood in their midst.

No ri, not even the ard ri, wielded such pervasive influence, such absolute power.

Padraic suffered through another gastric rebellion—they seemed to come every quarter hour or so—and tried not to dwell upon the bounding swells and the woe of sea . . . horizon . . . sky . . . horizon . . . sea . . . horizon . . . sky . . . horizon. He could see why Bridey was afraid they would broach if they shipped the oars for even a moment.

He watched Bridey row a few minutes before speaking. "You've seen him and heard him speak then."

"No. My stepfather went to hear him, but I did not. This was several years ago."

"Then how do you know what effect his speaking has?"

She shrugged between strokes. "'Tis so frequently spoken of among Christians. Everyone knows."

Padraic draped himself over the gunwale yet again. He wanted to explore in his mind the ramifications of this immense power the Christian Patrick wielded. But his mind felt much too ill to exercise itself in thought. He did not want to appear so feckless before this strong, hardy, patient girl. But his stomach made a fool of him, and there was nothing he could do about it.

In abject misery he raised his head. How far yet? He looked past Bridey's shoulder at the approaching mainland and wailed, "No!"

Awaiting them on the shore ahead, just below the brow of the hill, sat a dark rider on a huge black horse.

8

Ponies

Raw, cold wind. Mist nearly coarse enough to qualify as rain. This wasn't spring. This was winter in May. Cuinn shivered in his doubled wool shawl as he slogged through the wet grass between his quarters and the Great Hall. The Hill of Tara seemed to attract wind and bad weather. Cuinn's native Emhain Mhacha, though lying to the north, boasted a far fairer clime. Or perhaps Cuinn was simply embroidering the past with a greater beauty than it deserved. He tended to do that.

He poked his head in the door of the Great Hall. Empty. Wait. This was Blaine of Clones he was seeking. Therefore he was seeking in all the wrong places. Blaine would not be found in seats of importance any more than absolutely necessary. Cuinn turned away from the hall and slipped and slid his way down around the hill to the kitchens.

There sat Blaine on a wooden stool beside the bakery door. The cook, a broad, burly woman who probably slaughtered meat animals with her bare hands, leaned casually against the door jamb. A lovely aroma of barleycakes drifted down the breeze.

As Cuinn approached, Blaine grinned broadly and extended a wooden bowl and spoon. "Just in time, Cuinn! Declan has returned from Rome—he arrived last night. He's brought us a magnificent new sort of cabbage. Do try it!"

Cabbage. Cuinn was not an overly eager enthusiast of cabbage. He dipped his fingers into the bowl and tried a few shreds.

"Declan claims that the Emperor Diocletian himself developed this strain over a hundred years ago in Dalmatia, and it's been improved since." Blaine glowed. When food was involved, he always glowed. "What do you think?"

"I think it tastes like cabbage."

Blaine sniffed. "No wonder you are scrawny and perpetually cold. If you enjoyed food more, you would enjoy life more."

"I enjoy a fine ode, and thereby enjoy life more." Cuinn settled himself against the door jamb the cook was not occupying. The heat from the bakery washed out the door. Welcome warmth. "Do you ever, in any way, feel you distrust Muirdoch of Ailech?"

Blaine had already returned to his cabbage. He thoughtfully chewed a moment, not unlike a cow with her cud. "I can't say that I have. He's dark. He keeps his own counsel. But I've never seen reason to distrust him." He frowned at Cuinn. "Why?"

"He left yesterday morning seeking Padraic of Lambay."

"At our behest." Blaine tipped his head. His eyes narrowed. "You're not starting to become forgetful, are you?"

"You of perfect memory, do you recall his entourage?"

"The apprentice, Brian, of course—Brian knows the lad. And a hostler named Rowan—rather dark little man, but quick with horses. And that fellow from up near Carrowkeel."

"And what do you know of the man from Carrowkeel?"

Blaine shrugged. "A minor chieftain, renowned as a huntsman. There's a story about—apocryphal, I'm sure—that he's paid to hunt down wanted men, murderers his specialty."

"And Rowan the Hostler?"

"Besides handling the stables of most of the northern Ui Neill, I believe he breeds and trains—" Blaine stared at his cabbage bowl a long moment "—hunting dogs. Coursing hounds." He shook his head. "You're suggesting—rather you are drawing me into suggesting—that Muirdoch intends that the lad from Lambay not be returned whole."

"He is staunch in support of his own candidate. I believe we may have erred tragically in sending him."

"He would never stoop to duplicity, let alone murder. He is a brehon!" Blaine shook his head. "No."

"He is the Ui Neill's brehon. You and I would not stoop to murder, but we are not he. How far will he go to place the crown of the ard ri on his patron's head?"

Blaine laid his bowl aside, a few shreds of his beloved cabbage still in it. That rarely happened. "He's young. His political ardor hasn't had time to be mellowed by age."

"Nor has his enthusiasm for power. He is wise, but his wisdom is raw. Native. He's not had time to temper it."

Blaine sat forward, his elbows on his knees, and stared thoughtfully at the ground. "Which makes him a highly dangerous man. That is, if your suspicions be anywhere near well founded." Absently, he reached down and browsed those last shreds of cabbage. Munching, he looked up at Cuinn. "What do you propose?"

"You know how much I enjoy travel, but I see no other way. We take an assistant or two—not the full entourage by any means—and catch up to him. Then we stay with him every mile, to ensure his honesty and the lad's safety."

"Send the assistants with our letter."

"Even with a letter, they cannot command the full weight of our authority. Besides, letters get lost or damaged. And if the letters be lost, our assistants become mere feckless young men."

"I know." Blaine lurched to his feet and stretched his back. "But it was worth a try." He thanked the cook profusely. Obviously, this was not the first special dish she had ever prepared for him.

Blaine was not nearly so heavily built as his appetite would suggest. He was no longer trim and certainly not gaunt, but he carried himself with power yet, the way men in their prime still do. Cuinn the Stoat gathered in his cloak and tried ineffectively to scatter his envy. Skinny and small-boned his entire life, he was never as powerful physically as Blaine was now, and Blaine was no longer any paragon of heroic stature.

They sloshed through wet grass down toward the stables. Blaine counted on his fingers as they walked. "We'll have to inform the others of our plans and then . . ."

"I did so."

Blaine looked at him. "Then I suppose you've set our aides to preparing the victuals."

Cuinn nodded.

"And the horses. They're ready?"

"Should be."

"You were certain I was going to go along on this. I've always envied your second sight."

"Envy no more. When you've no real alternative and a man's

life is at stake, it's not a case of second sight. You're a just man. Yes, you'd go along."

"I never know whether you're complimenting me or manipulating me." Blaine grunted and stared ahead. "Not that there's all that much difference."

Down at the base of the hill, three lads sat on the rock wall that penned in the ponies. Under the shelters, five shaggy dun horses stood about lackadaisically. No doubt they realized they'd be working soon—they were saddled, after all—but they were certainly not eagerly champing at the bit to get on the road.

Neither was Cuinn, for all that.

The coarse mist thickened further into genuine rain.

* * *

It was raining on the far side of Ireland as well. Padraic hunched in the miserable drizzle and wrapped himself in the most wonderful cloak of self-pity. He bobbed in the middle of the ocean with the windchop tossing their curragh. It was nearly dark. They had been rowing for hours, and still his stomach refused to adjust to the wild ride. His black nemesis waited on the shore behind them. Heaven only knew what awaited them on the shore ahead. No shelter from the storm, no rest for his weary body, no haven for his soul.

He watched Bridey work the oars. She had to rest every quarter hour or so. The moment she paused, she would set the oars just so, both blades in the water, to brace against the dipping, lurching waves. Then, resolutely, stoically, she would begin again her mind-numbing labor.

A cloak of self-pity, and there's the pity of it, offers no protection against the rain. He was drenched and chilled to the bone. His fingertips were pink and wrinkled, he had been so wet so long.

He sighed, long and plaintively. "Has the wind shifted?"

"No. 'Tis still southerly."

"Then we're still headed, more or less, north. Don't you think you ought to hook back toward land soon? As we turn into the wind, I'll row, if you like."

"We're going toward land now. Ye see it behind me there, in the distance."

"But that's not the land where you live."

"Not yet."

Padraic frowned. "Bridey. Where are we going?"

"There be, ye might say, two fingers of land extending into the sea. Off the fingertip of the one be the Skelligs. That's the finger upon which m'stepparents have their farm. We be traveling across the bay from one finger to the other. To the Dingle."

"I understand that. But where are we going?"

She shrugged in midstroke. "'Twill take your black pursuer at least two days to get to the place we will reach ere morning. If, once we reach shore, we travel fast, and stay well to the north of the south shore, we should pass him and get behind him before he realizes we've left that finger of land. Ye see that a mountain ridge defines the land before us. I suggest we travel immediately to the north side of that ridge before proceeding eastward."

The idea did not sound at all good to Padraic. More than once he had tried to double back behind the brute. It just didn't work. But what else could he do?

He grimaced. "So then I shall continue east, and you will return south and home. Are you sure you can find home?"

"I'll not bother."

Padraic sat up straight. "What? Not go home?"

"Why should I?"

"Because . . . because it's . . . it's home. Home. You know."

"'Tis no home to me. True, I've spent most of m'life there. But home is where I was born, when I still had m'mum. Home is a crannog somewhere east of the Shannon's mouth. I'm sure, should I reach the general area, I can find m'way there again." She paused and braced her oars. "'Twill be to your benefit. Your pursuer will probably wait at m'rath for m'return, to quiz me or coerce me into telling him where ye went. M'stepfather has likely already sold the man m'information of your whereabouts. The longer he waits there, the safer yourself remains."

"But your parents."

"They be not m'parents, either of them. I told ye that."

"But . . ." Padraic stammered, at a loss for words.

She really ought to start rowing again. Whenever she stopped, the boat leaped and wallowed mercilessly. "M'mum—

m'real mum, that is—told me something of m'babyhood, and where we lived. And I remember a bit of it. But that's all I remember, ever, of any place save m'stepparents'. I've never been anywhere, nor done anything, nor learned a thing save milking and planting. I cannot even say all m'friends have gone off a-marrying, for I've been permitted no friends."

"No gaggles of girls a-giggling?" Giggling girls never ceased to fascinate Padraic.

"No such at all. Ye see?" She took up the oars again. "I can work on the farm day to day for ever and ever—for ye know they'd not change a thing if they'd the power to keep it the same—or I can go off adventuring, and perhaps even to marry. If I must toil day in and day out, I might as well toil for m'own profit as for m'stepparents'. Sure and they've received their recompense for raising me, and then some."

"It's a dangerous world. I know. I've been abroad through it."

"If I meet m'end, 'tis nothing lost. M'soul be safe with Jesus."

Padraic gaped. He stuttered. She said it with such confidence, with such a casual disregard for life. But was it disregard? Bridey of all people must love life, to delve into it so completely. Whatever she did, she did as if it were the most important thing in the world to be doing. She didn't laugh or smile much, but that could be corrected with a little cajoling by Padraic. He prided himself on his ability to amuse any face, from king to carved wooden fetish.

Safe with Jesus. What nonsense! Building on Skellig, for Jesus. What nonsense. Patrick out there somewhere, preaching Jesus, turning all Erin to Jesus. What nonsense!

Patrick and Padraic carried the same name exactly, though in different forms. Patrick was an ex-slave, Padraic the son of kings. Patrick hewed to nonsense. Padraic knew you need only attend to proper worship, avoid wickedness, promote fair play, and behave as a man in order to succeed in life.

Patrick was revered beyond reason by legions of people.

Padraic, friendless, was running for his life.

As darkness fell, the angle of the windchop seemed to change. Certainly it mounted higher. Padraic could see his immediate future—death by drowning as the leaky curragh inexorably

70

filled up, if a malign wave didn't tip them first. Bridey was nosing the leathern boat more or less diagonally across the waves now. She claimed she'd never left home. How did she presume to know what she was doing?

Padraic tried not to fall asleep. She needed him to bail periodically. His stomach needed him to go through the motions of leaning over the side, though he'd long since dispatched the last of that porridge.

She swatted him with an oar. "Bail."

He jerked awake. The boat lolled dangerously. He picked up the soggy leather bailer afloat in the bilge and began scooping. He noticed after five or ten minutes of work that the sky was beginning to lighten. So was the boat as the water level dropped to a respectable inch or two.

Another five minutes and he could see in the extreme gloom ahead the hint of a landform. The finger of land to the south, Bridey's home, had long since disappeared. Now a vague suggestion of mountains loomed ahead. Another quarter hour and Bridey brought the craft to within earshot of the new shore. Padraic listened to the harsh whisper of wind-driven waves breaking against offshore rocks.

And then, somewhere near shore in the darkness, a pony stallion whinnied. Like an unexpected ray of sunshine, the welcome sound burst into Padraic's heart to revive his dark, self-pitying spirits. It was a familiar sound, resonant with warm memories. Padraic even recognized the tenor of that bugling call, as if he spoke Horse as well as Erse. The stallion was gathering in his band, no doubt to lead them up to the day's pasturage.

The unmistakable voice cleared his thoughts and restored his hope. The world was not so upside-down as it sometimes seemed. A pony was behaving normally, predictably. Surely somewhere above the clouds, the stars stayed their courses, as did the cowering sun. Morning was dawning after all.

Padraic could probably swim ashore from here, and a horrid realization nearly unhorsed his thoughts. What if Bridey were intending to travel with him all the way? What if her quest for adventure meant partaking of his adventures? What if with her off-hand mention of marriage she had him in mind?

71

No. He certainly could not be slowed down and burdened by this naive girl-child, not if he would escape his pursuer once for all. And he had a very good chance at escape now.

The moment they reached shore, he must slip away somehow and be gone.

9

More Ponies

As brouhahas go, this one was better than average. More yelling, more blood, more mayhem, more dented helmets. And Gwynn, Queen Without a Throne, did enjoy a good brouhaha. It had started as battle practice and quickly escalated to friendly rivalry, to not-so-friendly rivalry, to fury.

Donn of the Moor sat in the mud with his legs asprawl, staring glassy-eyed. One unseasoned youngster wasn't going to get any more seasoning today. He lay by the empty picket line, out cold as a fish. Various other warriors and semi-warriors lay about, vanquished or nearly so.

The interesting contest raged between the leaders of Gwynn's two factions. Scanlon Too Skinny stood toe to toe with Donn of the Thicket, and neither man weakened enough to give way. They flailed with fists and clubs. Gwynn had already taken away their blades with a matronly "Both of you are too valuable to lose."

Donn ought to be winning, for Scanlon lacked Donn's bulk by half. But Scanlon was quick, and Scanlon was clever, which made the contest actually quite even. His name notwithstanding, Scanlon was solidly built too, if not compared to the mountainous Donn.

Gwynn sat back in her throne, a frame chair with stretched rawhide, hastily crafted. It served well. It had been Scanlon's idea.

Scanlon. She smiled slightly, remembering their first encounter. She recalled how swiftly he quelled his own astonishment as he rode out onto that open ridge to find her there. How quickly he resumed command of his coterie and dismissed them to the forest beyond, that he might interrogate this presumptuous stranger very carefully. Presumptuous stranger. His very words.

After all, she might be a spy from some other province, sent to determine the strength of the local ri. She might be a thief or murderess, bent on plunder in the area. One couldn't be too care-ful, Scanlon avowed.

Now, in addition to Donn and his minions—nine swords and seven families altogether—Gwynn owned the fealty and service of this latest band, those men who had been traveling west up over the slieve. Six seasoned warriors, four novices, and five families. Besides the men, all eager to improve their fortunes, Gwynn could press the twelve women into service if necessary. They were all fairly good in combat.

Not only that, a druid traveled with Scanlon Too Skinny. The druid had been attached to the same taoiseach Scanlon served. The druid was now attached to Gwynn.

A week ago she had only her stepson. Today she possessed, if not an army, at least a superior guerrilla band, not to mention a druid of her own.

Scanlon wheeled suddenly and bolted. With a joyous whoop, Donn took off after him to deliver the winning blow. Gwynn's heart sank. She had really been cheering, down inside, for Scan-lon to win.

The Donn roaring at his heels, the Scrawny One ran to the nearest family. A woman and two small children sat on a blanket as their caldron of lamb simmered beside them, watching the men practice their fighting skills. With a mighty sweep of his arm, Scan-lon shoved woman and children together off the blanket, snatched it up, and with a flick of the wrist swirled it over Donn's head.

The mountain howled. His great arms flailed to pull the cov-ering off his head. Too late. Scanlon snatched up the caldron by its bale and swung it in a high, broad arc. With a single muffled blow, the kettle drove Donn to the ground as a mallet would pound in a tent peg.

Scanlon stood erect with a smile. Casually, he returned the cauldron to its coals, barely a drop spilled.

Smugly, magnanimously, Scanlon helped the groggy moun-tain to his feet. "Excellent practice, comrade! You are a worthy foe and more!"

Donn swayed. He blinked, confused.

"We must do this again sometime!" Scanlon clapped Donn on the back.

Donn pitched forward face down.

Wagging her head, his broad, plenteous wife lurched to her feet and ambled over.

As Scanlon reached Gwynn's side, the Donn's goodwife was hauling her man to sitting.

Gwynn gave him the barest of nods. "You've just earned the rank of tactical commander. I trust you to think as quickly in the heat of a real skirmish."

"Thank you, lady. Your Connaughtmen are hardy." Scanlon hunkered down cross-legged to the left of Gwynn's throne.

To her right, the druid Dhuith, a gentle soul of rather slight build and rather dreamy countenance, sat at contented ease. He glanced up at her and nodded toward Aidan, off on the far slope. The lad sat sprawled aboard his roan mare, watching the action with detached bemusement. "Your snowy-haired son does not take part in practice."

"True. And what do you deduce from that?"

"Either he is better than anyone here or worse than everyone here."

She smiled. "And why do I not participate?"

Scanlon interjected, "No question there. Because, lady, you can best us all."

Clever fellow, this. She wished at least one of his people had been riding a stallion. She wanted to breed her mares, to get her livestock holdings back up to an acceptable level. Other than that slight lack, she saw nothing in his group to cavil about.

She addressed them both. "Dhuith, Scanlon. The truth, if you will. You served one of the strongest of the southern taoiseachs. Why did you shift allegiance from him to me?"

Dhuith smiled. "I studied for nearly two decades, mastering every detail. I was well commended by my masters. I have transcended time and visited the Otherworld. But I was one of four druids and not the chief. It would be many years before I could assume the full duties of a chief druid. By attaching to you I can assume that role instantly. I want to put my lore to work and use my powers fully."

Gwynn nodded. "And to my eternal benefit. Again and yet again, I welcome you."

Scanlon studied the wet dirt a few moments. "If I answer for my men and answer for myself they will be two different answers."

"Your men were in accord when they joined me. Their answer?"

"To better their fortunes. You proved your—" he groped for the word he wanted "—audacity. Your very attitude is a queen's. A few days later when Donn joined us at the river, and we heard his story, we knew we'd chosen well."

"And your own answer, Scanlon?"

He smiled. "I have two goals in life: pleasure of the moment, and glory."

"They are mutually exclusive?"

"Hardly, lady. They are one and the same and yet no way the same. The pleasure of the moment needs no further comment. As to the glory . . ." He shrugged amiably. "We shall see."

She pondered his answer. Her second husband had answered in like manner, that is, speaking eloquently even while saying nothing at all. It drove her to distraction while she was married to him. In Scanlon she found the trait charming.

From down by the river shore, a gaggle of prepuberty boys were calling to their mothers. The boys came struggling up the bank, laughing and boasting. "See!" They had speared a dozen salmon, fish half the size of the children.

There trooped the mothers down the hill to greet their sons, no doubt to lavish praise upon them. Already the women of Donn and the women of Scanlon were admixed as if they all belonged to one clan. Good! Good! When the women got on well together, the men would mesh well. Women always took the lead in these matters.

Gwynn sat back and permitted herself a quiet, enigmatic smile. She loved enigma; by appearing enigmatic she remained authoritative even if she were totally confused. Things were coming together very well. She was amassing an excellent power base if these warriors be any indication.

Two goals vied for her attention now, pleasure of the moment and glory notwithstanding. She must build a herd, the real wealth of Ireland, and she must establish a political base. The time-honored, most effective, way to build a herd was simply to steal someone's cattle. She now had the power to do it.

Too, she would scout the immediate area for political soft spots. Any ri whose subjects were dissatisfied, a tuath whose ri had just died and whose successor had not yet been named, any ri who seemed to be wearying of his present wife—Gwynn would alert herself to the first such opportunity and move upon it.

But that was tomorrow's problem. For the moment, she would content herself to be served and to eat salmon.

* * *

Miles to the south and west, Padraic paused for breath. It's hard to figure how far you've come when you're going straight up. And more's the pity that straight up is no progress at all when you have to go straight down the other side. The drizzle that had greeted him and Bridey when first they set foot upon this shore had given way to broken clouds.

And now he set forth anew, slipping and sliding up the steep, muddy track. He wasn't even sure that the trail was for people. It might simply be a cow path to high pastures. Extensive logging along both sides made it airy and open. In fact, this might be a skid road, a track down which they dragged logs for building and fuel. In that case, his highway to the top of the mountain could end abruptly at any point, wherever the logging stopped. That would certainly cramp his plans.

His goal was to crawl up into the mountains quite a way and hide, sleeping through the balance of the day. At sunset he would set forth again. If the broken clouds persisted or cleared somewhat, he would have enough moonlight to travel by. He could be well on his way to the other side of the mountains by morning and perhaps beyond the black rider for good this time.

Whom was he fooling? On at least seven other occasions he thought he had given that devil the slip. Why should this time succeed?

Because one escape effort, eventually, was going to have to succeed. It might as well be this one.

Padraic paused and looked all around. He needed shelter, somewhere he could curl up and sleep undetected. It appeared that the trees to either side beyond the clear-cut, some one hundred yards distant, were suitable for shelter.

Then his ears pricked, and his blood ran cold. He turned to face downhill. Someone was coming. He expected it to be horse's hooves—a huge horse's hooves. But it sounded like pony feet—many pony feet. Voices were conversing with lilting cheer.

Hastily Padraic moved off the path and stretched out in wet weeds behind a stump. That voice. It sounded almost like Bridey, but it couldn't be. For one thing, he had slipped away, leaving her alone with her curragh, the moment they touched shore. They were many miles separated by now. For another, this woman's voice was talking rapidly and excitedly, and Bridey had not used that many words in all the weeks Padraic had known her. Nor had she ever sounded so bright and cheerful.

Now if only these people were not accompanied by a ranging dog, his presence would remain a secret. He lay absolutely still, following the pony feet with his ears alone.

In spite of himself, his head rose cautiously. He had to look. That voice . . .

It *was* Bridey! She rode a dark, chubby pony up the muddy path. A foal followed doggedly behind her. Ahead of her, a man on a pony stallion led two other ponies.

"How long did it take ye?" she asked.

"Almost a year before I mastered it, working every evening. Summer went fastest, of course, because the sun was up so long. Bridey, it's the most satisfying thing I've ever done in my life."

"I want to so much! I can't wait to begin."

"Begin we shall, the moment we reach home." The fellow's voice spoke further, outlining something about, Padraic thought, Latin lessons, but that couldn't be.

Of course! What a smooth liar was Bridey of Currane! She actually had him believing that she knew no one on this shore—that she was leaving home and family with no prospects whatever before her. Look! Not only did she have friends here, but they obviously had been waiting for her.

And yet, had that black rider not been sitting on her home shore upon their return from the Skellig, they would not have come here. How could . . ? But . . . but . . . but . . . Padraic rose to his feet and staggered up out of the weeds. They tangled his ankles, mocking his agility. He heard the ponies and the soft conversation beyond the bend ahead. This man had to be a native of the area, therefore knew where he was going, and he was traveling upward. Padraic would follow him and be led up the best trail. All raths possessed haystacks and outbuildings. Should the fellow arrive at or pass a satisfactory rath, Padraic would pause there for the day.

A simple plan, fraught with a minimum of struggle and danger.

Minimum of struggle? The fellow on the pony stallion had no need to stop and draw breath. The pony did all the work. Padraic slipped and staggered and lurched through the mud, fighting to keep up with the fading noises on the track ahead.

He had very nearly lost all contact with them when he sensed they were turning aside to the left. The *trip-trap* and voices were moving up an even steeper grade, roughly northwest, without slowing.

The mountain rose ever steeper. He glimpsed them through the trees. Finally! At last! The fellow reined in his mount to rest it. Padraic could hear the ponies blowing even from this distance. He crept in closer, but not so close that they would hear his own labored breathing.

Although he could not pick out all their speech, he discerned words here and there. Bridey was anticipating learning how to read and write, it would seem. Somehow, Padraic assumed she had already done that. Most people who put on the cloak of Patrick's religion did so. On the other hand, when would she learn, and from whom would she be taught? Certainly not that jackanapes who fostered her.

They were on their way again, much too soon. Despite the cool breeze, Padraic was hot and sweaty. Far off to the right, the mountain's dense forest gave way to a bald, grassy knob. He felt sorely tempted to turn aside, slip away to that rath, and curl up in their haystack. No. He could go farther yet. He might as well make as much distance as possible.

But wait! He was being his own worst enemy. Minimum of struggle indeed! He had burdened himself with a maximum of struggle, for Bridey and her companion were obviously headed for the summit. Padraic had already climbed above most of the surrounding hills. He was huffing and puffing up the highest mountain in the area.

There had to be a pass through these hills that led down to the other side, and he probably had journeyed well beyond it by now. And yet no obvious trail to the north or northeast had offered that. One would think that the way over a pass would be broad enough to notice, for it would be used by numbers of travelers.

He was getting confused. And very tired.

Minimum of danger? That fond hope evaporated, driven away by barking dogs ahead. No doubt they were greeting the riders, but he must not venture closer, lest they detect him.

A pox on the luck! The dogs prevented his forward progress. Now he must double back, walking down the hill he had just won at the expense of so much sweat. He would have to go out to that rath he'd seen on the knob after all and spend the day there. He should have just stopped there the first time, when he was thinking about it.

Now the dogs were coming this way, barking enthusiastically.

Panicked, Padraic left the track and ran for the nearest tree. Unfortunately, although nearest, it was nowhere close by. He sprinted across the open clear-cut. He fell over a stump, regained his feet, tangled in a creeping vine, pulled his leg loose, ran harder.

He didn't have to look—he could hear. The dogs' voices were right here now! Their feet roared through the mat of thick, wet greenery. Padraic leaped against the trunk of a young oak. Desperately he shinned upward as jaws snapped at his heels. He scrambled to where he could perch on the first heavy limb.

He got the solid wood beneath his feet and rested, sucking in air. Terror drained him as much as did exertion. Round about the tree below, the dogs set up a happy cacophony of yapping. Some stood, some bounded back and forth, two simply sat. All craned their heads upward, watching him intently.

He had no idea how much time passed. The dogs tired of barking and bothered to announce only intermittently that he had been a fool to pass that rath. Perhaps this was a hunters' pack, with Padraic the fair game. Perhaps they guarded some major rath ahead. Did they belong to the man who accompanied Bridey? Certainly so, for they did not hesitate to leave that fellow and come galloping after Padraic. Were the man a stranger, they would have treed him as well.

Was Bridey a stranger? This as much as proved she was not.

Padraic heard voices and ponies uphill on the track. Five riders came into view down around the far bend. The dogs set up their barking again.

Was he terrified before? If that was terror, what was this? Padraic sat wedged among the limbs of a tree, at the total mercy of people who had no reason—no reason at all—to proffer mercy. Should he drop down among the dogs and run, he would be mutilated or killed. Should he remain up here, he would be mutilated or killed.

He climbed as high into the branches as he could manage. If he could get up among the leaves, not easily seen, those riders might assume the dogs had merely treed a pine marten.

As if dogs would come tearing down the hill in an excited pack to chase a pine marten.

He was doomed.

10

Stallions

No force on earth was better at creating mayhem than the Celtic warrior. The wee folk for all their mischief could not best him. The chaotic spirits of Sammhain were not his equal. No soldier of Rome, that city once mighty and now fallen, could match him. Five such warriors gathered beneath Padraic's lone oak.

He still clung to the nether branches, afraid any moment that the slim boughs might break. He could not see the men below, for the thick leaves. He prayed whatever gods who might be listening, the gods of oaks and good favor especially, that they not see him.

The fellows below were laughing as if at the richest jest of the year. "Why, look at that magnificent eagle up there!" "Isn't his a handsome plumage! I've always wanted an eagle feather for my cap." Roar, roar, roar. Hah, hah.

Padraic obviously had not gone unnoticed. He was safe from javelins, though, if not spears as well. The leaves would deflect such missiles. Perhaps a spear might penetrate the foliage, or a . . .

Gdunk. The whole tree vibrated. *Gdunk.* Again. The leaves rattled. *Gdunk. Gdunk. Gdunk.* The blows came faster. Just barely, Padraic discerned heads below, near the base. Creaking and cracking, the oak jarred. It leaned. Clearly, the men were using iron axes. Bronze blades dulled far too rapidly to cut through this hardwood trunk so fast.

Padraic, whose ancestral clan name, Slevin, declared him to be a child of the mountains, was about to meet his end at the hands of savage mountain men.

The tree shivered. The leaves rattled violently. It toppled so slowly, so majestically, that Padraic felt no sensation of falling at first. Then as the oak crashed to the ground, its branches bobbed wildly up and down. Padraic was flying. He slammed against the incredibly solid earth. Men laughed. Dogs barked. Ponies whinnied.

He considered leaping up and catching them by surprise. He might wrest a weapon from one of them. At least he could go down fighting, instead of lying here helpless, like a hedgehog in a bush. He commanded his body to leap up. It lay flaccid. He begged his body to breathe, at least. It sucked in shuddering breaths, not nearly enough to satisfy.

Someone kicked him, and another yanked him to his feet. His knees buckled, and they dragged him to a pony. A fellow directly behind him wrenched Padraic's arm back into a twist, to hold him in place. Padraic's body bowed; his arm shrieked silently in pain.

The pony's rider seized Padraic's hair and tipped his face back. "Your name, lad."

"P-p-peredur, lord." It was a name he had heard years ago in his captivity. "Of Louth." He ought to account for the eastern accent. From the corner of his eye he saw a dun stallion standing near, the mount of this fellow who gripped his arm so cruelly.

The horseman let go of his hair. Padraic's eyes rolled back in his head and his mouth dropped open. He sagged against the fellow behind as his knees gave way. The man released Padraic's arm, for he needed both hands to support the weight falling against him.

Padraic stood up instantly and snapped his head back. He felt it connect, heard the fellow's startled yowl. Gauging the man's position, Padraic kicked his foot back and upward, hard. As the fellow's arms dropped away, Padraic ran. He swung aboard the surprised dun stallion, dragged the pony's head aside, and dug in his heels. With a kick and a yell and a swat of the reins, Padraic was on his way down the hill toward freedom.

The stud pony's gait faltered slightly as the beast took the measure of the rider on his back. But Padraic had spent years tending the horses and ponies of his owner. As master of the stables he had managed the owner's wealth of horses and directed freemen as if they and not he were the slaves. The pony rightly recognized a rider of riders. His gait loosened and broadened as he stretched out to the trail.

Then from the party behind him came a long keening whistle. The pony skidded to a near halt and started to turn. Viciously, Padraic yanked him back to the downhill track. The whistle, piercing and insistent, rang out again, calling the pony to a halt. The little stud reared. He ducked his head and reversed ends.

Padraic knew when to quit arguing. He leaped off, abandoning the pony, and ran for the woods, out across the clear-cut. He heard the pony gallop cheerfully back to its master. The stud had won the dispute handily.

Padraic didn't think he'd reach the safety of the forest, and he didn't. He heard hooves behind him—and the dogs, all rushing at him.

A rider reached him even before the dogs did. One blow of the lead rider's foot sent him sprawling.

Laughing uproariously, the warriors put Padraic on lead with a rope around his neck and hauled him off up the hill. The nose of the rider who took up the stud pony still bled a little.

Padraic was tired. He was so tired. He stumbled along among the ponies, knowing full well he was about to be forced without resting to climb to the top of the mountain.

A voice up ahead hailed the company, and they hailed the voice. His captors left the track and plowed through the close green weeds of the clear-cut. The moment they stopped, Padraic sat down. He grabbed his lead line, so that they couldn't choke him, and stretched out flat in the wet weeds.

Now these men would hear about Keiran's search. Everyone heard about Keiran's search eventually. And they would sell Padraic to Keiran for some modest amount. He must lose no opportunity to escape.

But later.

He closed his eyes.

"Huh?" Bridey's sleepy voice was asking. "What?"

Bridey! Padraic forced his reluctant body to sitting. He recognized first the mare with foal that Bridey had been riding. It stood tethered, half asleep, nearby. So did the other ponies of that group. The man who accompanied Bridey was sitting on a log, munching on a chunk of bread and laughing.

Without a doubt, Bridey had been sound asleep beside the

log, the fellow's cloak spread out beneath her, for she sat on the cloak now, still groggy. She looked bleary-eyed at the leader of these warriors, and smiled.

Didn't she realize the moral danger—nay, the mortal danger—she was in just now? These men would . . . They had no compunctions about . . .

But she continued to smile. She nodded as the man spoke to her. Then, as the fellow moved aside and pointed to Padraic, she looked his way. The smile faded.

She lurched to her feet and walked over to Padraic, her arms akimbo.

The leader stepped in beside her left hand. "So you know this eagle."

She smiled wickedly. "I know him as an ill eagle."

All save Padraic laughed boisterously at her pun. They laughed all the more boisterously as she described Padraic's constant episodes of seasickness. The laughter died when she told how he summarily abandoned her the moment they touched shore.

Her original companion now stood at her right. He glared at Padraic. "She rowed the whole night through, covering many miles across open water in a coastal curragh, all because of you. Then you ran off and left her."

Padraic hauled himself stiffly to his feet. He could not feel less like standing. It would do no good to contradict Bridey's testimony, even if he could do so truthfully. Obviously she was the darling of this group.

"That is true, lord. I did."

"At least you admit it."

He spooned humility upon humility. "Churls are never proud to be churls, lord."

They laughed. Good! Padraic was making progress. At least now he enjoyed a bit of forbearance. People do not laugh at people they genuinely hate.

"Bridey," the leader asked, "is this churl a follower of Christ?"

"Hardly."

"Well! We'll have to change that." The leader clapped Padraic on the back. "Peredur of Louth, you are blessed beyond reason. You have fallen in among Christians, and that alone has saved your hide." He wheeled to Bridey. "Do you mind continuing on, or would you rather rest longer?"

"Let us continue on. I'm fine." She waded through the weeds back to her mare and swung aboard.

They put Padraic on the pony stallion. Its former rider chose one of the loose ponies accompanying the mare, and they headed up the track. Bridey's mare fell in behind Padraic.

He twisted to look at her. "Was this fellow waiting for you when we came ashore?"

"No. M'self stumbled upon him while seeking ye. Fool that I was, I feared ye were lost or ill. He was gathering his ponies off lower pasture. He asked, 'Be ye a Christian?' and I knew I was safe among friends."

"But you never met him."

"Ye've much to learn about the faith."

What was this? Patrick commanded such loyalty that men denied their basest instincts in deference to him? He agreed with the druidic precept that one must behave well. He kept a respectful distance from Bridey, for example. But that was survival. At home, she was surrounded by a circle of friends and relatives of her stepparents, people who would wreak ugly revenge upon any man who dishonored her. Here she moved with safety among total strangers, and no one to take up her cause should she be violated. This was all madness.

Or power. Padraic remembered vaguely the arguments he had received from Christians he met along the way, and there had been many. As one they agreed that Jesus Christ was the perfection of the druidic prophecies. They agreed that Padraic must embrace the faith if he wanted to go to heaven. Most of all, they agreed that in the Trinity alone—Jesus, His Father the ultimate God, and a vaguely defined Holy Spirit about which Padraic understood nothing—full power dwelled.

But all these purveyors of the power and promises of Christ had received their information from Patrick. What if Patrick was sadly in error? In profound error? A whole cult was springing up behind him, rife with power, and it might be disastrous power. Power from the wrong sources perhaps—from the black arts opposed to druidry.

Padraic tried to imagine Bridey involved in black arts of some sort. No. On the other hand, he could easily imagine her swayed by the false claims of a persuasive speaker—so many people were—and she had referred several times to Patrick's golden tongue. This was all getting very confounding.

What he really wanted to do was meet Patrick for himself. He was usually a good judge of persons. This Patrick, his namesake, intrigued him.

He turned again to face her. "You were talking to that fellow about learning to read and write, weren't you?"

"M'dream, at last, aye." And her blue eyes sparkled.

Sparkled. Never before had Padraic seen her face light up, let alone as happily as it did now. He twisted around frontward. He rode on, partly thinking and partly going to sleep. Mostly going to sleep, since heavy thought tended to put him to sleep.

Bridey snickered behind him. "Peredur of Louth. Indeed."

* * *

So peaceful they looked, those cows in brown and black, as they arrayed themselves out across the open lea to graze. So unsuspecting did the three herdsmen look as they huddled over an early morning fire nearby, stirring their porridge.

The rounded crowns of the slieves hid somewhere within a white overcast. Mist drifted in fingers across their forested slopes. Most of the vales and gaps, though, had been cleared, at least on this side of the hills. Pale green against the dark of the woodland, the clearings traced ragged lines, broad strokes, and little notches up from the hills' open feet. This particular grassy lea, one of the largest, extended nearly a quarter mile across.

The grazing cattle were quite scattered. That was less than ideal. It would be much faster and easier if her forces did not have to gather the cattle before driving them. But no matter. Gwynn watched from a rocky outcrop on the slope above the meadow.

Beside her, Dhuith the druid stood almost entranced, his eyes closed, his chin tilted upward. He was supposed to be recognizing and controlling any malevolent forces at work here, either wee folk or Otherworldly. He appeared to be asleep. Time would tell whether he was worth his salt. No doubt he was better than nothing, no matter how inexperienced or feckless he might be.

From across the way, Donn of the Thicket roared, "Charge!" and burst out of the woodland with his men and three of his women. Their ponies lunged and leaped across the tangled brush.

The herdsmen, taken completely unaware, sprang to their feet, scrambling for shields and spears. They made no move to defend the cattle. Rather, they crouched near their fire, back to back to back, and held their shields high to form a nearly unbroken wall about themselves. Their spears stuck straight up out of that little cup of armor. Why were they not resisting?

Gwynn realized belatedly what was happening. Her party had been spotted as it approached. The local ri knew she and her guerrillas were in the area. These herdsmen were not their cows' protectors. As if to confirm her analysis, one of the herdsmen blew a brass trumpet.

Here came the defenders, the reinforcements, the ri's mounted fighting force. They thundered into the meadow from the southwest on horses much larger than the Donn's ponies. Besides, Donn's ponies had only recently been stolen. They were not accustomed to their riders yet, nor were their riders accustomed to them. It was time for Gwynn's coup.

She raised her own trumpet to her lips and sent three bugling notes out across the lea. They rebounded from the slieve-side beyond. Even as they echoed across the valley, Scanlon Too Skinny and his crew charged out from the forest below her. Men and ponies together, a solid, welded unit of destruction, crashed forward against the defenders.

Gwynn could refrain no longer. With a howling cry that echoed as clearly as the trumpet blast, she drove her black mare forward, down off the rocky point and into the fray.

With their defenders on the scene, the three herdsmen had sprung to life. They speared one of Donn's men's ponies and were descending upon the unhorsed rider. He jumped to his feet, his shield up. But he carried only a javelin, a poor weapon for defense against three. Here was as good a place as any to begin.

The mare leaped over a fallen woman. As Gwynn kneed the pony directly toward Donn's man, she poised her battle-ax. She swung as she passed the first of the herdsmen, giving the haft a twist. The ax struck him squarely, dipped in a short, fast arc, and bounced off the skull of a second herdsman. The javelin of Donn's man dropped the third.

Gwynn shifted her attention to one of Scanlon's lackeys who seemed to be in trouble, being rushed by two of the ri's mounted warriors. With a stroke of her ax she hamstrung one of the horses, a stopgap measure to delay his attack. She disliked doing that—she wanted these horses as well as the cattle. They were excellent horses, robust and full-boned.

With a crash the hamstrung horse's hindquarters dropped, throwing its rider off backwards. The horse squealed and rolled to its side. Gwynn didn't have to watch—she knew from the angle of the fall that the horse's rump would pin the fellow's legs. Good. Gwynn would get to him later. Howling, she continued forward against his companion.

By all that's glorious, how she loved this!

The fellow turned and met her, thrusting with his lance, defending not his taoiseach's cattle but his very life. He had to cross over—he carried his lance in his right hand, and she was rushing his left side, her ax in her right hand, her reins in her left. He stabbed wildly. His blade caught her right shoulder even as she was swinging her ax, but the iron lance tip glanced away.

Gwynn brought up the ax at an angle he did not expect, an angle he could not defend against—from directly below. It would have taken off her own horse's head, but she wrenched the mare's head aside in time. He whipped his shield up in front of his face, an instinctive move and a useless one. Her ax blade sliced up behind the shield. She felt it connect solidly, heard him scream. Satisfied, she kept the mare pivoting as she turned her attention to that pinned rider.

She raised her bloody ax, but no need. Scanlon was here. With a grimace, he speared the fallen rider. He looked up at her then, squarely eye to eye, with victory burning bright in his face.

Together they turned their ponies back toward the melee, but the melee was over. If any of the adversary remained, they had quit the field. Casually, Scanlon returned to the hamstrung horse and with his sword slashed its throat. For some reason, that thoughtful gesture on his part touched her deeply.

Donn's people had bunched the terrified cattle and gathered the loose horses into the same herd. Now they drove the animals up over the gap, a pretty sight. Gwynn, Queen of Nowhere in Particular, now owned a good hundred head of cattle and at least a dozen more horses.

And she didn't want all this to end so soon. She yearned for more action, more cattle, more of everything. But already Scanlon's people had taken as trophies the heads they had earned and were headed over the hill after the purloined herd. Early morning, and already the day was done.

Scanlon's crack warriors had just proven themselves by leaping without hesitation upon a superior force and besting it. Whatever fighting men Gwynn acquired in the future, she would place them under the command of Scanlon's people. And that, so far as she was concerned, included Donn.

How did the flies find blood so rapidly? Half a dozen small black flies and a giant bluebottle buzzed about her ax blade. The battle smells clung close around her, fixed in place by the still air and lowering mist. Several of the dead had been disemboweled. Besides that, the pervasive smells of cattle lingered strong.

Scanlon left her side and rode back out across the field, sword in hand. Gwynn waited for him. She expected him to take more heads than just the one he severed so expertly.

He tied it to his saddle and rode in beside her, grinning. "So, lady, you take no heads?"

His horse stood at least two hands taller than her mare. She had to cock her head up and around to look at him. "If I collected every trophy due me, we would need a dozen chariots to carry them. There are better uses for chariots."

"I believe you, every word, for I've seen you. Tell me. Do ever you attack a woman in combat? You seemed to have been avoiding them today."

"On occasion, if one chances to get in my way. Given a choice, by and large I prefer to go for the big, fat donkeys, particularly them who most resemble my ex-husbands."

Then she reined in without thinking and gaped.

There was the stallion for her mares! The horse stood four-teen hands at least. Maybe fifteen. It was huge and gleaming black. What a sire to put to her black pony mare! To any mare!

His rider wore his two colors, a black tunic and cloak and vertically striped black-and-white trousers. A man of rank. Not only had he inlaid both bridle and sword in silver, he kept them polished. A man of pride. The two sagging panniers hung behind his saddle seat suggested he had traveled far. A man of strength.

He had materialized in the broad, open lea between Gwynn and Scanlon and her departing herd. He sat his horse casually, with confidence, on the slope before them and watched them approach. Now was when Gwynn needed her druid. Was he near?

"The boaire's champion, no doubt," Scanlon muttered, and he loosened his sword in its sheath.

"No doubt. The champion be hanged. I want that horse."

"As you wish, lady." Scanlon smirked.

Gwynn rode up nearly abreast the stranger and drew her mare to a halt near the magnificent stallion's left shoulder. Scan-lon pulled up at the horse's right.

The fellow ought to be intimidated by the fresh head hung from Scanlon's saddle if not by the swords and battle-ax. But his countenance remained mild, his sword sheathed. Of course, he sat a foot above anyone else, which surely did not damage in the least his feelings of confidence and pride.

Gwynn watched his face for any sign of fear or hostility and saw none. "Whose champion are you, that I might know whose cattle I have just taken?"

"No man's champion, at least in this part of Erin. Kieran of the Great Horse, your servant, Queen."

And the fellow did the obeisance due a queen. She began to wonder if she might not acquire the black stallion short of mur-dering this fellow.

"Your reason, then, for being here?"

"I'm hunting a runaway slave, Padraic of Lambay, whom I know to be somewhere in this area or to the west out on the peninsula."

Scanlon seemed nervous. Why should that be?

Gwynn ought keep an eye on them both, lest they come to blows and injure the horse. "Reward?"

"Considerable."

"How considerable?"

He smiled. "What is My Queen's desire?"

"Your stallion."

His eyes flicked momentarily to Scanlon. Then he seemed to dismiss the man and attended only Gwynn. "The reward would come from my ri, the man who owns the slave, and the horse isn't his. You're not the first person to covet this beast, nor would you be the first I ever killed defending him. I've struck deals with others for his services. Perhaps we can both win here."

In a fight, these two would either kill or maim each other, and Gwynn needed Scanlon. She must avoid an open one-on-one conflict. She needed this great horse too, but stud service would suffice if necessary. In fact, she could use this young man as well—so brash a warrior was always a powerful asset. If he failed to pass muster as a fighter, she could have him murdered by stealth without risking Donn or Scanlon. All sorts of options awaited the person bold enough to seize them. She couldn't lose so long as he lingered near—he and that horse.

She would question him closely about the escaped slave and join his search. Perhaps her druid could offer some insight through necromancy or divination. Of course, she would help him round up the errant lad if possible. There could be no better entry into the presence and the gratitude of Keiran's ri. And that was a step closer to a new throne.

11

Bees' Largesse

What was this penchant of Christians for climbing the highest rock? Not only to climb it, but to perch their raths and monasteries up there. The rath of Bridey's new friends made the perfect case in point. There it sat on the rounded crest of a miserably high hill, windy and difficult to get to. The farm was like any other. The house and stable nestled inside a protective wall of earth and rock. A palisade atop the wall kept wolves and foxes away from the livestock's throats. Outside the wall sat hayricks, the springhouse, the cookhouse, the butchering shed, the forge—all the lesser workplaces needed to keep a prosperous farm going.

Near it, even more exposed at the crest of the mountain, huddled the ri's small monastery. Within another earthen ring, the men and women of this weird cult prayed in a wooden hut, their oratory. They lived and studied in tiny hovels within the ring, their clochans. Padraic remembered Gallus discussing the same sort of arrangement on Skellig.

They traveled downhill for hours, eastward from the rath of Bridey's friend ("brother in Christ," she called him), and no bottom in sight. Her friend led the way, swinging his staff and laughing. He spouted nonsense syllables, and Bridey, following directly behind him, cheerily repeated after him. Padraic tagged along last, feeling left out. About the time they got through with one set, they began another. Roman alphabet. Greek alphabet. Why could not the Romans and the Greeks get together on so simple a thing?

Finally they leveled out into bottomland. Bridey's friend bade them farewell, laid hands upon them both, prayed in gibberish, and turned back toward his rath.

Now they walked in silence along level seashore. Apparently if Bridey did not have her alphabets to recite, she had nothing to say. To their left, a shallow, gentle surf washed lackadaisically across flat beaches. To their right rose wooded hills. If all the luck of Erin fell upon Padraic, those hills now separated him from his black pursuer.

He listened to the gulls circling above the shoreline simply because, even at this distance, they were louder than the travelers' footfalls.

Padraic excused himself for feeling a little cross. He jogged double-steps and moved in beside her. "Have you any notion at all where we're going?"

"M'mum's home was a crannog somewhere to the south and east of where the River Shannon narrows. So I am starting at the mouth of the Shannon, which you see here—" she waved a sun-tanned arm off toward the north "—to find where the river narrows. Then I shall walk south and east, asking as I go. Not so difficult."

"How do you know where the river meets the bay?"

She shook her head. "The river is the bay, as I understand. If we cut up across there we'll meet the end of it. We need not follow the whole shoreline around."

"Up through there?" Padraic frowned. "Terribly difficult. And dangerous. 'Tis a violent world we live in, and you haven't the slightest idea about the countryside. You've never been this way before. You don't realize what you're trying to do."

"I know exactly what I'm going to do. See." She stopped and squatted down on the path. "Findan and them explained it to me." In the loose dirt of the track she drew a cup shape that opened to the left. "This is the mouth of the Shannon to our left there. It appears as any other bay. Now the River Shannon—" she drew a line slanting down from the right and connected it to the closed bottom of the cup "—flows thusly out of the northeast and suddenly turns into a bay, if ye will."

She tapped the ground where the straight line met the curved line. "I shall use that as m'starting point."

Padraic shook his head. "Too vague. You'll never find it."

"Ye need not come with me. Go your way, Padraic-Peredur. Ye quit me once. Feel free to do so again if ye choose." She stood and continued on, marching smartly.

He fell in beside. "I'm ashamed of myself for it. I told you that. You need protection, or I would."

"Protection." She looked at him and snorted with disdain.

Disdain. She held him in contempt. Him. Padraic of Lambay, a prince among his people. She actually invited him to quit her again. Why didn't he?

Because she was a very useful person to be near. The clan was one's strength and glory, one's cradle and destiny, one's pleasure and duty. Outside the clan, a person was nothing. In essence, Padraic and Bridey were nothing, for they no longer had a clan. Bridey was seeking hers. But Bridey enjoyed resources even more efficient and useful than a clan connection—her brothers in Christ, as she called them.

Her brothers in Christ appeared out of nowhere to take care of her as the occasion demanded. She needed a bailer. They provided one at Skellig. She needed rest and lodging. They literally scooped her off the beach, mounted her upon a perfectly acceptable pony, and carried her away to food, shelter, and repose. She needed guidance on her journey. They set her upon the correct road and covered her (their very words) in prayer.

It was as if all the Christians in Erin possessed second sight, to know exactly what this woman needed and when and where to come forward with the gift. This largesse bestowed upon Bridey tended to benefit Padraic as well. It was as if he camped beneath a hive and received all the honey that dripped down. He was welcomed and fed on Skellig Michael, and he was welcomed and fed on the mountain.

Would that have happened were he not with Bridey? Possibly on Skellig. Certainly not on the mountain. It had never happened much in the past, either, regardless of how hard he worked at appearing to be a worthy recipient of largesse. No beehives in his past. He would be foolish indeed to separate himself again from this girl with the charmed existence.

And so he followed, having no better place to go and no better way to get there, hastening along the mouth of the Shannon toward the spot where the river narrowed.

* * *

"Where the Shannon narrows," Gwynn replied in answer to Kieran's question. "That area provides enough open space for our needs, and the fish are beginning to run. Our camp there is temporary, of course. There are a number of raths in the area—it's a rich piece of country—but they don't dare strike us, and we are diplomatically keeping our distance from them."

She need not tell him, because it was none of his business anyway, that she had moved from the River Corrib down to the Shannon to separate herself farther from her ex-husband's lands. Too, it was none of Kieran's concern that the ri tuathe around the mouth of the Corrib had been mounting enough resistance that it was wise to move on.

They rode in the van of Gwynn's fine new herd, leading the way to pastureland near their camp eighty miles to the northeast. Eighty miles was not far distant, but it would probably suffice. No, you never wanted to raid the cattle of your immediate neighbors unless you were firmly established in the area and had the power to do so. Gwynn was an interloper with, as yet, scant strength. Be nice to the neighbors. Raid their enemies' cattle instead. Not a bad rule of life.

Kieran of the Great Horse nodded. "How long do you plan to remain there?"

"For as long as I choose." She would not say that her choice depended upon finding an opportunity to exploit, or that she considered Kieran one of her better opportunities—at the very least an entrée to one. "Why do you think your runaway slave will come there, of all places?"

"I don't. How that rogue charms people into doing his bidding, I'll never know. Somehow he bewitched that girl into providing him a way across the bay. I could not follow him directly."

"So you lost him."

"Temporarily. I followed them by eye as best I could from shore. If they held to the course they were following when darkness fell, and I have no reason to believe they altered course, they put ashore just south of the mountain pass across the heart of the Dingle. What would be more natural than to hurry up over that pass and get the mountains between himself and me?"

"Precisely. So if I were he, I would not do what came naturally, for my pursuer can guess my actions. I would do the unexpected."

Kieran nodded. "The unexpected would be to travel east

along the south of the Dingle. But that would put him on a colli-
sion course with me. He knows the lay of the land forces me up
and around that way. As I was headed west across the Dingle, I
chanced upon a free cattleman who told of a distant neighbor's
encounter with an intruder. The stranger was hiding in an oak
tree. They chopped down the tree to capture him, then turned him
loose on this side of the hills. Humorous tale. He's coming north-
eastward, according to the boaire."

"And that is your man."

"That is my man, and apparently traveling this way. So rather
than waste time traveling west myself, then east again, I came
straight up in this direction."

"Ah. Then you have slipped around ahead of him. But if he
angles south and east . . ."

"He won't, for he thinks I'm south of him. He fears we'd cross
paths."

Gwynn made no further comment. She glanced at Scanlon on
her right.

Scanlon offered the tiniest flip of the eyebrow, an agreement
with her thoughts. They melded together well, she and Scanlon.

It sounded as if this Kieran leaned a little too heavily on his
own assumptions. Surely he knew the mind of his quarry better
than she did. On the other hand, he mentioned earlier he'd been
pursuing this rascal for a year. How hard can it be to catch a
slave? Maybe he wasn't as good a mind reader as he thought.

Summer solstice was coming up in a few weeks. She would
send her men and women out to gather with the area's druids and
filidh and gather the latest news. A stranger in the area was always
news. They could pinpoint the slave's whereabouts in a matter of
days that way. Too bad Kieran didn't think of that. Had he asked
around during Beltaine, he'd probably have the churl by now.

Kieran continued. "Now that I'm ahead of him, I'll alert all
the ris and raths along his path to bring him to me. This is my first
opportunity to be waiting for him."

"Offering that mysterious reward you mentioned, of course."

"Of course. Make it worth their while."

Gwynn listened for a moment to the lovely sound of four hundred cloven hooves behind her. Cattle. The first of what would no

doubt become a vast herd. "That's a lot of country to cover, just to send word around. Then you must be at some given place where they can bring you news. Or the slave, as the case may be. How do you purpose to handle that?"

"What would you suggest, Queen?"

Was Kieran mocking her? "You tell me."

Kieran's grand stallion thrust his nose down and sneezed mightily. Everything the horse did he did mightily. His great shaggy head swung high. He shook it and settled back to the trail.

Kieran spaced his words with obvious care. "I attach myself to you. Your people help me spread the word. I wait in your camp for the slave to be delivered."

"Who provides the reward? You have no cattle."

"You advance me three cows until I return the slave to his rightful owner, and I shall repay you four cows."

And while Kieran was attached to her, his stallion could be doing his job with Gwynn's mares. That business about advancing the reward was unacceptable, but no matter. She would adjust that detail when the need arose.

Scanlon, ever ready for a funny story, asked about the oak tree. The tale when told didn't strike Gwynn as being especially amusing, but she smiled enigmatically. What bothered her was, if this runaway was worth four cows' reward, why was he deemed of such little value that the people who caught him turned him loose again? Why was he not still in the service of the farmer who plucked him out of the oak?

There was much to this matter that Gwynn must uncover before she lent her name and forces to it.

* * *

"There is much more to the matter than what I described here." Cuinn of Emhain Mhacha lowered himself stiffly to sitting beside the fire. How he yearned for a warm, sunny day. His whole life long, his tiny frame and slim build had made him look frail. Today he felt frail. He hated riding horses. "We must attach ourselves to our emissary, Muirdoch, and assist him. It's not a job to do alone. We erred in sending him out with too little help."

The brehon of Kildare nodded sagely. A pudgy man who obviously ate well, he amply filled his cushion beside the fire. If Blaine of Clones, that hound who loved food, didn't envy the man, he probably ought to. The brehon of Kildare tucked his thick blond eyebrows together in thought. They relaxed and moved up into his forehead before settling back where they belonged. "Padraic of Lambay. A good hand with horses."

Cuinn's attention had been wandering. It snapped back to the conversation. "You know him."

"Only casually. Briefly. In the few short years since Brigid founded this monastery, it has become the crossroads of the world. That's why your Muirdoch stopped here, you see. He believed that if anyone had heard of the lad, we would. Obviously, he's right. Everyone comes through sooner or later. Padraic and Kieran. He did. You did.

"As you've no doubt heard, Brigid's generosity is legendary. Legendary. In fact, this generosity of hers—this compulsion to give away anything she lays hands upon, whether it be hers to give or not—has earned us a reputation far and wide as the place to receive largesse, so that draws folks also. To one and all, we are a great hive which constantly drips honey. When you meet her, you'll understand.

"But Kildare has long been a druidic center, even before Brigid—or any Christian influence, for that matter. They worshiped in the oak groves just down the road. Still do, I suspect, though we've been moving to discourage that in favor of the true worship, that of God and His Son.

"And we're a primary source of ritual mistletoe. Druids without sufficient mistletoe in their own area come from a hundred miles around to cut token sprigs. Speaking of generosity and largesse and all that, it makes a nice source of largesse for the raths round about, as they host druidic entourages. When you live near the hive, you enjoy the honey. Druids are generous too, you know. We see maybe—"

"About Padraic of Lambay. You say you know of him."

"Oh, yes. A quick and clever young man, and a boon to any household. Good worker. He was training some horses for us, and doing very well, when Kieran arrived. Padraic disappeared instantly. Kieran started upbraiding no less than Brigid herself for harboring a runaway slave, but Brigid put him instantly in his place. She may be generous to a fault, that woman, but she takes no nonsense from anybody. Of course, being a bishop in her own right, she need not. Still, it's unusual for a woman without military aspiration to be so solidly certain of herself. She claims it is Christ dwelling within and not she herself, but there's much iron in her backbone apart from Christ as well. Why, you should have seen—"

"Who is Kieran?"

"Kieran of the Great Horse. What an animal, that horse! I'm surprised he's remained alive this long. Kieran, I mean. Not the horse. You'd think some covetous ri would have driven a spear into Kieran's back and grabbed the horse by now. A stallion. And huge. Just huge." The tubby brehon spread his hands. "Feet this wide. I've not seen the likes in Erin in all my days. If you knew—"

"Kieran is a slave hunter, then. Under whom?"

"The fellow who owned him. Owned this Padraic, I mean. Now who was that? I'm sure Kieran said." The brehon's eyebrows popped up and drifted down, limiting his ability to appear stoic and dignified. They had a comic quality, those eyebrows, as if they either enjoyed thoughts of their own or were totally confused about the brehon's. "No, come to think of it, he neglected to say. I think I can see why. He would be afraid, this close to his ri's territory, that we would simply take the runaway to the ri and collect the reward ourselves, leaving Kieran with nothing. Understandable. Still, that doesn't help you much."

"When did this occur? When was the last you saw Padraic?"

"About nine or ten months ago. Right around Lughnassa. Yes, it would have to be then. August. He was working with the new colts, training them to lead and doing the first breaking with the one- and two-year-olds. Excellent hand with horses, that lad. I remember watching him. He was stripped to the waist, out in the paddock putting the colts through their paces. He had a strong resistance to the faith, as I recall, but—"

"You mean the Christian faith."

"Yes. He didn't seem to have a problem with the classic Brigid, the goddess. But he didn't seem to want to hear anything about our Brigid. I think he doesn't believe she should have taken the name of a goddess as her own, especially when she's representing Christ and not the old gods."

Cuinn frowned. "She didn't take the name. It was given her at birth, or am I mistaken?"

"That's quite true. He doesn't understand—doesn't want to. Such a clever lad in some regards and backward in others. Stubborn. He doesn't believe just anything he hears. He must be shown. I recall this one occasion when the abbot explained to him the importance of Jesus Christ's sacrifice given once and for all time for the forgiveness of sins. Now the abbot's a bit pompous at times, I allow, but he made an excellent defense. The lad did not embrace the truth. Of course, the lad has never met Brigid herself. That might sway him if nothing else does. She's a magnificent—"

He doesn't believe everything he hears. That was a perfect qualification for an ard ri who would lead wisely. The more Cuinn heard of this young man, the more firmly he believed that Padraic of Lambay ought to become the next high king.

But to accomplish that, they must first rein in Muirdoch and then—the hardest part—find the lad. And that would require days, perhaps weeks, in the saddle.

Cuinn hated horses.

12

Raven

"In the darkest hour, when the world has fallen silent and the moon has abandoned the night, other creatures stir. Although humankind adopted as its own the Erin aboveground, and the Tuatha da Danaan retreated to their domain belowground, certain druids have been known to reach the Otherworld and return to tell the tale. And certain of the otherworldlings roam abroad. Beware."

Padraic's mother said that, as she told him the tales of the wee folk, the wraiths and elves, the banshees. You might be walking along in the dark of night, minding your own affairs, and a withered old woman will suddenly be doddering at your side and pressing you for answers to weird riddles. They'd better be the right answers too! You never know when some feeble old woman might actually be the Morrigan, horrific queen of life and death, battle and procreation, youth and old age.

Padraic couldn't remember at the moment just what else. He did know she could transform her appearance to fit the situation, presenting herself as a stunning young woman with flame red hair or as a wrinkled hag with naught but gray wisps—or anything else she wished. Or she might just send forth her bird, the raven.

And the corridors between worlds? Caves, seeps, and springs. Passages between the lower earth and the upper world. Pinched and narrow ways that knew the footfalls of sinister creatures who roamed the dead of night.

Springs such as this one that Padraic sat beside. Right beside. Very, very close to.

The first-quarter moon was setting. It would be absolutely dark in minutes, for a coarse haze blotted out all but the bravest stars. And they were sitting beside a spring.

Bridey seemed not in the least nonplussed. She hunkered just downslope of the spring beside a little pool that had been dug out and walled around with stones. Ferns and hawthorns and wych elm crowded close about. She picked at the hem of her shift beneath her skirt, tearing away a bit of linen fabric.

"You know why druids consider springs to be holy places, don't you?" Padraic looked about, watching for lurking shadows and untoward movements.

"Aye, as does everybody. Yourself has no need to fear. No wraiths or gods shall come popping out. We're under the cover of prayer, ye know."

"Frankly, I feel rather exposed."

She sniffed, a sound of amusement somewhat short of a giggle. "That's because ye know not the power of the Holy Spirit yet. No evil forces can attack us, and the good ones don't want to. Ye could not be safer."

"Maybe. But I'd feel much safer if we were sitting somewhere else."

"Springs are holy to the saints as well." She had ripped away a square of linen. She stood up and crossed herself, a gesture Christians tended to make rather often. She snagged the square of fabric on a thorn of a head-high hawthorn. Scores of other bits of fabric hung on the bush, similarly skewered.

She knelt, then, and lowered her head in prayer.

Padraic knew she didn't speak Latin or Greek. Did God understand Gaelic? Did He even care to? She obviously thought so. Then why did the worshipers in Patrick's churches use those foreign tongues?

She took an inordinately long time at her prayers, while they lingered so very, very close to this spring—in the dead of night.

In fact, did not the Milesians, those first arriving Celts, and the Tuatha da Danaan fight their decisive battle in this area? The foot of the Slieve Mish, the mountains plugging the throat of the Dingle peninsula. That would make the local springs the corridors of choice, the entries closest to the place where the two races parted company. Padraic shuddered.

Finally she rose to her feet, crossing herself again, and shook out her skirts.

Padraic fell in behind her gratefully as they returned down a side trail to the main track and continued on their way.

Leafy branches wet with dew brushed their faces in the darkness, like clammy fingers. Six feet before and behind was about the limit of visibility. Even Bridey looked a bit ghostly in the non-light, with her long hair flowing loose. She spoke first, and that was not like her. "M'stepfather told of holy wells very near our rath. Less than a day's walk. And others within three days' walk. M'self was never taken to them, nor have I ever seen them."

"Magical wells that cure the sick?"

"So they say. Some of them. M'stepfather took a lame calf to one once—carried it the whole way. He gets lame calves often—pens his herd up too close at night. They get stepped upon."

"Did it cure the calf?"

"We don't know. The calf died on the way back home. Scours and probably starvation, I suspect, though m'stepfather said not. He did not take the cow along."

"So we'll never know if the wells are effective." Padraic smirked inside. He could not see how a spring or well that was an entry into the Otherworld could be beneficial.

Her voice sounded distant and sad. "When I was seven and broke m'leg trying to retrieve a lamb in the rocks, he would not take me. Said I was too heavy to carry. 'Twas a chance to test it, lost. So I suppose, no. We never will."

"Um—uh—how did you know that spring was up there?" Padraic couldn't shake the feeling they were being watched. Were a raven to croak just then, he would have shrunk into the ground.

"Findan told me about it. Patrick himself stopped by there, they say. Some are calling it Patrick's Well."

"Here? He was here?"

"Aye. He travels widely across the land, ye know. I remember when he passed near me stepparents', though I did not get to hear him m'self. He has quite a retinue with him, I hear—the sons of the taoiseachs and ri ruirechs, all following along after him to be educated."

That surprised Padraic, and it should not have. When a learned man passed through a district, it was assumed that he would contribute to the education of his host's sons. That was how princes' sons were educated. Somehow, though, Padraic envisioned Patrick as wandering about alone, wizened and eternally aged, walking along and jabbing his crozier into the dirt with each stride.

"If, as you claim, we're safe," Padraic persisted, "what did you pray about?"

"Guidance. To lead me to m'mum's crannog."

"And just like that, you think He'll do it. God, I mean."

"And why not?"

True. Why not? Why not do a favor for a follower of Patrick?

So Patrick had walked this track, paused at this well. Did he render it more holy than it used to be by drinking from it? For that matter, were there degrees of holiness?

A curious realization leaped upon Padraic's mind and muddled it. Up until this moment, the man Patrick had been an abstract, a name, an idea. Suddenly, Padraic grasped that Patrick was as real as Keiran and that he walked this moment in Erin. Somewhere. Padraic could go to meet him.

As much as he had daydreamed about seeing the man, the fact had never truly forced itself upon him that he could actually do so. At some time or other that man drank at this well and left his mark on this track. He was real. He was alive.

Padraic stopped abruptly and sucked in breath. A woman was seated on a low rock wall beside the path. An old woman. If this was the Morrigan, he was as good as dead. He dare not fail to recognize her as such, for that was the very failure that led in part to the hero Cu Chulainn's doom. Ravens did not normally fly by night. If a raven called . . .

Bridey stopped directly beside the woman and spoke gently. "Good night, grandam. Can we be of service to ye?"

"I was caught out past moonset and cannot see. The night became too dark for these aged eyes." The hag's voice rasped like rusted iron upon rusted iron.

"Ye may join us if ye choose. We're bound north to Creggaun, where the Shannon narrows."

No, no, no! cried Padraic's heart and soul. *If by chance this be the Morrigan, 'tis the last person we want to travel with!* But he dare not say that aloud.

"No, lass, I'm traveling southeast to Ballyneety."

Aaah. Saved.

"Can we assist ye then? I wouldn't care to leave ye alone here, and no one likely to come by."

The old woman's voice quavered a bit. "Why are yourselves out so late upon the track?"

"We paused a bit at Patrick's Well."

Padraic reflected ruefully that were Bridey fully honest, she would add, "And Padraic here sorely underestimated the time required to reach the rath to the north where we planned to stop." But she didn't.

The crone stood up. "Perhaps we might walk together until our ways part beyond yon hill." Bridey moved in beside her, and she laid a hand on Bridey's arm. Padraic walked along behind.

The old woman, who might or might not be supernatural—Padraic was reserving judgment on that—croaked, "And what will you be doing on the Shannon? You've kin there?"

Bridey proceeded to explain their quest. Actually it was Bridey's quest, and Padraic still wasn't certain just why he was so deeply wrapped up in it.

The old woman grunted periodically. Then she stopped so suddenly Padraic nearly bumped into her. They had arrived at the Y in the track.

She turned to Bridey. "You need not travel clear up to the Shannon before turning south again. The crannogs you seek, and there be several, are down on Lake Gur. I am guessing from your description of your mother that one of them is your destination. I believe I know one of your mother's cousins."

Bridey's huge lashes hid her eyes completely as she drew her brows together. "Gur. Gower. Garraugh. I remember something like that, very vaguely."

"The place goes by several other names. It's been the site of farming and herding since the very beginning, since the Milesians arrived."

And drove the Tuatha da Danaan belowground just a few miles to the west of us. Are you supernatural, old woman?

"Come with me," the crone croaked, "and I shall bring you within three miles of the place. If by chance it be not the place you seek, they will surely know the right one."

Bridey smiled, and the night brightened. "I am deeply in your debt, grandam! Yes. Thank you." She glanced at Padraic and frowned. "Why are you staring?"

"Nothing. Uh—no reason." Padraic raised his hands in a helpless gesture. They began walking, probably to the southeast, but Padraic could not tell in this formless night.

Amazing! Bridey had requested assistance. Assistance had just been delivered. And the old woman did not even seem to be a Christian. Either God used non-Christians at His pleasure, in which case He was very, very powerful indeed, or dark forces were at work here, leading Bridey astray.

Padraic had no notion which might be the case.

They walked throughout the night, something he would not have done by choice. The old woman paused at her lane, gave Bridey further directions, and apparently walked off toward her own house. Padraic and Bridey continued on.

First light washed mauve across the eastern sky as they emerged from the forest and stopped on the shore of a very small lake. The mud beneath their feet squished. Churned by the cloven hooves of many cattle, it led down to the water. Apparently this was where they came to drink.

Reeds grew in dense patches to either side of the mud, their stems glowing pink in the predawn light. The lake, utterly still, shone as brightly pink as did the sky. Silhouetted in black on the far side, a lakeside rath perched on the shore. Out in the water sat a crannog at one end and a crannog at the other.

Padraic had seen many such dwellings. The circular protective wall, which any rath ought to have, was built of poles and stakes sunk into the lake bottom. Wych elm branches wove in and out of the poles, basket-style, to form a high wall. The circle inside was filled with dirt, stones, debris, old logs—whatever the farmer found to build himself a flat plot of land above water level, out where there had been no land. The far crannog contained one round house within its wall. Its conical thatched roof barely protruded above the palisade. The near one had two.

Two dugout canoes, nothing more than split logs with the middles gouged out, floated motionless beside the palisade gate. Some crannogs slung a rope suspension bridge from the gate to a tree on shore. Not this one.

A spray of sparks burst up out of the palisade. Someone was rebuilding a fire from last night's embers. The gate opened. A man's voice hooted, and half a dozen cattle poured out the gate. They plunged without hesitation into the lake and began swimming this way, snorting and blowing, grunting, churning the lake surface into a vibrating mass of random ripples. The reflected sky light danced. Behind them, the boaire, or more probably his son or grandson, climbed down into a dugout and paddled after the cattle.

Padraic and Bridey pressed aside into the reeds. Instantly, Padraic sank into slack, watery mud almost to his knees. The cows staggered ashore. The lead animal swung her unwieldy head toward Padraic and Bridey, dipped it as she shied, and hastened on. In their turn, the others marked the interlopers in the reeds with a snort or a shy or the white of an eye and slopped noisily off toward pasturage. Their warm cow smell lingered as they passed.

The herder, a lad in his teens or so, beached his dugout and sloshed after his cows. His unruly hair stuck out, but that did not strike the eye nearly as forcefully as did his huge, protruding, front upper teeth. So intent was he to keep up with the cattle, he failed to mark Padraic and Bridey back in the reeds. Was he unobservant—the cows, after all, had noticed—or was he just dull?

Padraic struggled back to the path. "It's simply not natural!" He reached back to pull Bridey to firmer ground.

"What's not?"

"Crannogs. Lake dwellings. The object of building your house inside a high, encircling ring of earth or stone is to draw the goddess earth up snug around you. You store your parched grain in souterrains. Those tunnels and storage holes are inside the earth wall for a reason, you know—to let the goddess partake and protect. These people out on the lake—no earth wall drawn up around them. No souterrains. No earth goddess at all."

Bridey was shoving the heavy dugout back off the mud. She clambered inside and crawled to the far end. Her weight dipped that end and lifted this end off the mud.

Padraic climbed in, shoved off against the shore, and stepped forward far enough to free the boat bottom. "And the inconvenience. Getting into your boat every time you leave the house."

Bridey turned her back on Padraic and dipped an oar over the stern. With stately, sweeping strokes she began sculling. The boat bobbed in place a moment and then crept forward slowly. The speed picked up. "Just as inconvenient for raiders. Yourself has said, 'tis a dangerous and violent world."

Padraic watched the power in her sculling. "Aren't you getting tired yet?"

Her voice purred gently. "Nae, for I'm going home."

On the far shore, in a black treetop between the crannog and the brightening sky, a raven alighted and croaked lustily.

13

Pony Foals

She was two months late, she was very wobbly yet, and she was beautiful. For the third time she struggled up onto her spindly legs. It appeared for a moment that her mother's vigorous licking would knock her over again. But no. The gray mare moved in close beside her, and she started rooting. She found the teat, her lifeline, and began to suckle. Her dark, stubby little tail flicked up and down.

The gray mare regularly threw beautiful foals, and this little dun filly was bright and perfect in every way.

Gwynn leaned against an ash tree ten feet away, proudly watching the gray mare mother her foal. She heard familiar footfalls barely discernible behind her. She did not bother to turn and look. "Good morning, Scanlon."

The footfalls came heavier, so he had indeed been trying to sneak up on her. He even smirked as he did obeisance. Cheeky knave. He waved a hand toward the mare. "When did all this happen?"

"About an hour ago, I'd guess."

"So that's why you haven't been riding her. Aren't foals supposed to come earlier in the spring?"

"With her, it's any time. She tends to be hard to settle. I'm glad I'll be able to catch her in foal heat. When I fail to put her to a stallion in foal heat, she often takes months to settle."

He gazed out across the meadow in its early morning mist. "With that big black stud."

"Of course with that black stud."

Scanlon looked straight at her. "Don't you think you're getting fairly thick with the stud's master?"

She leveled upon him a glowering gaze. "You enjoy a certain unique position in my life, Scanlon, but that does not give you leave to question anything I do. It does not even give you the latitude for jealousy. Whether jealousy is warranted or not is none of your affair."

He started to mutter something.

But she was going on. "I deliberately give you and your crew a generous portion of goods and cattle taken by force of arms, and I shall continue to do so, for a reason. When you and yours are prospering, I prosper. Any time now, the opportunity to step in as a stranger in sovereignty will arise somewhere, and we'll seize it. Your prosperity will multiply then."

"Unless you decide to discard me. You picked me up with ease; you're confident, I'm sure, that you can unload me with ease. Perhaps even unload me and keep Dhuith."

"All the more reason to keep your proper place, as does Dhuith."

If he planned a reply, she would never know, for Donn's voice from the hillside interrupted them.

She shouted in answer and launched herself erect. Scanlon followed her up the trail from the open lea through the ash grove to the clearing where they camped.

Kieran of the Great Horse strode triumphantly across the beaten ground of the compound, smiling. He did hasty obeisance and dipped his head toward a frightened little woman on the far side. "Intelligence about my slave."

Gwynn settled into her rawhide throne and allowed a scowl to remain on her face as the woman was led before her. *Keep the woman worried. Don't let a smile betray your thoughts.*

Dhuith emerged from the trees behind her and stood silently, not in the circle of power and yet not out of it.

In her thirties, probably—middle-aged—the woman needed washing. Her hair needed attention. Her clothes needed work. She wore no torque, no ring, no gold of any other kind. She looked as if she did not receive enough good food to plump her to the fatness that nature intended for her. "Our clan is nearly extinct, and I have no sons," the woman began, "and my husband has no rank."

"Free man?"

"Yes, Queen."

"Go on."

"I travel from rath to rath, my daughters and I, helping with harvests and butchering. Because we have no ancestral land, and no tuatha of our own, we hope to establish ourselves with others, to marry the daughters well. Then in our dotage . . ." She stopped.

Gwynn waited.

The woman licked her lips and began again. "Because we get about so far and wide, we are considered—ah—a news source."

"You're a flaming gossip."

The woman quailed. "Yes, Queen. We learned about the slave named Padraic, and we learned that you and others here are seeking him."

"Well?"

"A boon from you, a small blessing, would make our lives much easier, Queen."

"The degree of blessing depends upon the strength of the information."

The woman weighed her chances of extracting a specific promise before the fact—Gwynn could see it going on inside her—and obviously decided, correctly, that they were nil. "Your Padraic came out of the Dingle, out of the southwest, and was seen approaching Patrick's Well. He told others that he plans to begin, from where the Shannon narrows, to seek a particular crannog. Which one I do not know. Names I do not know."

"Where the Shannon narrows. Right here."

"Or very close. Yes, Queen."

"When?"

"I am perhaps a day and a half ahead of him."

A maleficent smile spread across Keiran's face.

Gwynn was not about to pay the fellow's debts for him, including any reward to this woman. "If your information is accurate, and it leads to the capture of the slave, you'll be well rewarded. How will we find you if your intelligence bears us fruit?"

The woman brightened perceptibly. "The ri ruirech of Kerry will know."

"Attach yourself to some other ri. I just claimed a hundred of that fellow's cattle. We're not on speaking terms."

The woman came back instantly with "The taoiseach of Rath-keale?"

Gwynn nodded.

Two of Donn's young men led her off and sent her on her way.

Kieran stepped in close, beaming. "I'll need your people, mounted. Spread a wide net and let him walk into it. It won't be long now!"

"You'll handle it with Donn's people only. But not the Thicket. And all of Scanlon's stay here."

"My Queen . . ."

"I don't want to be sitting here bereft of spears when the ri ruirech of Kerry decides to come for his cows. This is one slave we are talking about, and if the woman's word be good, he's walking right into your open lap. Surely, good man, you can handle that."

"Of course, My Queen."

He hastened off, and Gwynn watched him go. He acted like a puppy chasing a bit of bacon. She must dig down to the bottom of this matter of Padraic the Slave versus Keiran the Eager Hunter and find the truth. She was beginning to look forward to meeting Padraic.

* * *

Padraic didn't mind earthen ring walls topped by palisades. They were natural. They made sense. He welcomed the embrace of the earth, the safety of the piked fence. A crannog was another thing altogether. He felt confined, pent up, masked from the rest of the world. You couldn't see anyone coming. The fact that you couldn't see anyone coming through an earthen wall either didn't matter. This was different.

This crannog, though, as confining as it might be, offered some small measure of security from dark nemeses on large black horses.

Padraic sat alone inside the woven wattle fence and felt the way its curvature wrapped around him. The only chore of the moment that the master of this rath felt inclined to offer Padraic was knife sharpening. So he sat with legs sprawled on either side of the whetstone, stroking an ax blade, a butcher knife, and a pruning hook by turns across the stone.

Over in the shade of the boaire's wattle house, Bridey sat chattering with another woman. The woman had known Bridey's mother, apparently, and a couple of cousins. In fact, everyone around Lough Gur seemed to know everyone else's cousin. The two carded wool as they talked, surrounded by great mounds of clean, white roving.

Padraic stood and stretched his stiff back. He had sat too long. He felt bleary from missing sleep all last night. He scooped up the sharpened tools.

The butcher knife he returned to the grandmother, who was boiling a joint of pork in a pot over a fire beside the house. Gram thanked him with a concave smile; she probably didn't have a tooth in her head. He buried the ax in the chopping block and left it there. He carried the hook out back.

His host, Conaire, was building a new tub behind the house along the fence. Conaire had dug out a rectangular hole and was in the process of lining it tightly with split planks. Bucka, his son, was helping, which probably doubled his time.

Bucka. This was the lad who had driven the cattle ashore this morning. In his flight, Padraic had met a number of people deficient in one respect or another, but rarely had he met a person deficient in so many respects at once. As a cowherd, Bucka was good for perhaps half a day. At noon Conaire sent his two daughters out to relieve Bucka, because Bucka could never get the cows to come home in the evening. Gram refused to let Bucka help with cooking—"Too clumshy," she explained, which Padraic took to mean "clumsy." Bucka did not shear sheep or, for that matter, handle sharp tools of any sort. He was not invited, Padraic learned, at planting time or harvest, and when he picked berries he ate more than he put in the basket.

What he did better than anything else was smile, with those enormous front teeth protruding. He smiled in greeting and smiled good-bye. He smiled when you told a good story and when you yelled at him. What was most amazing, every smile seemed sincere. He was the most perpetually happy person Padraic had ever known. And the stupidest.

Padraic was going to ask about other chores when he saw the pony mare. Dun colored, with a stiff dark mane, she looked like a blob of earth as she lay on her belly, her legs folded beneath.

"I've never seen a pony so thin and woebegone."

Conaire grunted. "She collapsed this morning. She's dying. We'll save the hide, but you see there's no meat left to butcher."

Beside her stood a listless foal, almost equally as skinny.

Padraic did not ask further about chores. He saw his mission. He rowed the dugout across to the mainland (what a nuisance, to live out on the water like this!) and gathered heads and leaves of the long grass that grew along the south bank.

Back in the encircling ring of the crannog, he chopped them into a pile of fine chaff. But what he really needed was a bone. For that he would approach the Gram.

She was cutting up dried apples with her newly sharpened knife.

"Gram! That pork joint—may I have the bone?"

She wrinkled her nose. "Mosht ladsh your age requesht the meat. You can wait for the evening meal."

"No, really. I'd like a bit of the bone, please. Please?"

With her wooden spoon she fished about in her pot and hooked out the joint.

"Ah, this is perfect!" Borrowing her big butcher knife, he scraped aside chunks of succulent pork, all oozing with juice, and with difficulty hacked away chips of the greasy bone. "You'll give me the rest of the bone after supper, please, will you?"

Leaving the joint and the Gram both a-shambles, he took his bone bits to the whetstone to cut and pound into powder. He stole a few handfuls of barley from the wicker granary by the house door. He pounded that down to coarse meal.

Finding a pot proved another chore. He ended up using the wooden bailer out of the dugout. In it he stirred his ingredients, plus water, into a thick slurry. He carried it to the pony mare.

She was not interested.

Force-feeding the pony took the better part of half an hour. He would press the mixture into the back of her mouth, then patiently stroke her throat until she swallowed more or less unintentionally. Another small dollop, another swallow.

Bridey came around the house with an oaken bucket of milk. "The wife wants me to try to feed the colt. She says it doesn't eat well but they want to save it if they can. Can you make it eat?"

"It's too young to do well on cow's milk. Let's try."

Padraic straddled the colt, holding it firmly with his knees, and tipped its head up. It was still small enough to fit between his legs. Bridey introduced the milk, a scooped handful at a time, and Padraic fought the foal's mouth open. She inserted her fingers so the foal would have something to suck on.

It worked, after a fashion. Padraic thought disconsolately of how a foal ought to eat—eagerly, with milk slurping and burbling in its whiskers.

He went back to the pony mare then and, in all, got perhaps half of the food mixture into her. He wrapped the other half in oilskin and slept with it, lest the dogs smell the bone and steal it.

The next morning before dawn, he awoke to song.

"I arise today through the strength of heaven." Bridey's voice. "Light of sun, radiance of moon . . ."

Another woman's voice joined hers. "Splendor of fire, speed of lightning, swiftness of wind . . ."

The boaire's husky voice chimed in. "Depth of sea, stability of earth, firmness of rock . . ."

The trio completed another several verses.

Music. Not a bad thing to awaken to.

Padraic forced himself up and out to check on his charge. The mare had not died yet. He fed her the remaining mix. He did not have to stroke her throat nearly as much today to make her eat.

He set about making the mare's daily portion. Why bone and eggshells acted as a good medicine for weakened mares and cows he had no idea. But they did. Curiously, they did nothing at all for male horses or cattle, gelded or not.

This would never do. It took him hours to prepare a day's gruel, and, if the mare survived, she would soon be eating three times this much. Who would be slow enough to spend hours pounding bones and barley and grass?

And then along came Bucka.

"Well, Bucka! You look delightfully cheerful this fine morning!" *Pound, pound, pound.*

Bucka grinned with those amazing front teeth.

Padraic pressed on. "You're so happy today you must have already completed your wise and foolish tasks. I congratulate you."

The grin faded somewhat. "Wise and foolish?"

"You know. As Bridey says, the wisdom of men is the foolishness of God. To do your wise deed and foolish deed to please God. That. You know."

"Well, uh . . ." Bucka closed his mouth as he frowned. "Bridey said that?"

"God said that, as I understand it." He thought Bridey often made up things she claimed God said.

"Oh." Bucka brightened. "I fed the hogs this morning, and now I'm taking the cattle out."

"There, you see? That's wise indeed! To fatten the hogs well means you'll have food for winter. And healthy cattle are the wealth and pride of any farmer. And your foolish deed?"

"Well, uh . . ."

Padraic nodded sagely. "It would be difficult indeed for a wise fellow such as yourself to think of foolish matters." He grinned. "No problem for me. I can think of foolish things with no trouble at all. For instance, I am gathering powdered bone and eggshells. The bigger the pile, the more foolish it will seem, I hope." Padraic frowned.

"'Tis ruddy foolish, all right." Bucka's voice hesitated. He watched the pounding in silence awhile, his good cheer melted away into a puckered brow. Like a moth to the flame he came, standing near and then stooping beside. He sat down close to the rock and the little pile of bone. "Do you suppose, friend, that foolish deeds can be stored ahead, like corn?"

"I don't know why not. You mean, do three in one day, and then have no need to do any for the next two?"

"Or catch up, if you missed a couple days."

"I don't see why not."

"It would be foolish to add to your pile there."

"Very."

Bucka grinned suddenly and leaped up. He returned moments later with two flat stones. His good cheer restored, he began pounding heartily.

14

Wolf's Counsel

" 'Twas huge, that grave. A stone barrow it was, a great heap of river rock forty strides long and ten strides wide, and not an inch short of that. The lads with Patrick paced it off, and they said, 'We cannot believe there would ever be a man this high.'

"And Patrick asked them, 'Do ye care to see him?'

"And they all said, 'Aye, we do,' but not without some trepidation, I assure ye. And so he struck a stone at one end of the barrow with his crozier, like so."

From his seat beside the fire, Rafe the Bear Hunter leaped up and assumed a dramatic stance, his left arm flung wide and his right holding an imaginary staff. He snapped his right arm forward, striking an imaginary boulder with a crozier that would have to be imaginary, for one could never imagine a fellow as rough-hewn as Rafe with the trappings of a gentle Christian.

It was not a matter of size. It was the whole manner of the fellow. It was not a matter of grooming. Rafe combed his rich brown beard and bathed as much as any man. It was the whole manner of the fellow. He looked, all in all, more like a brown bear than a man. The name Rafe meant "wolf counsel," and that was somehow exactly what Padraic would expect from him—the wisdom of wilderness and untouched places.

" 'Open, O Lord, the grace!' cried Patrick, as he signed the cross." Rafe's eyes went wide as he spread his hands. "Lo, and ye should've seen it! The boulders that formed that barrow shook and rattled. Then they begin pouring down the side of the pile, as the barrow starts coming apart. Years it lay there, mind ye, and nary a stone ever moved. Now this! The lads were terrified!

"A giant! A giant the likes ye've never seen arose whole. Erupted right out of those stones. Sure and that barrow forty paces long held but one man, and he was it, if he be called a man. 'Twas mortal, sure enough. And that fellow said, 'Blessed be ye, holy man, for ye have raised me even for one hour from many pains.'"

Pains? Bridey spoke of paradise. Padraic was gaining a whole new perspective on death. He did not particularly like it.

Rafe charged onward. "The giant could not walk abroad again, ye see, for sure and he would scare men to death. Why just his face alone would drive the gentry back belowground."

The gentry. The otherworldlings. The Morrigan and her powerful allies. They feared nothing and knew everything! Padraic gaped.

"And Patrick, bless him, he could not let even a monster lie in an eternity of pain. So he baptized the brute. And the moment the giant confessed God, he fell silent. Then they laid him once more down into his grave. Took all the lads and then some to do it, and the better part of the day to set the stones again in place. And praising God the whole time, they were."

From across the evening fire, Bridey gazed askance at Rafe. "M'self finds that a wee bit hard to swallow, good man. As if ye dipped a cupful from the well of truth and poured it into a vat of fancy."

Rafe shrugged and settled back to sitting. "As ye wish, good lady. 'Twas me cousin's son, who travels with Patrick as one of his disciples, who saw it firsthand. At Dichuil, it happened. Right near Dichuil. And ye know the stories, as how Patrick faced down the devil himself more than once. Raising a giant be no trick at all, once you've bested the devil."

Conaire's whole family sat around the fire, digesting Rafe's gift of fresh venison and feeling the cool touch of a thousand stars overhead. What a pleasant night it was. Padraic welcomed the change from gloom and rain.

Bucka, beside Padraic, obviously believed the story word for word, but then Bucka believed anything. Conaire seemed to have accepted it. His wife was smiling, his half grown girls giggling. The smallest child, a boy of six or seven, gazed rapt at the wild man. Gram had dozed off.

Why did Bridey question? She of all people ought to believe supernal stories about her favorite Christian. Padraic would have to examine her closely about that.

He tossed out an idle thought, testing, though it was no idle thought at all. "I've had a mind lately to find this Patrick, to meet him. 'Twould be interesting." He avoided looking at Bridey.

"'Twould indeed." Rafe bobbed his blond, shaggy head. "Many's the tale I've heard about him."

"I've heard he calls Armagh home—that is, in Ireland. He's a Briton, as I understand it." Padraic looked from face to face— except Bridey's.

"Armagh's a long way." Conaire glanced toward Padraic. "For them with no land and no responsibilities, I suppose 'twould not be so heavy a journey. Perilous, but not heavy. But for us who are tied so closely to land and family . . ." He let his voice trail away.

In that casual aside, did Padraic hear jealousy?

"Armagh? Clear off in Ulster?" Rafe shook his head. "Nay, he's in Connaught." He frowned in thought a moment. "Was the last I heard, anyway. I've not spoken to me cousin for a while."

Padraic had heard tales of Connaught. The primal Rafe would fit in there, if half the tales be true. "Where in Connaught? 'Tis a wild country with wild people—and vast."

"Ye'd likely have to enquire locally. Sure and beyond the Corrib."

The journey would take a minimum of two weeks of steady travel. And what about Keiran? The sparser the population, the easier Padraic was to find. Strangers show up more clearly in sparsely populated areas. "Armagh, however, is his seat. Right?"

"Right."

"Then I can simply go to Armagh and wait for him there."

"Eh, I suppose." Rafe pondered that a moment. "As I understand it, he's hardly ever there. But sure and he must come and go, to take care of matters there as well as roaming abroad on his mission journeys. And Tara. Tara's not far from Armagh, ye know. He drops by there now and again to dabble in politics and such. Politics." Rafe guffawed. "Now talk about facing down the devil! Politicians. Aye. Sooner or later, ye'd find him that way."

Sooner or later.

Padraic let it go at that, and the conversation drifted on to other things. Rafe spoke of wolves to the north of Lough Derg, and their depradations upon sheep. For the children he told again an apparently popular story about his encounter with a bear. Padraic would not have guessed a man that small could successfully wrestle a big brown bear into submission.

Amazing indeed.

Padraic decided as the fire died and sleep time neared that he would not approach Bridey. He would let her approach him. He checked once more on the dun mare, dragged his pile of sheepskins behind the house that he might sleep under the stars, and retired.

He awoke to loud slurping noises. Out in the compound beside the house, the dun mare's colt was eating. Copying Padraic's techniques, Bridey was clamping the colt between her knees and pumping cow's milk into him.

He was eating with much greater vigor today than when Padraic first laid eyes upon him. The mare looked better too. She stood now, occasionally flicking her tail, and even followed the feeding of her child with some interest.

Padraic rolled up his sheepskins, stored them, attended the sundry business of the morning, and joined Bridey as she was finishing with the colt.

On purpose. He did not look forward to this conversation.

He put a smile out front. "You're up early."

"M'usual habit."

"Not this early."

She glanced at him. "So ye're going a-seeking Patrick."

"To Armagh."

She released the colt and let the mother lick off her fingers. There was another good sign the mare was improving.

What should he say next? He would not bother with the patter with which he so often talked himself out of uncomfortable situations. She was onto him in that regard. With Bridey of Currane, clever talk and platitudes made no impression.

Out by the gate, the girls and their mother were finishing the milking. In minutes, Bucka would drive the cows out into the lake and across to pasture. The sun would rise. Gram would jam new wood into last night's embers as dancing sparks flew up to challenge the pedestrian sun. The day would wind its way henceforth from night to night.

And what would Padraic do?

"Conaire plans to put the mare out with the other horses today." Bridey wiped her hands on her skirt. "Do ye think 'tis wise?"

"She's got enough of her strength back, I'd say." He watched her face. "You're going to miss her."

Bridey shrugged noncommittally and wandered off with the empty milk basin.

What was going on here? Padraic pondered the lost-child look on Bridey's face and followed after her toward the gate.

With a hearty yell, Bucka drove the cattle through the opening. Wildly splashing, they hit the water, headed for shore. They would have headed for shore whether Bucka drove them or not, for there was no grass or forage on the crannog, and they were no doubt hungry—which rendered Bucka rather superfluous, and Padraic had suspected that all along.

But another yell came roaring from without. Padraic ran to the gate with Bridey at his heels.

The churning melee of swimming cattle had nearly capsized one of the dugouts. In it, Rafe was bringing a mass of reddish hair that had to be a deer. It was not quite dawn yet. Rafe had been up and out so early that he was already returning from a successful hunt.

Conaire had looped a rope over the pony colt's neck. His girls drove the mare out the gate behind the cattle. Well after she had taken to the water, the little horse realized belatedly that her baby was not behind her. She tried to turn around and swim back, but Bucka managed to thrust his dugout between her and the gate. He swatted her so viciously with an oar that he forced her head under momentarily. He jabbed at her, and jabbed again, until she finally turned and swam after the cattle. Only with Rafe's help, though, did Bucka get her headed ashore. Choking and gasping and totally spent, she dragged herself up onto the far bank and turned, calling toward her lost child.

The colt was blasting out one terrified whinny after another, a nearly continuous high-pitched squeal. He reared, kicked, and leaned back, pulling on the rope. He whipped his head violently back and forth, trying to break free and reach his mother.

Suddenly Padraic realized that Bridey was not watching anymore. Her face buried in her hands, she was sobbing. Her shoulders heaved. Never had he seen her express emotion so freely—and certainly never sorrow. She had seemed impervious to sorrow. The sight unnerved him.

Rafe carried in his deer on his shoulder, and the girls swung the gate shut. Conaire released the colt. Frantically it ran about the compound, galloping, galloping, calling and squealing, hearing its mother but unable to see her.

Conaire looked at Bridey. He looked at Padraic. Padraic looked at him. Obviously, neither of them had any notion of what to do. At a complete and fumbling loss, Padraic placed his arms around her.

She pressed in instantly against him and clung as if he were a floating log and she were drowning in the sea. So he drew her against himself and held her—and held her.

He waited until the shuddering sobs abated somewhat. "The colt isn't eating grass yet, and the mare's milk has dried up. He would starve ashore. It was for his own good that . . ." Padraic stopped. She knew that. He didn't have to tell her.

Worn out, the colt paused, quivering, beside the gate. From without, the mare's worried whinny came to him.

Muttering unwholesome comments under his breath, Conaire came waddling out of the house and opened the gate.

The mare burst into the compound, and the colt, squealing joyously, squeezed and squirmed against her. They nuzzled each other, and the mare shoved her nose into her baby here and there, checking for damage. The colt went immediately to her teat but gave it up in moments. Only then did the mare spraddle her legs and shake the lake water out of her hair.

Padraic snickered. "So Bucka is every bit as good at horse herding as he is at cow herding."

The reunion ought to delight her. Instead, her sobs renewed themselves.

One of Conaire's daughters came outside bringing Bridey a great square of linen. Bridey mumbled thanks and used it to wipe her face and clear her nose. The daughter frowned at Padraic as if he were the root of all this. She went back inside, probably still suspecting him of some dastardly deed.

Padraic led Bridey over to the firewood stacked against the

wicker palisade. The woodpile had settled against the hog cauldron in an unwieldy stack. He seated her upon the wood and perched himself on the cauldron. It was uncomfortable, but she leaned over and snugged her head against his shoulder as he wrapped an arm around her.

He let her sit quietly in her misery until he could harbor his questions silently no longer. Instead of making some clever comment, he said, simply, "Tell me."

"This is the very crannog where I was born, but 'twas smaller then. When Conaire took possession, he had to rebuild the house, so he went ahead and enlarged the whole compound. Conaire is very distantly related to me, of course. This is our clan territory."

She took a few deep breaths and continued. "Raiders from Connaught came one day. I was three or four, I suppose. I remember them coming in the gate. They seized m'mother and left me standing there. I heard her screaming m'name as they carried her away.

"I ran all about trying to find m'father, or a way to reach m'mother a-calling to me from out there . . ." Her voice broke again and dissolved into another spate of sobbing.

Padraic's heart ached for her. "Like the colt."

Her head nodded against his shoulder.

Like the frantic little colt.

Padraic understood now. "Except there was no reunion."

"No. Like that poor colt, but no reunion. They set the house ablaze—the smoke settled downward upon everything. I could not at first find the gate. And when I did, I could not follow, because I could not swim. Then m'father appeared and swam ashore holding me, and we left the area to join relatives in the Currane. A second cousin on his side, I think."

"How did your father escape death?"

"He hid. When they came he hid himself. He did not try the least bit to defend us. I remember looking back as we reached shore and seeing the thick black smoke settled over m'home."

"No brothers or sisters?"

She straightened somewhat. Except for an occasional shudder that caught her unawares, she seemed to be regaining her usual composure. The linen square was soaked. "Two sisters.

They were off in the hills with the sheep. I've no notion what became of Grydd—she was the oldest. The middle, Maeve, is at Kildare, they say."

"They. Conaire?"

"His wife. She knows all the clans in the area. Practically a fileh, she is." She cleared her nose again, but she did not bother to wipe her face. The linen was no drier than her tear-streaked cheeks. "She questioned me closely about the woman m'father married after, and how he died. She'll add that to the genealogies."

"Genealogy. Interesting. You never think of being part of one yourself. I mean—we're too young. We're not genealogical."

Bridey twisted to look at him squarely. The tears in those huge, opalescent eyes made her eyelashes seem darker and longer than ever. "Aye, the very thing. Padraic, this is the first time in m'whole life that I've felt connected to anyone. To a clan. 'Tis the first time in m'life that I've felt whole. 'Tis a satisfying feeling, a wonderful thing, that I cannot express in words. I've still no close members of m'clan about me, unless I find m'sister, but I'm in a genealogy. I am recited."

Padraic had been connected once, until the Behr came. But no fileh would recite his name. Now no one knew him. No one at all. "So what are you going to do? Stay here?"

"Go to Kildare. Seek Maeve." She grimaced weakly. "M'self was sore disappointed when ye declared ye're going to Armagh. That hurt me greatly. Then I realized ye've no reason to follow me about further. I've found me place. Yourself be still a-seeking." The grimace softened into a smile. "And escaping."

"And escaping. Keiran. My black hunter. Perhaps I can find refuge in Armagh. Perhaps he won't know to seek me there."

"Go to the church—Patrick's church—and seek sanctuary. They dare not enter a church to seize ye, under pain of eternal death."

"That black-hearted hunter would risk eternal death, I think, to get to me. Look how he's pursued me all these months."

"Relentless. Aye. I suspect ye present a challenge to him."

"A challenge." Charming.

The flask was uncorked, the bung pulled. Now that she was

talking, Bridey did not cease talking. She talked about her joy at finding her roots. She talked about her childhood and the heartless inattentions of her cowardly father.

Padraic's father had died a hero, valiantly defending his family against impossible odds. To act heroically is the single most important measure of a man. Padraic could not imagine living under the cloud of a father who hid to save himself.

Padraic let her talk. He inserted comments or grunts occasionally, to let her know he was listening. He wasn't really. He was planning his itinerary over the next month. He would tell everyone he was going to Armagh. He would get detailed directions for reaching Armagh. He would set off for Armagh. Up the road a safe distance he would hook west and head instead for Connaught.

Should Keiran track him here and enquire about, Keiran would hasten himself to Armagh.

And by then, Padraic would be well on his way to Connaught.

To find Patrick.

15

Dragonflies

A pox on bogs.

And Erin was covered with bogs.

Cuinn led his shaggy pony along a track two feet wide across what had to be one of Erin's grimmer bogs. Close at either hand crowded heather shrubs of various sorts. They tugged at the hem of his linen tunic and periodically snagged his wool cloak. Beneath the heath cover, a dark, slimy, quavering mat of moss extended in all directions—from where he had been to where he was going and forever, it seemed.

The unnatural openness bothered him too. Because trees cannot live and grow in the acrid soil of bogs, above the heath stretched nothing but empty sky. Light gray overcast arched unbroken from horizon to horizon. A clearing, a lea, a bottomland field was one thing. This was quite another. Cuinn felt exposed. Vulnerable. Uncossetted.

The brushwood track trembled beneath his feet as he, Blaine, and the three aides made their way. The roadway was nothing but tangled heath branches carelessly laced with coppiced hazel wands and wych elm. Now and then, across the very wet stretches, travelers had laid oak planks along the brushwood. Despite that the plank ends were often anchored by long pegs, they moved and picked up movement. Walking the planks, he could feel the complex rhythm of the ponies' hooves and the men's strides beneath his feet. It was unnatural.

The sheer number of dragonflies amazed and alarmed him. Dragonflies were unnatural too. "They are hunters, swift and fierce," Cuinn's teacher had told him, back when he was a lad like these aides behind him. "They never walk. They perch or they fly, poising in contemplation or soaring in joy, but they never plod along. They seize unwary insects in flight. They couple in flight.

Joy, lad. Compose yourself in contemplation, yes. But do not wait for joy. Go out and grasp it. No dragonfly waits for flight to come. He flies."

Taking that long-dead master's words to heart, yet another dragonfly zoomed near, its diaphanous wings aglitter. It whipped in a perfect half circle around the travelers and hovered a moment, then zipped away.

An island of normality loomed ahead, a small copse, solid land. How Cuinn hungered for a bit of solid land. They emerged from the bog track onto an open rise studded with small struggling trees, mostly poplar and alder. The ground beneath them had been browsed bare by the ponies of every traveler who passed. In fact, three ponies browsed this moment. They were picketed on lines at the far end of the copse.

Cuinn's aide led away their own ponies to drink from a dark, still pool lapping at the south shore of the thicket. A cloud of brown butterflies lifted off the mud as the ponies approached.

Cuinn greeted the travelers seated beneath an alder, a man and his wife. Their three small children left off play to cower by their mother's skirts. He sat down near them, reveling in the sheltering trees. This was the way the world should be—close and encompassing, not open and wide-skied.

Blaine of Clones hunkered down beside him.

The traveler smiled from face to face. "Brehons. Welcome to our district. You have a smaller retinue than usual."

Blaine smiled. "When speed is of the essence, the fewer the better. You're an artist, I'd guess. A metalworker. Your strong hands and those burn marks on your arms suggest it."

The traveler smiled again. "Reardon from Clonfert. I am a teacher of metalworkers."

"Indeed." Cuinn sat forward. "Would not a metalworker simply take an apprentice—a student—of his own?"

"Normally. But these are not normal times. So often a rath's artisan dies in battle or of disease. Whatever. The line is broken untimely. I train young men to step in. Occasionally I will train a girl, if her clan's geis does not prevent that. It is often taboo for women to handle iron, especially the iron of battle. I respect that."

Cuinn nodded. "So you travel widely."

"With my family. Yes."

"And you hear the news. My party and I are trying to catch up to another swift-moving brehon, Muirdoch. He in turn is seeking an escaped slave named Padraic of Lambay." There. The whole mission was laid out plainly.

Reardon nodded sagely. "This Muirdoch. He is a sour, beetling man, not given to humor."

Blaine roared a happy laugh. "The very fellow! Are we far behind?"

"Not really. Nor are you much distant from that other hunter of your Padraic, Kieran."

Cuinn frowned at Blaine. "Kieran!"

The metalworker looked confused. "You're not all of a common purpose?"

But Cuinn's mind was galloping. He asked Reardon, "What do you know about this Kieran?"

"Not much, really. I was passing through the territory of the Mulroney, having just completed the training of two of his boaires' sons. Let's see." He stared at his wife.

"The queen who's camped where the Shannon narrows," his wife prompted. "She's raiding into Kerry. That Kieran is associated with her."

Cuinn had not heard of any queen. "No association with the northern Ui Neill?"

"Who's he?" Reardon seemed as puzzled as anyone. "All I know is that the queen and this Kieran put out word in all the districts round about the Shannon to be watching for an escaped slave. They promised a fine reward for reliable intelligence. Spread the word far. They seem quite anxious to find him."

"And where did you meet Muirdoch?"

"Half a day's journey west of here. Less. You're nearly to the Shannon, you know. Another couple of days."

Cuinn could not believe he would ever travel again through other than a bog. "And you told Muirdoch about Padraic."

Again the man consulted his wife.

She nodded. "Yes. I definitely remember Reardon mentioning it. Your Muirdoch was asking about Padraic."

"Where the Shannon narrows." Blaine asked, "Is that easy to find?"

The wife snorted. "The queen certainly is. Taking over the region uninvited. Carved out a nice little niche for herself from some Kerry territory and some Connell territory up by the rapids. It's mostly a neutral seasonal fishing area, held in common by several clans. There she sits, stealing cattle and scaring the fish."

For some strange reason the woman's pique amused Cuinn. "An interloper, then."

"Out of Connaught, I'd guess, if I be any judge of speech. My Reardon here talked to one of her underlings, who spoke with a noticeable Connaught accent."

Perhaps Reardon had talked to the man, but the woman was the one listening.

The younger of Blaine's aides approached shyly, as if uncertain about joining. He carried a handful of tender green plants. No doubt he was seeking their identity. Of all the aides Cuinn had known in his long life, this lad seemed most curious about the world.

Cuinn rotated stiffly toward him and smiled. "Is our food waiting?"

The boy smiled. "Yes, lord. At your convenience."

"Is there enough for these folks as well?"

"Yes, lord."

Cuinn rotated back to a more comfortable position. He was going to be very stiff standing up; he could feel it already. "Then, fair Reardon, we invite you and your family to join us at our simple viands. Barley loaves, dried apples, and smoked fish."

Reardon glanced at his wife.

Instantly she started for her feet. "We would like that. I'm sorry we have nothing immediately at hand that we can contribute."

"No apology necessary." Cuinn reached out for the green plants in the lad's hand.

"This one is a water plant. The leaves stick right up out of the water in that little pond," the lad explained. He seemed proud of his find, and curious. "They're all over the pond. And this one—

the lovely yellow flowers ring the pond all about where the water meets the bank."

"The yellow flower, I believe, is asphodel. Six petals, you see. Like a lily." Cuinn handed that one back. He made it to his feet, lurching crazily. He turned the remaining plant, looking at it on all sides by rolling the stem between his fingers.

Under dappled closeness, they started for the pond shore and the aides. Cuinn pointed to the three-lobed leaf. "The druids' teaching plant. Some call this plant *shamrock*. Others call an altogether different plant the shamrock. I rather like reserving the name for the other, myself, for it grows widely. This is bogbean, and it grows only in bog water. Limited, you see." Limited to bogs. Distasteful, at the very least.

"The druids' teaching plant?"

Cuinn smiled. He had almost become a druid himself, until he shifted and undertook studies as a brehon. He touched each of the three lobes in turn. "Dew" (the central lobe), "because it's neither mist" (a side lobe) "nor rain" (the third lobe). "Mistletoc is neither plant nor tree. Fog is neither water nor air. The hawthorn is neither tall tree nor short shrub." He went down through a half dozen more recitations before his memory stumbled over that lesson from his distant childhood.

With a smile Reardon held out his hand.

Cuinn passed the bogbean to the metalworker. Was this man a druidic student?

Reardon recited only one triplet from the leaves. "The Father, the Son, the Holy Spirit. Three separate, yet three together. Each His own, yet each a part of the whole. Each different, yet all the same. The Holy Trinity."

"The Christ of Patrick." Cuinn now and again heard about the new faith. It was, in essence, nothing more than the culmination of druidism, he thought—a son of a god, serving man as must any true hero, dying that others might live. Such a golden-haired son had been promised by the druidic tradition since the beginning. Still, Cuinn was not ready to accept this Christ concept without much study and discussion. Who was to say the Christ was actually who He was represented to be?

He and Blaine queried the metalworker further regarding Muirdoch and the young slave Padraic, and learned little more. Muirdoch had traveled, apparently, directly to Kildare, found out what he needed to know, and now he was on his way to some vaguely defined geographic reference to the narrowing of a major river. For some reason, everyone assumed the slave would turn up there also—or be captured near there.

Very well. Cuinn would turn up there as well. Perhaps he would not have to spend quite so long in the saddle after all.

* * *

Padraic wished he had a pony. He'd give almost anything to be in the saddle now instead of walking. He had traveled northeast for two days straight. A blessing on the wife of Conaire—and on Conaire himself—for they had laden him with dried fruit, last year's nuts, and a pony's weight in barley cakes. The cakes were brittle—but soaked in stream water awhile, they tasted all right.

Bridey was apparently on her way to Kildare. What an amazing girl! Here was a young woman who was penned up at home her whole life like a wayward heifer. She broke loose, and now she was traveling all over Erin with nary a glance backward. There, see a courage of a different sort than that displayed by mere heroes! Hers was a courage of constancy. She plodded along day in and day out without the prospect of home. Padraic did so of necessity; what she did was voluntary and therefore all the more courageous.

He missed her. It was not her conversation he missed, for she often went hours between spates of talking. In fact, he rather liked that about her. So many girls yabbered constantly.

It wasn't her female attributes he missed, for he had tasted none of that with her. Somehow, it just did not seem right or comfortable to make any untoward suggestion to her. And now that he thought about it, he could not guess why that would be so. She was strong and nubile, athletic, and actually rather pretty when he thought about it. Hers was not a dazzling beauty; rather it was a comfortable attractiveness that made one proud to be seen with her—without making you worried that someone might stab you in the back so as to carry off your woman.

And with every step he took, he missed her more.

Two days northeast of Lough Gur, he had to be at least half a day beyond the wide embayment of the Shannon. Surely it would have narrowed down to normal river size by now as it hooked from its east-west direction to a north-south flow. He would turn west here and proceed northwest until he reached the river. Once across the Shannon, presumably via one of the narrow crossings, he would be on his way to Connaught to find Patrick.

And none—Kieran in particular—would be the wiser.

The forested track ran fairly straight between low hills and climbed over none of them. He was making good time. Now and then the trail passed a clearing. Occasionally he could see a rath with its surrounding cleared pasturage perched on the brow of a hill.

A blessing on the ri ruirechs of this region, whoever they might be. Padraic had not encountered bandits for quite some time, and regions with weak ris were infested with them. But then, bandits probably would not bother with him. He wore only one color and looked generally unkempt most of the time. He was a peasant, obviously—a lowly, valueless peasant.

Woof.

Padraic froze in midstep. Off to the right in the thicket—it did not sound like a boar or hog. He had passed several freshly churned-up places on the forest floor, though, indicating that hogs ranged nearby. And it wasn't a dog. He didn't think wolves made a sound like that. Besides, it was broad day. Foxes certainly didn't.

Woof.

Should he climb a tree or continue on? Loudly, he called, "Woof yourself, beastie!"

A familiar, raucous laugh burst out of the thicket.

Relief rushed over Padraic like a wave in high surf, leaving him weak-kneed. "Rafe! Where is the humor in frightening a lonely traveler half to death?!"

With a surprisingly minor amount of whishing and crunching, Rafe stepped out of the dense thicket. "Frightened? Ye didn't look frightened. I rather assumed, when ye made such a big thing out of going to Armagh, that ye'd head in the opposite direction before long. Going to Connaught, are ye?"

133

Rafe carried only his spear and a small leathern sack of supplies slung over his shoulder. He commenced walking, so Padraic fell in beside him on the track again.

"Aye. Why did you assume I'd go to Connaught?" So much for trying to be devious. Even this coarse bear hunter saw through him.

"I didn't, until I met y'r Kieran."

Padraic stared at him. He saw nothing in the shaggy, impassive face. "Now indeed you have frightened me half to death. Tell me the story."

Rafe smiled smugly. "I started north, thinking to go home. From a boaire of the Mulroney, not more than ten or twelve miles south of where the Shannon narrows, I learned that this Kieran of the Great Horse be seeking the likes of ye. Could be no other than y'rself, from the description. Did I say description? I spent the next half hour listening to the description of the great horse. Can't think of a more boring half hour in m'life."

"'Tis a huge beast of a stallion, all black, and well furnished with enameling and silver on its tack."

Rafe's head bobbed. "The very one. There, ye see? A sentence be sufficient. A whole half hour? Bah! This Kieran has attached himself to Queen Gwynn of Connaught, and her forces are joining his efforts."

"Why in the world would Queen Whoever be interested in me?"

"Or why would Kieran, for all that?"

"I was sold into slavery as a half-grown child. I escaped a year ago. Kieran is in the employ of my former master to bring me back. I suspect I have become his obsession. He'll not give up."

"Reward?"

"I'm sure. How much, I don't know. He's a swift, fierce hunter. He never rests, never walks. Always he's moving rapidly on that horse. Relentless, he is. Every time I think I've slipped away, he shows up. Like now. I fervently hoped I'd left him behind on the Dingle, and here he is. Two or three times he closed in so tightly he would have caught me if only he had dogs."

Rafe grunted. "Eh, well, they're camped right about on the very spot where ye'd be crossing the river, should ye continue in this direction. I suggest ye go to Armagh—or anywhere east. Ye're walking right into their hands, ye know."

"If I go farther north before turning west?"

"The bog trackways won't take ye where ye want to go, and the land east of the Shannon be nearly all bog north of here. Indeed, 'tis so open they'd spot ye miles away, even if ye could make y'r way along—which be next to impossible out there. 'Tis boggy to the west of the Shannon as well, but there are ways through it."

Rafe pondered nothing, staring straight ahead, his hirsute face empty.

Padraic waited. Apparently Rafe was done with whatever he had to say. "Kieran is obsessed with catching me. I have a few obsessions of my own."

"And they are . . ?" The bear hunter glanced at him.

"To evade Kieran—and to meet Patrick. To talk to Patrick himself."

"Well then, lad, ye've a problem. Traveling in the footsteps of Patrick, y're bound to step on Kieran's toes."

Padraic was rather afraid of just that.

Rafe frowned. "Why Patrick?"

"To see why he's turning all Erin upside down with his words and ideas. Christians from overseas have been preaching abroad the land for a hundred years. Why Patrick? Why now? What does he offer, and how does he do it? He's all I hear about."

"He's all ye're named for, I daresay."

"Why my father did that I don't know. He never said. I suppose someday he would have told me."

Rafe walked in silence, so Padraic lapsed into silence.

The way passed an open meadow. A flock of lapwings lifted off and flew away in gaudy splendor. A flock of brown dunnocks would not have had nearly the same effect. Two dragonflies whipped by. Water was near.

The track became softer, muddier. Horsetails lined it on either side now, and the trees opened up somewhat. Then, to the left, they opened up completely. Out beyond a vast and shimmering meadow of rank grass ran a river. Padraic could not see the water, but he could trace its course by the scattered clusters of birch and alder lining the riverbank.

Rafe's head snapped around, and he froze in place. Padraic stopped, listening.

The bear hunter pointed to a clump of ferns. "Down behind there! Hurry!"

Padraic waded out through horsetails and nettles, beyond the fern clump. He bellied out in the dank growth. Water in the soggy ground soaked up instantly through his tunic and trousers. He too could hear the sound now—ponies on the track ahead of them, coming down from the north. How had Rafe detected them so early?

And one of the animals was not a pony. Padraic's heart chilled as he heard the unmistakable *splack,* slow and heavy, of a very, very large horse.

The horse stopped. Kieran's haughty voice spoke. "Wild man, you are blocking our way."

"When I am content that ye do me no harm, elegant man, I shall gladly stand aside."

Padraic could hear the smirk in Kieran's tone. "You are safe, wild man. We're not seeking forest bears. We're seeking an escaped slave, Padraic of Lambay." Kieran's stallion sneezed heartily, drowning out part of his description of Padraic.

Rafe grunted. "And might there be some recompense for leading ye to this fair young man?"

Too late Padraic realized the folly of trusting the arm of man. As he thought frantically about the fastest way of escape, he wondered, *Just how mercenary is this bear hunter?*

"Four cows for his capture."

Four cows! Padraic's price came high indeed. No wonder Kieran was able to track him so deftly. Anyone would betray a slave for four cows. Now where would he go? Perhaps if he bolted up and raced away through the mire, the horse and ponies would be slow to follow. But then the men would simply dismount and pursue him on foot, intent upon winning four cows.

Rafe purred, "A handsome return for a slave that I would think be worth no more than three. I shall keep an eye open in m'travels. Where might I find ye?"

"Where the Shannon narrows, not five miles downstream of here. The camp of Queen Gwynn of Connaught."

"What would a queen of Connaught be doing camped at a fishing hole?"

"No business of yours, bear man."

"Possibly not, but it be business of yours. If I find your man and your camp has moved on, I'd like to know where next to look. Four cows is a handsome offer."

Kieran's voice hesitated only the slightest moment. "Her temporary summer residence. Her druid wishes to celebrate the solstice at a site in that area. We shall be there, probably, up through Lughnassa. The knave will be caught by then."

Rafe grunted again. "Thank ye, lord."

He must have stepped aside, for the horse and ponies took up the track again. The sound of their feet in the slick mud faded.

Long minutes later Rafe mumbled, "'Tis safe."

Padraic shoved himself to his feet. He was very wet, very cold, and a little stiff. He struggled out to the track. "Where now? They'll surely find me. There's no way to head east away from them, and they seem to be both to the north and south."

"I shall establish an evening's camp up ahead. Then if our dark elegance comes back this way, he'll not be suspicious, you see. Y'rself shall cower in the trees, well out of sight. Ye wish to go west, over the river. We shall do so, but not till dark."

"Why are you helping me?"

Rafe shrugged amiably. "And why not? Ye desire to find Patrick in Connaught. Connaught is the land I know best. I grew up there, m'self and m'fathers all. I be headed there now, and ye wish to go there now. Why would we not go together?"

"But you need only have pointed toward me, and you could have collected four cows."

Rafe snorted, a merry sort of sniff, and continued on north up the track, opposite the direction that Kieran had gone. "Now what would an old bear hunter do with four cows?"

16

Rivers

The importance of a person depends in part upon the number of important people surrounding that person. Gwynn's importance was improving day by day.

Her hall was temporary at best, an oval room built of woven wythes and poles like a crannog house. The thatched roof leaked, but it successfully deflected light rain and drizzle. And under that roof she could spread a banqueting table. Her hall was therefore complete.

This evening an impressive selection of people gathered at her banqueting table. She was practically duty bound to place her son, Aidan, at her right, when he arrived. If he was late this time, he could stay outside. That put Scanlon Too Skinny beyond Aidan one place to her right. She would much rather have placed him directly at her right, and she told him so beforehand.

She seated her druid at her left. Beyond Dhuith sat Donn of the Thicket and his son. There was not a warrior of hers here tonight of whom she was not proud.

Except, perhaps, Aidan, who seemed to have lost any zest for fighting that he might once have had. And he wasn't here yet.

Across from her, the distinguished guests included Kieran of the Great Horse (a semidistinguished guest, actually, but he looked elegant in his black tunic and silver trim) and a brehon from Ulster.

The brehon intrigued her. This Muirdoch glared at the world from beneath a black and perpetually puckered brow. He seemed preoccupied with the darkness of life, much more so than most brehons. He never smiled. Every word he spoke was weighted with meaning. Here was a wise man, far wiser than his youth would suggest. And Gwynn appreciated the dark outlook—she found herself slipping into it on occasion. She could work with this man.

His retinue impressed her as well. His aide, a student of the law named Brian, could be a match for Donn of the Thicket in a few years, if only he would train well. Unfortunately, studying the law would not give him any useful fighting skills.

Muirdoch's hostler, Rowan, was a dark little man like his master. Rowan himself was not particularly impressive to look at, but the coursing hounds he commanded were not only beautiful but effective. Muirdoch's gift to Gwynn was the wild boar they would now eat at her table, run down by those magnificent hounds in less than two hours.

About the minor taoiseach Muirdoch had brought along, Gwynn would reserve judgment. He was apparently renowned as a huntsman around his native Carrowkeel.

The banquet commenced without Aidan. So be it.

Gwynn set the ale tankard aside and looked from Muirdoch to Kieran and back. "So. My druid here, Dhuith, talks about streams of time that flow out of different mountains, yet empty into the same sea. You two rode on different rivers, rivers of time and place both, yet you arrive here at my door simultaneously. You two gentlemen both say you knew nothing of each other until you came, yet you both are resolutely seeking a seemingly insignificant lad. There is much more to this tale that I'd like to know about."

Kieran looked genuinely puzzled. "Until this hour, I thought I was the only one hunting him. And I don't believe my ri would send others out as well, although it's possible. I was supposed to hand him over in a few months and it's been over a year. Perhaps he became impatient."

Muirdoch merely looked put out, but then Gwynn suspected he usually looked put out. "I'm not associated with the man's ri. They're southern Ui Niell. I represent the northern branch."

"And you've not explained why you're so ardently searching for the slave."

"That is privy to my ri and certain other brehons. Not a matter of public interest. I seek him. I will reward the person who brings him to me. That's sufficient."

Gwynn smiled at the tankard. *Shrewd, this sour brehon.* "Yes, I suppose it is."

Donn's goodwife appeared at the far end of the hall. Why would she come in when she wasn't serving? When Gwynn looked at her she tipped her chin up. Gwynn nodded. She hurried forward, past the important personages, behind the table to whisper in Gwynn's ear.

"Thank you." *Intriguing! In fact, fascinating!* Gwynn dismissed the woman with a wave. "Scanlon, we have more guests outside, just arrived. Two brehons and their entourage. Greet them, bring them in, and seat them."

Scanlon arose from his wolfskin and strode out the door in that commanding, insouciant way of his. Gwynn loved to watch him move.

She smiled at Muirdoch. This was getting more interesting by the minute. "The rivers of time, the rivers of place, how they flow! I would assume these are friends and associates of yours. You came from Tara. These brehons are from Tara."

"Perhaps they bring word the lad has been found." His voice was tight, controlled.

"It takes two brehons to deliver such a message?"

She could not imagine two more disparate men than the brehons who entered the far door. One was a wisp of a fellow, aged and scrawny. He reminded Gwynn most of all of a stoat, with his pointy nose and lean line. He looked as if he ate once monthly. The other, robust and roly-poly, ate once hourly at least. His round, jovial face and shiny cheeks glowed with good health. They were presented to Gwynn as Cuinn of Emhain Mhacha (the stoat) and Blaine of Clones (the pudgy one).

She welcomed them and invited them to feast.

The men greeted Muirdoch enthusiastically and settled down beside him.

"This is excellent. Amazing!" Blaine wasted no time helping himself to the boar. "We feared we'd be traipsing all over Erin, and here, less than three weeks later, we sit down beside the man we're trying to find!"

"It all depends upon embarking upon the correct river." Gwynn smiled enigmatically. "Perhaps, esteemed gentlemen, you can tell me something about this Padraic of Lambay I keep hearing about. Particularly, I'm intrigued as to why so many fine people are hunting him."

The stoat answered because the pudge-ball's mouth was already filled with wheatcake and boar meat. "By lineage he's a prince. We wish to place him for consideration for an important position at Tara."

"An important position. What position?"

"Ard ri."

Gwynn kept her features relaxed. Her gut screamed, *High king!* That explained a lot. And it certainly presented brilliant opportunities. "As I understand it, brehons do not choose the high king. The council of ris chooses."

"We recommend. We feel he will be one of our better recommendations."

"Ah. Do they usually follow your recommendations?"

The stoat spent the next fifteen minutes discussing the administrative maneuvers around Tara and what they needed in the way of a candidate. No wonder he looked ready to blow away. He hadn't yet started to eat and his companion was on his second helping.

She looked at Kieran. "And of course you knew nothing about all this."

"I still don't, Queen. As far as I'm concerned, he's no more a prince than I am. I determined to take him back to his master, and I will do so."

"Not to Tara."

"Not Tara. His master lives near Stangford Lough."

She ought to run him through right there. Sure and she could not permit his deception to go unpunished. He had not been honest with her, and now he was lying to cover his duplicity. He would pay for that, and she suspected Scanlon would be more than happy to exact the payment. Her only question now was, should she turn Scanlon on him or take care of it herself? She would think about that—but not for very long.

The distinguished guests eventually took their leave. Gwynn ordered a marquee erected for their convenience. She would make every gesture possible to ingratiate them. After all, they represented Tara.

For formality's sake, Gwynn dismissed herself, but as the banqueting hall emptied she returned to her seat. Three of Donn's women brought rags and began cleaning up the long, wood-slab table. Gwynn ordered it left in place, since they would no doubt be using it again tomorrow. The women straightened the cushions and pelts, gathered up the bones and gristle lying about, and snuffed all the torches save the one near Gwynn's seat.

A white head appeared at the far end of the marquee. Aidan came in and sat down beside her on Scanlon's wolfskin. He sank back and leaned against the wall.

"So where have you been?"

He smiled enigmatically.

"Who's the dalliance?"

"Nobody from Scanlon's band."

Donn of the Moor's young wife. It had to be.

He continued, "I listened in on the conversation in here. The walls aren't all that thick. Do you believe Kieran, Mums?"

"Not for a minute." She snapped her fingers and ordered ale from one of the departing women. The girl disappeared briefly, came hustling back in, and filled the tankard. Gwynn dismissed her.

Aidan waited till she left. "What are you going to do?"

"I'm still thinking about it. How to draw the maximum amount of advantage out of this. I wish I knew eastern politics better." She looked at him. "How many ri tuathe hold sway in our Connaught?"

"Local kings? A score, perhaps. Two dozen at most." Aidan did not sip from the tankard. He quaffed.

"And of them, how many are ri ruirech?"

"My father is one, of course. Three other regional kings. Four."

"And how many can claim to be ard ri?"

Aidan looked at her oddly, as if she had just failed a lesson in elementary arithmetic. "Only one high king."

She nodded. "That, my son, will be you."

He stared at her, his eyes blinking. He shook his head. "Only Ui Neill hold that throne."

"No king rules simply because his father and grandfather did. Each must prove his own strength and valor. You know that. The brehons confirmed that today. This Padraic of Lambay is not of the Ui Neill. As a compromise candidate you offer exactly the same attributes as does this Padraic. Exactly the same."

"Mums, we're from Connaught."

"They're working very hard at uniting Erin under one head. Erin includes Connaught. If they hope to hold sway over Connaught, then a man of Connaught has just as great a chance for the high kingship as any of the Ui Neill. Greater, in fact, if they want unity as badly as they claim they do. That will be one of our basic arguments."

"And what if they find this Padraic? They will, you know."

"We find him first." Gwynn drew heavily from the tankard. "And remove him from consideration."

* * *

Nothing was quite so chilly as the River Shannon on the first night of summer. Padraic nearly froze his hands and feet swimming the mighty stream in the darkness. Shivering so hard his fingers would not obey his commands, he fished his clothes out of Rafe's leathern bag. It was not entirely waterproof, but they were still almost dry.

Rafe was dressed already, and Padraic hadn't begun. The hunter stretched casually. He was not shivering at all. "Ye're on the far side of a river from y'r pursuers. Safe for the moment. Want to stay here the night?"

"N-n-no. I w-w-want to walk a few m-m-miles to warm up f-f-first."

Rafe chuckled. "As ye wish. 'Tis no difference to me."

"R-r-rafe? Wh-wh-what goes w-w-woof?"

"Bear, lad. Ye never heard one?"

"N-n-nor seen one." Padraic could not get his belt fastened. No matter. He'd do it later. He pulled his cloak close around and trudged off up the trail behind Rafe. "All the b-b-bears are gone now. In the east."

"In the south too, aye. But not in Connaught. They're still around in Connaught. They take a sheep every now and then. I slay a bear in Connaught, I can trade the hide anywhere in Erin. High demand. I bought a slave girl with one last year. Just one is all I needed. Rare indeed, bearskins, and just about nobody has a bear geis."

Padraic believed that. Who would have a taboo against eating the flesh of an animal that no longer exists in your life? "Is the m-meat good?"

"Delicious! Very fat. Greasy, especially in autumn. One bear can keep a whole family in grease over winter."

The walk warmed him up eventually, and they stopped for the night.

They camped cold and continued on early next morning. But the next night, Rafe deemed them safely beyond any pursuers and with a flint struck a fire.

Padraic would have argued, "Ah, but you don't know Kieran! We're nowhere near far enough!" But then Rafe might allow another cold camp, and Padraic welcomed their fire too much to object. Here it was, the third night of summer, and the cold still ate into his bones.

Padraic missed the solstice observances, especially the fun and frolics of his early youth, back when life was simple and direct. Mum, father, kin, and friends. Missing solstice upset the march of days—one could not count them well.

Rafe put out snares before they retired and caught a hare for breakfast. That and some roasted roots he had dug along the way made a tasty repast.

Fortified, Padraic continued on with ever-improving elan. He was seeking Patrick! Very soon now he would determine the secret of Patrick's hold upon Ireland—and especially upon Bridey.

Especially upon Bridey.

17

Bear

This was the time of year the rowan tree paused between its glories. Its globs of white flowers had faded, and the vivid red berries not yet ripened. Still it posed handsomely with feather leaves against the cold, gray stone of the craggy pass. Rowan trees, when Padraic thought about it, did not really have a bad time of year.

He stopped and just stood on the track a few minutes, not so much for the view as for air. His lungs were throbbing. He gulped mighty breaths, and still they clamored for more. How did Rafe manage to stay ahead so handily? Rafe never wearied. Rafe never rested, except when Padraic quit.

From the crest of the pass Rafe called cheerfully.

Padraic answered with an unseemly epithet, not at all cheerfully. Why was Rafe in such a hurry? They were making good time. Why did he think they must make even better time? The River Corrib was behind them. They moved swiftly and steadily northwest toward what Rafe called a holy mountain. There, he assured Padraic, Patrick would be found.

The exhilarating wildness of this land amazed Padraic. He could see why Rafe, the Man of Wolf and Bear, would love it so. Oak and birch, ash and hazel—all the familiar trees—grew robust here, with a sort of sturdy abandon. Out on the treeless bogs, knee-high heathers shone gray and purple in the shifting light. For miles and miles and miles, Padraic saw nary a rath or even a cow. How many of these forested slopes never felt the tread of a human foot at all?

Game trails were the way to travel through these trackless hills. They followed the bases of mountains for the most part, skirting alongside the valley's open bogs. Here and there—in fact here, at the moment—they wound up over a mountain pass into another chain of hills and valleys as void of human life as the last.

Padraic lurched on up to the crest of the trail and stopped. "There's nothing to see. It's forest. I rather expected a view, Rafe."

Rafe chuckled. He sat on a gray boulder, unwinding the cord around his brogan. "Ye'd be discouraged if ye saw how far we yet must go. This way ye can guess."

"Wonderful. Planning to go barefoot?"

"Nae, I'm crippled, so I'm dumping a handful of stones out of m'shoe. Go on. M'self shall catch up promptly."

I'm sure you will. And pass me too. Padraic kept his thoughts to himself and started down the faint trace. He stopped. "Can I get lost?"

"Not so long as ye continue downhill. We'll pick up another game trail at the bottom. It should take us directly to the mountain. Aigli be not so far from here."

"Are there any people in Connaught at all?"

"A doon or two on the coast near the mountain, and raths besides. Sure and ye don't miss people already!"

"No." Padraic grinned. "But I'm afraid all the girls will miss me."

Rafe hooted and tossed a stone at him, but the throw went wild. If that was the size stone he had been walking on inside his boot, no wonder he was crippled.

Padraic groped his way perhaps a quarter mile down the strange trail and hesitated, not at all sure that he wasn't lost. He could see nothing for the forest. Should the way be this hard to find? What if Rafe was on the right track and Padraic was not and they had somehow become separated?

Then Rafe woofed behind him, and his silly bear grunt put Padraic's mind at ease. All was well. Why couldn't Rafe just say, "You're going the right way," like ordinary men?

Ferns on the trail ahead rustled. Padraic stopped cold and watched. That just might be dinner moving around in there. He wished Rafe with his spear were down here beside him, in case it was something tasty. Padraic was unarmed.

The ferns riffled again, and a small brown fur-ball waddled out into the open. Virtually fearless, it turned beady black eyes and an inquisitive nose toward Padraic. He had never seen a creature the likes of this one. Then, with a stabbing shock, he realized what he was looking at.

A bear cub.

And that woof behind him had not been Rafe.

He wheeled.

She had come up soundlessly to within ten feet of him. She stood up on her hind legs, her forelegs reaching, and she filled the mountainside. He could smell her hot, acrid breath. She woofed again, very deep and very throaty.

Then Padraic saw Rafe's spear shaft sink into her back. Whether she snarled or howled Padraic could not say—she hurtled toward him.

"Play dead! Play dead!" Rafe screamed from uphill beyond the bear.

Padraic let his knees melt and collapsed into the wet forest duff. He made his muscles relax. He forced his eyes closed. It was absolutely the hardest thing he had ever done in his life.

Her hot breath blasted his face as her jaws came down on his left arm, up near the shoulder. He stayed loose. He must stay loose. Stay dead. The paralysis of terror helped.

She picked him up—lifted him off the ground by that arm. She was going to rip his arm off, and then she was going to . . . Abruptly, she dropped him.

Padraic fell back into the dirt. The cub's little needle claws gouged into his ribs and side as it galumphed up over his inert body to rejoin its mother.

He slit his eyes open to confirm what his other mangled senses were telling him. The mother bear had turned away from him. She had turned to meet Rafe. Huge humps of shoulder bulged out of her shaggy coat. One of them was smeared shiny with bright red blood, fresh blood from Rafe's spear.

Rafe had come up behind her and yanked out the spear to use again. Padraic could barely see him beyond the massive horror of coarse hair and howls. She fell upon Rafe with her paws, huge as saddleblankets, flaying wildly.

Rafe roared his challenge, louder than the bear's frenzied cry. Padraic could see him brace, literally face to face, nose to nose with the beast, jabbing with his spear, jabbing, until the great hulk obscured Padraic's view and he could see no more.

He must divert the bear somehow. He had once saved a friend's life by diverting the attention of a charging bull long enough for his friend to scramble up a tree. He must do that now.

Instead, his arms shoved him to his feet, and his legs carried him to an elm among the ferns. He shinned up the smooth, cold trunk. His left arm gave out, then, and he hung in place, legs and one good arm clinging tightly to the lower limbs, the way burrs cling to wool.

Staggering, the she bear backed around to face Padraic, and he feared for one awful moment that she would come up the tree after him. Her entire front was blood soaked, and he had no idea whether the blood be hers or Rafe's.

The bear waved her bulky head from side to side, trying to dislodge Rafe's spear from her neck. Then she swung around and shuffled down the game trail, the spear still dragging. Her baby romped at her side, tripped over a root or stone, and tumbled. It fell in again behind her and bounded along at her heels. Padraic listened to them depart. She made far less noise than an animal the size of a bull ought to make. He clung as long as he could. Then his leg slipped free of the limb it was looped about, and he slid gracelessly down the trunk. The bark scuffed and scraped his cheek. His left arm would not function.

If she returned now, he was dead. He was too spent to climb out of her reach again. He stumbled to Rafe's side and dropped down heavily to sitting.

The wild man still breathed. The bear's teeth had put out an eye and ripped part of his face. Teeth or claws had shredded his scalp. Padraic had no idea what to do to help the man, nor any concept of where to begin.

Rafe's torn tunic moved slightly. Padraic flicked his eyes away. He knew what that meant. His own father had been eviscerated also.

An enormity of grief, bigger and more appalling than the bear, dropped upon Padraic and threatened to squeeze the life out of him. He could not move. He could not even weep. His father died by sword. So would Rafe, in a way. Fang and claw were just as sharp, just as effective. Padraic buried his father, and the horror of it flooded him anew. Soon he would bury Rafe.

Rafe's voice rasped, "Tell ye something." It was nearly a whisper.

Padraic leaned closer. He laid his good hand on Rafe's shoulder.

"Why I came with you." Rafe put spaces between nearly every word. They were exceedingly slow coming, and measured. "I want to meet Patrick too. Learn. How to save m'soul. Meet God."

Padraic said nothing, but already he knew what he must do. He would bury his friend in a long barrow, heaping the stones high to keep wild beasts at bay. Then he would go to the holy mountain and fetch Patrick himself.

"Bring him," Rafe whispered, confirming Padraic's determination. "He raised the giant. Let him raise me long enough to save m'soul. Aye?"

"Aye!"

Rafe looked content. "I'll be waiting." A tear trickled from his one eye left, but that was probably from pain. His face, what remained of it, relaxed. He smiled slightly. "Bear. She bear. The most ferocious animal alive. Not a bad way to go."

* * *

Kkkkkkkkkkkkkkkk.

Gwynn drew her ax blade across the whetstone again. *Kkkkkkkkkkkkkkkk.*

She glanced up at Aidan. The lad was supposed to be sparring with Donn of the Moor, that they both might improve their wrestling skills. Aidan was sitting under a tree tooting on those panpipes, and heaven knew where Donn had wandered off to.

With her earthen ring wall up, the place felt a little more like home. A good downpour would probably wash half the wall away the stockade wasn't even started yet—but the goddess earth hugged her now. The rest would follow.

Over under an ash just inside the ring sat her druid, Dhuith, with the two brehons. Gwynn knew better than to think they were discussing practical things. The conversation was much too eager, too animated, too intense. They were no doubt discussing some obscure point of philosophy or law.

How might Gwynn attach one of those brehons to her entourage? She'd take the stoat by preference. He seemed wiser, deeper. But she knew better than to discount the roly-poly Blaine. Get his mind fixed on practical issues, and he'd no doubt guide every bit as wisely as any other. She needed a brehon.

In fact, she needed a fileh too. A bard.

Every proper warlord, and Gwynn considered herself quite as proper as any, needed the complete complement of learned men. Of the three intellectual castes—the brehons to administer the law, the druids to administer the rites that kept men in tune with the rest of the world, and the filidh, who kept the genealogies and lore—she had only one so far.

In fact, she ought to think about getting a bishop too. Bishops and monks and monasteries were popular now throughout Ireland. Right and left, ris were establishing monasteries in their regions, usually either replacing the local druidic schools or as an adjunct to them. It elevated one's status considerably to have one's own center of learning.

It wouldn't really cost her anything. Once she established herself as a stranger in sovereignty over some clan area, and especially if she married into the clan, she would simply consecrate a piece of land and tell the monk or bishop to indulge his fancy. Let the monks do the building. Let them set up their school. Give them cull sheep and cattle now and then. Then the sons of the local clans would not have to leave the area to gain an education. She would keep the eager warriors, the youthful enthusiasts, at home.

Kkkkkkkkkkkkk.

Her blade was a sharp as it was going to be. Any more grinding and the edge would start to lay over. She looked up at the sound of horses.

Here came Scanlon with one of his men. The Too Skinny warrior dismissed his man and sent the fellow off. Scanlon rode over to Gwynn, slid off his horse and did a perfunctory obeisance. He was becoming a bit too casual.

"He's not in the area, lady. Your Kieran of the Great Horse has hopped upon his great horse and absconded."

"Ridiculous! How could he know we're planning to cut his

head off?" She gripped her ax a little tighter. "You're the only one I've discussed his demise with."

"And the only word I've spread among our people is that you want to talk to him. I don't think he's suspicious. But Donn says he apparently heard a rumor. A cattleman's slave claims she saw two men swim the Shannon at a ford north of here a couple nights ago. One of them looked like that Padraic—enough so that Kieran's probably halfway to Connaught now."

Not only was the future ard ri slipping through her grasp, so was that double-faced liar, not to mention his handsome stallion. She must quell her anger and think.

She grunted enigmatically. "Connaught. My country. Should Kieran catch his slave—finally—he won't come back down this way. He'll travel straight across Erin, using the more northerly tracks to Armagh. And I know where they are." She stood up. "We're breaking camp, Scanlon."

He smirked. "Across the Shannon."

She smiled. "Across the Shannon. Kieran can pursue his princely slave. We shall pursue Kieran. More precisely, we shall pursue his horse. I daresay that great horse will be a lot more noticeable in the countryside than is some half-grown slave."

* * *

The wind whistled as it tried to blow his hair off. The weather was changing. A thick cloud bank rested on the western horizon, and the sea far below, wind-churned, looked ripply. To the northeast, small islands hugged the eastern shore of a saltwater embayment. To the south lay the forested mountains Padraic had just traversed, mountains containing at least one bear.

And a grave.

Padraic stood utterly alone at the very top of a bare, conical mountain. Its trees had long since been cleared from the upper half, and most of the forest was gone from its base. Pastures had claimed the woodland at the bottom. Bonfires had taken the trees at the top. A great, blackened fire pit marked the highest point.

Padraic stood on Aigli, the holy mountain. Patrick did not. Now what?

He heard heavy breathing from somewhere below the crest,

and his first thought was *Bear!* His second thought chided him for his first thought and produced a third—*People.* Would this be Patrick?

Apparently not. It appeared to be a man and his wife, both of them middle-aged. If their clothes be any indication, they were comfortably situated cattle lessees from a medium-sized rath. Huffing and puffing, they completed the climb to the top of the hill. Immediately the woman marched over to the rim of the fire-pit, crossed herself, and began a lengthy prayer on bended knee, exactly as Bridey did. Her husband wandered about a bit looking, studying the view. Then he joined his wife in prayer. He finished the same time she did.

Only now, with the most important chores complete, did they acknowledge Padraic's presence. The woman sat down near the exceedingly steep north side. She smiled. "So you've come to walk in his footsteps also. Good. Good."

"I've come seeking him, actually."

"Mm." The boaire settled himself casually near his wife. "Patrick, you mean, of course."

"Yes." Padraic sat near them, but not too near. His arm hurt. It felt hot and sore to the touch where the bear's teeth had penetrated, and it throbbed whenever he exerted himself. Climbing this mountain had nearly killed him.

"Understandable." The cattleman looked out to the north. "You know, I'm sure, that this is the very spot where he drove out the last of Ireland's snakes."

"Snakes . . ." Padraic had never seen a snake. But then, he'd never seen a bear, either, until the day before yesterday. "No. I didn't know that."

"Sent them right over the side, right here, into the sea." The boaire nodded brusquely. "'Tis true. His holy mountain. Said so with his own lips. He spent six weeks up here in penance and prayer. By that he emulated Christ's forty days in the wilderness, you see. How long have you been in the faith, lad?"

"In the faith. Uh—not long. No."

The man studied him intently, and Padraic knew this man knew that the closest Padraic came to the faith of Patrick was watching others cross themselves.

But the man waved casually toward the huge firepit. "When Patrick arrived in Erin the second time. You know, I'm sure, that his first arrival was as a slave. Captured by Niall of the Nine Hostages and his raiders. They brought him from England. England's to the east, you know. He escaped . . ."

And so did Padraic.

" . . . home to England. Then God called him back, and now see the glory he's brought! Anyway, the second time he arrived, come Easter he built a great fire on the Hill of Slane. As the flames leaped into the sky, he declared all Erin for God the Father, Jesus Christ, and the Holy Spirit. Sure and 'twas glorious! That was the beginning."

"Were you there?"

"Aye, I was, and my wife here also. We were attending the equinox at Emhain Mhacha over to Ulster. Sometimes we'd journey down to Carman too, for Lughnassa. My wife used to race there, you know. Did very well."

"Race ponies, you mean?"

"No, women. Woman races. You have never been to Carman during Lughnassa? You ought. Anyway, we were prepared to return to Connaught, having traded some cattle and observed the equinox, when we heard of Patrick coming. 'Twas there we embraced the faith, on the spot. One of the first in Erin, I'm proud to say."

The wife spoke up. "We begged him to bring the faith into Connaught, and he did. He built a fire here on this mountain, just as he did on Slane Hill, and declared all Connaught for the Lord. Now when the faithful meet up here, we may build a fire to commemorate the arrival of the Word. 'Tis very moving."

"So he comes here periodically." And with Padraic's luck, he was between visits—or had just missed the Christian.

"Now and again." The boaire nodded. " 'Twas here recently."

Ah. Just as Padraic thought.

The boaire looked at his wife. "When would be the last time? Seven years? Eight? Not more than that."

Seven! Eight! "Where is he now? Do you know?"

"Mm." The man and woman frowned as one at nothing at all, their foreheads rippled in concentration. She mused, "He spent

153

some time in the lake country. There is an island out in Lough Derg, especially. More penance, as I recall. Down to Cashel, to bolster up the brethren."

"Armagh?" Padraic prompted.

"Armagh too, though he's hardly ever there."

The boaire nodded. "Cashel, most likely."

Cashel. Sometime in the last seven or eight years. Padraic sighed.

And while Patrick was driving out the snakes, why didn't he do the job right by driving out the bears?

18

Cow

Omnia Gallia en tres partes divisa est.
Gaul as a whole is divided into three parts.

Erin as a whole was divided into five—Connaught to the northwest, Ulster to the northeast, Leinster to the southeast, and Munster to the southwest. And then there was Meath, the middle, the peg that unified the parts.

Bridey liked the sense of completeness to that. Four corners and a middle. And somewhere in one of those corners—Munster being the latest one—Padraic the slave ran and ran.

Why did she think of him so frequently? He certainly never gave her a thought. If he did he would not have instantly abandoned her on the shore of the Dingle. He accompanied her only when it suited his purposes. Sure and that was clear enough!

"Eh, ye're mooning over some man again, girl." Bridey's older sister, Maeve, laughed. An oaken bucket in hand, she swung her legs over the low stone wall and crossed through the mud to Bridey.

Bridey paused from her milking to empty her bucket into Maeve's. The cows of Kildare produced an amazing amount of milk each, no doubt the fruit of daily prayers on their behalf. She tipped forward again on her stool, pressed her forehead to the cow's warm flank, and recommenced milking.

"Mooning over?" She grinned. "That's 'lunating' over."

Maeve cackled. "Most of us here had to struggle with Latin and Greek. Y'rself plays games with them." When Maeve talked to other sisters and initiates in the monastery, she carefully used the clear, urbane Gaelic pronunciation the learned classes used. With Bridey, just the two of them, she slipped comfortably into her rural southwest brogue.

Maeve was known as Pax here at Kildare. Many of the girls,

like Maeve, changed their names when they took orders. Bridey was not entering orders. She was only a student. Therefore she was called nothing fancy—Peace, or Grace, or Mercy. She was merely Bridey.

"And well I can afford to. Ye learned them because they're required of ye. I'm learning them because I wish to. 'Tis a powerful difference. Eh, Maeve, I do love this!"

"Ye love milking endless cows?"

"There be worse things to do in this life. And ye know ruddy well what I meant. I love the learning. 'Tis a dream come true."

"Dreams, aye. So whom were ye lunating over?"

Bridey snorted. "A man not worth the effort."

"None of them are."

"Padraic."

"Padraic! Do ye realize how many Padraics there are since Patrick arrived? Barrels full. Why couldn't ye fall in love with someone with a unique name? A heroic name, like Lugh or Mabon? One of a kind."

She was coming to the end of this one. With one hand she stripped as with the other she pressed the bag. "I hardly fell in love, Maeve. And he's no god, believe me. A slave. A runaway."

"Can't be!" Maeve studied the ground. "Padraic of . . . somewhere east, not far from Kildare here. Lambay. Lambay Island." She looked at Bridey.

And Bridey stared at her. All sorts of strange emotions rushed back and forth in her head, like panicked sheep running madly around in a fold as the wolf takes his pick. "How do you know him?!"

"I don't. 'Twas during m'rotation for serving Brigid. She received two brehons from Tara. I heard the whole conversation. They're looking for a brehon that had come through a day or two earlier, and all three of them are looking for this Padraic."

There couldn't be two Padraics of Lambay. What was going on here? "What about Kieran?"

"Kieran of Saighir? Bishop of Ossory? I don't know. They didn't mention him. He's not mixed up in that, is he?"

"No. Not that one. Three brehons seeking a mere slave!" Bridey shook her head. "Outlandish."

"Not so outlandish. He's actually a prince. They want him for some high office in Tara."

"A prince!" Bridey gaped. She abandoned the cow to her own devices and sat there on her stool, in the mud of the milking yard, to think about this. She reflected back on all that she remembered about him. Never did he mention anything about royal blood. Not once did he suggest he was highborn. If he knew his heritage he was keeping it a deep, deep secret. "You know—he may not realize why they want him. He may not know about his title."

"It's kind of hard to be a prince and not know it, Bridey."

"It could be, in this case. His parents died when he was very young. And they lived on that island. He was telling me one day about how his ancestors moved from the mountains out onto the island and supplanted some English refugees who had fled the Romans. His family, the Slevin, took over the land because it belonged to no other clan yet. Then usurpers from the mainland drove his family out in the same way. So it's possible."

Maeve grimaced. "Sounds like Erin, all right."

"Maeve, I must needs go to Armagh."

"And why so?"

"That's where he's going. Indeed, he's likely there now. I will find him there and tell him what I learned. Then he can go to Tara and receive the portion that is his. Don't you see? That will take care of his escaped-slave problem right there. He will be out from under the threat of Kieran then. Really, as far as I can see, it's the only way he can stop running from Kieran." Bridey leaped up. "Aye! The very thing. I am on my way to Armagh."

* * *

"I am on my way to Cashel." Padraic stood on the muddy bank of the Shannon and watched the ferry in the misty distance. Some enterprising soul had rigged ropes from this shore to a small island, thence to a sandbar, and from there to the far shore. Even with those two intermediate landfalls, the rope sagged beneath the surface for most of its length.

The ferry, a log raft of considerable proportions, was headed his way now. The operator had attached the raft to the strung-out rope with a great bone hook. With the rope as a guide to prevent his drifting downstream, he did not have to fight the current. He poled the craft with long easy movements, setting the pole into the bottom muck near the front of his raft and walking firmly to the back. Yank up the pole, walk to the front, and pole again.

Padraic pitied the man. With every crossing the fellow walked twice the width of the river. That was a lot of walking—the river looked to be more than a quarter mile wide here. And at the end of his day he was exactly at the point where he had started.

"Cashel, eh?" The traveler beside Padraic eyed him suspiciously. "Are you sure you aren't one of Queen Gwynn's people? Rumor has it she's coming back."

"I'm certain, having never heard of her." *Or was this the mysterious queen of Connaught who, according to Rafe, sought him?*

"Then you're not a Connaughtman. Been to the holy mountain?"

"As a matter of fact, yes." *And Patrick may have sanctified it, but he didn't remain there for long.*

"Then a Christian you are! We are brothers!" And the traveler, instantly shifting from suspicious to affectionate, clapped Padraic on the arm.

The wrong arm. The pain nearly made him faint. In fact, the fellow's jovial pat probably set it seeping again. Padraic kept his cloak pulled close over it. He could not afford to let word reach Kieran—however word always managed to reach Kieran—that he was less than wholly healthy.

The truth was he felt terrible. It had taken him longer by two days to return to the Shannon than it had taken to leave it, and he was a good twenty miles north of where he and Rafe had crossed westbound. It should have taken a day less time. He was no doubt fevered. The arm throbbed even when he lay still at night.

He kept his tone casual. "I understand Cashel is a Christian center now."

"Verily so. Once the king himself became a Christian—Oengus, that is—the whole rest of the area fell in line to be baptized. They've an important school there, and a monastery, of course."

"I thought an important druidic school was there."

"Aye, that too." The fellow smiled. "You know the why of that, don't you?"

158

"No. I don't think I do."

"Well, when the first Christians came to Ireland—that would be a couple generations ago—they built their churches and proceeded to tell us simple Irish country folk how to act and what to do. They set a bishop over us. Supposed to rule all of Erin, he was.

"You know the Irish are not about to put up with the likes of that. Everyone pretty much ignored him. The bishop, I mean. That would be Paulinus. He was the fellow assigned by Rome until Patrick got here. Sent, mind you. Not called, as Patrick was."

"One high bishop, like an ard ri. Like one high king over all Erin, you mean."

"Right. They're trying to do that too, and it's not meeting with any better success than the bishops had. Erin's not made that way. We're a land of many clans, and each as good as the other. So 'tis no wonder the church never got anywhere."

"Right. You can't impose new ideas from the outside. A friend of mine said that once." Rafe. *And now he's under a barrow of loose stones, waiting for Patrick. And the torque from around his neck, scratched by a bear's claws, is hidden inside my shirt.*

"Exactly. Patrick is English, you know. But he was a slave in Erin for years."

"So I hear." *Over and over and over.*

"Eh, and he knows how the system works in Erin. He knows whom to lavish with gifts and praise . . ."

"Bribery."

"That's what those lesser lights in Rome call it. Here it's the way you do business. You know that. Gifts and obeisance. For the right people, of course. Patrick converts the ris and nobles, and the rest of the tuathe fall in line. It pays handsomely to know how the system operates and then work with it.

"Clever, the way he goes about it. He takes a holy place. A standing stone, for instance, or a well. And makes it a Christian holy place. And the big druidic schools? He introduces them to the faith and lets them study it. Converts the whole school to Christian without a murmur."

"And that's why he's successful when no one else was, you're saying?"

"More than successful, for he's getting the aes dana behind him."

Aes dana. "The filidh and druids and brehons." The intellectuals of all Erin were espousing this faith. So were the common people, such as Bridey, and the nobles, such as Gallus and Pileatus and the others on Skellig Michael—Padraic was certain, just from the way he spoke and carried himself, that Gallus was a noble.

The Christian traveler rolled on, in full cry now on a topic he obviously loved. "When Patrick converted the king of Cashel, he converted all the south. Then he took the druidic school at Cashel and turned it into a monastic school, a school of the faith. 'Twas a glorious coup, and not a drop of blood spilt!"

The fellow's history essay continued as he enthusiastically described the persecutions and murders as the pre-Christian Roman government resisted the faith. If the faith was so splendid, why did Rome fight it so and try to stamp it out? The question was moot now. Tribes from the north had overrun Rome. Her glory was no more. Apparently her common sense was gone too.

Padraic didn't care, actually. He ceased to listen and merely grunted now and then when it seemed opportune. One way or another he would make it to Cashel. He would take refuge there in the Christian conclave. If Patrick did not come, or if he had left, Padraic would ask them to find the man or at least send him in the right direction. He did not want to go off seeking more wild geese.

The ferry bumped into the mudbank with a quiet, gentle *thub*. Instantly, twoscore sheep clattered off the raft onto the slippery track. Their shepherds ran behind, shouting orders the sheep did not heed. The whole baaing, woolly mass pattered away up the trace.

When the Connaughtman on top of Mount Aigli described this ferry to Padraic and how to find it, he said it was a service to God by one of the local ris. A service to God? The ri tuatha was responsible for the health of his land, always. Whatever good he managed to do would benefit his land, just as bad or negligent acts could cause disaster. Padraic understood that. He'd always understood that. But service to God?

He followed his Christian non-brother onto the raft, walking

160

with care from log to rough log. Two women led a cow aboard. Good. Padraic brushed aside some sheep drops and sat down behind the cow so that he could not be seen easily from the east shore. He pondered the concept of Patrick's God, a supreme father figure, lord of all, and no goddess in sight. That he did not understand.

By and by the ferry lurched, freeing itself from the mudbank, and began the slow crawl back across the river. The cow got over her initial nervousness, folded her legs, lay down, and fell asleep. Her mistresses sat head to head and chattered. The Christian struck up a conversation with the ferryman, his voice waxing and waning as the fellow poled back and forth, back and forth. Padraic dozed.

"What's that for?" one of the women asked, loudly and stridently.

Padraic opened his eyes.

The ferryman was waving a white rag above his head, apparently a signal to the east shore. "Letting them know I'm expecting dinner," he replied.

"Dinner, is it? Never saw you do that before." The woman returned to quiet conversation with her friend.

Kieran could not have alerted this ferryman, could he? He would not be waiting on the east shore, surely, though it would not surprise Padraic if he was. The black hunter enjoyed an abundance of second sight to be able to track Padraic so indefatigably.

In spite of his best efforts to remain alert, he drifted in and out of sleep. Then the ferry bumped to a standstill. They were there.

No, they weren't. The ferryman had grounded on a sandbar. Now he was shifting his hook from one rope to the next. He must wear out a hook a week, at least. He lifted off the sandbar only after all his passengers, the cow included, got up and walked over to the downstream side of the raft, tilting it alarmingly askew.

Padraic watched the far shore approach, apprehensively anticipating the appearance of a great black horse. Three women sat beside the track on the mudbank, awaiting a ride westward. Nothing else, not even a cow, populated the shore as far as Padraic could see to north and south.

He disembarked the moment the raft touched mud. He hastened up the slippery bank as his arm throbbed in protest. He paused, a bit dizzy, then hurried on. He crossed the grassy, open pasturage between river and forest and reached the shelter of the trees. Cool shade engulfed him, drew a protective cloak of green around him, bade him welcome. He was on his way to Cashel!

A lean, tough-looking warrior on a spirited little dun horse appeared from nowhere—from out of the welcoming greenery beside the track. He grinned wickedly. "You are Padraic of Lambay, an escaped slave."

Padraic's heart stopped. He kept the shock and terror inside and commanded his face to remain loose and friendly. "You are mistaken, lord. I am Peredur of Louth, a free man." With difficulty, he fished Rafe's torque from inside his tunic and held it up. Slaves did not have torques.

Two other riders moved in, one to either side of him.

"I am not mistaken. I am Scanlon Too Skinny, and you, my lad, are taken captive."

19

Dogs

If Kieran were a rational man he would admit he had lost the slave. Padraic of Lambay had completely and successfully hidden himself somewhere in the wilds of Connaught. Never before in this year of pursuit had Kieran ever lost him quite this badly.

But now he had the dogs.

Rowan the Hostler rode beside him. Rowan's remarkable coursing hounds ran along the track ahead, their ears cocked, their tails tense. Muirdoch knew what he was doing, bringing Rowan along. The dogs were not much good for picking up scent more than a day or two old, but once they took the trail they invariably ran their quarry down. Invariably. Kieran need only get within a day or so of Padraic, and he'd have him.

With a strange, yodeling bark, the lead bitch veered suddenly and crashed away through forest undergrowth. The other four dogs took up the chase, yapping exuberantly.

Rowan listened to the departing din a moment, his head cocked. "Hope you want hare for supper. That's what we're getting."

"Won't they tear a hare apart before we reach it?"

Rowan shrugged and grinned. "I was planning to cut it up anyway before I put it on the spit."

Kieran smiled as well. "I'll gather some tinder and strike a fire."

He rode out into a glade nearby and dismounted beneath a lone ash. What had opened up the forest here? Why did the trees press close upon each other all across the hillside and yet shrink back from this broad patch of quiet meadow? The waving grasses were just coming into seed, and summer wildflowers sprayed the meadow with white and gold. Kieran loosened his horse's saddle girth. The place was intensely still.

A solitary boulder, dark and rough, sat in very nearly the center of the meadow. Kieran prepared their fire bed near the boulder, that he and Rowan might lean back against it as they ate and rested. He arranged twigs and kindling, carefully set his tinder of moss, dry leaves, and lint beneath the twigs, and dug his flint out of the purse on his belt. He used his dagger to strike sparks. The tinder caught in less than five minutes of effort. Carefully, carefully, he nursed the glowing ember into flame.

Where was Rowan? His hounds should surely have caught the hare by now. Perhaps they were bringing down larger game.

Kieran tended his horse and fed the fire, building a fine bed of coals. One did not cook hare or any other meat over flame but over coals. Coals sealed in the juices and improved the flavor. They left none of the smoky essence open flame embued, which made all meat taste the same—like burned wood.

Kieran settled back against the boulder to wait. Rowan should have returned by now.

No breeze stirred, and yet the grass moved on the far side there. It bowed and returned to upright. Here on the east edge of the glade, the tall grass waved gently. A vagrant breeze, that was all. See? The grass in general did not move.

Where was Rowan?

Then Kieran noticed the faerie ring. He should have seen it the moment he arrived. Why did it escape his attention until now? Right beside this boulder, little mushrooms were arrayed in a nearly perfect circle. Off beyond the boulder on the other side, he spied another ring, a broken, irregular circle of fading brown mushrooms, their caps growing wet and slimy from age.

His fire faded suddenly. He must have been careless and put a piece of wet wood on it. Quickly he fed in some snapping-dry twigs. The flames improved. He happened to glance toward his horse. The stallion ought to be resting, his ears floppy, his neck relaxed. Instead he stood taut, ears up and head high. The black ears wigwagged. What did he detect?

Where was Rowan?

The silence hung so thick and heavy it half smothered him. He heard whispers in the grass, but he could not discern words. He would not look around anymore. He would tend his fire. Let the wee folk talk about him all they wished. He was doing nothing wrong.

Druids conducted their rites in groves and glades like this one. They made certain their site, wherever they chose, had as its center a sacred object, a natural object—a tree, a stone. To perform their rites, then, they formed a sacred circle around the object. Unlike some, Kieran could not feel the special forces of spiritual power residing in certain places as opposed to other places.

That was one reason he feared the gentry and the wee folk—he possessed no spiritual sensitivity. He could neither read nor discern them, but with their second sight and special powers they knew him intimately. They had all the advantage.

He felt extremely irritated, and for no reason. Come to think of it, he had ample reason. After more than a year of dogged pursuit, his quarry was for the first time beyond sight and scent. The three brehons were scouring the countryside around Lough Gur, where a stranger of the right description had been reported on a crannog. That high-and-mighty queen with a battle-ax thought Padraic was going to cross the Shannon eastbound somewhere to the north. Where she got that notion or why she persisted in it escaped him. That left him alone to dog the slave's footsteps.

And he had just lost the footsteps.

Faint voices made his skin crawl; voices just barely beyond the ear's ken whispered, *Beware.*

Beware of what, if anything? Of the wee folk? What other danger could there be?

Kieran sucked in air, a most unmanly reaction. In the dappled shadow of the ash tree, a beautiful young woman stood between him and his horse, silently watching him. He had neither seen movement nor noticed her approach. Never had he seen the likes of her before.

She wore black, a very feminine, flowing garment so intensely black that it must be dyed. The blackest of natural sheep's wool has a brown cast; this did not. His own black tunic, artfully woven, possessed a dark brown sheen in certain light. Even in this virtually still air, her long skirts lifted and floated as if in a breeze. Surely they could not be wool. The finest wool was not so fine as this. Her deep auburn hair floated as freely as the garment. And the skin—that icy-smooth, icy-white skin contrasted vividly with the rich chestnut of her hair.

Kieran instantly found himself awash in lust, and that was not at all like him. She stood quietly, so imperious and unafraid that he realized he dared not touch her. He walked to her until ten feet separated them and stopped to stare at her heavy silver torque. Its terminals were cunningly wrought death heads.

"Lady?" He yearned to reach out and touch her.

Beyond her, his stallion stood rigid, vibrant, his nose high and his eyes rolled so far back the whites showed. He snorted nervously. What was this?

Her voice, like her garment, floated soft and free on the quiet air. "You are gloating in a strength that is not yours, Kieran, and engaging in a pursuit that is beyond you. Seek a new strength and a new aim now, while you may."

"How do you know my strengths and my pursuits, lady?"

Her face slowly reshaped itself into a most tantalizing smile.

A dog barked. Kieran's horse nickered nervously. The stallion stood under the ash where Kieran had tied him, fifty feet from this stone, and Kieran was surprised that he still sat close by his fledgling fire, leaning back against the rock. The lady had vanished.

Rowan's coursing hounds came flouncing and panting out into the clearing about ten strides ahead of Rowan himself. Grinning, he tossed a half-grown pig beside the fire and swung down off his horse. "They ate the hare before I could reach them, but see what next they put up."

"Did you notice anyone in the trees as you approached here? Any movement at all?"

"Nobody around but us. No rath for miles, I'd say. Where the pigs come from is anyone's guess. Certainly not nearby." Rowan frowned. "Did you hear someone?"

"Probably not."

Rowan's hounds certainly gave no sign that they detected anything anywhere near Kieran's horse. They spread out and sniffed here and there about the glade. Then, one by one, they wandered over near Rowan's grazing horse and settled down in the tall grass to lick their feet. Kieran's black stud quieted down, but he never fully relaxed.

A dream. Aught but a dream.

Kieran thought about the vivid black of that magnificent woman against the gleaming black of his splendid horse. In his memory's eye the colors blended together even though the image of her remained sharp for a long time, as dreams so often do.

Late that night the overcast broke, permitting a gibbous moon to drift in and out the clouds. When the fire died to embers and the dogs slept, and Rowan snored in muted murmurs, Kieran again noticed the grass moving randomly here and there around the glade.

He didn't even want to think about it.

* * *

"Now what's this?" Aidan nodded off across the camp toward riders approaching from the south. He sat in the shade of Gwynn's marquee, whittling at another set of panpipes.

"Scanlon's back. And look what he's found." Gwynn smiled broadly inside but kept her facial expression enigmatic. She laid aside the braided bridle she was working on.

Scanlon's youngest warrior walked, leading his pony, and upon the pony sat a bedraggled youth of seventeen or eighteen, dressed in ragged brown. The others rode beside and behind the lad. Gwynn knew who it was.

With a maddeningly smug smile, Scanlon slid off his pony before Gwynn. He gestured roughly, and his party rode away across the compound, carrying away the captured slave.

Gwynn nodded. "Well done."

Scanlon did obeisance and flopped down to sitting at her feet. "Right where you said he'd be. He seems tired of running. Once the shock of capture wore off—and it wore off quickly—he resigned himself."

"So resigned that you neglected to chain him up. That's a gross oversight, not putting him in chains."

"I was going to, but I took pity. He has a sore arm, and he's ill."

"Ill?"

"Infection from a run-in with a bear."

She felt her eyebrows pop up. "You can see who won the skirmish. There he is, uneaten."

167

"My women are going to clean him up for you. He's a prince, after all. And I told them to get Dhuith on the job—you know, the usual potions and incantations. He should be ready for your audience in an hour or so."

"Thank you." She turned to Aidan. "Get off that panpipe chipping and fetch one of your tunics to the women for our ex-slave. He's a prince—we'll dress him like a prince."

Aidan stared at her. He opened his mouth, about to either contradict her or refuse. Then, apparently, he recognized her order as an order and shuffled off grudgingly to obey.

Gwynn wagged her head. "Can you imagine that little fop tangling with a bear?"

"The bear probably wouldn't have time to say grace before digging in."

Gwynn snickered. "You are speaking ill of the prince, knave."

"Forgive me, Queen." His tone of voice was as bantering as hers had been.

Scanlon's estimate of an hour was grossly understated. It was closer to four hours. Darkness came and with it the chill of a clearing night. Gwynn ordered fire in the banqueting hall and settled on her cushion to receive the slave prince there. So he was ill. She remembered the slack way he barely managed to keep his seat aboard the pony, and she placed her cushion facing the wall. Her own leaning board she propped against the wall behind his cushion.

Scanlon brought the lad to her as the departed sun's last pink was fading. He still had not put the runaway in irons. Either he possessed a lot more pity than she gave him credit for, or he already fully considered the boy a prince.

She was taken instantly by the lad's strength. Even in his temporary weakness, that strength showed through in the way he carried his arms and head. With a bath and a fresh shave and hair trim, he looked quite handsome. His eyes sparkled brightly, though part of that was probably due to fever.

Scanlon intoned, "Gwynn, Queen of Connemara. Padraic the Mountaineer, Prince of Lambay."

Padraic bowed to her, but he did not perform obeisance. He stood loosely, patiently, waiting.

She gestured toward the sheepskin across the fire from her. "Be seated there."

"Thank you, Queen." He settled upon the sheepskin and almost instantly relaxed back against the leaning board. His cheeks were flushed. Dhuith's incantations were slow to work.

Scanlon dropped down on his wolfskin uninvited, hard beside the lad. Gwynn let the lapse of protocol slide by.

"So you matched hugs with a bear." She studied the gold ring around Padraic's neck. "Your torque is nicely wrought. From whom did you steal it?"

He smiled. "I borrowed it, Queen, from a dead man who plans to return to life."

"May his plans come to fruit, that he might show us all the way."

He sat quietly, waiting, initiating nothing. Didn't his head burst with questions? Or was he simply so ill he was using all his strength just to stay awake?

"You don't seem frightened at all, runaway. Or even worried, for all that."

If his guard was up at all, he showed no sign of it. He smiled wanly, his body melted at rest against the board. "And that surprises me, Queen. A month ago, surely two months ago, I would be terrified and plotting my escape. A month ago my only aim was to evade the man who has been pursuing me, Kieran of the Great Horse. Suddenly that doesn't seem so very important anymore. I have other aims and desires now, and that one has slipped from prominence." He frowned. "I doubt that makes much sense."

"It makes very good sense. You're aware, I'm sure, that we have people all up and down the land watching for you."

He shot a bemused glance Scanlon's way. "And one of them found me. He says brehons are seeking me because of my royal blood. Something about a position of some sort at Tara."

She looked at Scanlon. "What's your impression? You've been talking to him."

"I'd say, from his actions and reactions when I mentioned it, that up to that moment he knew nothing about it. He was too sick and too addled to put up much of a front. I doubt he could be devious enough to give me a false impression. Besides, why would he? Royal blood is all to his advantage."

Gwynn stared at the lad's eyes. "Do you know Muirdoch, Cuinn, and Blaine, the brehons from Tara?"

"No." His eyes met hers fairly, without a flick. If he wasn't telling the truth he was a better liar than her second ex-husband ever was.

"They're out in the countryside seeking you now."

"Then I assume you're going to send someone out to tell them the search is over."

"Of course not. They're busily spreading the word to be on the lookout for you. I can't conceive of you getting away from us or even wanting to. But should you escape, the whole world will be waiting for you out there with arms outstretched."

"For over a year now, Queen, I have felt like the whole world is doing that. And Kieran is one of the seekers?"

"Not for long. He hid from me your princehood—that is, his real reason for seeking you. He led me to believe he was merely pursuing a common runaway slave. I do not tolerate liars."

"He may not have known."

"You would defend your tormenter?"

His face assumed a blank look for a moment before it spread into a wan smile. "That is what I was doing, wasn't it? I've changed more in the last month than ever I would have guessed. Amazing, what a she bear can do." He paused. "Or the power of Patrick."

20

Salmon

Is life more than eating, warring, and making love? Gwynn certainly hoped not. She sat in the shade of the ash tree at the far side of her temporary compound and watched Scanlon, out in the open area, work with the slave prince. Were she somehow pressed to choose between the three pastimes, she'd have a hard time indeed. Right now, she was eating a joint of chicken and watching Scanlon teach Padraic the use of ax and javelin. That's two of three, eating and warring, and that's not bad.

It stood to reason that the lad wouldn't have the slightest idea how to handle weapons. In slavery since ten or so, he would not have been permitted a weapon, let alone instructed in its use. Scanlon was an excellent coach. Ambidextrous himself, he worked the boy both right- and left-handed.

Padraic caught on almost instantly to every lesson offered. Not only was he quick, he showed remarkable aptitude. Dhuith's incantations had done their job—the lad seemed much sharper and more energetic this morning.

Scanlon stood with ax at ready, legs braced, and challenged Padraic to take him. The lad hesitated a moment. His tongue flicked across his lips. He lunged forward a step and swung his ax up as if to engage Scanlon. At the crucial moment just short of contact, he altered his grip on the ax to protect his face with the weapon instead of attacking. He thrust his right leg out, hooked his heel behind Scanlon's left knee, and yanked Scanlon's leg up. With a startled yelp, Scanlon staggered and tipped over onto his back.

Padraic mocked a swing of the ax toward Scanlon, pulling the blow two feet short of the mark. He stepped back respectfully and waited for the next lesson.

Gwynn roared. "Delightful! Beautiful!"

"Oh, yes, sure." Half in jest and half angry, Scanlon rolled to his feet and brushed himself off. "Just delightful."

Gwynn waved a hand toward one of the onlookers, Donn of the Moor. "Burn the tips of two staves and bring them." She nodded toward the gladiators. "Come. Rest."

The gladiators came. Scanlon sat down close to her right, still looking a bit abashed to have been caught by a simple childhood ploy. Padraic dropped into the cropped and beaten grass at her feet, utterly spent. He flattened out on his back and closed his eyes. He massaged his left arm absently.

Gwynn watched him a few moments. "Scanlon? Find Aidan for me."

Scanlon studied her a moment. He knew her thoughts; she could tell. Without comment he hopped up and walked off toward the encampment of Donn's people.

Gwynn watched the prostrate prince. "Did Scanlon describe the position the brehons seek for you?"

"No, Queen."

"Ard ri."

He opened his eyes and turned his head toward her. "May I speak my thoughts, Queen?"

"Please do."

"I think that's all a sham. I think Kieran enlisted you in his search for me, and now that you've captured me you're making a bit of fun at my expense. It's true that I belong to a line of royalty, so the joke has some basis. But the Slevin have never been considered for a seat beyond their province, nor have they sought any."

"Then why do I provide you with these lessons from Scanlon?"

"Why not? It's more entertaining than watching the grass grow, as you wait for Kieran's return."

Gwynn laughed. "You really do believe I'm going to turn you over to him."

"I've had a year of experience dodging just that very thing."

"Sit up and look at me."

He did so.

She locked him eye to eye. "Hear me, slave-prince. I will never surrender you into Kieran's hands or anyone else's. Is that understood?"

He held her eye for the longest time. She wished she could read what was going on inside that handsome young head, but his face remained stolid. "Then, Queen, either all my troubles are over, or I'm in deeper trouble than ever."

Again she laughed. "Here are the staves. Arise. Your rest is over."

And here came Aidan as well. Sullen as a bee whose honey has just been stolen, he glared at her. This was most uncharacteristic of her son. Usually Aidan approached life with a sunny insouciance. He had no cause to pout, unless Scanlon had just interrupted . . .

Of course. That was it.

Gwynn stood up and crossed to Donn of the Moor. She took the staves and hefted them. They were poles as big around as her wrist and taller than her head. They were too large and unwieldy for good close work. They permitted no finesse. Besides, Padraic's arm was probably quite weakened. No matter. These were the staves she had, their tips blackened in fire.

She handed one to Aidan and tossed the other to Padraic. "Aidan, I promised you the seat at Tara. Now earn it. The first man marked loses."

Aidan stared. "This simple churl? Mums, you should have been born a Roman. You like mismatched combats too well. Christians versus lions." He snorted and tossed his staff aside. "I'll fight worthy opponents, not this escapee."

With remarkable speed, the slave-prince swiped his staff across Aidan's chest, leaving behind a broken black streak. "According to the queen's rules, I win." He lowered his staff and looked at Gwynn. "Pray thee, may I go take a nap now, Queen?"

She laughed. "As you wish. You do seem a bit wearied. We'll get Dhuith to attend you again." Neither prince was going along with her plan. Why wasn't she angry?

Aidan glared. As Gwynn had rarely seen him pout, she had never seen him show this kind of ire. He exploded with a blasphemous name, dropped low to snatch up his staff, and continued back to his feet. He swung mightily, catching Padraic in the side. His blow sent the slave-prince reeling. Padraic sprawled in the grass.

Gasping, he hauled himself to his knees. He ought to be balancing his staff up by his face for protection. It practically lay on the ground, so low did he hold it.

Aidan lunged at him wildly, aiming with the blackened end. He would have fairly taken Padraic's head off with his charge, but the slave swung his staff along the ground. With a sharp crack, the weapon struck Aidan in the ankles, knocking both feet out from under him. Aidan slammed to the ground on his side. Padraic whipped his staff around and sent it whistling down upon Aidan's knuckles. It was an excellent move, particularly for one with no training or practice with the staff.

Aidan managed to hang onto his own staff as he rolled away from Padraic's blows. Both boys reached their feet at the same time. They faced off, staves high and gripped two-handed.

Aidan feinted; Padraic ducked. Aidan jabbed; Padraic parried.

Gwynn wished the slave-prince would take the offensive instead of reacting blindly to Aidan's angry attacks, although she could understand that he might not feel aggressive. His cheeks were flushed again, and she suspected it was fever more than exertion.

Aidan flicked the end of his staff around, a swift and sprightly move, to soundly thump Padraic's sore arm.

Gwynn caught her breath.

Padraic cried out a shapeless little "Aaah." His left hand opened. His arm dropped away, limp. He stood still a moment, stunned by pain. It was a bad moment to be standing still, for Aidan brought his staff about to deliver the finishing stroke.

But Padraic brought his staff around as well, stepping aside as he swung it one-handed. Quick as a cat he tucked the short end under his arm for leverage and literally fell forward at Aidan. The stubby, blackened point caught Aidan in the midsection, even as Aidan's staff was striking Padraic's right shoulder. Padraic staggered sideways, and Aidan staggered backwards. Aidan went down; Padraic did not.

Padraic made one last, telling lance-thrust with his staff, smearing a sharp black mark on Aidan's trousers to show exactly where he had hit. He turned to Gwynn, and the look on his face begged, *End this. Release me.*

Gwynn raised her hand. "It's over."

Aidan writhed on the ground as Scanlon roared with laughter. That was tactless of Scanlon, to laugh so at the feckless prince. But then, Gwynn was laughing too. "Scanlon, assist my son to his bothy. I'll want to talk to you then."

"Gladly." Scanlon hauled Aidan to his feet and tossed the lad over his shoulder, as he would a joint of beef. Thus did he carry the panpipe tooter off the field of combat.

Padraic let his staff drop and gripped his sore left arm. He waited in that casual stance of his, watching her.

She gestured toward her side. "Sit."

Padraic sat down cross-legged, more or less facing her.

She noticed traces of a brown fever line across his lips. "Cuinn, Muirdoch, and Blaine have never actually laid eyes on you, is that correct?"

"To the best of my knowledge, that is right."

"Neither has Kieran, is that right?"

"He would know me, but he's only seen me briefly a few times. He knows me mostly by description. I worked in the stables outside the wall. He stabled his own horse separately and cared for it himself."

Gwynn nodded. "Consider yourself blessed that I didn't carry through with my first plan. I was going to kill you and have Aidan take your place."

"I consider myself blessed and delighted, Queen. Pray thee, what stayed your hand?"

She studied him evenly. "Because you are ard ri material and Aidan is not. I would be a fool of fools if I slaughtered a possible high king and pampered a weakling. There's more to the qualifications than just bloodlines. A ri must be adept at warfare. He must be the strongest of the strong if he would earn respect, and no ri rules without respect. If I put any name forward for ard ri, it will be you and not he."

He grimaced. "My first impulse was right. I'm in deeper trouble now than ever. When your son finds out, he'll kill me."

"I want to strike a bargain with you, Padraic of Lambay. You'll need all the help you can get in a bid for the high kingship. Royal blood on both sides would be an immense boost to you, as would the support of strong arms. You already enjoy royal rank from the one side. I will declare you as close kin, giving you a legitimate claim to royalty on the other side."

He looked considerably more alert now than he had a moment ago. "At what benefit to me should I go along with our deception?"

"I'll support you, protect you, and train you myself."

"And the cost to me?"

"Hardly a cost. Seat me at your right side as adviser and coregent."

He pulled his knees up and draped his elbows upon them. He stared at the ground for a long time. By and by, he sighed heavily. "I can't see how I could lose. But then, frankly, I can't see anything at all right now. My head's a-muddle."

"You'll feel better soon. I'll have Dhuith get right on it."

He stared holes into the ground. Did he hear her platitudes at all? "I'm tired of running. So tired. I need support. And protection. Safety. I yearn for someone to build a wall around me, even if I only cowered behind it for a short while. A little rest . . ."

"Padraic."

He looked up at her.

"You're safe. Go rest."

This untrained slave who had just trounced her own princely son looked at her as would a half-grown child. "Thank you, beautiful lady." He dragged himself to his feet and wandered off toward Scanlon's encampment.

Gwynn sat back and permitted herself a quiet smile. If she didn't take the vacant throne of Tara one way, she'd do it another.

* * *

There are thrones, and there are thrones. The Bible lesson yesterday concerned the throne of God, to be approached through prayer. It was the day before yesterday that Maeve told Bridey about Padraic's expectations and prospects regarding the throne at Tara. This morning, first light, Bridey was on the road again, headed for Armagh, the "throne" of Patrick.

For no particular reason, as she walked along Bridey thought about her stepmother. A slave to the ale bucket, the woman was

176

virtually incompetent. Who handled the cooking and sweeping now that Bridey had left? Her stepfather spent his days in idle chatting with neighboring cattlemen. Who milked? Who drove the recalcitrant cattle from pasture to pasture? Who gathered eggs from all the hiding places here and there?

In a perverse way, she missed all that even as she hated it. She despised working constantly without a word of praise. Yet she missed the familiar routine that had been her life from childhood until now. And if it had not been for Padraic, she would still be working there, still drudging from day to day.

Strange and fascinating Padraic. Tormented. Cheery in the face of it all. At Kildare she made him a daily subject of fervent prayer. The farm had been her life for years and years, and she had known Padraic for only a few weeks. But she missed him far more.

Despite the yearning and the homesickness, she gloried in this new life. She worked as hard as ever. Harder, in fact, for she both served and studied. Besides, others kept calling upon her to help fix broken implements, of which there were many, and see to injured cattle and sheep, of which there were a few. Growing up, she had constantly dealt with old, broken implements, because her stepfather never got around to making new ones. And no amount of trips between Beltaine fires could save the livestock from his carelessness. Her stepparents' rath had been an excellent training ground for Kildare.

This morning she had rolled up her hairbrush inside her wool blanket. Now she carried the rolled blanket over her shoulder. This was much more than she'd taken when she first went off adventuring in Padraic's company. *The Lord provides.* It still amazed her.

To the east, the Wicklows loomed dark in their bumpy blanket of treetops. So far, so good. She wasn't lost yet. On the other hand, she'd been on the track less than an hour—not enough time yet to become thoroughly lost. Behind the Wicklows the sky washed gold, dawn-color.

Brigid, Bishop of Kildare, had herself blessed Bridey and sent her forth with detailed directions.

Brigid traveled to Armagh frequently, for she knew Patrick and the others there. Brigid had achieved a primacy no other woman in Erin enjoyed—a bishopric.

Brigid. Ah, sweet Brigid. Amazing Brigid. Brigid was generous beyond imagining. She had given Bridey this lovely hairbrush, and she'd done it so gracefully.

"Bridey, dear, your long braids are beautiful. Have you a good sow-bristle brush for that lovely hair?" This from a woman with thick and gleaming blonde tresses.

"Uh—no, m'm." This from a girl with mousy brown rope.

"Now you do. Your hair deserves it." And Brigid had handed Bridey her own brush. Bridey knew it was Brigid's own—some of Brigid's blonde hairs were still tangled in it.

When Brigid taught Scripture, it leaped to glowing life. When she prayed aloud, the prayers soared directly to God's right ear. Brigid was not only spiritually blessed and generous to the highest degree but breathtakingly beautiful as well. In short, Brigid was all the things Bridey dreamed of and more.

And now Bridey was walking away from Brigid and Kildare, at least for a while, all on account of a slave-prince who cared nothing for her.

Brigid's colaborers claimed she enjoyed second sight, that unique ability to see into the darkness of the future. Bridey pondered her parting words: "Bridey, dear, go where God takes you and do not fret. Greet Patrick for me."

Go where God takes you. Was this an instance of second sight, or did Brigid merely mean to stay close to God through Jesus? Did that parting statement perhaps preclude getting lost? Oh, Bridey devoutly hoped so!

Brigid promised the River Liffey to Bridey's right. Here it was, dancing in the dawn light. The salmon were running. Their silvery backs broke the surface every now and then. Bridey loved to watch the salmon leap riffles and falls, but the water lay flat along here. No falls, no riffles. It was too early in the day to catch one for supper. The fish would spoil and turn soft before nightfall.

When the river hooked eastward, she was to take the track to the left that would carry her north. She must be certain to catch a fish before she left the riverside. She rarely had a chance to catch salmon back home. Her stepmother did not particularly like fish of any kind, salmon included, and the nearest salmon stream lay some miles distant from the rath. At home, though, during the height of the run, Bridey would go out for a day, right after milking, and carry a basket over the slieve to the salmon stream on the other side. She would stand in the shallow water of a riffle, facing downstream with her legs spread, and wait. Sooner or later a salmon would come swimming within snatching distance.

Grab! Toss it up on shore beside the basket and wait for the next. Bridey smiled at the thought—and of the memory of cold rushing water, the slippery, wriggling weight of the fish, the hits and misses, the strange way water shifts what you think you see beneath its surface. It took Bridey years of practice before she could see a fish below the surface and accurately determine where it actually was.

A salmon leaped clear of the water, its tail flailing. It fell back in. Were Bridey standing out there, she would only have had to spread her skirt and the fish would have jumped right in her lap. An opportunity lost.

Then young men's voices chattered in the distance ahead, sending a sudden twinge of fear through her. She never felt comfortable around young men, Padraic excepted. She had no idea what having a brother might be like, but she suspected the relationship would be quite similar to that between herself and Padraic. Helping each other, putting up with each other, acting casually—she often dreamed, idly, of having a brother. Of course, a brother probably would not run off and leave her all alone on the shore of the Dingle. Or maybe he would. Who knows?

She really ought to fade into the forest on her left or into the streamside bushes between the track and the river. Let the young men pass, unaware of her. Then she would continue north, and they could wend their merry way south, none the wiser.

Here by streamside, tangled sedge, rushes, and horsetails grew at the base of a clump of birches. That would do nicely. She stepped down off the bank into the rushing water. Cold, cold water swirled against her legs to above the knee. She hiked her skirts high, lifted her blanket roll clear, and waded over among the rushes. Tall stalks and leaves and feathery horsetails completely obscured her from the view of anyone on the track. She stood, waiting, while her toes turned painfully cold.

Ten feet downstream, a monstrous salmon breached. Another fish glided by right beside her leg. Fish swam fin to fin from bank to bank. The school was practically thick enough to walk on.

"Look at that!" one lad called. Another shouted. Now here the young men all came, at least a half dozen of them, crashing through the weeds and brush and horsetails.

Bridey stood stock still and prayed. *Please, God, let them pass.*

One of them (he sounded like the same lad who exclaimed over the fish) cried, "There in the weeds! A girl!" A few laughed. Others smashed down the horsetails to take a look.

Bridey snapped around and yelled, "Go away! Ye're scaring them!" Then she let loose her skirts and blanket and turned her attention back to the water curling so swiftly around her legs. Her skirt and blanket wicked up chilly water instantly.

They watched her.

She watched the gray forms below. *Please, dear holy God, send one by!*

Grab! Her left hand connected with a tail. She managed with her right to dig her fingers in behind the gill cover, the only nons-lippery part on a fish. She hauled it up and clutched it to her chest as it flayed about desperately. She waded around the sedges and tossed it up onto the bank.

She scowled at the six rosy young faces staring at her. "A fine help ye all are. Ye may have that one for all y'r trouble. Take it and go, and leave this fisherman in peace." She sloshed back out into the river, but the run seemed to be ending. Fewer fish came by.

The lad who was so easily amazed and amused crowed about Bridey's stupendous feat of catching salmon with her bare hands. A few others, in manly tones, boasted of doing the same.

She wanted them to go away. Her skirt was soaked, her blanket getting wet. *Pray Thee, God, drive them away!*

God did not. One of them jumped down into the water and stepped into the current downstream of her. Obviously, he was going to show his companions his prowess.

Their spokesman ashore, not a bad-looking young fellow actually, called, "What is your name, pray thee, miss?"

"Bridey." She almost added the Currane and decided not to.

"Where are you from?"

"Kildare. Brigid's monastery."

The lad in the water turned and looked at her. He almost seemed disappointed. "A holy woman, then. One of Brigid's women."

"All women safe in Christ Jesus are holy."

He grimaced. "But not all holy women are untouchable. Brigid's are." He glanced back at his companions.

Bridey grabbed for a fish and missed.

The fellow ashore gripped a birch with one hand so as to hang out farther over the sedges. "Bridey of Kildare, come with us. We know the ogham, but we must needs learn the Greek and Roman alphabets before we reach home. We need a teacher."

"I be hardly more than a new student m'self."

"You know the alphabets?"

"Aye."

"That's what we need."

Bridey was about to protest further, but Brigid's admonition intruded on her thoughts. *Bridey, dear, go where God takes you and do not fret. Greet Patrick for me.* She pondered this in a new light. The admonition could easily be saying, *Patrick is not at Armagh. He's elsewhere. Go to him, not to Armagh.* If Padraic learned Patrick was elsewhere he would not go to Armagh either. He was seeking a man, not a place.

Bridey must place her trust and safety in God's hands now. She did so in prayer, bowing her face toward the river but not closing her eyes. Did she truly approach God's magnificent throne simply by asking favors of Him? If that be so, what a wonderful God He was!

She would have raised her eyes to the young man, but a sleek form caught her attention. *Grab!* She would have lost the fish, but she was able to flip it up into her skirt, enveloping it in wool. She got a good grip behind the gill covers and headed for shore.

She tossed the fish up on the bank and straightened to look the young man squarely in the eye. "I shall go with ye, lad, as a teacher and only as a teacher. Ye will learn y'r alphabets, if learn them ye would, and perhaps a little something about the nature of prayer, such as I received in m'own lessons."

"Excellent! Excellent. We prayed this morning that God send a teacher in our midst. And see what He has done!"

181

The fellow out in the stream managed to snag a fish and haul it ashore. They had more than enough salmon now to feed seven mouths.

Bridey splashed and staggered up onto the bank, her skirt heavy with water. She hated the feel of sopping wet fabric slapping against her legs, tripping her.

She stood erect. "Where be ye bound?"

"Cashel."

21

Shrew

Not only was this a banquet, it was a banquet in Padraic's honor. *This is not a thing that happens often,* he mused as he sat cross-legged on a wolfskin. The queen, seated between Padraic on her right and Scanlon on her left, presided with a robust enthusiasm Padraic rarely saw in a woman.

He was finally starting to get some life back himself. The bear had bitten him but once, and he was sick with infection and fever for nearly a week. Rafe had been bitten and raked repeatedly. When Rafe was raised to life, would he come back as a whole man, well in every regard, or as a victim of infection even sicker than Padraic? Padraic would soon find out. Perhaps he should take Dhuith along for the raising, to treat any fever present. No. If Patrick could raise the dead, he could surely cure a fever.

How much time did Padraic have? Presumably the giant had been dead for centuries. There must not be a time limitation. Still, he did not want to tarry. He had paused too long already. At any moment, Kieran would come riding back into the enclave of Gwynn and her cohorts. Then what?

Gwynn promised she would not let Kieran have him. Padraic was not about to glibly trust her word, though. The throne at Tara was about the only thing she talked about, grilling the brehons across the table from her for information. She said he was safe. He amended that to mean "safe as long as you fit into my plans for power and glory." He was not interested in power or glory. He was interested in freeing Rafe from the claws of death.

The purpose of the banquet was twofold. With it Gwynn officially introduced Padraic to the brehons who would conduct him to Tara for consideration as ard ri, and during it she announced her relationship to Padraic.

She made it sound quite convincing; for a moment even Padraic believed it. And a wild and glorious tale it was too, as she described losing track of her beloved sister only to discover she was granted the joy of gathering in her sister's son, her delightful nephew.

Delightful? After yesterday? Gwynn must have quite a warped sense of humor, or else she didn't care much about her son. Padraic suspected the latter.

He knew also, as surely as he knew the rain would fall, that the moment this shrew had insinuated herself into the Great Hall of Tara and secured her place, Padraic would become expendable. He still couldn't believe this Tara business anyway, but it must be true. Here were the brehons, seeking him.

And Brian! Talk about delightful—this *was* delightful. Padraic had not seen Brian since the burly pre-brehon went into training. They caught up on each other's news and lives for nearly an hour, hardly taking time to eat, as the people around them chewed food and discussed other things.

Across from him, the stoatlike brehon named Cuinn talked about the amazing way Patrick's religion was spreading among the druidic classes. Beside Cuinn, the round, harbor-seal-shaped Blaine talked about some vaguely different subject altogether. The two conversations meshed well enough, though, that each man probably thought he had the other's attention.

And then there sat Muirdoch, the dark brehon. Except for a complaint that he should never have allowed Kieran to take the dogs and his man Rowan, he remained virtually silent.

Suddenly, like the surf slapping rocks, thoughts of Bridey splashed across Padraic's mind. He heartily wished that she sat here now beside him. Silly goose. After the way he treated her, she wouldn't want to sit within a mile of him, and he didn't blame her. Yet the thought of her lingered, dancing lightly in the shadows of the torches.

Where was she now? Kildare, no doubt, reciting her alphabets.

Brian was handsome and young and powerful. Padraic did not mention anything about Bridey to Brian.

He struck up a conversation with Blaine of Clones, but with a corner of his ear he listened in on a quiet exchange between Queen Gwynn and her Scanlon. Did he hear that right? Gwynn was assigning Scanlon the task of seeing that their dark friend didn't bother them anymore. When she had mentioned to Padraic that she did not tolerate liars, she wasn't speaking idly. And when she warned Scanlon not to let the stallion be harmed, Padraic was absolutely certain about the identity of the dark friend. Muirdoch did not own a stallion.

Bridey remained on his mind, barely, but a confusion of other thoughts churned there too. Kieran of the Great Horse had pursued him relentlessly. He was the enemy of enemies. Whether he sought to kill Padraic at one time or not, he certainly wanted to capture him. Now, with this Tara business in the offing, Kieran would seek Padraic even more fervently. At least now he'd want Padraic alive at all costs.

And yet, look at these unwanted feelings Padraic suddenly entertained. Instantly the strongest urge to warn Kieran and protect him washed across Padraic. He didn't want Kieran to die by Scanlon's hand, and that was madness. It would solve all Padraic's problems—most of them, at any rate. Kieran's death worked to Padraic's advantage in every way.

Yet somehow he must prevent that death.

The stoat and seal turned their attention to him, then, and he had to put aside all his other tangled thoughts to concentrate on answering them. They asked him about the many places he had visited across Erin. How did he like them? Whom did he meet there?

My wise friends, I would have loved to tarry longer in many of those places, but I had to flee, with a dark nemesis hard on my heels. He would think of Bridey and Rafe tomorrow. Tonight he would laugh a little.

An hour after dark he excused himself to step outside. Stars twinkled through the haze overhead. They provided no light of any consequence, particularly since Padraic's eyes had still not adjusted from torchlight to starlight. He could see perhaps two feet, or three. Otherwise he had to grope his way. He would follow the wall, passing behind tents of Donn of the Thicket's people.

Suddenly he tangled in a clothesline. Why did women stretch their clotheslines all over? It was a trap, obviously, to catch some unwary male on his way to the facility. Men and boys talked about the ensnaring wiles of women—they ought to mention ensnaring clotheslines.

And then he froze. A familiar *clip-clop*—a hideously familiar *clip-clop*—was approaching the gate. A pony clattered up, and a pack of dogs. Padraic heard the great horse sidle as two feet landed on the ground. Kieran was back. Kieran might not survive the night.

Frantically, Padraic pawed through the linen clothes. Here—this woman's garment would probably fit. He slipped it on. And a tunic—he dragged a striped shawl off the line, tossed it around his head, and headed toward the gate.

The pony rider and his dogs made noise all the way across the compound. Padraic ignored them and instead followed the sound of the great horse.

"Kieran of the Great Horse." Padraic pitched his voice high. Kieran had not, to his knowledge, heard his voice before, at least not in the last few years. It was hard to speak softly and change pitch all at the same time.

"Yes?" Only stripes loomed in the blackness. The horse and darkness melted together into bobbing, disembodied silver bridle trim.

"Turn and flee. Instantly! The queen has ordered Scanlon Too Skinny to murder you."

"Why would . . ?" The rumbling voice paused. It was quite a manly voice, deep and menacing. "She thinks I was lying, doesn't she?"

"And she's afraid you'll take that Padraic lad away. She wants to use him to reach Tara. She has great plans for Tara."

"I don't doubt that. So she found the slave. Who actually caught him? Scanlon?"

"Aye." Padraic saw the vague stripes moving toward him. "Fly! Please."

Behind them, voices intruded. Padraic glanced back. So flimsy was Gwynn's great hall that torchlight leaked out in a thousand places. Silhouettes of three men moved across the light leaks.

The stripes paused a long moment. "Thank you, lady."

And then, thank all spirits and otherworldlings, Kieran swung aboard his black horse. He muttered a word of frustration, said, "No, wait . . ," and then apparently thought better of something. He turned his horse toward the gate.

Padraic heard Kieran's voice, heard someone else's, and the great horse clattered away into the night.

It was time to put aside his womanly attire. He took two steps and nearly fell on his face. His feet had tangled in some object. He groped around and picked it up. It was Kieran's fine woolen cloak, cloud soft. So that was the reason for his "No, wait."

Soon enough, Scanlon would learn from the guards that Kieran had come and gone again. But if this cloak turned up, Scanlon would know that the man had fled in haste. He would deduce that Kieran knew he was marked for death, that the great horseman had been warned.

Padraic found his way back to the clothesline. He draped the clothes back over the cords. He hung the cloak there too. This was Donn's camp. His women would not be likely to tell Scanlon they found a magnificent cloak on the line. If they were smart, they'd usurp it without a word.

Late the next morning, Donn's women took in their dry laundry. The cloak hung there by itself. As far as Padraic could see, Scanlon failed to notice.

* * *

"That's good! Very good!" Gwynn gave her ax a double twist. It swung up and around and would have taken off Padraic's head except that the ax was a blunt wooden dummy for practice purposes, she didn't put her full strength behind it, and he brought his own practice piece around in time to deflect the blow.

His parry was a move Gwynn must have tried a dozen times to teach Aidan. Her son had never caught on. Padraic picked it up the first time.

They were sparring out in the middle of the compound in sparkling morning sunshine. It was a perfect day. Gwynn had promised to provide Padraic training as well as protection. If he would make an excellent impression before the council of ris, he must know weapons and use them skillfully. He had a lot to learn in a short time.

Over on the sidelines, Padraic's friend Brian heckled, and cheered the queen on. One would think he would support his childhood friend. On the other hand, he was old enough to know better than to cheer against a queen. Too, Brian and Padraic had almost instantly regained that comfortable stage of friendship between young men that values banter and competition above nice words. Brian and Padraic were chums, and that said good things about Padraic's long-term loyalties.

Beside Brian, the brehons lounged beneath a tree watching. Their impression of young Padraic at the banquet last night had been extremely favorable, they claimed. "Bright," "well poised," "well traveled," and "knowledgeable" stood out among their praises. Now they were seeing the other side, the necessary physical skills of a ruler. And Padraic was not disappointing them in that regard either.

He had stripped to the waist and abandoned his boots. Despite that, his whole upper body glistened with sweat. It trickled in tiny rivulets down his face and pasted down his blond-brown hair. His cheeks glowed, but it was a healthy, rosy color.

The bear damage on his upper left arm intrigued Gwynn. The tooth marks—and deep they were—looked as if the bear had picked him up and thrown him. She couldn't get a good story out of him, though, and she couldn't figure out how he would survive an encounter like that. The open wounds had scabbed over firmly and one of the scabs was starting to peel. He'd carry white scars for the rest of his life. A mutilated man could not serve as king. Fortunately, battle scars of this sort did not count as a disqualifying blemish.

Good. If battle scars disqualified, no man worth his salt would be fit to serve. The best kings carried the marks of their daring and prowess.

Gwynn tucked her wooden ax in her belt on one side and her wooden sword in the other. She spread her arms wide. "All out!"

Padraic stepped back. "I dare not touch the queen."

"You certainly dare. This is a training session. Rest assured that Cu Chulainn dared touch Skatha, his instructor. All out."

The slave-prince hesitated, a bit slow to attack a queen. When she kicked out suddenly and sent him sprawling, he woke

188

up. They grappled for five minutes, and he gave as good as he got. Sweaty, he was worse than an eel to hang onto. She pulled her sword on him, and he parried with his ax, barely in the nick of time. He broke her sword; she broke his ax. It was an altogether successful and exhilarating climax to a highly instructive session.

Sweating and panting like plowhorses, they sat exhausted in the beaten dirt, laughing. Theoretically they were both dead, the victims of each other's weapons.

"My prince—" she grinned "—you need a bath."

The dirt stuck to his sweaty skin, making him a uniform gray. "And My Queen, you are not as fresh as once you were."

"You're fresh enough, knave, if mouths count for anything! We'll meet for another lesson this afternoon. You need work with the staff, despite that you nearly emasculated Aidan a few days ago."

He lurched to his feet and brushed himself off, a gesture akin to trying to scrape the mud off a pig with a toothpick. "If apologies are in order, Queen, I tender them."

"None are. Later."

She might be his weapons instructor, but he had the presence of mind to offer the obeisance due a queen. It was curious the way he so smoothly shifted from role of subject to role of student. That was a good thing for a king to have too—flexibility.

At the door of her bothy across the compound, she turned to look back at him. That nubile little wife of Donn of the Moor had materialized from nowhere. With coy smiles she was offering Padraic a drink from a water bucket. He was smiling at her. Did he realize she was married? For that matter, did he possess the moral fiber to care?

The brehons were watching too. Brian stood up, and they ordered him back down to sitting.

Gwynn halfway expected Donn of the Moor to come roaring into the picture. Scanlon mentioned that Donn was starting to suspect his wife's infidelity but had no idea who was cuckolding him.

Gwynn herself had heard some of the screaming matches between Donn and his wife. The little shrew must be an incredible aggravation to live with day in and day out. And look at her pouring on the sweetness and charm. She reached out and touched

Padraic's bear bite as they talked. She burst into a sudden laugh. Apparently she wasn't getting any more serious a story about that than Gwynn had.

The girl walked away, and here came the telling moment. Gwynn watched Padraic closely as he crossed to a hazel bush to get his tunic and boots. If he were interested at all, he would pause to watch the girl depart. He would at least glance her way once or twice. He did not. That pleased Gwynn immensely, and she had no idea why. After all, she didn't care whether the girl was cheating on Donn or not, and she didn't consider the girl a suitable mistress for her son, either.

So intent was she upon watching Padraic that she had failed to notice Aidan. The petulant towhead now stepped in front of Padraic before the slave-prince had walked six steps toward Scanlon's camp. Gwynn sighed. She could tell from Aidan's gestures that he was burning Padraic's ears, no doubt warning him to stay away from the girl.

Padraic was protesting disinterest. She could tell from the way his head moved. He shrugged and said something, grinning.

Whatever it was, the comment infuriated Aidan. The lad exploded with such vehemence that Gwynn had to assume he'd been into the ale bucket rather heavily. Time to put an end to this nonsense. Gwynn started forward.

Aidan lashed out suddenly with a fist, and Padraic ducked away barely in time, parrying the blow with tunic and boots. His own fist swung at Aidan and connected with a glancing blow. Aidan staggered backwards and took a sidestep to keep from falling. When he wheeled again to face Padraic, a burnished iron blade gleamed in his hand.

Gwynn heard "Usurper!" and "Mine!" as she broke into a trot.

The brehons were physically holding Brian down.

Aidan stabbed at Padraic low, either to disembowel or mutilate him. Padraic pulled out his wooden practice sword to defend himself. By the time Gwynn reached them, Aidan had cut three nicks in the coarse wood.

She grabbed Aidan's hair and yanked him in a wide arc, throwing him down.

He rolled to his knees. The fall had bent his blade neatly

perpendicular to the haft. He looked ludicrous holding a bent dagger, and Padraic looked heroic defending himself with a simple wooden stick.

Aidan roared, "He's stealing what's mine! And you're letting him!"

"You have to earn what's yours. But if you harm this prince, I'll kill you myself. Now quit making a spectacle of yourself! Get off somewhere and sober up."

What Aidan would have done were his dagger not bent at right angles, Gwynn could not guess. But it was, so with muttered threats and complaints, he backed down.

Padraic glanced at Gwynn. "As I said, a whole lot more trouble." He turned and left.

Still mumbling about mayhem, Aidan stalked off.

Gwynn returned to her bothy. On the way she noticed the black cloak that had been hanging on the line unattended since sun-up. She paused beside it and rubbed its fabric between her fingers. Excellent, excellent quality.

"Whose is this?" she asked, not too loudly.

Donn of the Thicket's rotund wife paused beside her tent and did a careless, hasty obeisance. "No one's that we know of, Queen. We thought 'twas the brehons', but they all have theirs." She went inside.

"Mm." Gwynn looked about, lifted the cloak off the line, and took it with her.

* * *

He is not your son. He is not your son.

The thought echoed over and over in Gwynn's head. She sat on her cushion, leaning against her backboard, and pondered the strange vicissitudes of life. People outside talked and laughed in the sweet glow of evening. Gwynn preferred the quiet darkness and solitude just now.

Aidan the panpipe tooter bore no relation to her at all save through her marriage to his father, now ended. In the greater scheme of things, he meant nothing positive. He meant a great deal to her life in negative ways. Should his dalliance with the wife of Donn of the Moor become generally known, the unity of

191

her armed band could be destroyed. She could not afford to permit her army to dissolve in discord.

Even worse loomed the possibility that he could rise up again against Padraic and mutilate the lad. Gwynn harbored no doubt that that was Aidan's intent. What a pity that would be, for Gwynn saw rich promise in Padraic Slevin of Lambay.

Not to mention the prospect of queen consort.

She had only one clear choice. She could order Scanlon to take care of Kieran—or any other awkward chore for that matter. This, though, was a deed she must perform herself.

The brehons and their entourage entered, so she greeted them. They were, after all, the emissaries of Tara. Scanlon wasn't back yet, but Donn of the Thicket was, so he sat at her left. Padraic had bathed. He looked quite handsome in clean garments. She seated him beyond her immediate right, leaving the nearest wolfskin for Aidan. Aidan did not appear. Women brought in the food. They filled the ale tankard, and the brehons passed it from man to man and back again. Dinner proceeded well. The guests were dismissed. All but the brehons left. Brehons, literally and figuratively, were a law unto themselves.

Gwynn sat about in her great hall until nightfall, sipping ale and listening to meaningless discussions about philosophy. Brehons were so very engaged in philosophy, and what use was it? None. Finally, about the time she decided she could no longer suppress her yawns, they excused themselves.

She spent the first hour of night darkness in her bothy sharpening her bronze dagger to a perfect edge. Were she of the shaving gender she could have used it for that. She dawdled at least another half hour in her quarters, waiting until she knew Aidan must be asleep. Totally asleep. She did not want him to know what killed him—especially not who.

She drew the finely spun black cloak up over her head. Her blonde hair tended to show up in any kind of light, even starlight. It must remain hidden. She walked out along the wall behind the marquee serving as her temporary great hall. She paused in the shadow of the ash tree awhile, listening. Over in Scanlon's tents someone was snoring. A dog barked briefly, not an alarmist sort of bark, and ceased. Other than that, silence.

She drew the tails of the woolen cloak across the front of her to shield her tunic from the blood that would spray. *Washing blood out of linen is such a chore. Washing blood out of wool is about as bad, but at least this deep black will not show stains.*

A horrid thought struck her. What if Aidan was not alone? She calmed herself. He had to be. Donn of the Moor was in camp tonight. Therefore his wife would sleep at his side.

No sounds, no movement. The guards on the wall were devoting their attentions to the world outside the gate, not the world within. She moved in behind Aidan's bothy and paused again to listen and watch. Very nearly she abandoned the whole idea. He was a likable fellow. He deserved a better end than a slit throat—and a far longer life. But he was more than just a nuisance. He was dangerous.

She drew her dagger and concealed it in the cloak, lest the metal blade pick up moonlight. She mentally rehearsed her movements. Confident then that she could act quickly and surely whether he was lying on his back, on his stomach, or on his side, she quietly slipped inside his bothy.

22

Dipper

He should have paused long enough to retrieve his cloak.

Kieran sat beside a rippling brook while his horse grazed at streamside. He should have taken the extra moment to slide off his horse, pick up the cloak, and remount. He was a fool to leave it.

Too late now. It remained behind in the camp of that self-styled queen. So did Padraic. Whether Kieran managed to get his cloak back or not was secondary. Getting Padraic back was the important thing.

The best Kieran could do, probably, was follow along at a distance as the queen and her entourage, including the brehons no doubt, traveled from the Shannon over to Tara. He could not hope to recover Padraic from that whole guerrilla band. But should some ri fall upon them and break up the guard, Kieran might have a chance at snatching Padraic away. Too, if Padraic showed his usual colors and escaped, Kieran could get on his track again immediately.

Would Padraic bolt, leaving behind a chance to become the high king? Kieran would not, but Kieran was sensible. Padraic had fled a perfectly acceptable situation—therefore Padraic was a twit. He just might bolt. And Kieran would be waiting to grab him.

Kieran's first order of business, however, was obtaining another cloak. He had almost frozen last night, trying to huddle under his saddle. Were he attached to a local ri, as was any retainer worth anything, there would be no problem. But his ri, and therefore his source for cloaks, lived a hundred and some miles away.

Out in the burbling brook, a big, plump, black bird with a white bib hopped onto a midstream rock. It looked like a giant wren in black and white, and it even acted like a wren. It bobbed as it flicked its short, perky upright tail. *Dipper* was its name. Kier-

194

an's druid back home claimed dippers could fly underwater. Kieran knew from observation that the bird often stayed underwater for a minute at a time, and he presumed it was foraging down there.

Its vivid black contrasting with the bright white reminded Kieran of that woman in black. In fact, the swishing tail on Kieran's horse could remind him of her. Sometimes he thought about her with no reminder at all. He wished the gentry, and that surely was what she was, could speak directly instead of in riddles. *You are gloating in a strength that is not yours and engaging in a pursuit that is beyond you. Seek a new strength and a new aim while you may.*

The dipper hopped off the rock into the roiling water, and Kieran could see no trace of it. Some moments later it popped out onto a boulder ten feet downstream.

Strange as it might be, the perky dipper fit into its realm perfectly. And Kieran fit just as comfortably into his. He too was clad in black and white. He too did not fit the usual definition for his kind. Retainer. Hunter. His tuath lay far, far behind him.

Gloating? He wasn't gloating. Sure and he was proud of his hunting skills and his resolve in recovering the runaway, but he didn't gloat as such. And of course his strength was his own. Whose else would it be?

Kieran heard voices and hooves in the distance. A party was riding this way along the streamside track. One of them would have an adequate cloak. He hurried to his horse, took up the reins, and swung aboard.

He rode out to the track and positioned his horse in the way, north-facing, just south of a sharp bend. He waited, noting with his ears the approaching pony clatter. They were in a hurry.

Young Donn of the Moor and two cohorts bucketed around the corner and dragged their ponies to a halt. They gaped, each reluctant to be the first to draw a weapon.

"I understand Scanlon is seeking me." Kieran watched their faces.

"True, but I'm not." Donn kept his right hand free and hovering near his sword hilt, Kieran noticed. "You are strictly his concern, not mine. I'm looking for Aidan. Have you seen him on this track?"

"I seem to have lost my cloak, and you have a good warm one there. An exchange of information for the cloak, pray thee."

"Is the information worth a cloak?"

"Probably not."

Donn exploded with a profanity and a bitter laugh. "I'd hate to see so fine a fellow suffer in the night cold. Here." He pulled his brooch and let his cloak tumble free of his shoulders. He whipped it around, let it fall by the track, and dropped his brooch down inside his tunic.

Kieran nodded. "I examined the track here as I passed this morning. Two riders on medium-sized ponies traveled southward rapidly, probably a little before dawn. That is the only activity I saw on this track that's less than two days old."

"That is he." Donn nodded. "He has a companion."

"Your face looks like you've just eaten raw nettles. I'd guess your soul feels about as pained. What's the story?"

"The queen entered Aidan's bothy after dark last night to ask him something or other and discovered he was gone. She instantly sent Scanlon to investigate. When I came off guard duty I found my wife gone as well. We are certain they absconded."

Kieran reined his horse well aside. "You have my deep and genuine sympathy, Donn of the Moor. May you catch them and work whatever justice you desire. I'm grateful for the cloak. My thanks."

Donn's face melted from caution and hostility to something akin to friendship, and Kieran perceived that with his words he had just won himself a comrade.

Donn nodded. "May all the gods and spirits build a wall of safety between you and the lout Scanlon."

Donn and his companions clattered away southbound.

Kieran sat a few moments analyzing all this. If Donn considered Scanlon a lout, which he was, then was Scanlon somehow implicated in the adulterous elopement? Those tangled webs were not Kieran's concern. He should have asked Donn about the queen's plans, but he didn't want to delay the distraught husband. Let Donn find Aidan. That panpipe-tooting little fop deserved anything they did to him.

And Gwynn, the power-hungry shrew, deserved to see her beloved son suffer. Kieran slid off his horse and put on the cloak. He had no fastener. He'd have to use a whittled pin until he could come by a brooch. No matter. At least now he could stay warm.

* * *

Eyes ablaze and nostrils flaring, he stood braced at the far end of his lunge line and dared the world to come. In the middle of the compound that was Gwynn's camp, a three-year-old pony stallion snorted at Padraic. On the other end of the lunge line, Padraic snorted back. He walked forward five feet, gathering in line, and stood still. He had stripped to the waist, despite that a brisk breeze chilled him. He didn't want to get his tunic wet, and his training plans today included a swim.

Beside his shoulder, Gwynn watched the stud pony. "Think you can keep that spirit in him? I need him broken, but I'd love to see him stay wild. Do you know what I mean?"

"I do, Queen. You want him tamed and untamed." Padraic kept his eyes on the horse. "Like Scanlon."

A pause. "I think we've discussed your impudent mouth."

"Several times. I shall desist if you wish."

She guffawed. "No, young prince, I think I prefer you saucy. Ride this pony to my door before nightfall, and any mare in my herd is yours."

"Were I to strike the hardest bargain, lady, I would ask the gray mare, for she has that lovely foal at her heels. But I'll not be greedy. The black mare will do."

"Indeed." With a snicker the queen walked away.

Padraic closed on the stud until three feet of lunge line connected them. He talked to the horse ten minutes, doing nothing but purr nonsense. When he stepped forward and raised a hand, the stud dipped his head aside violently. In addition to the loop around the horse's neck, Padraic threw a loop over the nose. He snugged it down tight. The stallion objected mightily, tossing his head, but he followed where led. He had no choice.

Padraic led him a quarter mile to the River Shannon. The stud had quieted considerably. He kept his nose in the air as stallions do, paying attention all around, but he walked at Padraic's right shoulder without balking.

Padraic kept walking down the slippery mudbank straight into the river. The horse stopped. Padraic backed up a step and led the horse at an angle into water above his knees. He let him drink. He waded on out, walking south with the current, pushing the horse farther and farther from shore.

Padraic watched the flow of water, picking out the channel. The pony stud was up to its breast now and getting nervous. With a gentle shove, Padraic pushed him out into the channel. The pony flailed and began to swim. His eyes rolled back.

Padraic supported himself in the water with a hand on the pony's withers. Every time the stud tried to turn ashore, Padraic wrenched its head away. Its face barely above the surface, the pony was forced to swim in the direction his head turned.

How long did they swim? Padraic didn't know, but he knew he was freezing in the intolerably cold water. No matter. He would just have to tolerate it. Snorting and snarfing, the pony began to tire. Padraic quietly slipped a leg across its submerged back. His weight nearly bore the pony under.

Up ahead, graceful curves in the rippled surface indicated a sandbar somewhere below the surface. The nearest shore lay several hundred yards to the east. Perfect. He guided the pony that way.

The stud's feet hit bottom, and he hauled himself onto the sandbar. The sand must be very loose beneath his hooves—he staggered, his back not more than six inches above the water. He flung his head, trying to no avail to free himself of that loop.

Still seated, his legs clamped firmly around the pony's barrel, Padraic let him rest. The pony tried to rear, but the soft sand beneath wouldn't let him. He could not buckjump without putting his head below the surface. Several times in his dancing and sidling he stepped off the sandbar into deeper water and dunked himself. Eventually, the stallion realized he could do nothing but squirm around tossing his head.

Enough rest. Padraic yelled and thumped his heels into the pony's ribs. Startled, the stud leaped forward into deep water, and they were swimming again.

Padraic let the horse exhaust himself thoroughly. By the time he turned the stud's head toward shore, the pony could barely stay up. Padraic would have liked to find another sandbar, but he could not. He would have to take his chances with solid land.

The pony hauled himself ashore, slipping and stumbling in the mud, and made a few feeble tries to dislodge his rider. The rider kept his head held high on a tight rein and made it point toward the camp, miles to the north. The pony began to run, but the tight hand and exhaustion combined to slow him to a walk. He tolerated the rider, eventually, because he was simply too tired to do otherwise.

Padraic now had but one small question: Should he hold the queen to her impetuous promise? No rath or encampment can survive long unless every member works, doing a part. Padraic's part was to break the colts and fillies and any ponies taken. He would have this stud worked into shape, and the defiant spirit intact, in a couple of weeks. With training, the sturdy stud would become a splendid warhorse. That was Padraic's expected contribution. Should he accept additional compensation?

On the other hand, he had no animal of his own. He could certainly use the mare.

Another question emerged: Should he ride the east shore of the river all the way up to the track that led to water's edge and then turn back down southerly to the camp? Or should he just cut cross-country here, pick up the trail south of the camp, and ride in northward? He could save almost a mile that way. He would do the latter. He reined the pony aside to eastward, cuing him with his knees as he turned his head, and took off cross-country away from the river.

These were the first leg cues the pony had ever felt. Padraic would use them consistently and frequently whenever he directed the little horse. They would soon become second nature to the animal.

Angling northeast, he found the northbound track as it passed through an oak grove. If the pony acted up now, or ran away, Padraic had no control. The loop over the stud's nose would do next to nothing to actually stop him. And trails, by offering direction, had a way of encouraging horses to run. From somewhere out on the creek to Padraic's right came the high, bursting, insistent notes of a dipper.

The stud was starting to recover a bit. He walked with his head up now, his nose no longer dragging the ground. His ears flicked back oftener than they perked forward. He was paying more attention to the rider on his back than to the trail ahead, and that was highly unusual for a stallion. Padraic clung tightly, waiting for an eruption that could occur any second now. Unless he kept his seat, he might not win that black mare after all.

The stud balked, dipped his head, and half reared. Padraic held him. They continued on for a few minutes. Padraic dare not dismount. He'd never make it back on. He should have stayed beside the river.

The stud tried to drop his head between his front legs and pitch, but Padraic kept the rope up short by gripping it and the mane together at the withers. The best the horse could do was kick his heels out behind.

Then he figured out that although he might not be able to dislodge the rider by buck-jumping, he need not walk along in docile resignation. He broke into a trot. Padraic kept the line in tight. The trot became a canter, and the canter lengthened into a gallop punctuated by occasional kicks. What little control Padraic had once enjoyed he had now pretty much lost.

The track abandoned the creek and angled out into open pasturage. A low woven wicker fence along the trail to the left kept traveling sheep and cattle out of the wheatfield behind it. Every few moments, the stud tried a crowhop to shake Padraic loose. This session with the stallion was fast ceasing to be fun.

Now Padraic was coming up quickly on a rider in the distance ahead. It couldn't be! It was!

"No!" Padraic hauled back ineffectively on the line. He was hurtling right toward his black nemesis, Kieran, and closing rapidly.

Kieran looked over his shoulder and swung his horse around instantly. He held his stallion dancing in place a moment and started in Padraic's direction. Whether or not he recognized Padraic by sight, he'd put two and two together quickly enough.

Padraic twisted the stud's head around to his left knee. The horse tried to shake his head and could not. He tried to dip it away. He slowed, chopped up and down, then altered course and lunged at the wicker fence.

His front legs cleared. The back legs knocked down a fence section. He galloped off across the field through its seedling wheat, cutting great chunks of dirt. Padraic glanced behind. Kieran's great horse cleared the wall handily. A race between Kieran's long-legged horse and this weary little stallion was no race at all. Padraic angled his pony toward the corner of the field where woodland grew right up to the wall. His pony was small enough to do fairly well in dense forest growth. Kieran's was possibly too large to weave well among the trees and overhanging branches. The forest was Padraic's only hope.

Bad turn of events: The weary pony could not clear this fence. He breasted it, his weight knocking the loose sticks down. He fell in a tangle of lead line and elm wythes and squeals.

Good turn of events: Padraic cleared the fence, sailing forward over the pony's neck and, with a resounding crash, entered the forest.

23

Mouse

Pain. Terror. Discouragement. The day was not ending nearly as well as Padraic had hoped. When it began he saw before himself the promise of a fine black mare. Now, his weary body battered, he faced instead the immediate prospect of capture and abduction.

He curled up tightly in what he hoped was an invisible ball beneath a clump of ferns. He wondered just how acute Kieran's sense of smell was. He certainly wasn't sweating enough to smell especially rank, but a good nose would find him. He was freezing, for his trousers, his only garment, were still wet from the swim in the river.

Sure and he dared not leap up and race away. That great horse would run him down in moments. So he lay quite still and prayed he would not start shivering, lest a fern frond tremble above him.

He heard the horse crashing here and there through the forest. The crashing stopped.

Kieran's voice called, "Padraic! Hear me. The queen has turned on me and on yourself as well. Scanlon is out to kill us both. A young woman warned me so last night. Your best bet for safety is with me. I'll protect you. Come out!"

A pink jay laughed from a treetop.

Padraic tried to work out where his best chances lay. With Kieran? Not a bit. Queen Gwynn? And there his thinking faltered. She had turned on Kieran, a supposed ally. She was certainly power mad. He could not trust her; he had assumed that from the start.

The brehons? They were totally trustworthy, except that the dark and moody Muirdoch gave Padraic an uneasy feeling. But they were too thickly involved with Gwynn and were essentially

202

without strength of arm themselves. Rowan and the hunter from Carrowkeel could not defend Padraic adequately, and even the mighty Brian would be overwhelmed by that horde. Padraic would give his very life defending Brian, and he knew Brian would do the same for him. At all costs, he must avoid bringing in Brian, for Brian's sake.

Kieran rode in his direction and stopped not fifty feet from Padraic. Loudly he repeated his message. Padraic heard other voices out by the field. Some of Gwynn's people had found the stallion and the broken fence. If, unlike Donn of the Moor, they were intent to kill Kieran, they knew he was here. Those huge hoofmarks in the wheat could have been made by one horse and one horse only. If they were aware that Padraic had taken the stallion out this morning, they knew Padraic was here also. Sure enough, here they came. Kieran's horse crashed off through the forest away from them.

Padraic stayed put. Pony feet splashed in standing water on the forest floor ten feet from his ferns. They crashed and rattled through the underbrush. He dared not peek out, but he recognized Donn of the Thicket's gravelly voice. Apparently they were assuming Kieran had captured Padraic. The chaotic noise faded.

Now was his moment to flee, while everyone's attentions were elsewhere. Kieran must evade his own pursuers—he could not give time to chasing Padraic just now. Padraic squirmed out from under the ferns.

When the stallion breasted the fence, Padraic had alighted in low bushes. It would have been a lovely, soft landing place had he been wearing his tunic and cloak. As it was, his bare upper body was covered with pricks and scratches.

He could not tell directions in the thick forest. Too little of the overcast sky showed. Kieran probably would flee to the southwest, to come out into river bottomland well below Gwynn's camp. Padraic half turned, orienting himself. That would make this direction southeast. He started off at a trot, dodging trees and brush, trying to warm up.

Padraic had learned that one is apt to walk in circles when traveling through featureless woodland. One way to avoid that is to drag a long pole behind you. The pole keeps you walking straight. Two problems prevented his doing that now—dragging a pole leaves a distinct trace that any fool can follow, and Padraic had no pole.

So he set his face toward a distant uniquely shaped tree, walked to it, and sighted toward another, tree after tree through the woodland. He crossed the track and paused only long enough to ascertain that Kieran had not come back down this way. He came to the little creek and did not hesitate to wade across. His trousers were wet anyway.

He came out into more open fields. Pausing on the edge of the forest, between bright and dark, he could tell now about where the sun hid. He skirted the forest margin so that he not get caught out in the open, ascertained true southeast, and began to walk.

His future as determined by three brehons lay behind him, and the past, Rafe's resurrection, lay ahead. He was on his way to Cashel.

* * *

My life is all a-shambles, mused Aidan, as he lay dying.

First that designing woman had led him astray. Aidan had never been led astray before. Then that Padraic didn't help at all. And then his mother turned on him by taking the part of the slave-prince. "Earn your right to rule." Yes. To be sure. Were all women so ambitious? Aidan was certain his status as a prince was what turned Donn's wife toward him. He was especially sure when she started to ply her wiles upon Padraic. And Padraic, smiling, had responded readily to her. Yes. Definitely ambition. Not love, as she claimed. No wonder she fought him so hard when he carried her off. She had promised to run off with him, and then Padraic entered the picture, and the promise was voided. Women. Bah!

And Padraic, that miserable cur. If he had not responded so eagerly to her advances, Aidan would not have had to elope with her so precipitately. He could have taken more time, as he'd originally intended. He would have planned their escape, their route, their honeymoon. But Padraic with his instant lust forced the issue.

Aidan planned when he left his mother's camp to follow the trails south and east to Cashel. There he would present himself to the Eoghanacht as a prince of Connemara and therefore a fellow enemy of the powers at Tara. He had promised Donn's wife status, and he would have delivered on that promise in the court at Cashel. Now look at what fate had dealt him.

Donn probably never would have caught up to him had not Aidan's bay mare drawn up lame. She had never lamed before. Such evil tricks the wee folk pull, for they were the ones who are ultimately responsible for the accidents and ill health of livestock. But then, Aidan had always understood what a twisted and perverse sense of humor the wee folk enjoyed, always at the expense of humankind.

Aidan could understand also that Donn might be upset. But Donn's vindictiveness should have been directed primarily at his wife, the instigator of all this. Certainly Donn had grossly overreacted with what he called, with a bitter grin, "my punishment of Aidan."

While his henchmen held Aidan fast and the perfidious woman watched, Donn had at one cruel stroke denied Aidan any chance to reign as a king anywhere, ever.

Now Aidan lay on his side beside the track where Donn had overtaken them, dying alone and unloved, and all for the sake of a beautiful, treacherous, ambitious woman. Two women. He might as well include his stepmother in the company.

It began to dawn on him then, as the sun drifted low, that he had not died yet. And he wanted intensely to die. With so much lost, present and future, he cared not a whit for life anymore. The most unjust of all unjustness had befallen him.

If wolves or hogs came upon him thus, they would be so maddened by blood lust they would tear him apart. Not a pleasant prospect. Dying was one thing. Being ripped apart was quite another.

Aidan sat up cautiously. Why must men be so cruel? Certainly it was a cruel world peopled by cruel men and cruel gentry and cruel wee folk. He knew that, but . . .

He stood, fainted, made his way to his feet again, and had to sit down, so dizzy and lightheaded was he. Along with his perfidious wife, Donn had taken away the bay mare, limp and all, and Aidan's leathern travel bag. In that departed bag resided his panpipes and spare clothes. Who would play the panpipes now?

His clothes were blood-soaked, his beautiful hair matted and filthy. He no longer resembled a prince in the least. After a few more false starts he managed to keep his feet under him. He began walking toward Cashel.

* * *

"'Twas when Jesus Christ Himself walked the earth that the devil was most agitated. The Holy Spirit was strong upon the land, you see, which situation always upsets the devil. Well, now. The devil came flying down from the north one day, and the Slieve Bloom Mountains—mountains far to the north there—stood in his way.

"Not for long, though, not for long. He took himself an enormous bite and bit a chunk right out of the mountains. You can see the gap there to this day. He passed through pretty as you please, and he spit out the mouthful of rock as he flew by here over our Golden Vale. Yourself be standing on that chunk of rock this moment."

This fellow in tattered cloak and ragged gray beard certainly appeared old enough to have been around to watch the devil do it. He leaned on his staff, nary a tooth in his head, and looked dignified.

Two of Bridey's companions stared rapt at the distance to the north and at the hill of soft white rock beneath their feet. Tell them the sun was an oil lamp painted yellow, and they'd believe you.

Three others smirked, not about to be led astray by this old fellow's tales.

The sixth glanced at Bridey, awaiting her lead. She was aught but a humble housemaid from the west. Why did these six strapping lads continually look to her for leadership?

"Eh, well," she mused, "it could be. But Brigid herself teaches that the Holy Spirit descended upon the likes of men only after Jesus rose up and away into heaven. Forty days after. Be ye certain that Jesus walked abroad when all this happened?"

"Sure and you would not call the word of a patriarch into question!"

"Never." Bridey with a cautious smile did her best to indicate that the matter was closed. "These six young men with me wish to attach themselves to the local school. And I seek a young fellow named Padraic of Lambay, who ought by now to be in the company of Patrick himself. Can ye direct us?"

The old man spat into the cropped grass of the steep hillside. His spitting was infinitely less epic than the devil's. "I suppose perhaps I could."

Bridey stood and waited patiently for him to break his own silence. She had learned that trick from Padraic.

He nodded presently. "The school is attached to the king's oratory on the far side of the ring wall there. As for the whereabouts of Patrick, that you'll have to ask the abbot who presides at the right hand of Oengus."

"Our deep thanks, kind patriarch. We wish God's very best blessings upon ye."

"Brigid, eh?" The old man glanced askance at Bridey's companions. "I thought the worst of you when you showed up with these. A girl ought be more circumspect, you know. But I know now that you're pure and holy, coming from Kildare."

Bridey did not bother to contradict him. She was tired of explaining that she was not one of Brigid's nuns—she was only a beginning student. *Let it by.*

She and her track mates bade the old man farewell and circled around to the gate in the ring wall. Either the devil had been careless in his biting or his teeth were woefully misaligned, for the level chunk of white rock was not at all even. On the one side it sloped steeply upward from the surrounding plain to its flat top. An old woman with a cane could climb that hill if need be. On the opposite side, though, the hillside dropped precipitously, virtually unscalable. And here on the top, with a commanding view of the plain all around, dwelt the heart and soul of the southland—Cashel, seat of the Eoghanacht, descendants of Eoghan Mor, the kings of Munster.

Bridey was standing where Patrick stood—where Patrick, Lord willing, was still standing close by. And Padraic. Had he arrived yet? She rehearsed in her mind for the hundredth time how she would break the news to him that he was no longer a fugitive but a prince.

They were told at the gate that no one was available to direct them. Somehow Bridey expected as much. Her six ex-pupils wandered off to the oratory against the far wall. Bridey pondered possibilities a few moments and sat down by a large rock inside the gate. She leaned back against the standing stone and folded her hands in her lap. She would wait. If no one helped her by nightfall, she'd walk out to one of the raths on the plain below and ask lodging.

The broken clouds had thickened into a dark overcast. The dull light muted colors in the outfield pastures stretching across the plain, but the greens hard beside her remained as bright as ever. The ground was littered with white stones and pea gravel—nay, the ground *was* white stones and pea gravel. From out of the cropped grass and rocks peeked shamrocks, their leaves vivid against the stones. What a peaceful setting Cashel was.

"Get away from there! How dare you?!" An earnest young man wearing an elaborately wrought torque came running out of the large circular stone building to the north.

Bridey sat still, calm on the outside and trembling inside. Sure and she must be doing something wrong, but she couldn't imagine what. "Good day. I come from Kildare. I'm seeking Patrick."

The fellow's bushy moustache totally hid his lips. "You're sitting on the stone of kings. This is where kings are inaugurated. It's sacred! You have to sit somewhere else."

Bridey hauled herself to her feet. "Eh, sorry. Sure and I would not care to inconvenience a king. Be there any kings waiting for me to move so that they can inaugurate?"

The young fellow hesitated, confused, and burst into raucous laughter. "You're from out west, I'd judge, from your accent."

"Very west. Just mainland of the Skelligs. M'name is Bridey of Currane, most lately of Kildare. Can ye direct me, pray thee, to find Patrick?"

"Perhaps, but 'tis a shade more complex than just walking up to the man."

"Eh, I was afraid so. The man I'm really seeking is Padraic of Lambay. He's come to find Patrick. Have ye heard of him?"

"Patrick I've heard of. Padraic of Lam—wherever, no. I am Declan." The bushy-lipped fellow glanced upwards at the overcast. "Kildare. Did you just arrive?"

"Aye."

"Half a chance of rain. Come, sit inside."

Feeling more than a bit uncomfortable and out of her element, she followed him into the round stone building. He gestured toward a sheepskin cushion ten feet from the door. She sat on it and settled back against the cold stone wall. This was certainly more comfortable than the inauguration stone, particularly since the half chance of rain became a whole chance a few minutes later.

The whole great stone building was a single room with a few split-plank wooden screens at the far side. Light came only from slitlike portals of dressed stone spaced along the wall. The mustachioed young man hastened out a back way. Two other mustachioed young men, their moustaches every bit as luxuriant as his, stood at either side of an empty stool. They wore nothing but striped trousers, ornate swords in equally ornate scabbards, and simple gold torques of twisted wire. There they stood, legs spread, arms behind them, guarding a vast, vacant room.

She listened to the rain drum outside. The tall, conical thatched roof did not leak. Her stepparents' had constantly leaked, as did the huts on the crannog, and she had always rather assumed all thatch leaked.

Her mind wandered immediately to Padraic, as it did anytime she cast it adrift. She wondered where that Kieran fellow was now and if he'd picked up Padraic's trail again. Surely not. That wonderful huge horse . . .

"Where is she?" A stentorian voice boomed across the great hall.

Bridey bolted to sitting upright. She had drifted to sleep. Her neck was so stiff she couldn't straighten her head for a moment. This was embarrassing. And frightening. She clambered to her feet and shook out her skirt.

"There you are." A man came striding toward her from across the hall, a man the likes of which she'd never seen. He was tall, a little darker than many, with a moustache even more magnificent than that Declan's or his guards'. His stride was stronger despite that he walked with something of a limp, his sword more ornate, his mien far more commanding. His cloak tails flowed out behind

209

him. And an elaborate cloak it was too, an intricate plaid in four colors. His trousers were striped in three colors. This had to be royalty of some sort.

He paused before her. "You're the nun who brought the six lads down from Kildare. Declan told me you were here."

"From Kildare, aye, but I be no—"

"A splendid job you did with those young saints. My abbot just examined them. They can't read and write yet—that's why they've come, of course—but they already have the alphabets down solid, and quite a bit about theology, the abbot claims. You're a fine teacher. I'm delighted you came. Welcome to Cashel and Munster."

The proper response was to thank him, but her words fell apart as they left her mouth, and she mumbled nonsense. She felt her cheeks flush and prayed it didn't show in this dim light.

Apparently it did. He chuckled with as much verve as he walked with. "My maid is preparing your bed in the guest quarters. Come along. You dine with us tonight. I want to hear all about Brigid."

Bridey sputtered something inane and fell in beside him. Her tongue, never brilliant but usually polite, failed her utterly.

* * *

Bridey did not eat in the refectory with the students, as she had assumed she would. She ate with royalty, something she would never in a million lifetimes have assumed for herself. She, Bridey of Currane, orphaned and stepped upon, dined with the Eoghanacht rulers of Munster, a little mouse in the company of eagles.

If only her stepfather could see her now (she held no such dreams about her stepmother—the lady would be too befogged by ale to comprehend, much less notice)! She who gathered eggs now drank not from a common cup, as ordinary people do, but from an individual clay tankard of her own. Each of the persons gathered round this royal table used his or her own cup. A lovely touch, and very elegant. She who herded swine and cattle was eating food—good food—prepared and presented by servants.

Oengus. No wonder his commanding presence forced all attention upon him. He filled any room he entered. And yet his wife, a bit on the rotund side, seemed not the least overpowered or dominated. She held her own, and cheerfully. She enjoyed an easy equality with her man that one did not often see in a couple.

The daughters of Oengus sparkled. His sons glowed with the same youth and vigor as their father, even the eight-year-old. And yes, it was as Bridey had suspected. There sat Declan among them.

Bridey was so obviously outshone by this august company that she decided from the beginning it was not worth putting on airs or trying to be highborn. She was simple Bridey, and Bridey she would remain.

Oengus cut a chunk off his lord's portion and handed it to Bridey. "You'll notice my druid is not in attendance here tonight."

Well, actually, no. Bridey had not noticed. She had no idea who ought to be in attendance.

Oengus continued. "He strongly opposed my espousing the Christ of Patrick, and he refuses to enter back in until I've renounced my baptism."

One of the sons chimed in proudly, "According to Patrick himself, my father is the first major king in Erin to be baptized."

Declan added, "Lots of ri tuathe, of course, and many a ri ruirech. But of the five kings of Erin, he alone."

Bridey smiled. "Then 'tis a rare wisdom ye display, lord. I proffer m'warmest regards and admiration."

"From a sister of Brigid, that's praise of the highest order." Oengus fairly beamed. "Now tell me. Is she as saintly as they say?"

A servant handed Bridey a chunk of wheaten bread. Bridey of Currane eating wheaten bread. Imagine. She smiled. "Eh, that depends whom ye ask. Ask her many pupils and disciples, of which I be one, and we'll all say, 'Aye! Saintly and more. She teaches from the depths of spiritual insight.' The Scripture whispers wonderful secrets in her ear, and she publishes them abroad to all who'll listen.

"But ask the sisters who work with her, and the abbess, who is a rather stiff and practical woman, and ye'll hear a different tale. Brigid distracts and frustrates them to no end with her giving. When she sees a need, she gives. If she sees no need, she's as likely as not to give anyway. For example, she discerned I owned no hairbrush, so she gave me hers."

"I heard a story—" Oengus paused to savor a morsel of pork "—that she gave away her father's very sword."

"And an elegant sword it was, lord, aye, worth several cumals, they say. She's a beautiful lady, but even in her youth she had that quirk about her—to give recklessly. Her father left her out in his pony wagon as he entered a house trying to arrange a bride price and marry her off. They could observe her beauty from the house, ye see, without being given his pony and cart, or whatever else came to her hand. But as he was inside, a beggar passed by, and she gave him the sword without a second thought. M'sister Maeve claims that's when her father threw up his hands and said, 'If ye care not to marry, don't. If I never get y'r bride price, I never do, but ye're costing me too much to keep.' And that's when she renounced marriage and established Kildare."

"That's about what I'd heard, but unconfirmed. Yes." Oengus nodded enthusiastically. "I'd love to make a pilgrimage up that way and meet her one day. She's still young, isn't she?"

"Aye, amazingly so for one who's building what she's built. A fine church, a great monastery, and now she's working on a library. Three books she has already, and two in preparation. 'Tis more than some men build in a lifetime."

"All built without real strength of arms."

"The Holy Spirit be arms enough, lord."

"Yes." Oengus's head bobbed. "Yes. And I pray each day that I be shown how to use wisely this power given me in the Spirit. My druid doesn't half understand the beauty and strength of Patrick's Christ."

The queen licked pork juice off her fingers. "You've met Patrick, have you?"

"Not yet, lady. No."

"Old. Feeble. Infirm. And yet he just keeps walking, with that crowd of princes tagging along. Now there's a testimony to the power of the Holy Spirit. Needs the help of his crozier to get around—uses it as a walking stick. But he gets around."

One of the daughters giggled. Her mother glanced at her reprovingly.

Declan laughed too. "Did you hear the story, lady? About the great king here getting baptized with Patrick's crozier?"

"Ye're the one!" Bridey wasn't sure whether she ought laugh or not. The mother seemed self-conscious about the whole thing, even as the children obviously considered it a jolly good tale. "Ye be quite the hero, lord, ye know. The monks and sisters at Kildare talk of it yet, and with no little amazement."

And that explained Oengus's limp. Patrick had felt a bit shaky as he was baptizing Oengus, so the story went, and leaned on his wrought iron crozier for support. His eyesight being less than perfect, he drove the crozier through Oengus's foot. That warrior of warriors, assuming it was all part of the ceremony, made not a peep of pain or protest.

"A hero! Among the monks and sisters at Kildare? Really?" Oengus beamed again.

"Aye, and even more a hero because ye've the courage to proclaim Christ." And now she asked the only question she really needed an answer to. "Be Patrick in this area yet, perhaps to instruct ye personally?"

"No. He's out on Beggary Island, with Ibar."

"He's not here then." Bridey's heart sank.

The wife cooed, "Oh, he'll be back, I'm sure, if you'd like to meet him. Ibar raised some sort of question about Patrick's credentials, and the old man is down talking to him. Trying to sort it out. Practical fellow, Patrick, when you think about it. And he speaks Gaelic with the same country twang you do."

Oengus tried unsuccessfully to hide his curiosity or at least temper it a bit. "Do you have a specific message for Patrick from Brigid?"

"Her greetings and blessings, of course. M'message be for a young man named Padraic, who is also seeking him. I was hoping to find Padraic by finding Patrick."

"Mm." Oengus seemed mildly disappointed. He brightened almost instantly. "Give me his description, and I'll tell my people to keep an eye out. We'll turn him up for you."

If the word Brigid heard up at the crannog be true, all the land round about the Shannon searched for Padraic. The brehons from Tara wanted him. Kieran sought him. And now Oengus, Cashel, and all the kingdom of Munster. 'Twas probably just Bridey's hard luck that the elusive lad had evaded them all by going to Armagh.

213

24

Otter

With a frantic lunge, Padraic grabbed the top stones of the wall. The dogs yapped hard at his heels. The stone under his right hand gave way, but the other held solid long enough for him to drag his legs up and over. He dropped to the cropped grass on the other side, ran as fast as he could to the creek barely visible in the moonlight, and plunged into the stream. He crouched there, only his face above water, as the cold creek soaked into his very skin and flowed all around him.

He turned slightly so that he could see the dogs. They did not enter the water after him. He had hoped and prayed the creek marked the boundary of this rath and apparently it did. The dogs were protecting their domain from the interloper—they had driven him off. Would they be content with that, or would they cross the creek after him if he climbed out on the far side? Best not to tempt luck, just in case the dogs did not mind swimming tonight. All he need do therefore was sit in this cold running water half the night until the dogs got tired and went home.

Padraic sighed heavily. He had rather liked dogs, and they liked him. He was fast developing a loathing for them.

By law and custom, a boaire and his wife each possessed four changes of clothes. Sure and any boaire in the district, then, could part with a tunic and cloak without suffering unduly. Simple solution: Take quiet, recondite advantage of some boaire's native generosity. But every time Padraic saw laundry on a line or draped across bushes, he invariably came up against farm dogs fiercely guarding the premises. He had gone two nights now without tunic or cloak, and he was about to spend a third not only shirtless but with soaking wet trousers.

What good fortune Padraic enjoyed that Lughnassa was nearly upon them. The latter part of July, temperatures were as high as they ever got, which wasn't saying much to a lad who was still naked from the midriff up. But it could as well be midwinter. He should thank Bridey's God for small blessings.

Bridey.

Padraic hungered to travel north to Kildare, to seek out Bridey. He missed her intensely, which was utterly foolish, and he hated himself for his foolishness.

Bridey and her God. They were so tightly intertwined he did not easily separate one from the other. That was not at all the way gods properly ought to be. Each deity handles the matters of his or her province. The spirits of the rivers, the forest, the land and its stones, all made war or sang in harmony with the human spirit. But they did not invade and possess, as did this God.

On the creekbank one of the dogs sat down, his ears perked toward Padraic. The others walked back and forth, sniffing, occasionally yipping. What if the boaire came out to investigate his dogs' interest?

Suddenly Padraic was seized with an inspiration worthy of a druid. He would test the power of Bridey's God. A druid could summon spirits and direct the forces of nature, at least to a certain extent. But Bridey claimed that any believer in Christ could pray to God for similar help in extremity, though she wasn't certain just how that worked.

Very well. Padraic cast his eyes skyward, since Bridey, following the pattern of Christians, addressed her God as Father in heaven. "I beg You in the name of Bridey Your believer to send the dogs away."

Nothing happened.

Mm. He had expected as much. You probably had to weave some sort of spell to work your will. You certainly couldn't expect to simply ask and receive. Druids wove spells all the time.

He thought about her comments. He thought about what the men on Skellig Michael said about the faith, Gallus and Pileatus and the others. He recast his request. "I beg You in the name of Jesus Christ to send the dogs away."

Upstream a hundred yards or so something large splashed—a fish leaping, most probably. Padraic looked that way but saw nothing in the filtered moonlight. Another splash.

The dogs were paying attention upstream now.

Padraic heard birdlike chattering, a curious babble. He'd heard it before, a long time ago, and it took him a moment to recall the source.

Otters. A family of otters was moving through. Now, nearly into August, the young of the year would surely be approaching adult size. Otters could be noisy anyway. No wonder it sounded like a gaggle of quarreling children. Squabbling and chirring to each other, they worked their way downstream in his direction. Another loud splash sounded much nearer.

One dog ran through the brush upstream. The otters' gabbling turned frantic instantly. The other dogs took off in that direction. From their triumphant yelping, Padraic discerned that the dogs had caught something exciting.

He sloshed ashore onto the dogs' side of the bank and with a glance over his shoulder ran back toward the rath. Up and over the rock wall he clambered and out across the cropped paddock. There was the week's washing spread out on bushes. He hesitated only a few brief moments to pull a cloak off a hazel bush near the gate.

He raced down the track that connected the rath with the main trail half a mile distant. He did not cease running when he reached the main track. He must get out of the dogs' territory before they lost interest in the otters. He caught his second wind and was able to run perhaps two miles farther before he slowed to a walk.

So far, no farmer or traveler knew he was in the area. He had knocked at no gate, halloed no one in the fields. He hid himself on those rare occasions when other travelers passed. He wanted to arrive at Cashel or nearly so before anyone realized that a lone traveler, a young man, was passing through. Kieran would have no clear way to trace him this time.

Not that Kieran needed a clear way. That black nemesis always just knew somehow. He regretted saving the man. How could he have been so foolish? He was thinking and doing a lot of foolish things lately.

Bridey.

And now he no doubt had Gwynn on his heels as well.

The moon was setting. He ought to call it a night soon, for he showed a marked tendency to lose the track and get thoroughly lost when he had no light by which to travel. Today he had eaten berries and some peeled rush roots. Tonight he would set out some snares. If he caught a hare or hedgehog he would think about risking contact with someone long enough to obtain some fire, for he had neither flint nor iron. He was accustomed by the rigors of this last year to traveling on an empty stomach. If he did not eat well soon, though, he would start to weaken. He could not afford that now.

Think how grand it would be! Imagine what it was going to be like to watch those stones go tumbling and rolling away, and then to see Rafe sit up!

* * *

They were, plain and simple, brigands of the coarsest sort. Base ruffians. Exiles. Criminals. Vagabonds. They were also the only people on the face of dear green Erin who had ever unreservedly embraced Aidan as a friend.

True, Aidan had chums as he was growing up. In adulthood, however, his childhood intimates all became either vassals or rivals. Aidan's father, certainly, never treated him like a valued relative. His natural mother was driven out early in his life, his stepmothers were distant. Only Gwynn came anywhere close to providing him the warmth of genuine affection, and she viewed him critically most of the time. And she hated his panpipes. That perfidious wife of Donn of the Moor was the worst of all. She had feigned closeness.

These people, though, accepted him for what he was, laughed at him and ridiculed him, and then freely extended the hand of friendship. His royal blood meant nothing to them one way or the other. He had never tasted this sort of freedom before, and he reveled in it.

They were highwaymen. Although they never said it, Aidan knew. Erin was filled with such as these. They were out seeking whom to rob when they came upon him by the side of the track. They dressed his wound skillfully. They applied balm and healing herbs. They provided him with clean clothes and a comfortable bed of rest in their camp. They plied him with good food and stolen ale. They listened attentively to his story.

He felt remarkably at home among these outlaws. That was a most curious thing too, because they certainly would have robbed him had Donn not taken away everything worth stealing. They probably would have killed or maimed him themselves. But his disaster saved him by evoking their pity and laughter.

As Aidan's grief and fury and horror abated, a new resolve grew inside him. He rehearsed it over and over in his mind. *If I cannot take the prince's part I will receive the hero's portion.*

The hero's portion. Yes.

He remained with them two weeks. On the night of Lughnassa he quietly slipped away and continued down to Cashel.

* * *

"Lughnassa. How I love Lughnassa." Oengus drew a bushel of air through that wondrous moustache. "For one thing, you don't freeze. I understand why we go out by night to observe the changes of season, but that doesn't make it any more pleasant."

They strolled out the ring wall gate, Bridey, Oengus, and his wife and children, in no great hurry to reach the druids' ring on the brow of the hill. 'Twas a lovely night, aflame with stars.

Bridey let her cloak hang loose in the warm breeze. "Might it not be, lord, that ye fancy Lughnassa so because the celebration goes on for two weeks running?"

The wife hooted. The children laughed.

Declan grinned. "Why sure and that would never have entered his mind."

Oengus gave his son an affectionate thump on the head.

Declan was crowding quite close to Bridey. It made her a bit uncomfortable. But no one else seemed to notice, and the children actually bumped into each other on occasion, so that must be the way of things around here. She held her peace.

Oengus's ample wife chuckled from deep within her extensive bosom. "The truth is, he gets cold easily. I don't. I suppose that's why Imbolc is my favorite. The candles glittering on the water. Don't you think?"

"M'self has never celebrated Imbolc, lady."

"You are named for dear Brigid! And you never celebrate her special time?"

"M'stepparents left me home to tend the stock. The first of February is always a bad time to leave the rath. The sheep are starting to lamb. M'stepfather's sheep tend to have more trouble with lambing than do some, and we must watch them closely. And we're planting the first of the garden then, of course."

"I don't doubt a bit that your stepfather finds trouble dogging him every step, if he neglects to participate fully in the fire festivals. Participation means bringing the children. Raising them from infancy to attune themselves to the land."

"Eh, 'tis exactly what the abbot was discussing this morning, lady. Training up the children in the way they should go."

Oengus turned to her, beaming. "So! In the Scripture."

"Aye, lord."

"Good. Good."

A man so hungry for the pure word of God ought to employ the abbot or one of the abbot's assistants to teach him privately, Bridey thought. She understood that the man must present a faultless, invincible face to friend and foe alike, but not being able to read was hardly a weakness. And it was certainly reversible. If a humble farm maid from Currane could learn to read and in turn teach others, sure and the king of Munster should not have a bit of trouble.

Bridey still could not understand why she was ensconced in the company of royalty. By day she had spent the last week and some at the abbot's school with her six traveling companions, studying and learning. Late into each night she dined with the king's family and conversed with them. More than once she found herself explaining some element of theology she had herself learned only that day.

And to all who came, the king presented her as the emissary from Kildare, no matter how often she explained she was not one of Brigid's nuns. "Nonsense," was Oengus's stock reply. "You come from there with her blessing. You are therefore her emissary."

"What about you, Bridey?" the king's wife asked. "Lughnassa is the time of wedding, the season of marriage. We have seven weddings planned for tonight. Do you plan to marry?"

"Brigid herself eschews marriage."

"Aye, and you told us that the words of her mouth were 'To remain unmarried is my choice because I was called to it. That does not make it anyone else's choice. Each must answer his or her calling.' What is your calling?"

And Bridey answered truthfully, "I don't know yet."

* * *

To marry or not to marry. Every time she made the decision one way or the other, it turned out to be the wrong choice. And Gwynn of Connemara, Queen of Currently Somewhere on the Shannon, was looking at the decision yet again. She thought about the men, good men, over the years whom she decided not to marry. She could be a happy wife with half a dozen sturdy children now, if she'd taken that prince out on Achill. She deemed him too slow and gentle at the time, yet his people chose him as ri ruirech scant months after she left him.

And the men she married that she should never have—ah, that would fill one of the Christians' precious books and more! Her latest husband, for instance. She probably should have established a fast outside his door in an attempt to get some of her cattle back. He had usurped them illegally by any honest brehon's opinion. She didn't. She had been too hurt, too angry. It was too late now. How do you know before the fact which lover will turn on you and rob you? Gwynn had had no luck at all with second sight.

She watched Scanlon drilling some young men from a band who called themselves the Fermagh. Whether Scanlon enticed the Fermagh to join Gwynn's cause or coerced them, the Fermagh plus a few other roving bands of highwaymen had swelled Gwynn's army to nearly threescore. Scanlon was ambitious, as was Gwynn's latest ex-husband. But unlike that churl's, Scanlon's ambitions meshed nicely with hers. Scanlon and Gwynn together pursued the same aims as allies, not rivals.

She would gain much and risk much in a union with the Too Skinny one. So should she marry Scanlon or not? The age-old question remained unanswered.

She got up from her wolfskin beneath an oak and wandered

the quarter mile down to a little creek burbling merrily toward the Shannon. She felt restless. Things were going wrong with her world.

Kieran had escaped her grasp because of treachery within her own ranks. She had no idea which woman warned him, but one of the guards on the wall swore he talked to a woman moments before he fled. She would find that witch one way or another, and the best way would be to recapture Kieran and see who came to him.

Padraic still was not netted. How could the little fool turn his back on Gwynn's aegis, or on a chance at reigning as high king at Tara? Incredible! Nothing could be more important. Obviously his inability to think was a serious strike against him. Still, he had the potential. Now all they had to do was find him—sift through all of Erin, a huge pile of grain, to recover one tiny kernel.

And Aidan. Donn of the Moor would say nothing about her stepson other than "He chose not to return with us." Donn was being altogether too possessive of his woman. In most clans, men and women mixed freely, husbands and wives together in common. The idea of one woman exclusively united to a single man was alien. And Donn had carried it to an extreme. She ought to punish him, but she was uncertain exactly what to punish him for. No one, including his wife, would provide word number one about the fate of Aidan, except to assure her that he was last seen alive.

She watched the pink and orange light from the setting sun dance on the crystal waters. The small brook spoke to her far more clearly and affectionately than did the ponderous Shannon. Besides, she much preferred water one could conveniently wade across. She abhorred barriers of any sort.

Over in the sacred ring a hundred feet away, Dhuith was assembling worshipers. He still performed the usual functions of a druid—he had done a fine job of presiding over Lughnassa just past—but he had almost totally incorporated Christian exercises into the nonfestal worship he conducted every Saturday. Gwynn had attended two or three such offerings, and she bored quickly of the tedium of hearing something in Greek and then listening to its Gaelic translation. Why not just do it in Gaelic and be done?

Gwynn saw the three brehons from Tara among the people

assembling. Were they Christians, or were they simply investigating the claims of Patrick? Brehons seemed to approach everything in life as an intellectual exercise. So did druids, after a manner.

She listened to the antiphony of the lay leader directing the worshipers in their hymns while another voice intoned the prayers. It was actually rather pretty. She heard a fluid joy there, ebbing and flowing with the prayers and music. That was another reason she stayed away from those Christian offerings—right now she didn't want some cricket chirping, "Joy! Joy!" in her ear when her heart and soul felt no joy. And there she was back again to her original unanswerable question.

A soft, rustling *whoosh* across the creek captured her attention. An otter had emerged from its tree-root den. Amazingly flexible and smooth, it traced a serpentine path through the grass and weeds from land to water. Its size startled her. Many a time had she seen otters, and their sheer size always startled her. They were so large to be able to flow so gracefully and bend so easily.

The otter poured itself down a mudbank and disappeared beneath the water. Moments later it popped to the surface with a bream in its mouth.

Here came a companion. It bounded forward on tiny legs, looping along in more a gambol than a run, down to the bank. As it plunged into the water, the first otter quickly gobbled its bream. By the time the second otter surfaced, the fish was gone.

Gwynn smiled. She could relate to that. Seize whatever you can and use whatever you are able, for others are bound to want your prize.

The otters commenced to scold and chase each other. Gwynn suspected their behavior was more courtship than pique. Otters possessed the same lusts that mankind did. That was not surprising. The druids taught of life beyond death—that life is not the snuffing of a soul but simply the exchange of one form for another. That was probably why the magical boat of the sea spirit Manannen MacLir could anticipate human thoughts, or why the great bull of Cooley could think such thoughts. Souls passed to and from the Otherworld; everyone knew that. Possibly they passed to and from other forms of this world as well. Perhaps that's what made the Christian theories so attractive to druids.

Where would Gwynn's eternal soul reside, were she to die this moment? Actually, those otters right there were not a bad choice if she had to choose a form. See how they fit so splendidly into their preferred world, the water. And how, though their short legs were hardly useful for running, they ran all the same. Clever creatures too, to catch fish in the fishes' own medium and to read each other's thoughts, as that bream-catcher obviously had.

No, an otter wouldn't be bad at all.

"There you are." Scanlon came crashing down off the hill through the rank streamside growth.

The otters fled. They simply disappeared, here one moment and gone without a trace the next. That was another score in their favor.

Scanlon hunkered down in the weeds close beside Gwynn, facing away from the stream. He kept his voice low. "I can't get a thing out of Donn of the Moor concerning Aidan. Think we should go look for him?"

"Torture's unwise, I suppose."

He nodded. "They're talking about bolting if I cause them much more trouble. And if they do, Donn of the Thicket will go with them."

"Torture's perfectly acceptable practice."

"So is justice, and the two Donns think they're right."

"Bah. All the men in Erin think they themselves are right, to the exclusion of everyone else's opinion. And only half of them are. Less than half. Those who oppose women are almost always wrong."

Scanlon wrinkled his nose. "If you expect me to address that, you don't know me well after all. What are your long-term plans? I assume you have some."

"Two otters. They began on the land but hastened straightway to the water. Why? Because water is their natural realm, the place they fit best. A good philosophy, Scanlon."

"You're going to hasten straightway to your natural realm."

"So far we've been rather clumsily casting about, seeking a clan in turmoil. Enter into that picture as a stranger in sovereignty and take over."

"Or marry in."

"Or marry in. Something. How foolish, my Too Skinny one! Here we are groping around for some small out-of-the-way kingdom while the throne at Tara stands vacant."

"Isn't that a bit presumptuous of a queen with no people?"

"Ah, but Scanlon, thanks to you I have people. A considerable fighting force. You and I, co-regent." She watched his face a moment. "What did you have in mind?"

"Nothing so grandiose, though I vow I like your plan better. Mine was to travel down to Cashel and look for a wedge among the Eoghanacht in which to insinuate ourselves. They would be more amenable to us than anyone up here, because they're on unfriendly terms with the Ui Neill. The king at Cashel is as much an ard ri as is the man at Tara."

She nodded. "And while there, seek out Aidan."

"I'm worried about the silly little panpipe tooter. If Donn says he's alive, he's alive. Donn is honorable. But you can wager any kingdom in Erin that they didn't leave him in pristine condition."

She sighed. Aidan had, after all, abandoned his father's heritage and pinned all his hopes for advancement upon her. Still, she didn't really relish traveling to Cashel. The king there was, so far as she knew, young and vigorous yet. That throne would not open for a while. It was a pity that Cashel and Tara lay essentially at opposite ends of Erin.

"You're no help at all, Scanlon Too Skinny. I sat down here with one hard choice to make. Now I have two."

Choices. In some ways it would be so much easier to be an otter.

25

Rocks

Why ride the grandest, most magnificent horse in all Erin, if you don't intend to travel fast and far? Kieran reminded himself of that periodically. And he often pointed out to himself how far and swiftly he had come, as he nursed the open sore on the inside of his right leg where a flaw in his saddle cover rubbed him. Kieran welcomed any moment wherein he could sit on something that didn't move. He savored such a moment just now.

He sat leaning back against an ancient trackside oak and watched his horse crop grass ten feet away. "Brown hair, early manhood, no tunic. That was he. And all he wanted was fire?"

"No tunic, right. Just a cloak and trousers." The farmer seated beside him nodded slowly. "Said he'd snared a hare and wanted to cook it. I gave him a brand and half a loaf of barleycake, and he left. With great thanks, I might add. Polite young man, and bright. Cheery."

"And well he should be, chosen to a throne in Ulster. Now I have only to reach him to tell him of his fortune. Did he ask directions or anything of the sort? Give some indication where he was headed?"

"Asked no directions as such." The farmer scratched his bearded cheek. "He walked off southward, on the track to Cashel."

"Mm. Any hint or suggestion that he had some purpose in Cashel?"

"You tell me he's a prince. Cashel's the seat of the royal family. Why wouldn't he go there?"

"Good point." Kieran lurched to his feet. He still had a loaf of barleycake in his travel bag and some boiled pork wrapped in greased hide. He would not ask food here. The information was more than sufficient.

The farmer stood up also. "Not thinking of hiring your stallion out, are you?"

"I'd be happy to on my way back north in two weeks or so. Shall I drop by?"

"Do that. Perhaps we can make an arrangement."

Kieran left the fellow then, with effusive thanks. After all, he could be as polite and cheery as the next man—or the last one, as the case might be. He swung aboard his stud and headed south, less than three days behind Padraic.

* * *

Sure and she should have gone to Armagh after all. And that left Bridey in a quandary. When the six youths found her in that creek, she believed the Lord was directing her to Cashel. His hand protected her the whole way. He blessed her by helping her provide those young saints what they needed. And yet Patrick was not here, had not been here for some time, and was most likely on his way north now. She dreaded having to take to the road again alone. Bad things happened to lone travelers. But she could see no way out of it.

Perhaps she ought simply to let Padraic meet whatever fate lurked in his way. Sooner or later he would find out. Perhaps he knew already. He might be in Tara this very moment receiving the allegiance of all the kings of the north.

And here she sat on the rock of Cashel.

The beautiful plain they called the Golden Vale, dreamy in the haze of late summer, stretched out to the north and west. The blue-gray slieves beyond seemed farther away today than usual. What a pleasant view this rock below Oengus's ring wall afforded. Bridey liked its position as well. Off the breast of the hill, this small outcropping rock could not be seen from Oengus's wall, and the noise of the settlement on top did not reach down here. Nestled in the hillside, it afforded both beauty for the spirit and quiet for the heart.

Out in the broad vale, cattle and sheep grazed in open green pastures. Amid the few rock walls, garden plots lay silent in the sun, safe from roaming livestock, soaking up warmth and growth. Women and children and men, sometimes in pairs and sometimes alone, moved up and down the trail that stretched across the plain toward the north. Did they see Bridey seated on the side of the hill? Probably not. Several seemed to look this way, but sure and they must be admiring Oengus's white rock house on the top. 'Twas an amazing thing, if all you were accustomed to was a woven wicker crannog or a house of mud and pales.

Dainty swallows shared the sky with heavy black rooks, dipping and wheeling in free flight overhead. Total contrast, the tiny birds and the great. Total contrast too, the weightlessness of birds and the solid hulk of bedrock. Bridey yearned to be a bird. She would wing her way to Kildare and hide herself forever after behind its silent walls, studying in peace.

She would fly on north to Tara and seek out Padraic.

She would coast on silent wings to the crannog of her birth, which was actually quite close to here—a third the distance to Kildare.

Fly? She would sit on this stupid white rock until she rotted. The druids and Patrick agreed heartily that the soul lives on beyond death. The druids, though, were sure that souls returned to this world when they died in the Otherworld, just as they journeyed to the Otherworld when they died here. Brigid, however, taught from Scripture that it is for man once to die and then the judgment. There was no return. Bridey would never be a bird therefore, or a spirit in the rocks and trees, or any other thing. She was Bridey, plain and simple, yesterday, today, and forever.

"Good day."

Bridey jumped. She twisted around to look at the speaker. "Well, Declan! Ye move about with all the noise of an ant in a fleece."

The king's middle son laughed and sat down on the rock beside her. "Dreaming or planning?"

"A bit of both. And y'rself?"

"The same." He seemed not the least bashful about pressing close to her. "Oengus praises the depth of your wisdom, you know. He doesn't say it to your face, but he claims you have a wonderful grasp of things spiritual. The abbot says the same. He says you catch onto deep matters instantly."

"Ye call y'r father 'Oengus'?"

227

"He's not my father by blood. I'm fostered. My father is a ri ruirech down south. That's why he named me Declan. For Declan of Ardmore, you see. I'm Declan of Clonmel—or will be some day in the annals."

That seemed presumptuous. He was assuming he would be remembered in the epic stories one day, but then every lad spins that dream. She let it by. "All these Declans about are confusing to me. And all the Colmans."

Declan tittered. He didn't chuckle or even giggle. He tittered. Bridey liked the lad quite well except for his ridiculous titter. "Four Colmans that I know of, and three Declans, aye. I'm named for the one that started the monastery before ever Patrick entered Munster."

"Patrick was not the first here to preach Christ?" Bridey turned to study him. Now she really was confused.

"Oh, no." Declan counted on his fingers thoughtfully. "Let's see. Besides Declan, there's Ailbe, at Emly. Ciaran at Saigir. Abban of Moyarney. Ibar. They all came before Patrick, mostly to the south of Cashel. But he's the one who made the impression on Oengus."

"I've heard he's a splendid speaker and apologist."

"More than that. He knows Gaelic ways. When he arrived at Cashel with his retinue—there had to be twenty-five or thirty young men, sons of taoiseachs and kings—he looked like an important man. A learned man. You know how Oengus admires learning. He gave the proper gifts. He took the druids' knowledge and expanded it, showing how Jesus Christ is the culmination of druidism. Aye, he's a speaker, the likes you've never seen. But 'twas his Gaelic ways that are winning the world."

Bridey smiled. "I would like to think 'twas Jesus Christ winning the world."

"You know what I mean." He tittered again, then sobered. "A week or so ago, when we were walking out to the first night of Lughnassa, you told the Mum that you didn't know whether you ought marry. Do you mean, you have no clear direction?"

"Exactly that. I thought I had direction to come here, and now I be not so sure at all. I've no idea whether I'm following God, or whether I'm outside His will. 'Tis a confusing time for me."

"So whom would you marry if you married? That Padraic? Is that why you want to find him?"

She snorted. "Not at all. He's a prince, and princes don't often marry milkmaids. I've an important message for him, that's all. Information given to me at Kildare."

"Princes marry anyone they please. You know that."

"I said 'not often.' Besides, he cares very little for me. I've proof enough of that."

"I'm a prince, and I'll marry a milkmaid if I choose. And I care."

"About what?"

"About you! That's why I'm very pleased that God told me you are the woman for me."

Bridey gaped at him. "Why did He not mention any such to me? Ye'd think He'd mention it to m'self as well."

"Perhaps He did. You just said you can't discern the will of God. He may be shouting in your ear this very moment, and you don't hear Him."

"I be not that deaf spiritually."

"But you don't know."

He had a point there. This was all whirling at her much too fast. She felt crowded, breathless.

He pressed on. "My father and his father were ri ruirech, and with my fosterage here with Oengus, there's no reason the council would not give me the kingdom next. My clan's territory extends from Knockmealdown to the sea, except for a bit on the coast that's the Garvans'. You cannot do better than I in all Erin."

Oh, can't I? You have no aspirations to the high throne of Tara. On the other hand, Padraic had no aspirations toward Bridey.

She stood, mostly to get away from him. "Perhaps I cannot do better, but I must consider these things awhile. 'Tis far too quickly ye've put all this to me."

"Then here is something more to consider." He reached out and drew her to him, and, perhaps because it had never happened before, she had no idea that a kiss was coming. Came it did, filtered through that plenteous moustache. She pushed away. He persisted.

229

She panicked. What if someone observed this? What would they think of Brigid and of the Jesus Christ Bridey was supposed to be serving? She tried to shake her head, but his left hand gripped the back of it securely.

She managed to wrench away, then, and made a valiant effort to step back. "Declan, stop it!"

"I want you to know without a doubt how much I care about you."

"If ye cared, ye wouldn't press the issue! Someone will see and—"

"No one will see. And I told you I'm a prince. If I say I want a milkmaid, I may have a milkmaid."

From the hillside above them, the most wonderful voice in Erin called, "I too am a prince, and I say you can't have that milkmaid."

Padraic! Of all the people in the world, there stood Padraic, rock solid! He wore trousers and cloak only—no tunic and no weapon. But somehow he appeared so commanding, so formidable, he didn't really need a visible weapon.

Bridey grinned irrepressibly. She could not bring her cheeks together, so wide did her grin spread. Padraic! He was here!

Declan stepped back. "I thought you said you weren't considering this fellow." He looked up at Padraic. "You're the Padraic she was seeking. I can tell."

"Seeking me?" Padraic looked at Bridey. "We have a lot of catching up to do. I didn't know that. I thought you would be at Kildare. I was going to go there."

Did Declan see he was pressing his suit in vain? Bridey certainly hoped so. She backed up a step and started to climb the hill toward Padraic and safety.

Declan grabbed her arm.

She wheeled on him. "Don't. I don't want to see ye get hurt."

"Hurt?" Declan frowned, as if it were totally beyond ken that he might lose a fight.

"Aye." She jerked her arm free. "Padraic of Lambay is invincible. Everyone of the Ui Neill knows that. 'Tis high time the word spread down here as well." She scrambled up the grassy slope then, rapidly, desperately, and she did not pause until she stood in safety just uphill of Padraic.

Padraic's voice sounded deeper than she remembered it. "A man of honor never forces his attentions on a woman, young prince. You know that. I'm glad I happened by to remind you. Go in peace."

With a wary eye, Declan climbed the hill, watching Padraic as a hare watches a wolf. The moment Declan passed, Padraic too began the climb up through the cropped grass. Bridey pressed close to his arm all the way.

Padraic. Of all people, of all times. *Padraic.* Her heart sang a muddled song, knowing she had just been blessed lavishly by God—call it a miracle, perhaps—and not knowing in the slightest how all this came about.

As they neared the crest he did not seem at all winded. "I was coming south down the track, across the vale toward the mount here, and I saw you walk down over the side and sit on that rock. I don't know how I knew, but I knew it was you. Sure and I wasn't expecting you here, of all places. But it just looked like you somehow. I would have reached you much sooner, but I had to swing all the way around to the south side to climb up onto the hill."

"That's amazing. Miraculous. Aye, a miracle indeed, for I could discern no faces on the travelers I saw below." She stopped and turned to face him. Her heart was thumping, and not from the climb. "Padraic? Be ye that interested in me, truly, that ye'd pick me out at such a distance when ye were not expecting me?"

He grinned that endearing, boyish grin of his. "Apparently so. But had you asked me that an hour ago, I would have said, 'Nonsense.'"

She bobbed her head, her heart doing happy little jigs, and started off toward the round house. She must present him to Oengus immediately. "And a most glorious nonsense it is!"

* * *

A scant mile from the Rock of Cashel, Aidan Prince of Connaught stood at the rim of a quiet pool and studied his reflection. He'd lost weight, and he hadn't been heavy to start with. Other than that, he looked just like the Aidan of old, like any prince or hero. He knelt to sip a drink from the dark water and stood again. Beyond this pool in an alder grove, Cashel loomed. He could just so see it through the leaves.

Two hundred years ago or thereabout, Cormac MacAirt drove out from Tara a people called the Deisi. Part of the Deisi traveled over the sea to Wales, 'twas said, and the other part came south here to Cashel. The Deisi became the power behind the Eoghan-achta, and together the two tribes ruled the south. For obvious reasons therefore, neither Deisi nor Eoghanacht wasted any affection upon Tara and its Ui Neill.

The people of Connaught viewed the Ui Neill in a similarly dim light. The Connaughtmen and Ulstermen had been feuding in fact and fable for centuries. The legendary Cu Chulainn himself, an Ulsterman, chose as his enemies the warriors of Connaught. Aidan and Oengus of Cashel therefore shared a common loathing for a common enemy. He would use that historical wedge now, that bit of commonality, to insinuate himself into the court of Cashel.

He left the pool behind and began the last short walk to the gate of Cashel. He had been a fool to pin his hopes on an exiled queen, just as he had been a fool to pin his affections on a design-ing woman. But he had learned from his mistakes. Painfully, tragi-cally so. From now on, Aidan of Connaught would progress by his own hand.

He could see why they would call this plain the Golden Vale. The setting sun burnished it to glowing. And there on its rocky outcrop sat the heart of the south. He approached the first of the visible guards, a powerful young man with a bare chest and wire-bound torque.

The white-haired prince addressed the guard. "Aidan, a prince of Connaught, to greet Oengus."

The young man shouted up the hill, announcing not Aidan's name but apparently his own. He nodded to Aidan.

By steps and degrees, Aidan moved from base of mount to top of mount along a torturous trail. Were he an attacker sneaking through the dead of night, he could never make it up through this narrow tangle of white rocks—which, of course, was the intent.

On top, at the gate in the ring wall, a warder stepped forward. Aidan introduced himself yet again.

The warder smiled. "Word has preceded you. Oengus, ard ri, king of Cashel welcomes you. A feast is just now commencing.

Your presence will add great luster to this festive occasion, prince. Enter into the largesse of your lord."

A feast? Lughnassa was over and past. Autumnal equinox wasn't coming for another month yet.

"My thanks to the lord of Cashel, Oengus. Why a feast this time of year?" Aidan followed the old man toward the door of a great round stone house. Light poured out the slit windows along the wall.

"To welcome another royal, Padraic of Lambay, a prince of the Slevin."

Aidan's legs stopped moving as his mouth dropped open. Here? And then he saw in a flash what that conniver was up to. *Of course! Padraic learns from Gwynn about his prospects as high king. But he is only one of seven candidates. So he obtains Gwynn's support. Then he races down here and enlists the Eoghanacht in his bid for power. What promises did he make Oengus?* Aidan shuddered to think.

Blindly he followed the old man inside. They had rearranged seating to provide Aidan a place among the royals. Sure enough, it was the Padraic, sitting there at Oengus's right just beyond a large woman who was no doubt Oengus's wife. How many state dinners had Aidan attended in his life, and always at the place of honor near his father? Now he was relegated to last-in-line among royals.

While Padraic, a slave, sat in greater honor.

It suddenly occurred to Aidan that Oengus would not know about the slave part of Padraic's background. And should Aidan be so crass as to bring that up, Padraic could not in honor deny it. He did obeisance to Oengus and sat down with a smile on the wolfskin provided him. His only decision now: when and under what circumstance would he bring up the matter of escape from slavery.

Oengus looked about. "Who among here counts himself as friend to our new guest?"

Padraic replied, "I count myself the friend of Aidan MacGhervin of Connaught, and stepson of Gwynn of Connemara. I'm delighted you're here, friend!" He dipped a beaker of ale in salute toward Aidan. He seemed not the least hostile or reserved. But then he needn't be. He wasn't the one who actually succumbed to that woman's wiles. He never got past the point of intending to.

Aidan picked up a tankard and dipped it toward Padraic.

Oengus rose to his feet. "Who claims the hero's portion?"

One day, Aidan would. Not today. Perhaps sixty persons sat at meat in this hall, men and women in equal proportion. A dozen retainers, all handsome young men stripped to the waist and armed with splendid swords, stood along the wall with arms folded and legs apart. Their identical gold wire torques glittered.

Among all these people there had to be some fine stories, and there were. One by one, half a dozen men and two women stood and declared their right to the best meat by telling the best tale.

Why didn't Padraic mention the bear incident? He had the scars to prove it, although one's honor depended upon one's honesty and no other proof was required. Could it be that his bear attack was somehow dishonorable or, at the least, unheroic? Aidan couldn't picture so dramatic a survival as being anything short of heroic. He ought to get to the root of that tale one way or another. There had to be much more than met the eye.

When a warrior of the Garvan described his encounter with a boar, and he armed only with his dagger, people oohed and aahed, and Oengus granted him the hero's seat and portion. No one challenged. The feast was on.

Aidan leaned forward and called to Padraic, "What about the bear, friend? Surely you have a just claim to the hero's portion."

Padraic grinned. "Hardly. This man ate his enemy the boar. Mine—the bear—is still running around in the woods, healthy and happy."

Beside Padraic sat a rather plain girl in peasant's dress and long brown braids. If this was Padraic's lady of the moment, his taste in women had slipped considerably since he smiled back at the beautiful wife of Donn of the Moor.

She looked at Padraic curiously. "Bear?"

"And such there be yet in Connaught. Aidan, have you and your brothers ever gone bear hunting?"

Well, to tell the truth, they had. So Aidan repeated a couple of hunting tales of savage bears, only slightly embroidering the damage they can inflict upon the dogs and horses. He intuited that, in this heroic company, humor would take him much farther than could bravado, so he embellished the comic elements.

It worked. By the end of the evening, everyone was more than half drunk on ale, everyone was laughing, no one had risen up in fury to attack anyone (a normal prospect at feasts such as this), and Aidan was warmly accepted into the company of the Eoghan-achta. Thanks to this evening he had more or less stumbled into, he was well on his way to winning the support of the most powerful king in Erin.

Eat that, ambitious women!

26

Mosquitoes

Probably part of Padraic's success with horses was due to the fact that he could think like a horse. The saving grace was that horses could not think like Padraic. He leaned on the rock wall of Oengus's main paddock. With this fractious pony he would need all the edge he could get.

He watched the nervous dun mare standing alone in the paddock with her legs braced wide. He had never seen her before, but he knew that defiant stance. "She hates being caught up, and she's made a game of it. When I bring in the rope, she'll run around from end to end to avoid me, staying as far away as she can. I'll cut her off by taking the short distance across the paddock. Sooner or later, she'll start pausing to sniff at tufts of grass beside the paddock walls. About five minutes from now, she'll let me put the rope over her head."

Oengus responded with a bemused grunt. "Go at it."

Padraic stepped inside the gate. He heard rocks grate on one another as Bridey perched herself on the wall. The wooden gate groaned beneath Oengus's weight as he draped himself casually upon it.

Padraic walked toward the mare. She bolted and ran along the inside of the wall to the far end of the circular paddock. He walked toward her. She galloped around the perimeter to the other end. Without raising his hand or his voice, he strolled about, cutting the corner, always pushing her, never speeding up. Relentlessly he walked her down.

The spates of galloping shortened. They slowed to trots. She would dip her head down, nip at a bit of grass in a rock crevice, jog off again. Five minutes after he stepped into the paddock, Padraic laid his hand on her rump. She wheeled and jogged to the other side. He followed. Five minutes and twenty seconds after he stepped into the paddock, she stood still as he slipped the rope over her neck.

He led her over to Bridey and reached a hand out. "A pebble, pray thee?"

Bridey gave him one of the small round pebbles she was holding for him.

He flipped a loop over the mare's nose and snugged it up. She stood with her head high, her nostrils flared, expecting trouble—expecting to make trouble too. He dropped the pebble down into her ear and swiftly swung aboard her. By the time the distracted horse had shaken the pebble out of her ear, he had his fingers firmly wound in her mane near her withers as he gripped the rope.

She could not lower her head to pitch. She sidled and reared and bolted and lunged, but she could not drop her head to buckjump. Ten minutes of earnest effort and she gave up trying to dislodge him. She stood still near the stone wall, frustrated, her flanks and shoulders lathered.

Padraic slid off her and led her to the gate. "Next time will be easier, and the next time after that easier still."

Grinning, Oengus undraped himself and stood aside. His hostler opened the gate, and Padraic led the mare out. He handed her over to the man and joined Oengus.

The king began a casual stroll up the path away from the paddocks, his limp more pronounced on this upslope. Bridey followed at his one side and Padraic at the other. "So it's all in knowing the mind of a horse."

"Aye, lord."

Oengus chuckled. "You can walk any horse down that way?"

"No, lord. It works on her because she's been handled—been around men. Broken to lead. A truly wild horse will drop of exhaustion before he'll let you get near that way."

"God does the same with people, do you realize that? He knows how they think and uses it to direct them. So does Patrick, for all that. For instance, Patrick said, 'Build your monastery here on Cashel, right here by the standing stone. The holiest ground.'"

"And indeed 'tis holy ground." Padraic saw Aidan's white head in the distance, up by the trail to the top of the rock.

Oengus's stride, even with the sore foot, was twice a normal man's. "But you see what he's doing? He blesses all such places to the cause of God. For the worship of God by Christians. The sacred wells and groves, the standing stones, the druids' circles—they've all been used for centuries."

"I understand what you're saying." Padraic couldn't see who Aidan was talking to. "The people are already accustomed to coming to those spots for prayer and worship. Rather than force people to accept new places, something people are loathe to do, use the existing holy places for the worship of the true God."

Bridey spoke up, something she rarely did. "And when he stepped forward and lit the druids' Beltaine fires on the Hill of Slane, dedicating them not to Bel but to Christ, that would be the same thing, aye?"

Oengus boomed, "Exactly! Exactly! Now who's this?"

Padraic drew a deep breath. He knew the dark man who had joined Aidan up ahead.

Kieran of the Great horse.

Padraic stood in the safety of Oengus of Cashel, and still he quavered with fear.

Aidan looked as smug as a stoat with a mouthful of chicken feathers. Beside him, Kieran smiled broadly as Padraic approached. His stallion sidled uneasily behind him. Aidan did obeisance as the king approached. Kieran hastily did likewise.

"Ah! Of course!" Oengus walked right past Aidan and Kieran, a kingly prerogative apparently, to admire the huge black horse. "You're Kieran of the Great Horse. You'd have to be. Only horse like this in Erin. Padraic told me all about you. He told me about this magnificent beast as well, and every word true. I thought he was exaggerating. Not the least!"

Kieran had lost his ready smile. "So you know about me."

"And that escaped slave business? Oh, yes. He told me all about it. I was rather hoping you'd find your way here. Your horse is standing at stud, I trust. Available?"

"As you wish, lord. May I make an offer: my stud's service for a year in return for the escaped slave. Think of the herd you'll have five years from now!"

"Nonsense. I've already sent a contingent north to Padraic's owner to pay his ransom fee and be done with it. Happy to. Your horse is a separate business, between you and me." Oengus brightened. "Did you know Patrick was a slave for some years up in Ulster and escaped back to Britain?"

"Yes, I did." Kieran sounded wearied by the topic.

If Oengus noticed, he was polite enough not to mention it. "When Patrick returned to Erin as a missionary, his first order of business—actually, his second . . . no, third—anyway, he straightway went up to his old rath to pay his ransom fee to his former owner, a man named Milchu. Milchu heard he was coming and was so frightened he closed himself inside his house and set fire to it. Immolated himself. We're never going to know what dark reasons that man had for doing so. One of the mysteries of the faith."

Padraic noticed that Aidan too had lost his happy smile. And he recalled now that, at the banquet last night, Aidan had mentioned something about slavery a couple of times, though Oengus paid scant attention. If he didn't know better, Padraic would think Aidan was being vindictive somehow. But surely the prince of Connemara would have no reason to cause Padraic trouble, unless he were somehow in the employ of Kieran. That must be it. Kieran must have recruited Aidan to help round him up.

Kieran looked stricken. "That then was the northbound body of warriors who passed me a day or so ago. Twelve cows with them."

"The very same." Oengus signaled one of the guards. The man came running. "Take this man's horse to the stables and treat it as one of my own. Kieran, Aidan—join us for a tip of ale and a quiet chat. I want to know more about that horse. Coming, Padraic? Bridey?"

Padraic glanced at Bridey's face and bobbed his head. "We'll be along in a moment. Our thanks, lord." He waited until they had ambled off out of earshot before he turned to Bridey. "You look shocked. Whatever happened?"

"'Tis over. I didn't know he was paying your ransom. 'Tis over! Ye be no fugitive anymore. I don't . . . I just feel so . . . ended. Relieved. I . . ." Tears streamed down her face.

Why did good news so often bring tears to women's eyes? Padraic had never figured that out. He did recognize, though, when a woman was past talking. He gathered her in against him tightly, wrapping his arms close around her. With one hand he pressed her head against his chest, and he listened in amazement as she wept with joy for him.

* * *

Cuinn of Emhain Mhacha had missed the races. Emhain Mhacha's were the finest horse races in the world, and Cuinn missed them this year. Emhain Mhacha was named for the Mare Goddess, the powerful goddess of fertility, cereals, and horses. And that, in a phrase, was all mankind really ought expect from life—horses, bread, and progeny. The races were dedicated to her honor. They were an event not to be missed. And here sat Cuinn in a swamp.

Not a swamp. A bog. A wet place, nonetheless, with mosquitoes everywhere. One cannot celebrate Lughnassa well anywhere save at Emhain Mhacha. Certainly not in a sun-drenched, insect-infested bog.

The slight little brehon sat on his cloak in the shade of an alder, the only tree in twenty miles and growing on the only solid earthen hillock in twenty miles, as he watched Gwynn's minions file by. Moving this unwieldy mass of people from point to point took hours. She was accumulating a considerable army, and a formidable one, if these women fought half as well as did their men.

As the warriors rode past, the heads on their saddles bothered him, as severed heads always did. He accepted that they were the legitimate trophies of war, and everyone did it. Still-... still ... Perhaps it was simply his abhorrence at the thought that his own head might hang someday from someone's horse trappings. Who would take the head of a brehon? He shuddered.

Blaine claimed, and Cuinn just about had to concur, that Gwynn with her army could not be trusted. Dhuith, her druid, seemed level-headed, but he was, after all, in her employ. The best checkrein on her activities was the brehons from Tara traveling with her. She would not step seriously out of line so long as they were watching over her shoulder.

Besides, with the slave-prince fled, Gwynn's outriders had a better chance by far of turning him up than did the brehons. Cuinn knew it was true, but that didn't mollify him in the least. Because he was bound to this lengthy retinue, he had missed the races at Emhain Mhacha.

He swatted a mosquito on his arm as he surveyed the red bumps all over him.

A brushwood trackway, a woven mat of coppiced hazel three feet wide, provided the trail across the bog. Men and horses, cattle and hogs, all had to walk the track single file. Only children and chickens could walk two by two, and the chickens were carried. Threading hundreds of cattle and a couple hundred people across a bog one at a time took half of forever.

Somewhere at the head of the line rode Muirdoch and young Brian with the queen. Half a day in advance of the retinue, Rowan and the hunter from Carrowkeel ranged out with the dogs, providing meat for the entourage. Cuinn and Blaine, somehow, had ended up near the back. Brehons were not accustomed to dragging along at the rear of things.

Blaine stood and extended his arms high as he flexed his back, stretching everything except his pot-belly. "Time to move on, I suppose."

"I suppose." Cuinn stood, not the least ready to move on. He folded his cloak across his saddle skin, grateful for any bit of extra padding. "You would think, when the breeders are looking to improve horses, that they'd breed for broader backs. Narrow backs are fine on chariot horses. But riding stock . . ." He let his complaint die a-borning and swung up onto his scruffy horse.

Blaine always gave the impression that he ought to be carrying the pony, not riding it. He was certainly broader. He thwacked his gelding in the ribs with his heels and pushed it into the line ahead of a warrior and his family. The warrior stopped to allow Cuinn and their assistants to fall in behind Blaine. Cuinn was back out in the bog, under the relentless sun of a late-August day, surrounded by heath no higher than one's knees.

"What do you think of Dhuith's theology?" Cuinn sought in vain a comfortable seat, and he'd been on the track less than a minute. He slapped a mosquito on his leg.

"I like it." Blaine twisted around to talk easier. "One perfect divine Son, sacrificed to provide satisfaction to one perfect supreme God. Frankly, I can't think of a thing wrong with it. What about you?"

"The Otherworld is my only problem with it. I don't think he deals adequately with the Otherworld."

"Eternal life."

A glistening dragonfly zipped in close, hesitated and zipped away. Amazing things, dragonflies. Cuinn always half feared some dragonfly would smack into him as it dashed about at high speed, but that had never happened.

"Aye, but under what circumstances? I personally know druids who have broken through to the Otherworld and returned. We all know that the gentry pass back and forth. But Dhuith claims once you're there, you're there." Cuinn wondered if they weren't giving this trackway too much of a workout, all these hundreds of animals and people beating upon it. The matting shifted ominously beneath his pony's feet.

"Dragonfly nymphs." Blaine didn't seem to feel the least uncomfortable riding. He perched on his horse with casual ease. But then, he had all that extra natural padding. "You know about dragonfly nymphs. They live a long time as creeping creatures beneath the stream. No wings, no good eyes. Then one day they climb up a reed, split their skin down the back, and out emerges a dragonfly. Wings, everything."

"Yes, I know that. Is this one of Dhuith's illustrations?"

"And an excellent one. Now think about that creature beneath the water. It cannot have the slightest idea about flight, or sunlight, or any such thing. All it knows is the gloom of its water life beneath the rocks. You see the application, don't you? We are like that underwater nymph, unable to know what lies in our future. Death is the nymph creeping out of the water. From the mundane to the glorious, from crawling to flight. Beautiful, is it not?"

"Beautiful." Sure and the dragonfly would not want to return to its lowly existence beneath the rocks even if it could, once it tasted the joy and freedom of flight. If dragonflies ate mosquitoes, as the druids claimed, there were not nearly enough dragonflies. What dragonflies there were could certainly feast to their hearts' content here.

Cuinn worked on the illustration for perhaps half an hour, mulling its ramifications. The more he pondered it, the better it seemed.

"Oh-oh . . ." Blaine up ahead sat forward suddenly on his horse, his fat legs wrapped around it, his shoulders hunched. His pony staggered, whether from Blaine's shift of weight or something else Cuinn could not see. Now his own pony lurched.

With startled, piercing whinnies, the ponies ahead jumped about. Cuinn's mare slipped out from under him. The track was giving way, cracking, breaking, tipping up. Cuinn landed on his side in a heather shrub. It bowed and broke, spilling him into slimy, soggy moss. A cloud of gnats and mosquitoes rose up off the slime.

A pox on bogs.

27

Hare

His head howled. His ribs and belly screamed rhythmically. His neck moaned. All Padraic had intended to do was walk out to the rim of the Rock of Cashel and watch the sun set. Now he suffered mightily in pain and darkness, shaken like a rat in a dog's mouth. Oh, how his head howled.

He squirmed, trying to make his ribs quit hurting. The wild jostling slowed, and he recognized the rhythm as a horse's walk. He could hear hoofbeats, and he recognized them. Kieran's stallion. No other horse plodded so purposefully.

He squirmed again. He was draped like a sack of stones across the withers of the great horse, his legs hanging down one side and his arms down the other. No wonder his ribs hurt, riding on that bony withers. His wrists were bound, and he was wrapped in his cloak so that he could see nothing. What was going on? And his head, how it howled.

The horse stopped. A heavy hand shoved on his shoulder, and he slid backward off the horse, legs downward. He flopped into mud and lay still, putting all his efforts into breathing. He heard the stud's huge feet near his head and the feet of a smaller horse beyond.

Kieran yanked the cloak away. "Ready to ride?"

"No." Padraic lay still. The night was nearly complete in this dark woodland. He could see virtually nothing. Gently he twisted his head until he could touch the back of it with his wrists. He found there a knot the size of a hog's head.

Kieran kicked Padraic's ribs. "Up."

"And to think I warned you of Gwynn's murderous intent. I should have let you hang about her camp long enough to receive Scanlon's cold iron in your back. What a fool I was."

"What . . ?"

Padraic shifted into a higher pitch of voice. "Ooh, Kieran, since I don't have second sight I didn't know you're going to cause me all manner of pain and trouble, so I'll don this woman's garb and warn you away."

Kieran roared.

Padraic opened his eyes to make certain it was laughter.

It was. The black nemesis reached down and yanked Padraic to his feet. "I'd not in a thousand years suspect you of being my benefactor that night. For weeks I've been puzzling over which woman's fancy I tickled that she warned me like that. Why did you do it?"

"A splendid question with no answer." Padraic tried to stand erect, but he kept tipping dizzily.

Kieran grabbed two fistfuls of tunic and piloted Padraic to a pony beyond the great horse. "Come on. I didn't hit you that hard. Up." He gave Padraic a rough boost.

Padraic slid onto the pony's back and very nearly slid on over the other side. He gripped a hank of mane in his cold, stiff, tingling fingers. The cords on his wrists were much too tight.

Kieran ran a rope between Padraic's arms and tied it in a loose loop around the pony's neck. There was no way Padraic could jump off and slip away.

Kieran mounted, and away they went. He led the pony forth at a vicious trot. Padraic bounced like a boat in a storm until he managed to get his knees up and adjusted to the pony's rapid, jarring gait.

His head . . .

"Why are you doing this? I'm free. You know that."

Silence. Kieran was concentrating, apparently, on keeping to the track in the darkness. No doubt he knew the moon would be up in a few minutes. It would be bright enough that they could travel the night through.

Padraic's head . . .

"I see." Padraic was talking simply because it was the only way he was going to hear a friendly voice. "You're going to slip past Oengus's contingent and get home ahead of them. That way you can collect your reward for returning me, before our master knows the ransom fee is coming. How much were you promised?"

"Ten cows."

"I'm flattered." Padraic was also being shaken to bits.

"Oengus thinks you're worth twelve. I think everyone has you greatly overvalued."

"Oh, I don't know. You're alive right now because of me."

"And you just said yourself 'twas a foolish act."

Sure and Padraic couldn't dispute that. He still thought so. And yet, in a curious way he didn't.

His main concern now was escape. He couldn't manage that yet, the way Kieran had roped him to the pony. He felt like a hare in a snare, ready to leap and flee but tied helpless. Perhaps if they passed close enough to Oengus's contingent he could cry out or break away.

"S-something else occurs to me." Padraic let the pony's ragged gait make his voice stutter and jar, a not-so-subtle hint to slow down. "When you present me for your reward, what's to keep me from telling my master that the ransom is on the way? He'll not want to part with ten cows if he doesn't have to."

"You won't. I'll see to that."

That sounded ominous. Padraic decided not to press the matter.

Kieran slowed the animals to a walk eventually, not to spare Padraic's howling head, presumably, but to give the horses a rest. This was going to be a long, long ride.

* * *

Bridey felt near tears again. She really must try to be braver. She represented Jesus Christ and Kildare. But the enormity of all this . . . and poor Padraic . . .

She had never ridden in a chariot before, and she was not certain this was her favorite mode of transport. It was, however, certainly better than rowing a curragh.

On the wooden floor at the front knelt the charioteer, a burly little man with broad, heavy hands. Beside Bridey stood Oengus. All the jouncing and bouncing kept Bridey off balance. Oengus obviously was accustomed to riding thus. He flexed his knees slightly and didn't lurch in the least.

They rattled along the track, their two horses barreling on at a canter. Tall Oengus missed most of the low-hanging tree limbs, barely, but leaves slapped his face now and then. It was all very exciting in a way. If Bridey were less distraught she would probably be enjoying it better.

Oengus talked about traveling fast. They certainly were. With a retinue of ten crack horsemen and two chariots, Oengus was burning up the trail. Bridey almost feared they would kill the horses.

Up ahead the track opened into cropped pastureland. The two lead riders hauled to a stop. The chariot ahead of this one, the one carrying Aidan of Connaught, rolled to a halt. The charioteer drew the king's chariot in behind. Oengus leaped out and strode to the front, limping a bit more than usual.

Bridey hopped down and ran up beside Oengus. Unless someone told her to go away, she wanted to miss nothing.

They had arrived at a crossroads. A track just as heavily traveled as theirs intersected at nearly right angles. The lead riders had dismounted. They were bent nearly double, examining the dirt closely along both tracks.

The older of the two snapped erect and shook his head. "Impossible to say, lord. Grainan here thinks your ransom traveled the north road. I'm inclined to agree. Cattle were driven in two directions here, but that's the logical one for our people. Good grazing the whole way for night camps. No trace of the great horse. I'd guess he took another track, probably headed north along that way, up the coast." And he waved an arm.

Oengus grimaced. "No way to catch up to him. He's no doubt faster than we, or as fast. But . . ." He clapped his hands together. "We can get there very shortly after he does."

Bridey pondered the situation for only a moment. Either God was whispering instructions to her, or her muddled mind was issuing orders of its own. "My lord, ye'll stop at Kildare on y'r way back south, aye?"

"Aye."

"I feel compelled to travel to Kildare now, m'self. 'Tis only a few miles to the east there. Then I shall come north behind ye." She looked at Oengus helplessly. "I cannot tell ye why I feel this."

He smiled. "No need to explain. Go where you feel sent. We'll stay on Padraic's trail."

247

"I give ye all thanks, lord." On impulse she grabbed his hand and kissed it. She started immediately down the eastward trail at a run. When she glanced back to wave farewell, the chariots had already lurched into motion again, northbound.

Why was she doing this? She had no idea whether her feeling of God's leading was genuine. She slowed to a walk, panting and sweating, until she should catch her second wind. She must bring herself to the throne of God as Brigid had instructed. She was about to ask His guidance and help again—and with no confidence at all in her ability to hear Him.

Along the valley road, most of the trees had given way to pastureland. Hard beside the track, a bed of shamrocks spread out across the ditch and melded in among the cropped grass. Cattle and sheep grazed about on either hand.

It was getting late. Golden light and long shadows stretched out before her. What if night overtook her before she reached Kildare? What if highwaymen seized her unprotected? What if . . ?

What if that figure of a woman on the track really was Brigid herself just a quarter mile ahead? Bridey's heart leaped into her throat as she broke into a wild, flailing run. "Lady? Lady?!"

The figure stopped and wheeled. Lovely golden hair tumbled down her back as she let her light cloak slide off her head.

It was!

Only after Bridey babbled praise to God for several minutes as she ran did she remember that one is supposed to sing praise to God for miracles. She was too breathless to sing, her heart too filled with joy. She almost literally fell upon the prioress of Kildare monastery, sobbing.

Brigid's firm arms held her a few minutes, then gently turned her aside. "Let us sit a moment, Bridey, child. You look absolutely distraught. I was not expecting you for days."

Still sweating and breathless, Bridey stumbled to the roadside and dropped down on a shamrock-carpeted slope. And then she realized what she'd just heard. "Lady? You were expecting me?"

"I've seen several disturbing things in vision these last few days. You are coming with a king."

"Oengus of Cashel. He continued on. He's in a rush. He'll

stop at Kildare on his way back." Bridey wiped her tear-streaked face on the hem of her skirt.

"Oh, dear. I had a fine linen square with me this morning, but I gave it to an old woman earlier. I'm sorry I've none to give you. Now tell me. What is this about a captive prince in mortal danger, riding through darkness with tingling fingers?"

Bridey frowned. "Padraic! That's Padraic. He's alive, aye, lady? Y'r second sight saw him alive?"

"Yes, but the vision wasn't clear or direct. Tell me about him."

"He's a prince of the Slevin who—"

"I know that part. Lately."

"Lately. He was going to join Oengus early in the morning to work on a difficult dun mare. A problem horse. He's a splendid breaker and trainer of horses. He didn't appear, and when Oengus sent his steward to investigate, it appeared Padraic hadn't slept in his bed that night. So they put an expert tracker to reading the ground all about—the tracks on the ground, ye know?"

"Aye." Brigid watched Bridey's face intently, with penetrating blue eyes that saw beyond vision. It was mildly distracting.

Bridey continued, "The tracker says Padraic walked casually out across the Rock on the preceding evening. Someone approaching from behind knocked him down and carried him to a huge horse. There be only one horse that size in Munster, so we know whose it was. His name is Kieran. Kieran on his great horse, with an extra pony in tow, rode north in the night—long gone by morning when the tracker reported his findings. But Oengus called out two chariots and a guard and took off after him anyway. We're certain this Kieran abducted him—and likely to earn a prize for returning him to his owner."

Brigid nodded thoughtfully. "That explains much of what I've seen. Good. Good. You will continue on tomorrow. You must go to Tara."

"Not Louth, where his master lives? Not Armagh?" And, since the topic seemed to be enigmas, "Lady, ye told me to go where God takes me, and to greet Patrick for ye. God has not led me to Patrick."

Brigid smiled. "Then you're not at the end of your quest yet."

That certainly made sense. Bridey hadn't thought of it quite that way. Kildare seemed so much like home, so much like the end of a journey, it never occurred to her that she was still in the middle of the trek.

Brigid climbed to her feet, so Bridey followed. They started east along the road.

Brigid smiled suddenly. "I'm so glad you've found love."

"Love? Ye mean as in man and woman?"

"Certainly. Your love for God we both know about already. Padraic. He's declared his love, hasn't he?"

"Well, er . . . when he arrived at Cashel we spent two days simply sitting and talking, catching up on each other's lives, ye might say. He avowed that he thought about me all the time. I suppose for a man that's akin to declaring love."

"The best you get, most of the time."

"Lady, do ye see my whole future?"

"No. What I see are little bits and pieces, as if you passed an open window and glimpsed what is inside."

"So ye see pieces of the future."

"And why not? I ask God daily for guidance. I pray daily for the Holy Spirit's hand on my life, as do you yourself. This happens to be the way the Holy Spirit guides me. You, He will guide in a way that is uniquely your own." Brigid quickened her step a little. "Let's hasten, so as to arrive in time for supper. You must get an early start, and I want you well fed. Also, I've a package for you to take with you."

"A package?"

"Remember that fine linen we worked with in the long evenings, and how nicely it spun out? I wove it into a winding cloth. You'll take that with you."

Bridey's heart did a flip. "A burial cloth! For someone dying. You want me to take burial clothes along . . ." If this was typical of bits and pieces of the future, Bridey didn't want to know about it.

Brigid laughed. "Not for your Padraic, dear Bridey." She sobered instantly into a profound sadness. "For Patrick."

28

Ants

The gate had been ripped off the ring wall. It lay, cast aside, six feet away. Outside the wall, black piles of ash and charred wood marked what used to be the kitchens and sheds. Even the granaries had been torched. Amid the stench of decay, animal bones and scraps of hide lay strewn about. Flies buzzed.

Padraic stepped inside the ring wall. The house had been burned. The fire had not consumed the thick thatch completely, but what was left lay in a rank heap inside the circle of ashes. In the light drizzle, it all stank like smoke, though the fires were out, the ashes cold now.

Fifteen months ago, when Padraic fled, this prosperous rath of the Dealgan boasted hundreds of cattle, horses, and sheep. His wealthy master leased hundreds of cattle more to boaires in the area round about. Now the only things Padraic saw alive, besides thousands of flies, were some hawfinches in the coppiced hazels by the brook, and a few jackdaws.

And ants. He had forgotten about the ants. As always, the place was alive with black ants in the grass and on the wall.

The raiders must have destroyed the rath not long ago—spring or early summer—because the barley and gardens had been planted. But they were unkempt and weedy.

Padraic drew a deep, deep breath. "Now what?"

"I don't know." Kieran surveyed the horror with a stricken look on his face. "I suppose we should rummage around in that and see if he and the lady were still inside when the roof fell."

"I suppose so." Padraic could not feel less like doing so. "We'll have to make new handles for the pitchforks. The toolshed burned."

So had the stables, and at least one horse had died inside, judging from the fly swarms. Padraic didn't want to know which one. He had his favorites.

Kieran stumbled a bit walking to the ring of ashes that had been the house. "Never mind. It's been done. It's all churned up in here." He brushed past Padraic and walked outside the wall. For long minutes he stared off at the familiar hills surrounding them.

The rath, with its earthen ring wall perched on the curve of the hilltop, sat in a beautiful location. Excellent pasturage surrounded it. Good water flowed hard by. The master, Dealgan of Cross Keys, had four grown sons and two daughters. Why didn't one of them come in and rebuild?

Padraic wandered over and stood near Kieran. "Who do you suppose will come in and take over?"

"Some boaire's son, probably. What's left in our bag, do you remember?"

"Half a loaf of barleycake and that oat bread the farmer's wife gave you to try."

"No need to build a fire, then."

Good. There's been more than enough of that already. Padraic followed Kieran off to the protection of the lone oak by the creek. It was nearly dry there yet. As usual, Kieran tied the tether line around Padraic's waist and fastened him thereby to a convenient bush.

Padraic flopped down on his back beside the great gnarled trunk and watched the amazing density of sheltering leaves move about overhead. "Many's the hour I spent in my youth up in this very tree. I'd sit on that limb right up there and think about my parents. I'd daydream that things were different. Better." He grimaced and raised his bound wrists, a gesture. "I'm still dreaming."

Kieran settled himself by the trunk and leaned back against its harshness. "As do we all. The ten cows I would have received for your return were going to be the start of a prosperous life for myself. A couple of them would be a gift to Aneen's father. You remember Aneen?"

"Aye."

Kieran gazed off at the plundered farmstead awhile. "Amazing, isn't it, that any Irishmen at all ever reach old age? Not even the toughest and luckiest are guaranteed a long life. Dealgan was as tough and as lucky as they come." He glanced at Padraic. "So were your parents."

"How would you know that?"

"I knew them."

Padraic sat up and stared at him. "When?"

"My foster father and I met them at Tara, at that big enclave with all the ris. You and a sister had some sort of illness. I forget what—anyway, it was serious enough that they left you two home. Your father talked about fostering you to my foster father. Nothing but praise for you, he had. 'As bright and clever as his namesake,' your father claimed. I was old enough that I attached myself to Dealgan soon after. Then a year later the Behr came."

"My namesake. Patrick."

"Your parents were Christians, both of them. Among the first, too. Apparently they heard Patrick soon after he arrived in Erin. Not his oration on the Hill of Slane—not that early—but not very long after that."

Padraic sat stunned. His parents. Bridey's faith.

He didn't remember much about his childhood on Lambay—not nearly as much as he remembered of his formative years on this rath. He remembered that his parents had followed the traditional seasons of the druidic year, coming to the mainland eight times annually because no druid lived on Lambay. He remembered his mother's laughter, and her lap.

And then the Behr came—in the same way someone, Behr or others, descended upon this Dealgan rath.

A sense of loss engulfed him. So much loss. Bitter loss. Irretrievable loss.

"When the Dealgan bought me, what was the ransom price?"

"Three cows. The usual cumal. He increased the price as you got older."

"Until now I'm overvalued. So you say." Padraic dropped back to lying in the uncropped grass. His parents were Christians. He should have suspected. And Kieran considered them tough and lucky. For some odd reason that made him feel very good.

Out of nowhere an ant paraded across the front of his tunic, up near his neck. He brushed it off.

Kieran lurched suddenly to his feet. Padraic half expected to get kicked again. A flash of terror robbed him of speech, for when Kieran grabbed Padraic's arm, he was brandishing his dagger.

With a stroke he drew the blade up between Padraic's wrists, cutting the cords, taking only a little skin off the left wrist and palm.

He slung himself carelessly back into his seat by the oak trunk. "Go to Tara. See if you can be high king. Who knows? It could happen. Maybe one of us at least can make his dreams come true."

Padraic sat up and rubbed his wrists, and rubbed them, and rubbed them. "What are you going to do? Attach to some other taoiseach?"

"I don't know." Kieran looked at him. "Listen to the message I received: 'You're gloating in a strength that isn't yours and engaging in a pursuit that's beyond you. Seek a new strength and a new aim while you may.' What does that mean to you?"

"It's a riddle?"

"I don't know. Is it?"

Padraic pondered awhile. "Sounds like something Bridey would come up with. Bridey spouts the Christian theology. All real strength comes through Jesus Christ. That's what it sounds like. Where'd you get it?"

"The Morrigan."

Padraic stared at him. He recalled the old woman he and Bridey befriended on the road to Lough Gur. Just thinking about the gentry made him feel uneasy. But there was no ignoring any message they delivered.

The misting rain was beginning to penetrate the leafy cover, dripping on their patch below the oak. The pesky ants had found Padraic now and crawled here and there in his clothes. He was doing more brushing and swatting than thinking.

He climbed to his feet and picked at the knot in his tether line. "If you have nothing better to do, come with me to Tara. All the kings and taoiseachs of the Ui Neill will be there, electing their ard ri. Sure and you can attach to someone there. And if you wish, come along then to Kildare."

Kieran hauled to standing and stretched. "Why Kildare?"

"Because at Kildare will be a lady you have met, though only casually. She is of very plain appearance on the outside and extremely beautiful on the inside. She is also very gifted with inner sight, and she may just have the answer to your riddle."

* * *

As he looked at the solid line of warriors arrayed across the hill, each spear and sword ready to slay him, Aidan regretted giving up his panpipes in favor of becoming a hero.

He stood in Oengus's second chariot, trying not to let his nerves show, as Oengus's two aides strode across the pasture toward the alien army. Like ants between the wall and the honeypot, the warriors lined out across the hill. They looked to be at least a hundred strong, each mounted on a fairly fresh pony. Oengus's contingent was a tenth that, and the horses were tired. Ten on one? The chariots would help, but not much.

Even from here, Aidan could see severed heads hanging from their horses' trappings. That line of weapons and weapon-wielders was no ordinary band of highwaymen.

One of the warriors rode forward from the alien line to receive the aides. They conversed. Grainan signaled to Oengus.

As he hopped down out of his chariot, Oengus paused long enough to signal "Come" to Aidan.

Oengus strode across the grass, proud and strong, and his confidence boosted Aidan's a little as he followed close behind.

From the other line, a burly man with a bright plaid cloak and a moustache almost as statuesque as Oengus's dismounted and walked down the hill to join the group. From his commanding demeanor Aidan understood instantly that he was the leader of this band of a hundred. Aidan's father never commanded that kind of presence. Aidan recognized for the first time the meaning of petty king as opposed to high king. Aidan came from a line of very petty kings.

It became obvious to him as he approached that these two kings knew each other, though they were not friends. They greeted each other coolly, formally. Neither performed obeisance.

Oengus dipped his head toward Aidan. "Aidan of Connemara, a prince of Connaught, accompanying me on this quest."

No one seemed to expect any response from Aidan, so he offered none.

"And what is your quest, Oengus?" asked the moustache.

"I was entertaining a guest in my home, a prince of the Slevin. A retainer from the northern Ui Neill, a man named Keiran of the Great Horse, kidnapped my guest and fled north. I have come to rescue him. That's my only purpose in entering your province, but I will rescue him."

"Why would he kidnap the guest of a high king?"

"For personal gain. It's a long story. I'm sure he feels safe, that he's confident I wouldn't pursue him into a province that's not mine."

The moustache smirked. "And here you are."

"But not to stay. I'm passing through. His destination is a rath of the Dealgan. Therefore it's mine." Where did Oengus get the tribe Dealgan? From Padraic himself most probably. Apparently Padraic had spilled out to Oengus his whole story, every bit. Aidan would never have done that, but he had to admit that the tactic of being candid had certainly worked well.

"Up to the east of Tara?"

"Somewhere in that area. I'll have to ask when I get near."

"You're going to snatch this Kieran right out from under the Ui Neill, in their very heart."

"As I said, it's a matter of honor. They can't honorably shelter him. A guest, by all that's holy!"

The king of the Lagin nodded and studied the ground. He looked at his aide. "We're talking about the same one, right?"

The aide nodded.

The Laginman stroked his moustache a moment. "We've a problem. Rather, you've a problem. That branch of the Dealgan exists no more. Raiders burned them out this last spring."

"How do you know?"

"Forces of the Ui Neill entered my borders claiming they were pursuing the raiders. Specified the victims. My people rebuffed them."

Oengus grunted. He studied the grassy sward a moment, frowning. "Where will Kieran go next, once he discovers the Dealgan are gone? Is there a remnant of the Dealgan, and, if so, where would they go?"

"I'd guess any survivors would migrate down to the coast to join the other branch of the clan. Or go to Tara."

"Then I'll go first to Tara. It's closer. Are the Lagin with me or

against me?" Oengus seemed ready to take on these hundred Lagin on the spot, and that terrified Aidan.

"If he'd seized one of your tuathe, or even one of your family,
I'd tell you to go home. But to seize a guest from under your
roof—that's another matter. The Lagin are with you."

Aidan might be from Connaught, but he knew a bit of the
political affairs of the midlands. The Lagin were trying to hold
their own bit of territory here in Leinster, resisting annexation by
either the ard ri at Cashel or the ard ri at Tara. Both purposed to
unite Erin under one seat. Connaught sat far to the northwest, out
of the way, and had to be traveled to. Connaught therefore had
little to fear from the ambitions of others. The lands of the Lagin,
though, lay as a buffer between the two contentious realms.

Not a comfortable place to be.

Oengus nodded, turned on his heel, and presented his back
to the Lagin. The king's word was sufficient. Aidan, the prince of
Connaught, without a voice in the matter, turned also and followed Oengus back to the chariots.

He braved a question. "Why did you invite me to the conversation, lord?"

"To imply by your presence that this is a matter transcending
provincial borders—a matter of honor, not politics, in which all
tribes ought unite. Even foreigners."

"Is everything you do that carefully considered?"

"Yes." Oengus paused before leaping up into his chariot.
"That, prince, is why I am king."

29

Winds

With the dust cloud of what had to be an army approaching from the northwest, and the Eoghanacht guard and two chariots almost certainly somewhere close by, and that contingent of screaming warriors pouring out the gate toward her, this did not seem to Bridey the most propitious of times to visit Tara.

There was no place to run, of course. She froze in place and watched helplessly as the warriors from Tara's gate streamed toward her.

Most were stripped to the waist; some wore no clothes at all. Their brightly burnished torques caught the waning sun and glinted like stars. They were ready to do battle. They ran with axes or spears in hand, shields at their sides. Still yelling, they swept past her down the hill.

Within a hundred feet of the gate, she stepped well away from the track, for she could hear chariot wheels inside Tara's great earthen wall. Here they came, creaking, clanking, their iron wheel-rims clattering on the stones, their eager horses lunging. What magnificent men, the cream of Tara's guard, rode in them behind their charioteers!

Bridey waited until the dust settled in the track before she continued up the way to the gate. That dust cloud at the far end of the vale must indeed be an army—they would never send so many chariots and forces out against Oengus's mere dozen men and two chariots. Besides, if Oengus were coming here he would approach from the northeast, not the northwest. Surely he was days ahead of her and in Louth by now. Two different people had already told Bridey that Padraic's old rath was destroyed. Surely Oengus, a king, would hear. Where would he seek Padraic next? Did the ex–slave-prince ride at his side yet? Bridey abhorred unanswerable questions, and she had been assailed with a host of them lately.

She saw smoke rising from the vale beyond the hill, and she walked past the gate to the hillcrest. An army encamped on the plain. A ragged, temporary sort of palisade surrounded simple brush shelters. The smoke of more than a dozen fires drifted northeast. That would mean perhaps a hundred warriors. The election of an ard ri certainly drew crowds.

She had returned to within ten feet of the gate when she leaped aside again. Another chariot was coming—just one this time. She gasped. Oengus's chariot! It bucketed out the gate, accompanied by four outriders, and that white-haired prince of Connaught rode in it. The prince did not appear to notice Bridey by the gate, but that certainly didn't surprise her. He was a strange young man under the best of circumstances, and she suspected these circumstances were highly unusual.

She announced herself as Bridey of Kildare to the guard on the gate and was directed instantly inside.

Another bare-chested young retainer stepped forward. "They're expecting you." He turned on his heel and marched off toward the nearer of two large buildings, a great rectangular hall. *They're expecting me?* She fell in behind him.

He ushered her into a vast, dark banqueting hall. A pall of smoke hung below the roof and several men sat about the fire in the middle of the room. One of them was Oengus.

He stood as Bridey approached. "Here she is." With a broad smile he strode over to her and led her by the hand to the company around the fire. "The emissary from Brigid at Kildare."

From the shadows along the wall, a young man came running with a sheepskin cushion. He positioned it at Oengus's right. Since Oengus was the only face here she knew, she made a generalized obeisance all around and sat down. She was never going to get used to this emissary business, or to the honors that the title seemed to carry.

Bridey nodded from face to face. "Brigid sends God's blessings and her warmest greetings to all here. She begs you all to act in love toward one another and put aside pettiness. She senses danger here, though she knows not why, and asks all present to act circumspectly."

"Her second sight is highly regarded as coming from God,"

a bald, gray-bearded man commented. "That's exactly what we have here. A danger, and a need to act circumspectly. Most of us here fail to see eye to eye." He exuded the same kind of riveting presence that Oengus did. In fact, every man in this circle acted like a king. Bridey felt very, very small.

Oengus smiled. "Quite an august gathering, though, when you think about it. Bridey of Kildare, the man on my left is high king of the Lagin. His force is camped to the north just over the hill there, along with my people."

Should she speak or hold her peace? She was an emissary. She would speak like an emissary. "I'll be carrying a report back to Brigid, and it ought be complete. I thought, lord, that the midlands did not care to associate with the Ui Neill. You would take part in electing an ard ri?"

The king of Lagin shook his head. "Tell Brigid I'm not in the area for that. It's another matter. A matter of honor."

Oengus nodded toward a man across the fire. "The ri ruirech of Trim. The fellow on his right, the king of the southern Ui Neill." He paused, then nodded toward the bald man with the luxuriant gray beard. "MacNiall, a direct descendant of Niall of the Nine hostages—high king of Tara."

It took Bridey a moment to digest the implications of that. "So the selection has been made."

"During the gathering for Lughnassa a few weeks ago." The king of Trim sounded much older than he looked, with a rough and gravelly voice. "Since Lughnassa is a time of joining, a wedding of diverse thoughts—a time of maturity, if you will—we thought it appropriate to make the selection then and try to maintain some accord."

The king of the southern Ui Neill, on the other hand, sounded younger than he looked. "Besides, everyone was here then for the horse races. It's getting so that the races here are better than the ones at Emhain Mhacha."

"Not the ones at Carman," said the king of Trim, and everyone chuckled appreciatively.

Bridey had never attended the woman races at Carman, nor the horse races anywhere else for that matter. They didn't sound particularly appealing. But then, she wasn't a man. "That be most of the peoples of Erin here in this place, if ye count Aidan as representing Connaught. He left just now, with others."

MacNiall nodded. "Scouts reported that an army of Connaughtmen is approaching. We're sending out some forces to show them a little fang. Aidan is going out there because he thinks he knows who they are."

"And that be circumspect?" Bridey looked from face to face.

"More so than falling upon them with weapons flying. See what they intend first."

"The Eoghanachta, the Lagin, Connaught." Oengus grunted in that way of his. "It seems, MacNiall, that the winds of chance have blown a diverse lot your way during your first days of office."

A lot of warriors to fend off, if need be. No one said it. No one had to.

The ard ri, the king Padraic would never be, wagged his head. "Lucky me."

One of the retainers stepped in within ten feet of the fire and spoke. "Muirdoch, brehon of the Ui Neill, has arrived, lord."

"Muirdoch." The ard ri snorted. "So where was he when I needed him? He was supposed to be the one who nominated me to the council. Muirdoch of the Ui Neill is welcome."

A dark, sullen fellow came forward, a somewhat younger man than Bridey would expect a brehon to be. He did obeisance before the new high king and settled onto a fine goatskin the lads along the wall provided. He nodded to MacNiall. "They told me of your new joy and responsibility. My warmest congratulations. I'm sorry I couldn't be here to participate."

"So am I. Where were you?"

"Trying to track down the runaway slave at the behest of the gathering of brehons. We found him. Possibly he'll be good material someday, but right now he lacks maturity and sound judgment."

Bridey glanced at Oengus. Had Padraic mentioned brehons in his lengthy tale? Apparently he had. And, just as apparently, Oengus did not agree in the least with Muirdoch's assessment.

Muirdoch lapsed into a story about Padraic foolishly fleeing and Kieran setting out in pursuit. He described Gwynn of Connemara in much the same terms as had Padraic—grasping, conniving, power-hungry. Then he announced in a long, rambling narrative that Gwynn, Padraic's aunt, had arrived at the gate. When Padraic arrived, presumably in the hands of Kieran, she intended to stand at his side during his election.

Oengus knew the truth. How did he regard this interesting fable? Bridey couldn't tell from his face. "Connaughtmen," he rumbled. "They always have been a little slow to catch onto things. What does she intend to do now that Padraic is no longer a candidate? Any hints?"

Muirdoch shook his head. "I don't think that possibility ever crossed her mind. I came on ahead. Cuinn and Blaine are with her."

The ard ri's eyebrows shot up. "Attached to her?"

"No. Keeping an eye on her. So far, she's been on her best behavior for the brehons from Tara. What now, I don't know."

"Lucky, lucky me. Is she strong enough to make a try for the throne by force?"

"If the force that roared past me as I came in are all the warriors you have on hand, she could be."

Oengus rubbed his cheek awhile in thought. He looked at the king of Lagin. "The last thing we need is Connaught meddling in the affairs of Tara."

The king of Lagin gave the barest of nods.

Oengus straightened. "You have our strength as well against Connaught."

Is this what kings considered acting circumspectly? No wonder Brigid had sensed danger here.

The king of Lagin didn't look pleased. "The prince from Connemara. It will be interesting to see where that Aidan stands."

* * *

Aidan stood braced in Oengus's chariot, feeling rather like a king himself. He still had not healed completely, but he would endure because he had to. No one of the Eoghanachta knew about his mutilation. To the best of his ability he would make certain none did. That might well mean silencing Donn of the Moor early on.

In the distance ahead, MacNiall's warriors were lining out

across the crest of a defensible rise, presenting a wall of shields and weapons against Gwynn's approach. Aidan's chariot closed quickly.

Probably because chariots were not much used in the rough terrain of his father's mountain fastness, he had forgotten how swift they could be for bringing warriors up to the front lines. He directed his charioteer to the center of the line.

Gwynn's army had grown considerably since Aidan's elopement. She must have close to two hundred people behind her now. Quite a herd of livestock followed at the rear too. A busy group, her raiders. She rode with all the command and dignity of Oengus himself. Aidan felt a sharp thrill of pride, even if she was not his kin by blood.

At her right rode Scanlon Too Skinny. There was a day not long ago when Aidan rode there. On her left, Donn of the Thicket, looking faintly ridiculous, perched upon a pony much too small for him. And at his side, his son. What was Donn of the Moor thinking as he watched Aidan approach in a king's chariot?

The two brehons from Tara, the stoat and the roly-poly one, rode with their entourage at the fore, as one would expect brehons to do. With the stoat leading, the group pushed through the defensive line without the least hesitation and rode on toward Tara. As the *clip-clop* of their ponies' hooves faded over the top of the hill, Aidan heard the stoat saying, "I cannot begin to tell you, Blaine, how good it feels to return to—"

Fifty feet short of the hillcrest, Scanlon and Donn stopped. Gwynn rode forward alone, with all the light-hearted presence of a warrior who could wipe out this entire defensive line single-handedly if she cared to. In spite of himself, Aidan didn't doubt for a moment that she could.

She drew her black mare to a halt six feet from the line and smiled enigmatically. "Aidan."

"Mums."

From the three men arrayed before her in chariots, she instantly and correctly picked out the high king's commander of forces. "Gwynn, a queen of Connemara, seeking to sojourn. My nephew is a candidate for high king."

Aidan knew what the orders were. Bring the leaders, hold the army at bay. He sent his charioteer forward to his mother's side and called to her favorite, "Scanlon. You're more than capable of making appropriate arrangements, I'm sure." He smiled at his stepmother. "Mums?"

Gracefully she slid from her mare's back and, her ax hooked upon her shoulder, stepped up into the chariot.

"Tara," said Aidan simply. His charioteer swung the rig around. The line parted for them, and they were off, clattering across the hillside.

The sun would be down in another hour. It washed the hills and valleys in its unique liquid gold. The open vale stretched out. Tara's distant hill stood bold against the sky.

"You've come up in the world since last I saw you." Gwynn studied him thoughtfully.

"And I plan to rise further still. Your numbers have improved."

"Scanlon's a good recruiter."

Should he mention it now or later? He mentioned it now. "When Donn returned to your camp, you didn't come looking for me."

"Into the provinces of the Lagin and the Eoghanacht? Hardly. I was less than a hundred strong then. I was forced by that circumstance—lack of strength—to leave you to your own resources. Obviously, your resources are formidable. Have they chosen the high king yet?"

"Yes, and it's not Padraic. Someone from the northern Ui Neill, so your efforts have gone for naught." Aidan felt incredibly royal, riding along in this chariot.

"We shall see."

Aidan fully intended to present her as his stepmother through her marriage to Ghervin of Connemara. Somehow, his presentation ended up being "My mother, Gwynn, Queen of Connemara."

Despite all his bold resolutions never again to be influenced by an ambitious female, Aidan was once more the humble lackey, standing in the whim and shadow of a women.

30

Fox

Had Padraic realized how far it was from the Dealgan south to Tara, he would have thought of some way to travel besides riding a small pony behind that great horse. Sure and the thirty miles was no fun on a stubby-legged pony that repeatedly broke into a sudden and always unexpected jog, trying to keep up with Kieran's huge stud. The black beast tended to walk fast anyway.

Padraic had never been to Tara. Kieran had. Kieran pointed out the stockade and buildings on the hill ahead. Curling listlessly, the smoke of dozens of fires rose from encampments spread across the vale. Perhaps these were the tents of the ris and taoiseachs who had come to Tara to choose a high king. Padraic kept telling himself he had no chance at such a stroke of fortune, but his heart didn't listen. It pounded anyway.

For a center of bustling activity, the place felt deadly quiet. A few warriors and women, none geared for either feasting or battle, paused to watch the great horse pass.

"Feels strange," Kieran muttered.

So. Padraic wasn't the only one to sense the uneasiness. They climbed the rutted trail up the hill. Padraic realized halfway up the slope that the ruts were probably cut by chariots, not wagons. He had always felt uncomfortable around chariots.

The gate guards stepped aside even before Padraic finished saying his name. That was more than just odd—it was ominous. People stood around inside the compound, watching.

This was the largest ring wall enclosure Padraic had ever been in. A low outer wall protected what was probably a huge, rectangular banqueting hall. Inside the main ring wall and palisade loomed the great round house that was the heart and soul of northern Erin. High king. Here.

Padraic slid off his pony, grateful to feel solid ground beneath his feet again. He heard Kieran hit the ground just behind him. They led the horses toward the two guards outside the round house door.

From the gate behind them, from the building before them, from behind the granaries stepped armed warriors. They converged upon Kieran and Padraic from all directions, a solid, enclosing wall.

Kieran muttered, "Padraic, I don't think they're taking your candidacy seriously."

"The story of my life, my black nemesis. Nobody ever takes me seriously." Without really thinking, Padraic swung around back to back with Kieran. He heard Kieran's ornate sword swish as it left its scabbard.

From out of the round house strode Oengus. Padraic broke into a grin. The grin melted away as he watched the ard ri's face. Oengus was not pleased.

Behind him came an equally imposing bald man with a gray beard, and beside him Gwynn, of all people! Her strange, white-haired son followed along behind her. All were armed. Even Gwynn carried her favorite ax hooked over her shoulder. Nobody looked friendly.

"Padraic, I'm disappointed in you." And Oengus appeared very much as if he meant it.

"That makes me intensely sorry, lord, for not only do I owe you a great deal, I admire you immensely. How so?"

"I hastened here thinking you were abducted. It's obvious from the way the two of you rode in here just now that you walked away from my hospitality of your free will, without so much as saying good-bye."

What could he say? If Padraic denied it, sure and his denial would sound hollow and insincere. He'd seem simply to be squirming. But if he did not deny it . . .

Kieran wheeled to face Oengus. "He did not walk away from your hospitality. Your first guess was right. I abducted him. The transgression is mine alone. We're together now because the man who would have paid me for his return is dead. Padraic's worthless to me so I freed him, and we came here, both of us, to better our fortunes if possible."

"My scouts have been reporting on your approach for hours. Your horse is a little hard to miss. You two ride together, in friendship."

Padraic raised his hands, a gesture of helplessness. "Not friendship. Safety. Two traveling the roads are twice as safe as one traveling alone, especially for me. He has that sturdy sword, and I have no weapon at all."

"Pity," Oengus rumbled ominously, "because you're going to need one."

"Padraic!" Gwynn barked it out. Quick as a cat she tossed him her ax.

He caught it and swung it up instantly, guarding his face and chest. This was better than a sword. At least he'd had a little instruction and practice with an ax.

Kieran stepped around back to back with Padraic again and raised his voice. "I understand you think I lied to you, Queen. That's not so. I knew nothing about any high king business, though I've always known he was a prince. Dealgan promised me ten cows for his return. We thought I'd have him back in a month or less. The chase became . . . it was . . .

"My Queen, have you ever hungered for something so much you live it and eat it and drink it and you can't think of anything else? That was my pursuit of Padraic. There came a time when the ten cows didn't matter anymore. Only catching him mattered. That was my state when I joined you where the Shannon narrows. Fifteen months it took me, and journeying from Connaught to Cashel, but I caught him. I caught him! I never lied to you. I don't lie."

Oengus snorted through that wondrous moustache. "So you caught him, is it? By your own mouth you admit you violated my hospitality."

"The only thing in the world for me was handing him over to Dealgan. I thought of nothing else—particularly not consequences. I took him back, lord. I took him back to the rath. I completed my task."

"At the expense of my hospitality and therefore my honor. I won't let that by. When a guest comes under my roof, he's safe. Padraic. Move aside."

Why Padraic did not, he had no idea. Even when his lips

gave form to his thoughts, he didn't understand. "He's an honorable man. I'll stand with him."

It was clear that Oengus didn't understand either. He opened his mouth, probably to rage, but Gwynn spoke up.

"May I suggest, lord, a test of heroes. Kieran versus a champion of your choice."

Oengus brightened. "Not a bad idea at all. An excellent, time-honored way to settle an issue."

Kieran's voice rang bravely. "Bring me your best, lord high king. I'll gladly prove my honor."

Padraic glanced about. That Scanlon Too Skinny wasn't here—he would be the most dangerous. Oengus was certainly dangerous, but he probably wouldn't expose himself to possible injury. He'd assign one of his warriors. Donn of the Thicket was big and strong, but slow. And Aidan? Hardly. There was, of course—

"Padraic."

Oengus said his name again, and it wasn't to ask him to step aside.

"Me?!"

"You claim to owe me much. Repay by championing my honor. Neither of you leaves this inner wall." Oengus's voice dripped poison. "To the death." He stepped back.

Instantly Padraic swung a half turn in place, his ax high, and just in time, because that sword was slashing toward him. Its hilt clunked against the ax handle, and the flat of its blade rang against the ax head. That fox wasn't going to take his time pouncing on the mouse—not when their lives were at stake.

Padraic and Kieran. Apparently only one of them would see his dreams. How had he ever gotten into this?

Padraic gave way to Kieran's first attack of sword-slinging, parrying the blows as he backed off. He wanted that sword to break against his ax, but it was damascened iron. Not much chance. Such swords often bent, though, without too much provocation. Padraic wasn't lucky enough for that to happen, either.

Kieran shifted tactics. He kept his blade level and stabbed forward with it. That was a much more difficult thrust to parry. Padraic needed a shield badly. He couldn't use the ax aggressive-

268

ly without losing the defense it offered. He stepped away backwards more rapidly than he had before, backing and sidling toward the surrounding circle of warriors. They moved casually aside.

He lunged suddenly at a nearby fellow, grabbed the man's shield in both hands, and swung shield and fellow together out into the space between himself and Kieran. The fellow yelled in surprise and terror. Padraic jerked on the shield and almost lost his grip with the hand that held shield and ax together. He'd either break the fellow's arm or shake it loose from there. Which happened he didn't know, but the shield came away in his hands as the warrior fell back against Kieran. Padraic wheeled around a full circle and at last faced his nemesis on somewhat an equal footing.

Now it was Kieran who needed a shield. He dropped back, a step here and a step there, but he was surprisingly good at protecting himself even while keeping that blade coming at Padraic.

And Padraic, as he saw a dozen little tricks played out successfully against him, realized how fatally he was outmatched. He was a horseman and a slave, not a warrior. He had not a chance here against even the most artless of these fighters, and Kieran was one of the best. If he would have any chance at all, he must outfox the fox, and that was highly unlikely.

The sword parried Padraic's ax, whipped around in a tight circle, and stabbed at Padraic's side. Its point ripped along the inside of his right arm. His right hand opened. His ax fell away. He dared not pause to assess the damage. He tried not to think about surviving this encounter one-handed as he bolted away. Kieran was hard on his heels.

The centerpiece of the compound was the standing stone, the sacred spot where kings were crowned. MacNiall received the joy and responsibility of ard ri there a fortnight ago. Taller than it was broad, all pitted and weatherworn, it stood silently awaiting the next king. Padraic leaped upon it, clung to its wedge-shaped top with his shield arm and braced his left leg against its smooth side. With his right leg he lashed out at Kieran.

His foot caught Kieran in the neck and sent him staggering backwards, but he didn't fall. Though the kick was essentially worthless, it spoiled Kieran's aim. His fine sword clanged against the rock. Sparks flew.

Padraic reversed directions, leaping away from the rock with a push of his left leg. He hit the ground running and raced for the ring wall. He dared not go over it. Oengus had said, "Inside the wall." Should he venture outside, or run, the whole compound would hunt him down. Kieran chased after him yelling.

Padraic was hoping to wear Kieran down a little, but it was he himself who was tiring. He snatched up a stout stick of birch firewood from the woodpile against the wall. His right hand obeyed the command to hang onto it, but a weird combination of pain and numbness robbed his fingers of feeling. His whole hand and arm were not much more responsive than the club they wielded.

He scrambled up onto the mound and braced his back against the wooden palisade atop the earthbank. With the shield he could defend against the sword's strokes, and with the flailing firewood he aimed for Kieran's head and knuckles. If he could just break a couple of Kieran's fingers, the sword would lose effectiveness.

Kieran seemed more careful now with his attack, more considered. He stabbed at Padraic less frequently and with greater purpose. Was he getting wearier or just smarter? He was sweating profusely in that black wool tunic.

With his sword Kieran knocked the birchwood club out of Padraic's hand.

Padraic slid his left arm out of the loops of the shield and with a howling shout flung it, flat front-side forward, directly at Kieran's face. Kieran had to fall back.

Padraic leaped off the bank and ran across the compound. He heard Kieran right behind him. Fifteen feet beyond the standing stone he dived forward and skidded on his belly across the loose dirt. Kieran's triumphant yell ululated to heaven as Padraic went down.

Padraic had gauged the slide exactly right. His hands dragged to a halt inches from Gwynn's neglected ax. He grabbed it two-handed and rolled. As he swung it toward Kieran he gave it that twist that Gwynn had taught him. The ax missed Kieran on its first swipe, looped back on the twist, and bit solidly into his ribs.

Kieran grunted like a pig stuck in mud. His knees buckled, and he dropped. Padraic yanked the ax away and swung it wide. He fully intended to chop off Kieran's sword hand while he had the chance. He could not. He pulled the stroke, the ax swished harmlessly on a wide arc, and Padraic brought it up to the basic guard position in front of him. With one foot he kicked the sword away from Kieran's reach.

It was over.

The bystanders had all fallen well back, maintaining their view of the scene but staying clear of harm's way. They moved in closer again, some braver than others, tightening the circle.

Oengus walked in almost beside his two champions. "To the death."

Padraic watched Kieran a moment. The nemesis made a few valiant tries at sitting up. His eyes glassed over, he fell onto his back and closed his eyes. His breath came in long, painful, labored gulps.

Padraic faced Oengus squarely. "You have the power of life and death over me. Over all of us. That's what 'high king' means. But you can't make me kill. That's still my choice, and I choose not to. I've been playing mouse to this man's fox for fifteen months, and I know his strength and character. He may be my nemesis, but he's worthy. I won't kill him."

"It's kill or die."

"I know that." Still holding it two-handed, for he could not trust the grip in his right, Padraic lowered the bloody ax, letting it sling loosely from his fingers. He was insane. He knew he was insane, and he regretted this insanity. The rest of the world was insane too, and Padraic regretted that as well.

Oengus himself drew his sword. His face burned red with fury.

"A boon before I die." Padraic stood quietly, and much more peacefully than he would have guessed of himself.

"That is . . ?"

"In Connaught, on the track down the north side of the last set of hills south of the mountain where Patrick drove the snakes out of Erin—a new barrow is there, perhaps halfway down the hill, a fresh grave of stones heaped high. In that grave lies the man who saved my life from the bear. He's waiting for Patrick to come raise him from death. Send Patrick, I pray thee, to raise up Rafe the Wolf's Counsel out of that barrow, as he raised the giant at Dichuil. Catching me was Kieran's greatest hunger. Helping Rafe is mine. I owe him my life and yearn to return his to him. Rafe is waiting, lord."

Oengus stared. Of all the requests he may have anticipated hearing, that obviously was not one he expected.

The voice of an angel called out, "Oengus."

Bridey! What was she doing here? She ought to be in Kildare. If not Kildare, then Cashel.

She stepped in front of Oengus, between him and Padraic and the prostrate Kieran. That foolish angel! A high king could run an angel through with as much impunity as he could kill an ex-slave.

"Oengus," she said quietly, "define 'grace' for me."

The king scowled at her, sullen. "More blessings than one deserves."

Did he follow her thoughts? Padraic certainly did not.

"And 'mercy,' lord, pray thee?"

"Less punishment than one deserves. My honor is at stake here, woman."

"Aye, it is. Christ's life was being unjustly forfeited. All the same He forgave His torturers. To grant God's grace and mercy to someone who only mildly offends ye is very nice, and very safe, and no real sacrifice on y'r own part. Now I call upon ye to grant God's grace and mercy to two men when y'r very honor be the question."

"Nothing is more important than one's honor."

"Christ is. Ye're called to a higher standard now, lord. Ye be a man of Christ."

Oengus fumed. His sword tip never wavered. "You know I'm justified in taking you down as well, for preventing me from fulfilling my word."

"Aye." The angel's voice remained light and easy.

Padraic could see only the back of Bridey's head. Her shoulders were squared, but she was not tensed at all nor did she fidget. The simple milkmaid from Currane opposed the most powerful man in Erin without indicating the least bit of nervousness.

And in that Padraic saw Patrick. Patrick served Jesus Christ, and more than once in that capacity he had encountered kings. Kings presented scant challenge to a man who faced down the devil himself. He operated not in his own strength but God's, and with God's strength he raised the dead. Patrick was no magician. He was a servant. Therein lay his power—and Bridey's.

Oengus glared. Was he thinking? Scheming? Figuring out how to slay Padraic without killing her as she stood between them? He must have been framing his speech, for he used the careful, measured Gaelic of a brehon delivering verdicts. "I declare my honor to be satisfied. Therefore I'm sparing these two, granting God's grace and mercy upon them. I praise this woman for showing me the mind of Jesus Christ in the matter."

As he sheathed his sword, Oengus looked past Bridey at Padraic. "Go quickly. Find Patrick, raise your friend from the grave, and then come to me in Cashel."

Another compelling thought jolted Padraic. Kieran had just been saved by a strength that was not his.

Or was he saved? The king of the Lagin stepped forward from the circle of onlookers. "I'm astounded! The Eoghanachta are renowned for their ruthlessness. Yet Oengus here has declared his honor satisfied short of blood. Who is this Jesus Christ, and what is His secret power, that He would change one of Erin's reputed heroes into a soft, fluffy little grandmother?"

Oengus turned to the king and smiled. Padraic's blood froze at the sight of that smile. Smiles were supposed to be warm and friendly. Oengus's smile, cold and cruel, chilled to the bone. He didn't gather himself. He didn't prepare. He simply rotated a quarter turn and thrust his sword through the middle of the king of Lagin.

Bridey cried out, a muted wail.

All over the compound, amid war cries and screams, fighting erupted. The least offense sets off a Celtic warrior, and killing a king cannot be considered least. Padraic swung the ax up to ready.

A moment ago he had thought the fight was over. It was only just beginning.

31

Storm

The trained Celtic warrior fights with the strength of a bull, the stamina of a horse, the rage of the stormy sea, the determination of a terrier, the cunning of a cat, and the common sense of an absolute idiot.

Gwynn stood astonished and bemused as the whole inner compound of Tara erupted into a titanic melee. She had no idea exactly who was setting upon whom. There were only a dozen Eoghanachta altogether, but far more than a dozen men were fighting. The Ui Neill were taking the side of the Eoghanacht, their casual, on-again-off-again enemies, against the Lagin, their immediate and far more dangerous enemies. With whom her own Connaughtmen were casting their lot was anybody's guess. Probably they themselves didn't know, but they loved a good brouhaha more than any.

She knew whom she herself would fight beside. She would dig into the fray and assume her people would take her lead sooner or later.

The only person in the field without a ghost of a chance was that little girl with the long brown braids who successfully stood up to Oengus MacEoghan of Cashel. She obviously had never received any training at all as a fighter, for not only did she not try to seize a weapon of some sort, she stood there like a dunce with her hands pressed to her face, aghast, shouting, "No!"

Padraic grabbed her and pulled her in behind the protection of his ax. Oengus swung around beside him. Without so much as conferring about a plan of action, they began working their way toward the gate, conducting the girl to safety.

Gwynn charged forward, sword and shield ready, and fell in beside Oengus. They really needed three people if they were going to protect the girl adequately.

Padraic! What splendid native talent this lad possessed! With her bronze ax he bested a trained fighting man with a damascened sword, and the only instruction he had received was from her. *Sure and it makes an instructor proud, something like that!*

Padraic grabbed up the shield of a fallen fighter. His right arm was going to give out soon. She could see the bright blood running down it. Two of Oengus's minions joined them, and the going got easier.

Near the gate, Scanlon had engaged a young fellow with pimples. He skewered the upstart and wheeled to yell at Gwynn, "Whose side are you on?"

"Ui Neill! So are you."

"You're insane!" He locked hilts with the Ui Neill swordsman coming at him, tussled, and shoved the man backwards, free. "I'm on your side, she says!" he shouted and turned to engage another slavering swordsman. The Ui Neill warrior fell in beside him as if they'd always been the best of friends.

Gwynn and her compatriots moved outside the main gate and down through the outer compound past the banqueting hall. Fighting had spread out here beyond the confines of the ring walls and down into the encampments in the valley. Gwynn's people were camped to the northwest of Tara, and the Lagin who came in with Oengus were settled more or less to the northeast. That temporary encampment between them was probably the home-grown Ui Neill guard that MacNiall was using to enforce and cement his tenuous hold as the new ard ri.

Tents and brush shelters burned in all three encampments. Black smoke spread out across the vale and obscured the churning melee, but it screened none of the screams and war cries.

Literally by strength of arm, Padraic, Oengus and their comrades ushered the girl down the hill toward the stables. Oengus was surrounded by seven of his fighting force now, not including Gwynn and Padraic. Most likely they were about all that was left of the dozen or so he started with.

Oengus headed for his horses. They were picketed between two chariots a couple of hundred feet downslope of the walls. Nice horses they were, well fleshed and alert.

The seven arrayed themselves in a solid defensive perimeter

around Oengus and his picket line. Gwynn took her place on the defense line among them, but there didn't seem to be much action in this particular spot.

Padraic and the girl fell instantly to work helping the charioteers harness the chariot teams. Was there romance here? If not there ought to be, so closely and comfortably did they work together. Sure and they were both excellent hands with horses, as well. The chariots readied, they turned immediately to saddling the guards' mounts.

Padraic ceased using his right arm and hand at all. He bridled a small perky gelding using only his left. Gwynn saw but still could not figure out just how he managed that.

Somehow the new ard ri, MacNiall, ended up here on horseback with a couple of retainers. His sword was bloody to the hilt, and blood had sprayed across his horse's chest and the leg of his trousers.

"So you're leaving, Oengus, just as the party is getting interesting." He slid off his stud horse.

"And I can't understand why I am."

"Ah, but lord!" That brown-braided girl paused beside the off horse of Oengus's chariot. "Do ye not see? 'Tis a splendid thing y're doing, and I'm very proud of you."

Oengus snorted, and it sounded derisive.

She pressed on. "Eternal life is a gift from God to you. Ye did not earn the right to be called His own, any more than an infant would. Ye accepted it. He'll never abandon ye once y're His. Now y're dead to—"

"I know, I know. Buried with Him in His death, raised with Him in His resurrection."

"That and more, lord! A new person, safe in His hands. Dead to sin and the evil of the past. The old person would not have had the strength to resist that fatal foolishness within the walls."

"Running away from a fight, though . . ." Oengus shook his head.

"Ye found Padraic as ye intended, and ye satisfied y'r honor, including the slur by the king of Lagin. Y've left nothing important undone. 'Tis simply a matter that ye're not partaking of the foolishness which followed, foolishness that be none of y'r own doing."

Oengus nodded. "A higher standard, you said." He turned to the MacNiall. "As we discussed, the joint meeting next year. Have your people work on it, as will I."

MacNiall nodded. "Gwynn? Might as well bring Connaught in on the talks—see if we can all do some good for each other."

"Anytime." Gwynn smiled enigmatically. Being enigmatic wasn't hard this time. She had not the remotest idea what these two were talking about.

MacNiall asked, "Going home?"

Oengus nodded.

"Don't you have a brother-in-law up here someplace?"

"Enda, over by Drogheda."

"Enda?" the brown-haired girl blurted. "Did he not establish the first of our monasteries? He's . . . he's quite famous at Kildare for his church-building." The child had much to learn about addressing kings.

Oengus didn't seem to take it amiss. "Aye, he's a church builder. This isn't generally spread abroad yet, but I just gave him Aran to build a monastery there. My sister claims he's thinking of calling it Killeany. It's going to be a glorious center of learning, to rival Kildare."

"Good! Good!" The girl beamed. "We need all such we can get, aye?"

"Aye!" Oengus seemed absolutely awash in the Christian faith. He was otherwise such a sensible man.

MacNiall thanked Oengus for the twelve cows. Oengus thanked MacNiall for the hospitality. It was a cordial parting all around, considering that Oengus had started this whole ruckus by running his sword through the king of Lagin. On the other hand, neither man wasted any love on the Lagin.

Oengus leaped into his chariot and paused to look at the girl. "Aren't you coming? I'll take you to Kildare."

She shook her head. "Ye remember I've miles to go yet, lord. I've the parcel from Brigid to deliver to Patrick."

He smiled, then, and asked God's blessing on her, and she asked God's blessing on him. The Eoghanachta clattered away, all of them.

MacNiall handed his horse off to one of his retainers. "Came down for a better mount. This beast bolts too easily."

Gwynn smiled, warmly and definitely, not enigmatically, at the magnificent royal. The bald pate notwithstanding, he was a beautiful specimen of manhood. "I've just the mount for you, lord. She's battle-hardened, to match your courage and skill. Padraic? You know my black mare. Fetch it from those tents down there." She waved an arm toward her stable compound on the hillside yon.

"Aye, Queen." Gripping his arm, the lad trotted off toward Gwynn's camp. The brown-haired girl ran along at his side.

"Your favorite?" MacNiall asked.

"And she'll be yours as well. Padraic is quick and knows his way around there. She'll be here momentarily." Someone ought to say something to fill the awkward space of time until Padraic returned. And so, in sultry tones, Gwynn purred warmly, "I understand, my lord MacNiall, that you are currently unmarried."

* * *

Aidan had no idea why he was doing this. As the storm of battle raged all around, he gripped both of Kieran's ankles securely and dragged him across the open compound. He had thought at first of simply helping the fellow to his feet and escorting him to safety, but Kieran was past walking. He tended to babble, and his eyes kept rolling up into the back of his head.

Aidan kept going, through the ornate doors into the cool darkness of the great hall and on to the fire in the center of the room. Unattended, it was about burned out. A feeble blue flame licked across the coals every now and then.

Aidan applied his dagger to the fellow's black tunic and rather hated doing so, so finely spun was the wool. A shame, to hack up so gorgeous a piece. On the other hand, it was spoiled past mending.

His mother's bronze ax had taken out at least one rib and probably two. Fortunately, however, Kieran was not breathing bloody froth. His skin, pasty white and wet with sweat, looked bad, but Aidan had seen worse in men who subsequently lived.

He bound the wound temporarily with strips of the black tunic. He tucked sheepskins and wolfskins under Kieran and over him and around him, cocooning him in warmth. The warmer the man stayed, the better he'd do. It might be late August outside, but in this dark and gloomy building it felt like March.

Aidan needed help, but the aides and retainers had all abandoned the hall. He had orders to give. He didn't even know where to go to find the things he wanted.

A figure, a white shadow against the dark walls, loomed at the far end.

"Lad!" Aidan called. "Linen for bandages, water, and mead sweetened with honey. Quickly!"

The shadow hastened out the back way. Aidan spent the wait rejuvenating the fire. He had it blazing again by the time the retainer returned with a basket of supplies.

Aidan felt his mouth drop open. "I'm sorry. I would never have issued orders at a brehon, had I realized it was you."

Cuinn of Emhain Mhacha grinned. "I suspected as much. This fire is worth it. Just so long as this remains the only fire." As he settled onto bare earth beside the blaze, he glanced at the rafters all around. "Not the safest place to bring our fallen warrior. There's scant protection in a building they'll likely burn down at their first opportunity."

"If they torch the building, we'll drag him back outside. And you'll get warm at last." Aidan decided Kieran could spare a wolfskin. He pulled one from beneath the warrior's legs and passed it to Cuinn.

"Indeed." The old man spread the skin and with a grateful sigh settled upon it, as close to the fire as he could get. He watched awhile as Aidan rummaged through the basket. "The goods there are from the hospital. So is the mead."

"You have a hospital here?"

"They do. I'm from Emhain Mhacha, remember. I'll be going home in a few days. I would have done so by now—Blaine has left already—but I so dread getting upon another horse. I was rather holding out for a chariot or a litter. If MacNiall be a man with a heart, I may get one yet. And you, prince of Connaught—what are your plans?"

"I don't know. I'm examining several options." Aidan let his voice trickle away, for his mind was not on his speech but on the contents of the basket. Here were the dressings he needed, a full pot of salt, and a phial of some sort of chopped leaves. And the mead. He tasted it. Well sweetened. Just what Kieran needed.

"The phial." Cuinn pointed. "The hospital has as practitioners its own herbalists and bonesetters. No need to bring your own or rely upon old women who may or may not remember which plants are best." Cuinn lapsed into silence and watched.

Aidan wished the old man would help, but he wasn't about to embarrass himself again by asking boons of a brehon. With only his own strength he worked at tidying up the fallen hero. Hero? This man shared Aidan's shame—they both had been bested by an ex-slave they should have been able to subdue handily.

He started at the top, so to speak, wiping off the dirt and blood from first the man's head, then his arms and body, and his legs. That taken care of, he trimmed the ragged edges of the wound itself with his dagger, then bound the fellow's gash with salt and linen.

Only after the job was completed did Cuinn venture, "Pity you're a prince."

"How so?"

"Your talents as a surgeon will be wasted as you take over some petty domain. You're very good. Very good."

"I've had enough practice patching up my brothers in our youth. They share both my father's love of ale and his total disregard for limb. And don't worry about my becoming ri."

"Attach yourself to the hospital here. Better yet, come over to Armagh or Emhain Mhacha, and we'll set you up one of your own."

Aidan looked at him. Was the odd little stoat serious? Apparently he was. Setting bones and binding wounds. Aidan had never considered that as a way to spend a life. On the other hand, if you were halfway good at it—and Aidan was—the heroes would come to you.

Lots of danger loomed along with the best joints of meat at feasts. The hero who owed his life to a man's medical skills, however, would be more than happy to share his hero's portion. There was most of the honor right there, with none of the danger.

No one need know of Aidan's mutilation. And even if they did, it wouldn't matter. He would be valued for his services.

Kieran was awake and somewhat alert again, so Aidan offered him some honeyed mead. But Aidan was still preoccupied with Cuinn's suggestion. The more he considered it, the better it looked.

The storm of battle outside seemed to be abating. There was another advantage to this new prospect: wound-binders and bonesetters were much too valuable to risk on the field of battle. Just as he was doing this very minute, he could honorably avoid conflicts. That was a happy thought, since he was never very good at winning them. Even better, he need not study for twelve to twenty years to become one of the aes dana—a fileh, a druid, or a brehon—and that was the only other way to avoid battle.

"Yes." He turned to Cuinn and nodded. "Let's do that."

32

Earth

Were those seagulls circling with raucous calls mourning the passing winter, or complaining because Padraic had just wrung the neck of one of their kind and dismembered it, or laughing at him because he was totally, hopelessly lost? Bridey was looking to him for guidance. He had just guided her to land's end and no prospect of finding Patrick.

He stood on a ragged bit of elevated land and gazed out over the countryside, trying to make heads or tails of the directions they'd been given. The body of water before them looked like a lake and acted like the ocean. The far shore did not seem so distant that you couldn't swim to it if you had to, but the sea churned wildly from southeast to northwest through the narrow channel. The current was much too strong and unpredictable to swim. It was seawater too, with seaweed and mussels clinging to a sheltered embayment in the shore. Was that far shore a peninsula or an island? The gulls laughed.

Somewhere near here, Patrick's nephews at the church in Armagh assured them Patrick was working. "Try Dichu at Saul," they suggested. But previous to that, another nephew of Patrick's, Loman at the church of Trim, had claimed, "You didn't miss him by far. He was through not long ago. Sure and he's back at Armagh by now." If Loman was wrong, why ought Padraic believe that the others were right? No one knew where Patrick was, because he was always a step or two ahead of everyone else.

"I suppose," Bridey mused, "this is the Strangford Lough they talked about." She didn't seem confident. She turned their seagull on its roasting stick above the coals. "If it is, this is where he first came ashore when he returned to Erin as a servant of Christ."

Most of the trees were gone, even on the mountain hard behind them. Raths in abundance, a thousand close-trimmed rings of earth, studded the land as far as the eye could see. Padraic had heard that the north country was rich farmland, but he had not expected quite so many farms. Every rath had its walled-in truck patch and its grainfields. The patches and fields lay brown against the green, plowed but not yet planted. Spring planting would not begin for some weeks yet. The rest of the terrain looked smooth as fine wool, grazed short by thousands of fat cattle and sheep.

"Southwest of the narrows." Padraic was so very tired of seeking, of traveling, of living hand to mouth off the countryside. He wanted to simply sit still. He wanted to lie stretched out upon the earth long enough to feel her gentle, soothing voice speak lullabies to his weary spirit. "So how do we know where the narrows are?"

"We step up to a convenient rath and ask." Bridey always said that. Were it up to Bridey, they would travel from rath to rath to rath all the way across Erin, without missing a one.

Padraic sat down cross-legged by their little fire. "It seems strange not having to wonder if Kieran is coming at me just over the hill."

"I still can't understand why MacNiall attached him as a retainer before even he knew if the lad would live or die. Usually, ye know, ye test a fellow's prowess before ye take him on as MacNiall did."

"Oh, come, Bridey! Stop and think."

The corner of her mouth turned up. "Oh, of course. The horse."

"I'd wager MacNiall doesn't care the least about Kieran. 'Tis the horse. He's discontent with his herd—the war horses in particular—and wants to improve the line." He stared at the cooking seagull parts. "They're not nearly as big without feathers as they would appear when they're flying, are they?"

"Ye and y'r snares."

"How was I to know a seagull would swoop through?"

She pulled the tiny wing—the minuscule wing—off the stick and licked it. "Have ye tasted seagull before?"

"Not really."

"'Tis about the same as a bit of harness leather that's been soaked in rancid fish oil for a week or two. No matter that it's small. 'Tis all y'r own." She stood up. "Enough of this traveling as ye used to travel when Kieran pursued ye. Ye may continue thus. I shall meet ye at Patrick's side." She picked up her bundle and marched off cross-country, up and around the hill.

"Bridey? Bridey!" Padraic scrambled to his feet. He scooped up his leathern travel bag and ran after her. By the time he caught up she was halfway round the hillock. She could move fast when she had the mind to. "Bridey, I'm doing the best I can. I've never been up this way before."

"Neither have I, but I can do no worse than y'rself. And I might just do a good bit better."

"It's too dangerous. No. Don't go traveling across these hills alone."

"Then come along if ye wish." She never wavered. Straight as a spear shaft she headed for a rath that perched on a gentle slope perhaps half a mile beyond a brook to the southeast.

Padraic heaved a sigh and fell in beside her. "Why are you so stubborn?"

"Stubborn? I be cold and hungry and weary, Padraic. Stubborn, no. Done with this aimless blundering about, yes. We shall call on this rath ahead and beg their hospitality. We shall eat a bit of barleycake and sleep on sheepskins. We shall enquire as to where Patrick might be. If they have no direct knowledge of him, we shall ask the location of Dichu's church in Saul. If they know not his whereabouts there, we shall go down to Oengus's brother-in-law Enda, at Drogheda. We shall tackle the task with method. No more flopping mindlessly across the earth like a salmon on a rock."

What could he say?

They had waited six months for Patrick to turn up at either Armagh or Tara, spending the winter at Tara. Two different messengers claimed he intended to. Padraic greatly feared that the old man decided for some reason to travel over to Connaught. He certainly wouldn't want to turn around and go right back there once he came home.

And now here was Bridey, rebelling.

In the flat, shallow vale between this hill and that rath ran a small brook. On either side of the brook stretched extensive plowed fields. Fieldworkers were closing them in with woven brushwood fences, as farmers did with grainfields everywhere to keep out roaming cattle and pigs and sheep.

This was excellent farmland, level enough to plow easily without a lot of staggering and stumbling across hillsides. Padraic hated trying to plow a straight furrow across a very un-straight field. Too, when the grain came ripe they would be able to use a harvester. On level land, a pony at the back of a wheeled carriage could shove it along without difficulty. The toothed iron blade along the front would catch up the grain heads as it passed through them, cutting them off. And on really flat land, the grain heads tumbled back into the bin behind the blade without sliding out into the dirt. The field boys then could cut and sheaf the straw at their leisure. Many's the sheaf of straw Padraic bound in his youth.

But that was for six months from now. Right now, they were putting up fence.

Bridey led the way down to the brook, hiked her skirts, and waded across.

Padraic tried to skip from stone to stone, slipped, and got wet to the knees anyway. "You know, he could be down at Louth. Mochta's monastery. Mochta's a nephew too, you know. We mustn't discount that possibility."

The damp cool breeze of March, unique to that month some-how, carried the plowed-earth smell that was also unique to March. April did not feel the same. The clammy cold of February lay be-hind them. Padraic ought to feel the renewal of spring that came with Umbolc last month. He didn't. He felt cold and bone tired.

Without comment Bridey plodded forward doggedly across the field and walked directly up to the man driving tall alder stakes into the soft earth. "Good evening, lord. We've traveled from Armagh, Kildare, and Tara, trying to find Patrick, and we desperately seek an evening's rest and victuals."

"Kildare, is it? You've come to the right place." The farmer looked askance at Padraic. "You too, I assume."

"If you would, lord." Padraic kept forgetting that he no longer had to conceal his plans and whereabouts—that he could travel openly.

An assistant, possibly a slave as Padraic once was, was basket-weaving thin, whippy elm wythes between the upright stakes. Someone was being a bit lax here; the weaving at the bottom was so loose that piglets could probably squeeze through. But Padraic was not about to criticize.

The man left fence-making to his people and led the way home. This rath did not have a gate set in its earthen wall. The pile of brush beside the walkway would simply be moved into the gap come nightfall. In the morning, part of it would be burned as fuel and the rest of the pile moved aside so that people could again pass in and out. Sometime during the day, it would be replenished. The dogs came charging out, snarling and barking. How Padraic hated dogs! With a cheery word and a smile, Bridey greeted them. They snarled at Padraic. They backed away from Bridey and regarded her with a quiet caution, not the least hostile. The farmer ordered them off and conducted Bridey inside.

No doubt alerted by the dogs, the goodwife appeared at her doorway. The farmer returned to his field, and the woman invited Bridey in instantly.

She invited Padraic as well, more or less as an afterthought. He never understood how women could do that—establish immediate rapport even as they made the men feel as smart and useful as a parchment plowshare. He sat by the center fire as his stomach growled and the women chatted happily.

As he dozed, he vaguely realized he was far wearier than he had admitted. Ever since he lost all that blood in Oengus's brouhaha, he had trouble making it through the day without falling asleep. It had been a long, hard winter. He found it next to impossible to keep up with Bridey. Now here were half a dozen small children rushing in and out, laughing and crying, fussing and fighting, and their noise couldn't keep him awake.

The farmer returned home an hour later, as the sun was tossing its last golden rays across the hillsides. Finally Padraic had someone to talk to who would talk to him, and he found himself too weary to make intelligent conversation.

They ate a wonderful lamb stew from a common pot and sopped fresh barleycake in the gravy.

The farmer considered himself something of an authority on

the history of Christians in Erin. He described, no doubt for the hundredth time, how Dichu of Lecale, the local ri, bitterly opposed Patrick before being swayed by signs and miracles. He and his druids became Patrick's first converts, and he gave Patrick the very church at Saul to which Bridey and Padraic would travel on the morrow. Bridey hung upon his every word. Padraic became bored halfway through the poorly told tale.

On the other hand, Padraic had also seen more of Erin than this man ever would, including many of the places the fellow discussed so freely. Perhaps a bit smugly, Padraic mentioned, "I grew up in Louth. I knew that Mochta, in the monastery at Louth, was a nephew of Patrick's, but I didn't realize Loman at Trim was too."

The man laughed. "It pays to be a relative! Melchu, his brother, bishop of Ardagh. Muinis and Rioch, both nephews. So is Mel, the bishop of Armagh. Not a brother to Loman, though. Sons of different sisters of Patrick's."

"Mel!" The wife sneered. "Patrick should spend less time riding all over Erin in that chariot and spend more time keeping an eye on Armagh."

The farmer explained. "Mel let his aunt, Lupait, move into his quarters, if you hear my meaning. And by 'aunt' I hardly mean a dotty old lady. Patrick insisted they live apart. Does no good to insist if you be not there to enforce it."

Bridey smiled. "Sure and if he spent more time at Armagh, we likely would have caught up to him by now, aye?"

Outside, the dogs set up a royal furor. The farmer looked at Padraic as he climbed to his feet.

Padraic knew what he had to do. He must aid in the rath's defense, if things came to that. A guest came under as much protection as any of the host's immediate family and must help protect the home as diligently as did his host. Padraic was wearing the sword Gwynn had given him as a parting gift. He wished she'd given him the bronze ax; he knew what to do with that.

They stepped out into the night, the farmer with his ax and Padraic with drawn sword. They stood a moment as their eyes adjusted. Padraic tried to get the feel of the earth and the night, but the dogs' noise drowned out subtleties. The farmer called out.

A voice answered from beyond the brush in the gateway. Bridey stood in the doorway. "Padraic?"

"He said something about Kildare, Bridey."

"I thought that's what I heard." She called, "Conleth?"

The voice responded enthusiastically.

"He's a metalworker." Bridey crowded in beside Padraic. "A wonderful artist. He made the beautiful screens in the sanctuary at Kildare. And he's Brigid's spiritual director."

"I've heard of him!" The farmer yelled at his wife, "Call off the dogs!" and tore away the brush from the gateway. From the house, the wife summoned the dogs, promising them tasty tidbits. Not even the dogs ate seagull.

Padraic tried to help, but Bridey did more. A wizened little man stepped through the gap in the brushwood, and Bridey fell instantly upon his neck. They babbled and greeted each other. Padraic felt strangely left out.

Conleth held Bridey at arm's length. "Brigid says it's soon. I came up in hopes of seeing him again."

She sighed. "Will we reach him in time, do ye suppose?"

"Sure and we will! He's at Saul, she says." Conleth looked at the farmer. "Saul is close, is it not?"

"Very. What does Brigid say is soon?"

"Patrick's death."

The farmer stood agape for a moment. "We'll leave on the morrow before first light. I'll take you there myself."

Patrick's death. Padraic, as weary as he was, had trouble sleeping that night. He was provided with a wonderful bed of sheepskins and still he couldn't sleep. What about Rafe?

Bridey prayed. Very well, he would pray. In the heavy silence of the night, when even the crickets were hushed, he knelt in the position he'd so often seen Christians take. He clasped his hands and begged God to spare Patrick long enough to make one last trip to Connaught. Padraic would drive the chariot himself, if only God would send Patrick. He finished it with the sign of the cross, just to make sure.

Then he lay with his eyes wide open and thought about Rafe, rotting in a grave near Mount Aigli, awaiting the touch of Patrick. Rafe, who offered such wisdom about life. Rafe, who approached life and love with hearty élan. Rafe, all man. Rafe, who saved Padraic's life at the cost of his own.

Would Padraic ever give his life for another? He very nearly did, defending Kieran. That still amazed and confused him.

In the silence he could almost hear the gentle voice of the earth giving rest to his soul.

But only almost.

33

Sky

He was a hare, and dogs were pursuing him as he flew over walls and through thickets. On they came at his heels. He was a horse, and the dogs had become bears. He would not have guessed bears could run as fast as horses. His leg was giving out, the front right one.

The farmer kicked him. He'd dozed off after all. Time to go to the church at Saul.

They ate dry barleycake on the way as they walked. The heavy dew of early spring soaked everything, Padraic's shoes included. Dunnocks chirped here and there in the bushes as they passed, and pipits ran about in the grass ahead of them, but the time of singing of birds was not quite come yet.

They arrived before noon. Padraic recognized the church at Saul without the farmer's having to tell him it was that set of wooden buildings in the distance. The wooden church, another building, and a cluster of mud clochans, monks' quarters, crowded together inside the ring wall. The earth goddess seemed to draw up protectively around this Christian enclave, even more so because the earthen wall was without a palisade.

The earth itself held Padraic close to her bosom. That told Padraic something more about the man. *Please, Father in heaven, let Patrick come to Connaught!*

Two dozen young men just outside the gate watched with downcast faces as the party approached. Padraic remembered that Patrick traveled with an extensive retinue of young men, sons of ris and taoiseachs, who were receiving an education.

Bridey and Conleth greeted them and continued on inside. Padraic followed. The farmer hesitated but a moment and entered the gate as well.

It was deathly still here. Men and women who walked from

290

building to building murmured together or said nothing at all. Bridey and Conleth seemed to know where to go. Probably all such church complexes were laid out much alike.

A middle-aged fellow came around the corner and stopped. A broad smile popped out and faded. "Conleth! You got here. Is Brigid coming?"

"I'm sorry, no. But she knows." Conleth presented Brigid and the farmer and couldn't think of Padraic's name. He introduced this fellow as Benen, who would no doubt succeed Patrick to the primacy of Erin. Everyone seemed very comfortable with each other. Except Padraic. He merely felt uneasy and out of step with the world.

"Come." Benen led the emissaries from Kildare inside the far building, and Padraic was not barred. The farmer trooped in with the party, his eyes wide, drinking in every detail.

Somehow Padraic had expected a heroic figure, a massive man who could face down the very devil and bring kings to bay. Patrick had traveled to every corner of Erin, as had Padraic. Up to Connaught, to Mount Aigli, to drive out the snakes (but not the bears) and strengthen his believers. Down to Cashel to bring the Eoghanachta into his fold, Oengus foremost. Through Leinster, preaching, equipping the hermits and farmers who would carry on the word. To Meath and Kildare, setting Brigid upon her steadfast course. Here into Ulster, his beginning and his end.

But on a raised pallet in the corner, a feeble old man lay on his side dozing. No heroic proportion. No stentorian voice. No clear eye and sharp tongue. The old man opened his watery eyes as they entered his presence. He greeted Conleth, his old friend, enthusiastically. Enthusiasm was a relative term—he grunted and murmured a few words, which was apparently the most energy he could expend. He met Bridey of Kildare just as enthusiastically. He laid a trembling crab-claw hand upon hers and blessed her. No one bothered to present Padraic or the farmer.

Then Benen ushered them all back out.

Padraic wandered out to the gate. It looked so peaceful, with cattle grazing and sheep at rest. He gazed awhile across the lush green meadows, until his eyes blurred so hot he could not see. So that was that. He should have insisted upon an audience with the man. He should have begged the old fellow to at least say the words that would raise up Rafe. That was all it would take. A few words. Even if Patrick didn't travel all the way to Connaught—and you could see by looking at him that he'd never step into a chariot again—he could at least say the words. Maybe loan Padraic his crozier. And Padraic didn't insist, didn't ask, because he was too . . . too what? Certainly not shy. He'd never been shy a day in his life. Not awestruck—not of that sorry heap of old age. Too what, then?

The man who raised the dead could not raise himself.

Someone had dragged a dead alder up against the earth wall just outside the gate, gouging out the new spring grass and shamrocks around the wall, making ragged brown wounds in the earth. It was too small a tree for good lumber. Firewood. The trunk lay in three or four pieces, hacked apart by a person who didn't do well with an ax. It was a nice ax too, iron with a heavy, solid head, standing propped against the log.

Padraic picked up the ax and took a test swing down against one of the trunk sections. The blade needed sharpening, but it cut well enough. He swung again. Again. *Chunk. Chunk.* He cut through the trunk in a couple of blows and laid into the arm-length piece that was left. He swung harder. Harder. The chips flew fast enough to sting his legs through his trousers.

He felt his fury building, and he didn't care.

The man who raised the dead could not raise himself!

This was all for naught. Rafe had died forever. Padraic would die forever. Patrick was about to. *Chunk! Chunk! Chunk!*

He chopped and chopped until his weakened right arm quit and his hand would not grip the ax. He shifted to his left. *Chunk! Chunk! Kglug.* The handle broke. The ax head went sailing.

He dropped what was left of the ax handle, sat down on the soft earth upon the green grass and shamrocks, and wept. He drew his knees up and laid his arms across them to make a headrest. His head, like life, was too heavy to hold up.

The grass whispered beside him. He recognized Bridey by her scent, a sweet and natural woman smell, as she settled beside him and draped an arm over his shoulders. He didn't want her there, but he said nothing for fear she might go away.

And that was crazy. He was crazy. He had gone mad, and now there was nothing left for him but to be the sacrifice at the next fire festival. Vernal equinox, not a fire festival, was coming up next. Then Beltaine.

Quietly, she said, "I'm sorry ye will not get to take him to Connaught."

"Rafe didn't have to attack the she-bear. He came at her from behind with his spear, and not a hope of killing her that way, just to get her off me. He died for me."

"So did Jesus."

What did one say to that? Padraic shuddered. Sobs still caught him unawares.

"Because Jesus was raised, all believers will be. All of us, safe in heaven. 'Tis the blessed hope, Padraic."

"I could so picture those round river rocks rolling down off his barrow, and up he sits. It would've been glorious."

"Heaven's the place to wake up, Padraic, with all the angels singing a welcome. There's glory!"

"Rafe wasn't a believer."

"He heard not the word directly, and that was m'fault as much as anyone's. I recall his faith was the equal of what he'd received. There be many in Erin not yet of the faith. 'Tis coming."

"But not for Rafe. He was so sure that Patrick could raise him back up. He totally believed that."

"And y'self, Padraic. Do ye believe Patrick could?"

"Certainly. He did it."

"Those be tales. There are tales, and there are tales. Some be true, some be true in part, some be pure fancy. What if that were all just fancy?"

Padraic shook his head. The sight of the dying man teased and taunted him. *He who raised the dead could not raise himself.*

"He's but a mortal, like us all, whose body is dying. Whence would come his power to do something like that?"

Padraic watched her face. She was the one who knew these sorts of things. She was studying him, awaiting his answer. This was an examination of some sort—she was testing him.

He pondered the question. His head offered no answer; it

was his heart that came up with one. "It would be the power of the Master he serves, the Son of God, Jesus Christ."

She cocked her head. "Do ye truly believe that, Padraic?" He almost heard, behind her words, *Surely, simpleton, you do not believe such rubbish.*

Yes, he did. Rafe had believed that Patrick could raise him up without apparently recognizing the source of such power. It had to have a source, and the source was certainly not the man Patrick himself. He would not let this girl talk him out of it.

"I truly do." He bobbed his head. "Yes, I do."

"Eh, Padraic!" She startled him with a sudden, gladsome hug. Then she sat back and studied him, her opalescent eyes sparkling. "The very thing, Padraic! I saw ye at prayer in the dark last night. But mere faith be not sufficient. It must be faith in Someone, and ye've placed it squarely where it ought to go."

He dropped his heavy head back down to resting on his crossed arms. "Scant help that is for Rafe. His faith was in Patrick alone, as far as I can tell." So near, and so far. "Jesus Christ died for me. I accept that. But Rafe died for me too, and I've let him down."

She fell silent.

Suddenly Padraic didn't want to talk about this anymore. Sadness flooded him unbearably. In fact everything weighed too heavily. Everything.

He wiped his face on the hem of his tunic and looked at her. "What will you do now?"

She appeared put off stride to have the subject shifted to herself. She stammered. "I don't know. What do you plan to do now?"

"I don't know. I'm a prince. Seek out the Slevin maybe. They're my tuathe, after all. I thought you wanted to study at Kildare."

"I want to live there forever. I doubt I will, but 'tis m'dream."

"Brigid won't marry, you say. Does that mean you can't either?"

"Of course I can. In fact, m'sister be thinking about it. The monks and sisters marry. Sometimes to each other. Mostly to other people."

"Good." Padraic felt his cheeks flush. "I mean, that's good."

Another withered old man—the world was full of them—came shuffling up the track toward the gate here. The two gray-haired men accompanying him seemed grim. As he approached, the fellow looked less withered. The scars on his arms suggested he was a metalworker. His burly hands, so out of place on an old man, looked strong even yet.

He stopped beside Bridey and Padraic. "A blessing upon you both, Bridey and Padraic." He signed the cross and continued on in through the gate.

Padraic leaped to his feet. "I never saw him before. You must have . . ."

"Nor I either. Sure and he's a man of God." Bridey scrambled to her feet. "'Tis a sign, Padraic! Something momentous is happening."

They followed the old fellow inside, from spring sun into filtered darkness. Padraic's breastbone fluttered.

Benen was outside the door of Patrick's chamber. He spread that beneficent smile across his face again. "Tassach! It's been a long time. Thank you. Bless you for coming. Of all the workers and friends he's loved, he loves you best. I can't think of another man who ought do this."

"A sorry task, but a joyful one. Think of the crowns he's about to receive."

"Aye, and aye again." Benen led the man into Patrick's presence.

Padraic and Bridey entered too, for no one barred their way. Bridey simply stood there. Padraic took her elbow and guided her in behind them. Until someone chased them away, they would watch. He had to see.

Benen knelt at Padraic's head and stroked the old man's cheek. "Tassach is here."

Patrick made no move save for feebly raising the claw hand. Tassach took it in his own burly one.

Tassach then began a low, droning litany in, Padraic guessed, Greek or Latin. From his gestures, and the signs he occasionally made, Padraic would surmise they were the words spoken to a dying man. He glanced at Bridey and knew he'd guessed right.

Tears poured down her cheeks. This girl who had never known the man mourned his passing. This woman who had never heard him speak was eagerly and happily devoting herself to his God.

Padraic drew her in close against his side. She wrapped a strong young arm tightly around his waist and snugged her head in against his shoulder. It occurred to him suddenly—and this was a ridiculous time for it to do so—that he no longer felt the restlessness that had plagued him.

Tassach, Benen, Conleth, the five or six others here, and Bridey as well, all wept openly. Padraic found himself mourning the old man too. He had come so far. This wasn't what he expected to find, but somehow it seemed now to be right.

Bridey began the song Padraic heard her sing on her crannog near the Shannon—one of Patrick's own hymns, she once claimed. "I arise today through the strength of heaven. Light of sun . . ."

The others joined in, raising joyful voices through their tears. "Radiance of moon, splendor of fire . . ."

And all the angels in heaven sang a welcome.